NEW YORK TIMES BES[T]

SHARON SALA

BROKE-ASS WOMEN'S CLUB

RosettaBooks®
New York, 2021

This is a work of fiction. Names, characters, places, and incidents are either the products of the author's imagination or are used fictionally. Any resemblance to actual persons (living or dead), events, or locations is entirely coincidental.

Cover Art by Kim Killion, The Killion Group
Interior format by Brian Skulnik
Edited by Deborah Grace Staley, www.writebytheocean.com

ISBN (paperback): 978-0-7953-5346-8
ISBN (e-Pub): 978-0-7953-5345-1

www.RosettaBooks.com

This book is for every woman who finds herself on the hard side of life through no actions of her own.

I dedicate it to the strong ones who refused to quit.

You are my sisters. And you are not alone.

CHAPTER ONE

David Logan was a player.

A man pushing fifty-five who looked forty, behaving like he had yet to turn thirty. He was six feet of handsome with brown eyes and the beginnings of a silver streak growing in his hair. He still hadn't decided if the look was aging or giving him a dash of distinction, but either way, it was there.

He was a field rep for a well-known pharmaceutical company, with a territory covering the southern half of the state of Missouri.

He had a woman in St. Louis, a woman in Kansas City, a woman in Springfield, and a woman in Columbia, which meant always having a woman in his bed, no matter what part of the state he was working.

The quirk that kept his adrenaline flowing was that they were all his wives. It was the ultimate game, but he was a player, and they were the pieces in his game of life. He made good money but dividing it four ways was never enough. He'd already depleted the personal savings of three of his wives without bothering to let them know and had become adept at slipping money out of one checking account to cover bills in another. Like playing Russian Roulette with two blondes, a brunette, and a redhead.

But since Janie, his redhead, had her own bookkeeping business, he'd been leery of juggling their funds, because he knew she would discover it. However, he'd gotten himself into a bind last month, and with a little forgery, he'd moved her personal savings to keep the other three households afloat. He had a big bonus day coming and planned to begin putting the money back before she discovered it was gone.

It was nearing the end of May.

David had been working the St. Louis area for almost a week, and it was time for him to head southeast. He was packing, getting ready to leave, and Janie was fussing with his suits and clean shirts, always making sure he had everything he needed for the time he would be gone.

"David, darling, I'm putting in a few extra shirts... just in case," she said.

David smiled, poked a finger through one of the red curls above her forehead, then ran a finger down the side of her face.

"You, my love, are the best. I don't know what I'd do without you. I'm going to miss you so much. I'll text every night. Oh... and don't forget, the plumber is coming tomorrow to see about that garbage disposal, so be watching for his text."

Janie hugged him. "Thank you for always taking such good care of me."

"It's what I do," David said, then closed his suitcase and picked it up off the bed. "Come walk me to the door."

And so she did, falling into his embrace and goodbye kiss, then standing in the doorway and waving until his car was out of sight.

Only then did she go down the hall to her office to begin her workday.

Within moments of getting on the interstate, David Logan shifted to his David Lowry alias and was on the phone with his third wife, Gretchen, in Springfield.

She answered breathlessly.

"David! Darling. What a perfect way to begin my day."

He chuckled. "You are such a sweetheart. I just wanted to give you a heads up that I'm headed your way today."

"Wonderful! Will you be here tonight?"

"Yes. I think I have about a week's worth of work in the area, so we have some special time ahead of us."

"I'm so excited! Have a great day. I can't wait to get you home!"

"I can't wait to get there," David said. "See you soon."

After that, he put his phone on Bluetooth and headed south.

Less than an hour out of St. Louis, he drove straight into a thunderstorm, turned his wipers on high, and found an oldies station on Sirius XM.

The traffic was steady, and David was driving seventy. He was singing "Blue Eyes Crying in the Rain" with Willie Nelson and keeping up with the traffic when his cellphone rang. When he saw it was his second wife, Bettina Lee, who knew him as her husband, David Lee, from Kansas City, he let it go to voicemail. A few seconds later, it rang again, and he rolled his eyes. It was his fourth wife, Pauline Lord, in Columbia. He loved his women, but he often wondered what the hell had he been thinking?

All of a sudden, a semi came flying past him in the fast lane, and he was abruptly awash in water. It hit the driver's side window so hard and fast, it startled him into thinking he was about to get side swiped.

He swerved, and when he did, his car hydroplaned and spun him to the left, right into the fast lane of traffic, into the path of another fully loaded semi.

It took a rescue squad two hours to get his car out from under the truck, and then peel what was left of him out of it. He was identified by the driver's license in his wallet, which happened to still be David Logan, and the tag number on his car, which was registered to the company he worked for. Then they found a briefcase wedged partially beneath the seat with three more driver's licenses, all with his photo, but with different names: David Lee, David Lowry, and David Lord. At that point, it became the responsibility of the Missouri Highway Patrol to find his next of kin and to notify the local police to see if any of his aliases turned up in open crimes.

A detective named Fairfield got the file dumped on his desk, shuffled through it, and began a search on David Logan, David Lee, David Lowry, and David Lord. What he discovered was shocking. The man had different Social Security numbers for each name, which led him to believe it was a case of stolen identities. But further investigation revealed that while the man had been using Social Security numbers of deceased men, he'd been paying taxes on all four identities. He also discovered David Logan had a rented mailbox in a post office in St. Louis, where the mail for his aliases was being sent.

The detective was floored. David Logan wasn't just a bigamist. He was a skilled conman who knew his way around the systems it took to hide what he was doing. Now he had to find out if he had next of kin under any of his other names.

That's when he found the four wives and didn't know who to call first. In the end, it didn't matter. They all had to be notified. After that, it was up to David Logan's first wife to claim and bury him, although he was in so many pieces, there would have been enough to go around.

It was just after lunch when the doorbell rang.

Janie was mopping up a spill on the kitchen floor, and when she heard it ring, was glad for the momentary reprieve. She leaned the mop against the cabinet, ran her fingers through her curls to get them off her forehead, and hurried through the hall to answer.

What she didn't expect to see were the two Missouri Highway Patrolmen standing on her doorstep. And she still wasn't processing what she was seeing until they asked for her by name.

"Janie Logan?"

"Yes, I'm Janie," she said.

"Mrs. Logan, I'm Officer Danfield from the Missouri Highway Patrol, and this is my partner, Officer Kirby. May we come in?"

"Yes, of course," she said, and led them to the living room. As soon as she was seated, Danfield delivered the blow.

"Mrs. Logan, I am sorry to tell you that your husband was in a car accident on I-44, and he did not survive."

Janie gasped. "No! Please, no! Are you sure it was David?"

"Yes, ma'am. His remains are with the coroner, and you will be notified when they will be released for burial. Please accept our sincere condolences."

Tears were rolling. "Oh, my God. He just left the house this morning. How did this happen?"

"It was raining. Apparently, his vehicle hydroplaned and spun him into another lane of traffic and in the path of an oncoming semi. He did not suffer."

Janie moaned, then covered her face and started sobbing.

Danfield looked at his partner, then grimaced.

"I'm sorry, ma'am, but I'm afraid there's more."

Death had already written its own story on her face when she looked up. She was devastated and broken, already envisioning the coming years alone, and they were telling her there was more?

"How can there be more? He's dead," she sobbed.

"There is one other thing you need to know. You are David Logan's legal wife, but you're not his only one."

It was like cold water in the face. "What the hell do you mean... I'm not his only wife?"

"David Logan has been living under three other assumed names with three other wives in the state of Missouri. Your husband was a bigamist."

Shock rolled through her in waves, and then she was on her feet and screaming in their faces.

"I don't believe you!"

"I'm sorry, ma'am, but it's true. Obviously, none of you knew about each other, but as we speak, there are officers knocking on their doors right about now, telling them exactly what we're telling you. And they will be just as shocked, and hurt, and sad, and they're going to be feeling just like you are right now. My sympathies are with all of you. The coroner's office will be in touch. Is there anyone we can call for you, so you won't be alone?"

Janie shook her head. "No. Oh, my God. I don't know how to feel! This is unbelievable."

"Yes, ma'am," Danfield said, and then they stood. "We'll see ourselves out."

Janie heard the door open and close, but she couldn't bring herself to move. She couldn't absorb what she'd just been told and still think of the man she'd thought was hers. This was the biggest tragedy of her life. It was the biggest shock of her life. And she had a feeling it was going to be the biggest embarrassment, as well.

And then she thought of the other three women, and her heart broke just a little for them. They'd all been living a lie. The homes they'd made with him—the lives they'd shared with him. It had all been a sham.

She needed to call her lawyer. This was going to be a mess she couldn't mop up.

Bettina Lee was a forty-closer-to-fifty-something blonde who fancied herself a lookalike for actress Jennifer Lawrence.

She had just returned from shopping and was in her driveway unloading groceries when a highway patrol car pulled up behind her, and two uniformed officers got out.

"Ma'am, are you Bettina Lee?"

She tucked a stray lock of blonde hair behind her ear and took off her sunglasses.

"Yes. I'm Bettina Lee."

"May we speak to you inside?"

Her heart was beginning to pound. Something bad had happened. But to who? *David? My son? My daughter?*

"Let us help you carry in your bags," they said, and took them from her arms. They followed her inside and set them on the hall table.

Bettina's stomach was in knots as she led them into the living room, then dropped into the nearest chair.

They sat facing her, and then gave her the news.

She gasped, and then she moaned, and then dissolved into tears, but when they dropped the bigamist bomb, another kind of shock rolled through her.

"What do you mean? Three other wives?"

"Your husband was a bigamist. His body is in the morgue and will be released to the legal wife."

"Is it me?" she asked.

"No, ma'am, it is not. But you will be notified when the body is released, and to what funeral home."

Bettina threw up her hands. "Oh my God! Is this a joke? This can't be happening."

And yet, it had happened, and it was still happening. She was so hurt and so furious that if David wasn't already dead, she would have killed him.

Gretchen Lowry was getting ready for David's arrival tonight. She'd cleaned the house, put fresh sheets on their bed, and had a cherry pie baking in the oven. It was his favorite. As soon as the pie came out of the oven, she was going to shower and shampoo her hair. David always told her how much he loved her long blonde hair and the elegance of her long neck and heart-shaped face. But he especially liked for her to wear her hair down when she was wearing nothing at all, and the thought of making love with him tonight made her shiver.

She had just poured herself some iced tea and was thinking about something to snack on when her doorbell rang. She took a quick sip and then went to answer it. Seeing two uniformed officers from the Missouri Highway Patrol on the doorstep felt like a physical blow.

"Gretchen Lowry?"

"Noooo," she moaned, and staggered backward.

They grabbed her before she could fall and helped her into a chair in the living room, then sat on the sofa.

"Ma'am, are you Gretchen Lowry?"

She nodded, her hands fisted in her lap. "Is it David? Did something happen to my husband?"

"Yes, ma'am. We're sorry to tell you—"

After that, everything faded. Gretchen heard them, and the

words, and knew that today was the end of joy as she'd known it.

The details were horrifying. She couldn't fathom her darling David's life ending in such a devastating fashion. Tears were rolling down her cheeks as she struggled to catch her breath. She didn't know what to do. How to make sense of this nightmare and still be alive in the world.

And then the officers took her grief and wrung every ounce of empathy from her soul. She heard them relating David's deceit, then shrieked like she'd just been stabbed. After that, she went numb. They were still talking when the timer went off in the kitchen. David's pie was done, and so was he.

"Is this all?" she asked.

"Yes, ma'am. Is there someone we can call so you won't be alone?"

She shook her head. "No. I'll make calls later."

"Yes, ma'am. We're so sorry for—"

"Please see yourselves out. I need to get a pie out of the oven," she mumbled, and walked out of the room.

Pauline Lord had been up since four a.m., working on a website for her latest client. She finally finished what she was doing around nine and went to shower and get dressed. Designing websites from home was her sideline. She didn't make a lot of money at it, but enough to keep her medical insurance paid and have a little money on the side. The fear of not having insurance came from watching her grandparents die without it. She'd had the same carrier and policy since her first marriage, which had ended in divorce. And when she and David had married, she'd opted out of being on his policy because she'd wanted to keep the one she had.

By the time she got to the kitchen to eat, she'd missed breakfast and decided to call it brunch. After eating, she went back to the computer and worked some more, then hours later, got up, stretching to ease the tension in her back and legs as she meandered through their house.

She wished David was here. She missed him. But she'd known his job and his hours when they'd married. When she thought about it, her life hadn't changed much from what it had been before, when she was the divorcee with no family. Except she was no longer in the efficiency apartment barely making ends meet. Now, she had this wonderful home and space—so much space—but still mostly alone.

She ended up later in front of the bathroom mirror, debating as to whether she should let her bangs grow out or trim them back to a decent length. David loved her long dark hair. She wouldn't cut the length, but she was just about to trim her bangs when the doorbell rang.

"Saved by the bell," she said, then laughed at her own joke and went to see who was at the door.

Two Missouri Highway Patrolmen were on the doorstep.

"Ma'am, are you Pauline Lee?"

It was the look in their eyes. Stark terror washed through her, and all she could do was nod.

"May we come inside?" they asked.

She was beginning to shake. "Is it David? Did something happen to my husband?"

"Please, ma'am. May we come inside?"

"Oh my God! It is David!" she moaned, and fainted.

When she came to, she was lying on the sofa, and the two officers were bending over her. One officer was holding her hand, and the other had a cold cloth on her forehead. She shoved it off her forehead and sat up.

"What happened?"

They both stepped back and took a seat. "You fainted."

Pauline felt cold from the inside out. It was shock. She couldn't quit shivering and wrapped her arms around herself to keep from coming undone.

"I know that! What happened to my husband?"

And then they told her, and it was even worse than she had imagined. When she asked when she could see him, they skirted the issue, and then delivered a final blow."

Pauline raised her head, certain she'd misunderstood what she'd just heard.

"What?"

The officer sighed. "Your husband, the man you knew as David Lord, was a bigamist. There are three other wives. You will be notified by the coroner when the remains are released, and to which funeral home, but it will be up to the legal wife to receive them."

"This can't be happening," Pauline mumbled. "Do the other women know?"

"You are all being notified today."

Pauline sat, staring at a smudge on the toe of the officer's shoe. The grief she'd felt only moments earlier was frozen somewhere inside of her now. She didn't know how to feel, or what to do. David had always taken care of everything. But her reality had changed within the space of one breath. She didn't have the luxury of grief or anger.

But when she saw the sympathy and pity on their faces, in that moment, she hated David Lord, or whoever the hell he was, as she had never hated before. She gripped the arms of her chair and then stood up, like a drowning woman coming up for air. She didn't know how long she could tread water, but she wasn't dead yet.

"Thank you for coming. I'll see you out."

She stood in the doorway until they were gone, then closed it and turned, listening to the quiet. She would never see David again. She would never hear his voice, or share his bed, or come apart in his arms again. And in knowing that, she also had to accept, she'd never known him at all.

By nightfall, the shock of his deceit had turned into anger and despair for all four of the women.

Janie was alone in the dark, staring out her living room window at the streetlights beyond, and the passing traffic. Shattered didn't cover her emotional state, and she couldn't stop thinking of the three other women.

And how he'd gone from one bed to the other without a hint of guilt. He'd cheated on her—on all of them. The horrible part was that the others probably felt the same way about her.

She was tired. So tired. But she couldn't bring herself to sleep in the bed they'd shared. He'd sullied every aspect of their marriage. Finally, she stretched out on the sofa, pulled an afghan over her, and closed her eyes.

Bettina Lee had cried herself sick before scouring every nook and cranny of their house, looking for anything that would explain this nightmare. She kept thinking they'd made a mistake identifying the body. Because of the damage to his body, they'd used the identification they'd found in the wallet and the car registration. But what if some stranger had robbed David and he was the driver who'd wrecked the car? What if David was somewhere hurt and lost, waiting for help to come, and no one was looking because they thought he was dead?

She got online and checked their bank account, then broke out in a cold sweat when she saw how much money was missing from the last time she'd checked. There was hardly any money left in it.

Conned. She'd been conned. And she assumed the other women had, too.

She wandered through the rooms of their house, wondering what the other women looked like. Were they younger? Prettier? And why so many? Maybe they were well-to-do. Maybe that's why he'd done it. Conning all of them. Bettina had nothing to bring to the marriage but herself, yet he'd taken her anyway. Nothing made sense.

She was so sad she couldn't think. All she knew was that he was the second man she'd given her heart to, and the second man to break it by cheating and lies.

Gretchen Lowry was in the kitchen, scraping the bottom of a quart of ice cream. Her tongue was numb from the cold, but she just kept eating. She couldn't really feel it because she was numb all over from the shock of her husband's deceit. She felt like the biggest dumbass walking for ever trusting him. She could find a job, but not in time to save their home. She'd buried her first husband years ago, and now it was about to happen again. Only this time she didn't have the right. Because they weren't legally married.

She kept asking herself why he'd felt the need to keep adding women to his life. Was there something lacking in her, or was something lacking in David that kept him feeling unsatisfied? And if so, why the hell had he kept up this charade?

Gretchen was hurt and angry and confused, and she didn't know how she was supposed to feel about his death. All she knew was the anchor in her life had just been cut, and she was adrift in the hell he'd left behind.

Pauline Lord couldn't quit shaking. She was as alone in the world as a person could be now. Her mother had abandoned her when she was a kid by taking her to her grandparents' house for the weekend, but she had never returned. They had raised her with all the love they'd had to give, but they'd been gone for years. She had one failed marriage and had been on her own for years when she'd met David.

His appearance in her life had felt like a gift. After years of being alone and with no one to trust, he'd come striding into her life like a White Knight and hade swept her off her feet.

She'd taken this betrayal as more proof that she wasn't worth loving.

She didn't know what a nervous breakdown felt like, but she was bordering on coming undone, in a way she never had before, and was so scared that she'd never be able to put herself together again.

Six days later, the wives were facing yet another similar truth.

David had raided their personal savings and had moved money from their checking accounts with no indication of where it had gone. But, knowing what they knew now, they suspected he'd juggled all their monies to keep each household afloat. It was hard to imagine how frantic he must have been at times, trying to keep all the balls in the air to not give himself away. They still didn't understand why he'd chosen to marry so many women, or why they'd never caught on that it had happened.

Janie was appalled at how naïve she'd been. She was a bookkeeper! She should have known all this was happening. But now she understood why he'd always insisted on filing taxes separately.

However, her lawyer was thorough in all he'd found out, and there was nothing left to doubt. The lawyer had discovered a private mailbox rented in David's name at the post office. And Janie also discovered there was a safety deposit box at their bank she'd known nothing about. While she was wondering how to access them, a policeman showed up with a box containing David's personal belongings. The man expressed his sympathy, asked her to sign for it, and left.

Her hands were shaking as she carried the box into the kitchen and began removing the contents. It was like going through a junk box at a tag sale, looking at the remnants of someone else's life.

His wallet was there and four sets of key rings. Each set had a personalized fob. Logan. Lee. Lowry, and Lord. And then she saw the driver's licenses and understood how he'd gotten away with it. He'd been living under four different names.

One of the keyrings had a key to a safety deposit box, and somewhere on them was likely a key to the private mailbox, too. But since she had no access to the safety deposit box, she'd have to get her lawyer to go with her to the bank to deal with all that.

He had already informed her that her savings was gone. Her husband had embezzled it a little less than a month ago, and she hadn't had time to catch the absence of the missing money. Her only saving grace was that the house she lived in was hers, inherited from her father twenty years ago, and there was a trust fund that went with it—something David had not been able to access.

She wouldn't go bankrupt. She wouldn't lose her home. But she'd lost faith in herself. She'd fallen for someone who hadn't really existed.

It was the rage in her that led her through the house, removing every vestige of his presence, taking down pictures, digging his toiletries from the bath, and trashing them. Then on to their closet, yanking everything of his off hangers. His suits, his pants, his summer shirts, his shoes and belts, his winter coat, the hat he liked to wear fishing. Pulling everything that was his out of drawers. She wanted every trace of him gone.

She boxed and bagged, sometimes crying so hard she could barely see, and carried it all out to the verandah. So many bags. So many boxes. Ten years of a life with a man she'd never known.

And then she called a friend who ran a shelter, and he sent a van and a couple of workers to pick it all up. She watched from the window as they made trip after trip from the porch to the van and back again, and then they left, taking the remnants of her husband with them.

She turned away from the window and started up the hall, then stopped in the foyer, listening to the quiet and closed her eyes, standing there until the silence became a roar within her before she could make herself move. David wasn't the only one who'd died. He'd taken a piece of her with him.

Bettina was embarrassed that she'd fallen for a conman.

Now that fact was coming home to roost. She had a stack of bills she couldn't pay and no job. She was going to lose their home and was in such a state of shock she couldn't think how to move forward, or what to do about the debt. His clothes still hanging in the closet were a constant reminder of who'd gotten her in this dilemma, and in a fit of rage, she headed for the bedroom, screaming and crying as she began pulling down suits and shirts still hanging from the rods.

"You son-of-a-bitch! You worthless, lying piece of trash!" she sobbed, digging out his underwear and socks from the dresser drawers. "I will not be sorry you are dead."

Then she grabbed a trash can and began dumping all his toiletries from the bathroom drawers and shelves, before stuffing all of the clothes into trash bags, then dragging them through the house and out to her car.

She took off to the Salvation Army, crying all the way. Her first husband had cheated on her with her best friend then married her, and now this man she'd been married to for seven years had been a cheater, too. She still hadn't decided who the bigger losers were. The men she'd married or herself for saying, "I do."

Gretchen was enraged by what he'd done to her. The money from her first husband's life insurance policy had been put into a savings account long before she'd met David, and the money she'd had from her job as a bank teller before they'd married was gone, too. She still didn't know how he'd gotten to it, but it was obviously a case of embezzlement and forgery.

She was a woman wronged—humiliated and trying to separate the grief she still felt from the reality of who he'd really been.

There was barely enough money left in their checking account to get through the next two months. She didn't have a job, and it wouldn't be long before she was also out of a home. She was sick to her stomach. Sick at heart. And sick of the reminders of his presence all over the house. It was time for a cleansing, but it was harder than she could have imagined.

It took four trips to get his things out of the house, and then she got in the car, laid her head on the steering wheel, and cried until the rage was gone. Then she drove it all to Goodwill.

Pauline was still in shock, moving through each day as if somehow this horrible thing would just go away. Her hands trembled as she wrote out checks for the bills that were due, knowing she was never going to be able to keep their home. Her saving grace was having the small income from web design and filing their taxes separately.

But there was no satisfaction in knowing he was dead.

He'd played his game, had all the fun, and escaped retribution.

Her emotions ran hot, and then cold, and then went flat, like a tire. She was in limbo, waiting for the last shoe to fall.

And when it finally fell, it landed on every wife's head.

David in all his incarnations had always reassured each wife that he had a life insurance policy should something ever happen to him. He'd shown each one where the policy was, and how to access it. Then when they had, their requests for assistance were all met with the same response.

He'd let the policies lapse.

At that point, Pauline lost it.

"You got off easy, you sorry bastard. All you had to do was die. You left us to drown in your lies. For the rest of my life, I will regret I ever saw your face."

Then she bagged up the clothing and donated it to a homeless shelter.

After she got home, the house felt different. Or maybe the difference she felt was in her. Removing him from the house was the only revenge she would ever get, but it was the beginning of starting over.

Janie was resolved about the lapsed personal life insurance policy. It was a shock, and yet it wasn't. He'd lied about so much, that this was just one more thing to accept.

And then she got a call from the pharmaceutical company David had worked for, expressing their sympathies, and informing her that they had a fifty-thousand-dollar life insurance policy on all their reps, which doubled if it was an accidental death. And since she was the recipient listed on the policy, she would be receiving the money in a timely fashion. It didn't come close to replacing what he'd stolen, but right now, a hundred thousand dollars was huge.

Bettina was shattered. Heartbroken, and needing to hear familiar voices. She got her son and daughter on a conference call to let them know what had happened.

They'd been short with her when she'd told them of his death, and that her money was gone, like they were afraid she'd want them to take care of her now, which pissed her off. She was perfectly capable of taking care of herself.

She already knew her son, Joe, had never liked David, and her daughter, Patty, had been holding a grudge ever since Bettina's divorce from their father, Gary Vale. But she was still their mother and hoping for empathy, so she called them again.

"Hi, Mom. I'm here. What's wrong now?" Joe asked.

Bettina frowned. "Let me get Patty on the other line. I don't want to have to say this twice." And then she let Patty into the call. "Okay, honey. Joe's on with us."

"Hey, Sis," Joe said.

"Hi, Joe. How's everything going?"

Bettina sighed. "Joe's business is not the reason for this call."

"So-rrry", Patty drawled. "What's wrong now?"

Bettina eyes welled. "Interesting. That's exactly what Joe asked. Thank you both for your concern. I just found out that David let the life insurance policy lapse. I just wanted to hear a kind voice."

"Oh, my God!" Joe muttered. "I told you he was bad news."

"For real," Patty said. "I never liked him from the start. Dad would never have done that to you."

Bettina's eyes welled, and before she could stop herself, she was screaming.

"You're right. Dad didn't steal my money. He just broke my heart, lied his ass off to me for five years while he was cheating on me with my best friend, then dumped me. Don't ever mention his name to me again."

Their silence was deafening. Nobody said, *I'm sorry, Mom.* Nobody offered her a room. Neither offered to come be with her in her time of grief. And in that moment, the pain of their rejection was too much.

Without saying another word, she hung up, then turned toward the window and stared out into the street, watching cars driving by and people walking on the sidewalks, just living their lives, and wondered what was going to happen to her.

Her phone began to ring, but when she saw Joe's name on Caller ID and didn't answer. She didn't want to talk to her children. She didn't much like the cold, judgmental people they had become.

Gretchen had a sister, Erin, in California. She had already called her with the news of David's death, and the sordid tale of what was happening. But when she did, Erin had the actual nerve to laugh.

It was the final straw for Gretchen. She hung up on her, mentally vowing to never speak to her again, so when she found out about her savings being gone, and that the life insurance policy had lapsed, she didn't bother to let her know. It was already obvious she wouldn't care.

Pauline was alone again. A two-time loser. And now, at the age of forty-five, she was so shattered by the deception and the continuing bad news, that she knew she would never trust another man as long as she lived.

It was just after the first of June when they all finally got the call.

David's remains had been released to McLaughlin Funeral Home in St. Louis, Missouri, to a woman named Janie Logan. And to their surprise, at Janie Logan's request, they had all been invited to gather with her there, the day after tomorrow, at 1:30 p.m.

Bettina went straight to her closet after the call to make sure her black mini dress was clean. She felt obliged to show off her best attributes without realizing how desperate that was going to appear.

Gretchen hated to spend the money, but she called her hair stylist and made an appointment for tomorrow, anyway. She wasn't going to meet the other wives looking as haggard as she felt.

Pauline went to the bathroom with scissors and trimmed her bangs, then made sure her black slacks and blazer were clean.

As for Janie, she knew the invitations had been delivered along with the calls, and that's all that mattered. She wanted to see them. To see the faces of the other women he had loved. They were, in a manner of speaking, all part of a family now, without ever having been given a choice, or voiced their permission.

CHAPTER TWO

Janie woke up the morning of the gathering with a knot in her stomach and went through the first half of the day in a daze, trying to decide whether to appear as a widow, or the pissed-off woman that she was.

In the end, she just wore a fitted black dress, which drew attention to her bust size, but from the age of fifteen, there had never been a way to ignore it. Black had always been a good choice for her. It left the eye to move immediately to her fair skin and red curls.

She'd spent the better part of an hour on her makeup, and chose shoes that made her taller, because it was hard to be formidable when you had a turned-up nose, big blue eyes, and were only five feet tall.

David had called her his little pixie.

She thought of him now as the lying son-of-a-bitch.

As the one who'd issued the invitations to the other wives, she arrived early at the funeral home. It would have been the height of rudeness not to be on hand. By fate alone, he'd married her first, but they'd loved him, too. She didn't know if any of them would come, but if they did, they had a right to be a part of this.

The director was sympathetic to their situation and had set enough chairs in the visitation room so that they could have privacy and be together in their grief.

And so, she sat, staring at the sealed casket, unwavering in the choice she'd made to put him in the equivalent of a plain pine box. Gutted from the rage growing within her, she was devoid of sympathy for his fate. And with each passing day as another lie was revealed, it fed that rage until it was all that was left within her. Her eyes suddenly blurred with unshed tears, but there was no empathy in her voice.

"You were so pretty on the outside, but oh David... how well you hid your ugly, lying heart."

And then she heard footsteps out in the lobby, and the director's voice.

"In here, Mrs. Lane."

So, at least one came, Janie thought, and stood, watching as a tall, elegant woman with long dark hair walked into the room. She was wearing black slacks, a white silk blouse, and a black blazer.

Janie stood up and held out her hand. "I'm Janie Logan"

"I'm Pauline Lord," Pauline said, and grasped her hand, feeling the firm grip before she quickly let go, and eyed the little woman with the fiery red hair. Her first instinct was to trust her. Her second was that she would have liked her on sight, had they not been meeting this way.

Then Pauline turned toward the plain, non-descript casket without a single arrangement of flowers around it, blinked, and then looked back at her.

"You're pissed too, aren't you?"

Janie shrugged. "I guess it shows. Please, have a seat."

Pauline sat, and within moments, the funeral director escorted two more women into the room. Both blondes with pretty faces. Both graciously endowed. Both wearing black. The physical distance they kept between each other was evidence of how uncomfortable they felt about even being here.

Janie sighed. David certainly had an eye for beauties, and she wondered what the hell he'd ever seen in her. But she repeated her greeting as she went to meet them.

"I'm Janie Logan. Thank you for coming."

Bettina's black mini dress set off her fine legs and blonde hair, while the dipping neckline accentuated the generous girth of her breasts.

"I'm Bettina Lee. Thank you for including us."

"How could I not?" Janie said, and then turned to the other woman. "Hello. I'm Janie," and again, held out her hand.

Gretchen's blonde up-do was elegant, accenting her long neck and pretty face. She was also dressed in a tight black dress with a slit up past her knee, and a neckline revealing the womanly figure beneath.

"I'm Gretchen Lowry," she said, and then looked at the casket. "That about sums him up, doesn't it?"

Janie ignored the comment and pointed to the chairs.

"Shall we sit for a bit? I think we need to talk, but they have these chairs all lined up facing the casket. Let's circle our wagons and see where we're at," she said.

They each grabbed a chair and pulled it around until they had unconsciously formed a small, united circle, facing each other.

Bettina had a wry, bawdy sense of humor, and as she was looking at all of them, finding the obvious physical similarities made her snort.

"Well, I guess we can all agree that he was into boobs."

Shocked by the need to laugh, they didn't bother to hold back. The quick outburst of laughter behind closed doors was the beginning of a litany of revelations.

Janie sighed. She'd had a feeling this would be good for all of them, and she'd been right. "I also see we're all wearing identical pearl earrings. I don't suppose they were a wedding gift?"

The other three immediately touched their ear lobes and then rolled their eyes.

"Oh my God," Pauline muttered.

Gretchen sighed. "I always thought he was so unique in his choices of gifts, and now I find he was buying in quantity."

Bettina gasped, and then her face got hot. "So, we all got pearl earrings for a wedding gift. But did you also get something else? Oh... how did he put it? Here, darling... a little something for your lonely nights when I'm away from home?"

There was a mutual gasp, and then the realization of what she'd said sunk in.

"Does it run on D batteries?" Janie asked.

"Oh gawdamighty," Gretchen mumbled.

Pauline rolled her eyes. "Are you serious?"

"He did, didn't he?" Bettina muttered. "He gave all of us vibrators—for a freaking wedding gift."

Gretchen rolled her eyes. "No wonder he was too tired to get it up."

They clasped their hands over their mouths to keep from laughing again, and then stared at each other in disbelief.

Silence grew, but Janie knew laughter was only part of what would take them past the disaster David Logan had caused.

"Did you come into the marriage with any kind of money or savings?" she asked.

"Not me," Bettina said. "But our personal bank account is nearly empty."

Janie glanced at the other two. "Are your savings gone?"

Pauline burst into tears. "Yes, I had a little savings, but everything is gone."

Gretchen bit her lip to keep from crying. "I had life insurance money put back from my first husband's death. It's gone. My sister laughed at me when I told her what had happened. I will never speak to her again."

Bettina's eyes welled. Tears rolled, taking carefully applied makeup with them. "I have two grown children. A son and a daughter. I haven't seen them in seven years. They disapproved of me and hated him. I called them when I found out he'd been killed, scared out of my mind in shock and grief, and all they had to say was 'I told you so.' I hung up and cried myself to sleep."

Their revelations had released an anger in Janie, too, and now she was crying.

"I don't have any living relatives, and only a few friends. Some of them know he died, but it's weird. No one came to see me. One person sent flowers. A client of mine who owns a flower shop. But no one else called. They don't know the whole story, but it obviously didn't matter, so I guess they weren't such good friends, after all."

Bettina wiped her eyes, angry all over again.

"He vetted us like the con man he was! He looked for lonely women hungry for attention. Women who wanted to belong to someone. We were easy marks for kind words and a pretty face!"

Hearing their truth wasn't easy, but hearing it said aloud gave validity to what they'd been feeling.

"Well, he's not pretty anymore," Janie muttered. "And what's left of him is in that box behind you... I don't know how you feel about this, but you need to know that it is my responsibility to deal with the remains."

"Are you having a funeral?" Pauline asked.

Janie frowned. "Funerals are for saying goodbye to people you love. A way of honoring them. He had no honor. He stole our money. He lied to all of us. And hell no, I'm not doing that. When I leave here today, it will be the last time I see this place. He's being cremated. I don't want his ashes. Do any of you?"

Gretchen burst into tears again. "I have to find a job, so I'll have money to find somewhere to live, and the last thing I'd want is to take him with me. So, that's a no for me."

Bettina shuddered. "I've already faced the fact that I can't keep the place we leased. I don't want the bastard."

Pauline shook her head. "I don't have family. I work online building websites, but he stole all my reserves, and I won't come close to making enough to pay deposits so I can move or support myself. In about a month, I'm going to be homeless."

At that moment, the skin crawled on the back of Janie's neck. She sat quietly, seeing past the facade with which they'd arrived, to the broken people they were beneath. They hadn't meant to be connected to each other, but now they were.

She thought of her home—a huge, two-story house with a full basement and an attic of epic proportions, situated in the historic district of St. Louis. She was the third generation of Duvalls to be living there. It was hers, free and clear... and it was empty, except for her. She took a deep breath and started talking before she could change her mind.

"I have an offer to make. I inherited my family home over twenty years ago. I'm the third generation to be living in it. David just moved in when we married, and fortunately, could not get his hands on it. But it's huge... and there is a second floor with four large bedrooms and two Jack and Jill bathrooms just sitting there gathering dust. My bed and bath are downstairs. I have an office there and a bookkeeping business. I have space, and I'm not going to be evicted. If we were comfortable being married to him, then we should be able to find a way to be comfortable with each other."

Pauline went pale and then reeled in her seat so fast the other three feared she was going to pass out.

Gretchen reached out to steady her. "Are you all right?"

Pauline grasped Janie's wrist, as if she needed the connection to hear the answer.

"Are you offering us a place to live?"

Janie nodded. "Yes. For as long as you want or need, even if we grow old together there, it will be fine with me."

"But what if we don't get along?" Bettina asked.

Janie shrugged. "Family doesn't always agree, but if they care enough about each other, they find a way to get past the rough spots."

"Oh my God. Oh my God," Pauline said, and then burst into tears.

Janie felt a wave of emotion wash through her. This was the right thing to do. She stood. "Group hug," she said, and opened her arms.

Moments later, the widows of David Logan were in a four-way embrace, crying and hugging, and for the first time since their devastating news, getting a glimpse of salvation.

In height, Pauline towered over Janie, but right now, the little red-head was a giant to Pauline.

"No wonder he loved you," she said.

Janie shook her head. "He didn't know the meaning of love. Now, how about you all following me to my place so you can finish deciding for yourselves?"

"Yes, yes, please," Pauline said.

"I'm in," Bettina added.

"So am I," Gretchen said.

There was a quiet tap on the door before it opened to the director. He was standing on the threshold with an odd expression on his face. The women had been in there for over an hour now, and while the employees of the funeral home hadn't been able to hear what was being said among the women, they'd heard the laughter and they'd heard crying, and they didn't know what to make of it.

"Ladies, I was wondering if you'd all come to a decision as to what kind of service you wish to have?"

Janie didn't blink.

"We have all come to the same conclusion. He doesn't get a service, and we don't want him. Cremate the body, dump the ashes, and send me the bill. And we're leaving now. We're going home."

The director was aghast. Never in all his years had he ever been delivered such an ultimatum.

"Are you certain this is what you want?"

Janie's cheeks were flushed in anger. "What we wanted was an honest husband. Instead, we got a crooked bigamist who stole our savings, lied to all of us, and destroyed our lives. Burn and dump him. Period."

The director stepped back to keep from being mowed down, then glanced back inside the viewing room, and shook his head. Even the deceased reaped what they'd sown.

Janie left the funeral home so full of rage she was sick to her stomach. She gave the women her address should they get separated in traffic, then purposefully drove slow, hoping they wouldn't lose her.

She didn't know what fresh hell might come her way by turning her home into a refuge for a bunch of broke-ass women, but she did know she would have never sleep soundly again if she had stayed silent. She wasn't guilty of anything, and neither were they. They'd just had the misfortune to fall for a lying conman with a pretty face.

Finally, she reached her neighborhood, and the sight of home gave her courage. She wasn't the only member of her ancestors to have suffered setbacks and sorrows, but with no other heirs waiting in the wings, she was going to be the last. She gained nothing by holing up in there alone, and she wasn't leaving this world like a stray dog with its tail tucked between its legs.

She pulled in beneath the double-wide portico, then got out to wait for the others to get parked beside and behind her. The driveway went through the portico and made a loop back out onto the street, so whoever was parked in front took the loop, and whoever had parked behind other cars, backed out onto the street.

They were shocked by the size of it, and she could see it on their faces. It was a grand old house, but it didn't run itself, and it would be touch and go financially with three more people under the roof.

"Oh my God!" Bettina whispered, as she got out of her car.

"It's beautiful," Pauline said, as she walked up behind her.

Gretchen just kept staring. It was a mansion. A massive red brick house with a verandah that ran the length of the structure, and ornate turrets and gables on the rooftop.

"It's just home to me," Janie said. She had her house key in her hand as they followed her up into the house, with the sounds of their heels echoing on the marbled floor of the foyer. "You can tell the age of the place by the architecture, but everything that mattered was updated and begging for the sounds of life within the walls. Follow me, and I'll give you the grand tour downstairs, and then we'll go upstairs to the beds and baths."

She took them through the living room, pointing out a massive gas fireplace at one end of the room and all the built-in shelves laden with antiques and family treasures on either side of it. Then she walked them to the library and across the hall to her office.

"I have sixteen clients, and they are fairly large accounts. I think I'll make enough to keep things moving," Janie said.

"Oh! We would work, too!" Pauline said. "I can design websites anywhere. I'll work on my computer in the bedroom. We wouldn't stay here without making a contribution!"

"For sure," Bettina said, and Gretchen nodded in agreement.

Janie breathed a quick sigh of relief, pleased to hear their eagerness to make this succeed.

"That would be hugely helpful," Janie said. "If you'll follow me, I'll show you the dining room on the way to the kitchen."

They followed, staring open-mouthed at the elegant chandelier hanging over a long cherry dining table and the dozen chairs around it, and at the matching sideboard and china cabinet, filled with what appeared to be a twelve-place setting of china.

Then she moved on into a roomy eat-in kitchen with a large white rustic table surrounded by armless, straight-back chairs, and more cabinets than they'd ever seen in one space. They each stroked a hand across the smooth surface of the white quartz countertops, then enviously eyed the butler's pantry and a large utility room beyond.

Janie walked them out the back door onto a verandah that was a twin to the front, with a deep porch running the length of the building. Out here, the grounds beyond the house were huge and covered in a thick carpet of green grass with paved walkways that wound through the flower beds, and the bushes beyond.

"The roses! Oh, my word!" Gretchen said. "Do you do all this yourself?"

"I tend the flowers because I love them, but there's a company who mows and weeds for me. I couldn't possibly do it all," Janie said, and took them back into the center of the house, pointing out the long hallway beyond the stairs.

"My bedroom and bath are at the end of that hall," and then she stopped and kicked off her heels. "I can't stand these a moment longer. Now, upstairs we go, and see what rooms appeal to each of you. They're all about the same size, but decorated differently, so let's see what you think."

"My feet hurt, too," Bettina said.

"Then kick off your shoes," Janie said, and one by one, the four women in black removed the fancy shoes that they'd worn to impress and walked up the grand staircase in their bare feet. Once they reached the head of the stairs, Janie paused, pointing to the door on the right.

"This leads to the blue room. The one across the hall is the lilac room. Then the other two doors at the far end of the hall are the yellow room and the red room. As I said before, there's a Jack and Jill bathroom for the lilac and yellow bedrooms, and another for the red and blue bedrooms in between them.

"Blue is my favorite color," Pauline said.

"I love lilac," Bettina said.

Gretchen sighed. "Yellow is a happy color. It's my favorite."

Janie smiled. "Sounds like you have already settled one issue." Then she opened the door to the red room and led the way in.

There was a large, antique four-poster bed against the far wall, along with a matching dresser and armoire in convenient proximity and a flat-screen television hanging on the wall opposite the bed. And in a sitting area, there was a small love seat, a writing desk and chair, and a lamp.

Then Janie pointed to the closet door.

"Most of these old houses had tiny closets, or none at all because they kept their clothes in armoires and dressers, but my father remodeled them years ago. They all have decent size walk-in closets. Have a look. Open doors and drawers. Pauline, check out the extra bedroom while you're looking. You could move things around and use it for your office if you want. I'm going to the kitchen to get out some snacks. I haven't been hungry in days, but I feel better right now. When you've finished looking at all the rooms, come join me. We'll sit at the kitchen table and talk some more."

"Thank you, Janie. Thank you," Gretchen said.

Janie paused, then shook her head. "No. Thank you," and then she was gone.

The three women looked at each other and then burst into tears.

"I dreaded coming today, but look at the blessing that was waiting," Gretchen said.

Pauline nodded. "I have been scared to death ever since I found out my savings was gone."

"David didn't have any morals, but he had good taste in women," Bettina said. "I think we can do this. Now, Janie gave us free rein, so let's check all this out."

Janie had shopped yesterday on the off chance they might choose to come here after meeting at the funeral home. She was nervous, and at the same time, elated. If they did this together, she was certain they could survive what had been done to them, so she began making little sandwiches and getting out a fruit tray, then she set places at the kitchen table.

By the time they came into the kitchen, they were chatting.

She looked up, smiling. "Something has obviously pleased you."

"You pleased us! You have given us hope! We will never be able to thank you enough," Bettina said.

"We are gratefully taking you up on your offer, and the spare bedroom would be perfect for an office. There's already a desk and chair in it, and lots of room," Pauline added.

"But we want to assure you that we're all ready to find work to help make this happen," Gretchen added.

Janie took a quick breath. She meant to speak, but the words were suddenly stuck in her throat, then the tears welled and rolled.

"Don't cry, sweetie!" they all cried, and gathered around her, wrapping her up in their embrace.

After that, they ate and talked until the food was gone, and their plans were made.

"I know it will be hard giving up your own places," Janie said. "And, while I want you to live here as if this was your home, you might not feel that way, and that's okay. It won't hurt my feelings. Just consider this your—your..." Janie was struggling to put a name to their situation, and finally threw up her hands. "Oh, I don't know. For lack of a better word... your clubhouse. Men of a certain social status go to the country club for socializing and golf and conducting business. So, this will be *our* clubhouse, where we come for comfort and safety and know we have a place to rest. This house has been the Duvall estate for three generations, but as of today, it's going to be the Broke-Ass Women's Club. And we're going to survive what happened to us and persevere in spite of it, because that's what women do best."

They laughed, and then they cried, exhausted from the upheaval of the day, and from knowing the burdens they'd come with had just been taken off their shoulders by the smallest among them.

"The Broke-Ass Women's Club it is!" Bettina said. "Now all we have to do is go home and pack."

They all agreed selling their furniture and household items only made sense. None of it held sentimental value, and the money would be a little nest egg to tide them over until they found jobs in St. Louis.

"I'm selling everything except my personal clothing and my mother's silver," Gretchen said.

"Pack it and bring it with you," Janie said. "There's room in the attic to store anything you want to keep."

Bettina and Pauline both spoke up, agreeing they had a few family keepsakes that they would bring, and it was settled. By the time they were getting ready to leave, they weren't strangers anymore. They were women connected because of a tragedy and a crime.

"Drive safe!" Janie said, as they were getting back into their cars. "Call me when you get home, so I'll know you made it."

"We will, we will," they all said as they waved goodbye.

Then one by one, they drove through the portico and back onto the street—all too soon out of sight.

Janie closed the door, then turned around. The house seemed too empty and too quiet now that they were gone. She moved through the foyer, pausing before heading down the hall to her bedroom to change, and made a mental note to tell the cleaning service to ready the upstairs for residents.

Then she spoke aloud, so the house would know.

"They'll be back, and it will be good."

A couple of days later, Janie was at work in her office when her business phone rang. She hit Save on a spreadsheet, and then reached for the phone without checking Caller ID.

"Hello?"

"Hello. May I speak to Janie Logan?"

"This is Janie."

"Mrs. Logan, I'm Bruce Ledbetter, with the *Dispatch*. First, please accept my sympathies on the loss of your husband. We're doing a piece on your deceased husband's bigamy situation, and would like to get some comments from you regard—"

Janie hung up. She wasn't surprised, but it had been long enough since the accident that she thought they might have let it slide. Obviously, someone had spilled the beans. Likely someone from the funeral home. Bigamy was news-worthy, and here she was.

So, now this would be local news, and knowing the state of the nation these days, it might tickle fancies enough to make national news as well.

She immediately sent all three of the girls a heads-up text not to give interviews, or the media would hound them forever, and then got up. She needed to clear her head before she went back to work and went outside to her garden. She filled a bird bath, dead-headed some roses, then sat down on a little bench beneath a massive oak at the back of the property and finally leaned back and closed her eyes.

Birds were singing. The air was warm on her face. A sense of peace moved through her, and as it did, she let go and cried. Tears were healing, and the Good Lord knew she was in need of that. She had been conned and swindled, and now everyone who knew her would know it, too.

The next morning, she opened the paper and saw the headline and photos beneath.

THE DEATH OF A BIGAMIST – Four women share tragedy.

"Well shit," Janie muttered, and stuffed the last bite of her cinnamon toast into her mouth. "Thank you, David, for the ass you were. You've left a mighty stink behind you for the rest of us to clean up."

The next day, Janie headed to the bank to meet her lawyer, James Bedford. There would be witnesses necessary to the opening of David's safety deposit box, and all the contents would be listed as she removed them, then a copy of the list would go to her, her lawyer, James Bedford, and to the bank.

She arrived with her chin up and her emotions shuttered. There'd be no histrionics for David Logan. He didn't deserve them.

She handed the key to a bank officer, and he, his secretary, Janie, and her lawyer proceeded into the vault, unlocked David's safety deposit box, and pulled it out. Then Janie's lawyer began removing the items one at a time, giving the secretary time to list them.

The items were shocking. Four separate birth certificates, one for each of his aliases, with a Social Security card paperclipped to each one, and all with different numbers on them. There was a manila envelope with all manner of paperwork supporting them, and a notebook with phone numbers and initials beside each one.

Bedford frowned. "Getting identification like this doesn't come cheap."

There were four small plastic baggies, each with a different woman's name written on it. Each baggie contained identical ruby rings in different sizes, still in the little black velvet gift boxes.

Janie snorted. "Jesus. Talk about shopping in bulk. Christmas presents, I presume."

Bedford grimaced. He knew Janie was hurting, but there was nothing to be done but get this over with, and finally they finished.

"What do I do with this shit?" Janie asked.

"I'll take possession on your behalf until we're sure this has all been settled, and the police are satisfied. But there's no Will, and it's becoming apparent the man owned nothing, so there's nothing to probate."

Janie nodded, and as soon as she departed, went straight to the post office, removed the accumulated mail in his private box, informed the postmaster that the owner, her husband, was deceased, and went home.

For the next seven days, everywhere Janie went, she was accosted by people she knew, wanting all the gory details of her life. She was prodded for information by her clients, even by a clerk at her pharmacy. She was heart-sick, fed up, and carrying the burden of shame and rage to the point that she finally lost it.

It was Thursday. The cleaning service was at her house on their regular schedule, but today she'd added to it. After she'd given them directions as to what she wanted done upstairs such as changing the bedding on the beds then to prepare the basement for the storm season, she left to run errands.

One stop at the dry cleaners.

A stop at her local pharmacy.

A trip to the supermarket.

And then on the way home she noticed she was running low on fuel, so she pulled into a gas station. She took her credit card and keys as she got out, then locked the car behind her before moving to the pumps. She had the gas cap off and was in the act of refueling when a car pulled up on the other side of the pumps.

One look at who it was, and she groaned. Brad Dunning was someone she'd gone to school with. She immediately turned her back to him, hoping he wouldn't see her, and focused on the fuel running into her tank. But her hopes were dashed when she heard him say her name.

"Janie! Hello there!"

She looked over her shoulder. "Oh. Hi, Brad. How are Tish and the kids?"

"Oh, they're fine," he said, and circled the pumps, then leaned against the back end of her SUV and crossed his arms, as if settling in for a visit. "I wanted to express my condolences for your loss. Tish and I are so sorry."

"Thanks," she said, and breathed a sigh of relief as the pump kicked off. She quickly replaced the nozzle, got her receipt, and screwed the gas cap back on, but Brad seemed to have forgotten he was supposed to be refueling his own car.

"So," Brad said, and then winked at her. "I know this is personal, but did you have any idea that—"

It was the wink that undid her. She interrupted him in mid-sentence.

"Brad! Do me a favor and stop talking! Yes, it's personal, which means, none of your damn business! I have seen you off and on all over the city for the past twenty years, but not once have you ever felt the need to speak to me. And now, during the worst time of my life, you want to chat?"

Shock registered, but Brad Dunning didn't know he'd unleashed the Kraken.

Janie threw up her hands in a gesture of defeat as the tone of her voice shifted into *shout*.

"It has become painfully apparent to me, and even more shocking than finding out I'd been married to a con man, that I had been led to believe I also have friends. Because apparently, *I don't!* Friends don't pry when someone dies. They bring food. They send flowers. They just show up and ask if I need any help. Guess how many pies showed on my doorstep? *None!*" And now she was screaming. "No flowers of sympathy! No sympathy cards in the mail. *None!* So, you take your curiosity and your nose out of my business and shove it straight up your ashoutss! Now get off my car! I'm going home!"

When she took the first step toward him, Brad Dunning jumped and ran.

Janie huffed her little self into the car, and drove away from the station without looking back, and the farther away she drove, the more she began coming undone—cursing fate, and David Logan, and Brad Dunning, and every other fair-weather friend who dared claim a connection to her. She was too mad to cry. All she wanted was the comfort and sanctity of home.

The cleaning service was still there when she got back, so she began carrying in the groceries, and then went back for the pieces she'd picked up from the dry cleaners. She began putting everything away. The longer she worked, the more frustration that came out.

She was standing in the pantry, shoving cans of vegetables on the shelves, when she lost it again.

"Damn you, David Logan. Your deceit was unforgivable... But I only knew you ten years. Fuck the people I grew up with. I knew them all of my life."

By the time the cleaning service left, the house was shining. She could smell lemon oil in every room, and the order of everything in its place gave her a sense of peace. She couldn't control people's actions, but she could control her reactions to them. Today had been

an anomaly. The pressure of all that had happened had made her lose her cool. She couldn't do that again. She wouldn't give them the satisfaction.

And she, by God, had something to look forward to. She wasn't going to be alone much longer. She'd been raised Episcopalian, but life had given her sister-wives, and she had never been one to refuse a gift.

CHAPTER THREE

Pauline was the first to arrive.

She came two weeks later, and Janie helped her move her belongings into the blue bedroom, then her computer and files into the red bedroom which would become her office. They stored a couple of her boxes in the attic, and then Janie gave her a key to the house. She was settled in before nightfall, and they ate dinner together in the kitchen. Because Janie cooked, Pauline insisted on cleaning up.

"Please," Pauline said. "I want to. I need to be another arm, not a burden."

Janie nodded. "I get that, and the help is appreciated. I'll be in the office for a bit finishing up a little work, and then I'm going to have an early night. The house is yours to roam as you please," she said, and then impulsively hugged Pauline before she left the room.

Pauline was too surprised to return the favor, and she turned to the dishes in the sink, blinking back tears. Once she was finished, she took a cold bottle of water up to her room and began unpacking the last suitcase she'd brought with her. By the time she was finished, she was exhausted. So, she showered, put on a pair of clean pajamas, and crawled in between crisp, clean sheets. The moment her head hit the pillow, she smelled lavender. Just like the sheets that used to be on her bed at her grandparents' when she was a child.

It was the perfect end to a long, stressful day. There were no words for how grateful she was to Janie, and no way to express how broken she felt. The man she'd loved had stabbed her in the back when she wasn't looking. She missed him to the point of agony, and at the same time, hated everything he'd done to her—to all of them.

She closed her eyes and cried herself to sleep.

Eight days later, Gretchen arrived, and again, it didn't take long to get her moved into the yellow bedroom, store a couple of boxes in the attic, and get a key to the house. Making dinner together later was no longer a task, it was becoming a party.

Gretchen loved order, and the old adage of "a place for everything, and everything in its place" showed.

Janie emptied cans of petite diced tomatoes into a pan, while Pauline was put water on to boil the pasta.

"Hey, Gretchen. The spices are in the cabinet to the left of the sink. Would you get some basil and oregano for me?" Janie asked.

"Sure," Gretchen said, and opened the cabinet, only to be faced with a large assortment of spice jars all in a jumble. She began pulling out the jars one by one until she found the herbs and gave them to Janie. Then without thinking, she took the rest of them out, and put them back on the shelf in alphabetical order. And when Janie sent her to the pantry for a small can of tomato paste, she quickly delivered it, then went back and sorted cans into alphabetical order, too.

Pauline saw what she was doing and grinned.

"Girl, you are way too organized for me. Whatever you do, don't rearrange my office. I have a method to my chaos."

Gretchen paused, suddenly afraid that she had done something wrong.

"Oh, I'm sorry. I did that without asking. It's just my OCD on alert," she said.

Janie shook her head. "No ma'am. Don't ever apologize for being you. I think the Good Lord sent you to put me back together. I've been alone so long that I quit paying attention to that."

Then both girls stopped and stared at Janie.

"Did you just hear what you said?" Gretchen asked.

Janie frowned. "What do you mean?"

Pauline sighed. "You just said you'd been alone so long. Is that how you felt, too? Alone, I mean? Before all this happened, that's how I felt. I was married, but still always on my own."

Janie's eyes welled. "I didn't realize I'd said that. A subconscious brain fart, I guess."

They looked away from her tears.

"I'll take that explanation any day over admitting I was scammed," Gretchen said.

And they laughed again.

After that, they finished cooking, and the evening came and went.

Two days later, Bettina arrived. Coming from Kansas City, she also had the farthest to drive, but she arrived with a broken finger and a black eye from a fall she'd had three days earlier. Because of her broken finger, it had taken her forever to load her things into the car. Then she'd cried most of the way to St. Louis from the pain and frustration. But the moment she got out and the girls saw her, she was enveloped in sympathy and hugs.

"Oh honey! What happened?" Janie cried.

"I fell over a damn box," Bettina said, then broke into tears all over again.

"Bless your heart!" Pauline said.

"We'll get your stuff," Gretchen said. "It won't take the three of us anytime to get you moved in."

"I'm so sorry," Bettina said, as the tears kept rolling. "I didn't intend to arrive as an invalid. I feel like a fool."

"You go inside. We'll tend to this," Janie said. "Oh... I left your key to the house on your dresser."

"I'll take a load as I go," Bettina said.

"You take yourself and your purse and hush," Gretchen added.

Within a couple of hours, they had Bettina's clothing in the closet and the dresser, her suitcases put up, and the boxes she's brought stored up in the attic. After that, they went downstairs, gathering at the kitchen table with cookies and cold drinks to catch up on the drama they'd each gone through in selling their things.

"People are unbelievable," Gretchen said. "I had two full bedroom sets, nice ones with matching dressers, and this woman actually had the nerve to offer me a measly hundred dollars for both sets."

Pauline frowned. "No way! What did you do?"

"I told her I'd already been conned enough in this lifetime, and to get her stingy ass out of my house," Gretchen said.

They nodded, still sharing her indignation.

Bettina couldn't quit looking around the table. Unable to believe she was really here—doing this. Living with David's other wives instead of him. Not that she would have wanted him back, but there was a hole in her heart where his place used to be, and she didn't yet know how to fill it.

However, now that she wasn't driving and had taken some pain meds, she was more comfortable than she'd been all day. The pea-nut-butter cookies were good, but the camaraderie was better. She'd been anxious about how this situation was going to play out and had envisioned a repeat of high school slumber parties, but this felt comforting. Like being with sisters. She reached for another cookie, then waved it in the air, punctuating her story about moving.

"I had a buyer for my dining room furniture, but she wanted to give me a check and something told me, don't take it. So, I told her it was cash or Venmo. She got angry, but I stood my ground. And while she was still having herself a fit, and cursing me out in my own dining room, another buyer showed up and offered cash, and I took it. Right in front of her. The look on that woman's face was priceless."

Janie laughed and listened, watching their faces, seeing them without makeup, without artifice of any kind. Just forty-something women who knew who they were, with nothing to prove.

After their first dinner together was over that night and the kitchen cleaned up, the women were hesitant, not quite certain what they should do next. Was everything under this roof to be done together, or were they free to make their own choices?

Then Janie answered the question before they could ask.

"I'm going outside. The roses need watering, and now that the sun is going down, the air will be cooler. This is home. Do what you feel like doing. Sit out on the back verandah. Watch TV in the living room or retire to your rooms and watch TV there if you're needing some alone time. We're all used to spending lots of days alone, so there's no need to feel like we have now become a herd."

The idea of a herd made them laugh.

Janie loved the sound of their laughter and kept on talking. "There are books galore in the library. Poker chips and decks of cards in the sideboard, and there are several board games on the shelf below. Monopoly and the like."

Gretchen stilled. "Did you play Monopoly?"

Bettina sat up a little straighter. "With him?"

"He was a horrible loser. He had to win, or he was mad," Pauline said.

Janie was stunned and her expression showed it.

"Well shit. I suppose we'll be running into this information for-ever. And frankly, I don't enjoy that game. I did it for him."

"Same," they echoed.

Janie walked over to the sideboard, pulled out the Monopoly box, and headed for the back door.

"What are you doing?" Bettina asked.

"Going to water roses. I'm just taking out the trash along the way."

"I'm going to bed, maybe watch a little TV," Bettina said. "It's been a long day for me."

"I'm going to watch TV in bed," Pauline said.

"Me, too," Bettina said.

Janie nodded. "Oh... Bettina, the other girls know this, but I'll say it again for you. Nobody is required to get up in this house until they're ready, and when you do, feel free to eat what you want. If you want to cook yourself some breakfast, it's in the fridge. If you just want cereal and coffee, all the fixings are in the pantry."

"We add what we need to a grocery list," Pauline said, pointing to a pad on the table, and we donate to the pantry fund, then one of us makes the grocery run for the house."

"Got it," Bettina said. "Right now, I'm hoping this black eye fades soon. I hate the looks I'm getting. I just know everyone thinks I'm a victim of abuse."

Gretchen frowned. "Well, you were abused, in a way. We all were. So, wear that black eye proudly, girl, because we're still here, and he's not."

Bettina sighed. "You're right. I need to get over worrying how I look. I used to have all kinds of confidence in myself, and I'm going to again. I had all these plans to start job hunting immediately, and now here I am looking like I was in a bar brawl." They laughed, which made Bettina smile. "Well, I do."

"It's okay. There's nothing wrong with us. You can just hold down the fort here until you're all better," Janie said.

"I can do that," Bettina said, already feeling better about herself.

After that, they dispersed, leaving Janie to her flowers.

She went out with the Monopoly game, dumped it in the garbage can, and then picked up the garden hose and began watering the bushes, moving about the yard as she worked. When she neared the back of the property where the Rose of Sharon bushes were blooming, she heard a door slam and sighed.

That would be Florence Lane, her neighbor to the west. She was nosy and something of a busybody, but she was also a lonely widow, stuck with a son and family living with her, and Janie felt sorry for her, too. Since her husband's death, Florence no longer knew quite where she belonged and kept trying to find her path in life again.

Janie didn't want to talk. She didn't want to answer questions, but she also didn't want to be rude. As she heard her coming up the path, she just gritted her teeth and prepared herself to be grilled.

And then Florence called out.

"Yoohoo! Hello neighbor!"

Janie turned around, pretending surprise.

"Oh, hi Florence. Nice evening, isn't it?"

"A little steamy for my comfort," Florence said.

Janie nodded and kept the water running, but Florence persisted.

"I feel so sorry for you after all that embarrassing news coverage. I just wanted to see how you're doing. Do you plan to have a memorial service for dear David?"

Janie winced. Pity pissed her off.

"You don't need to feel sorry for me. I'm going to be fine. No, there will be no services, but thank you for asking."

Florence frowned. "No service? But why?"

Janie turned off the water. She wasn't going to lie to cover up his crimes. And she wasn't going to let anyone else make her feel guilty about it.

"I would have assumed, since you have obviously read the sordid story in the paper, that there is no such thing as 'dear David', and you would have the grace not to speak of it. It appears my assumption was wrong."

Florence flushed, then looked away.

"Well, I didn't want to seem—"

Janie swallowed past the lump in her throat. "He was a conman. He lied to four decent women, stole their life savings, and played with their lives. Why the hell would I honor that?"

"Of course. I just... Well, never mind."

"Yes. Never mind," Janie said.

Not to be deterred, Florence started over.

"I see you have company. It's so important to be supported during times like this."

Janie sighed. The woman was not going to stop. "They're not company. They live here now."

"Oh! Well, I'll say. I can't wait to meet them. Are they part of your Duvall family?"

"No. They're David's other wives. He stole their money and a good deal of mine. He left them broke and homeless. I have a home. Now they do, too."

Florence's eyes widened and her mouth dropped.

"Why would you live with *them*?"

Janie frowned. "There is not a damn thing wrong with us. The obvious question to be asked is why did we live with *him*? Now, excuse me, but I need to finish before it gets dark," Janie said, turned her back on her neighbor, and picked up the hose.

When she heard a door slam again, she knew Florence had gone back inside, and would have bet money she was already on the phone calling everyone she knew about what she'd been told.

Whatever.

Janie watered until it was too dark to see what she was doing, then dragged the hose back to the hydrant and turned off the faucet. She was listening to St. Louis at night as she coiled up the hose when she happened to look up and saw the lights shining from the second-floor windows. Even in the red bedroom, which meant Pauline was working. Those windows had been dark for more years than she could remember, and now they were alit from within. The house was alive again, and it made her feel good.

Janie sighed and began picking her way up the shadowy path to the house, and then inside, locking up downstairs, turning off lights as she went, and pausing at the bottom of the stairs to listen.

She could faintly hear the televisions and imagined them in their nightwear, tucked safely into their beds. It felt good not to be in this house all alone. The month of June was nearly over. Subsistence for two of them was still an unknown, but they were finally under one roof.

One step at a time, girl. One step at a time.

It was Wednesday. The first day of July.

During the ensuing days, Bettina's black eye faded, and Pauline quit crying at the drop of a hat. She had finished the website she'd was building when she moved and was elated to have two new clients.

Gretchen and Bettina had been job hunting for the better part of two weeks, participating in an abundance of Zoom interviews between them, but it was Gretchen who finally got a call to come in for an in-person interview. Everyone was excited for her and began helping her pick out her outfit.

Pauline did her hair, and Janie loaned her a purse.

Bettina was watching as she dressed, and when Gretchen went into her jewelry box to look for jewelry, Bettina quickly spoke up.

"Girl, don't wear those pearl earrings."

They all stopped, turned to look at Bettina, and then burst out laughing.

Gretchen nodded. "Right! No pearls."

A short while later, she was headed out the door. "Wish me luck, y'all."

"Luck!" they shouted.

Gretchen shook her head, but she felt bolstered by their desire for her to succeed.

"You're all impossible," she said.

"Maybe," Bettina said. "But we're also irreplaceable."

They bunched up in the doorway to watch her leave, and then closed the door.

"I'm nervous for her," Pauline said.

"Oh God, me, too," Bettina added.

"I have cookies," Janie said.

Pauline gave them a thumbs up. "When in doubt, eat! I'm up for a cookie or three."

"I'll get the drinks. What's your pleasure?" Bettina asked.

"As long as it's not sweet, I'll always have iced tea," Janie said.

"Me, too," Pauline said.

"Let's sit on the back verandah," Janie said. "The azaleas are blooming, and they are a sight to see."

So, they took their drinks, and a plate of cookies and went outside.

The day was already hot, but the iced tea was cold. There was a breeze, and they were in the shade as they settled into chairs around a small table with their snacks.

"To Gretchen!" they said, and toasted her with cookies.

"And to us!" Janie added, and they toasted again, then took a big bite.

They sat in mutual silence for a few moments as they finished off their cookies while taking in the view of the blooming azaleas.

"My favorites are that lavender shade," Janie said.

Bettina pointed. "I like that dark pink."

Pauline was still in awe of the elegance of the whole property.

"You are so lucky to have grown up here," she said.

Janie gazed out across the grounds, trying to imagine how it would appear to strangers.

"I know, but I never saw it through your eyes. You know what I mean? When you're little, whatever is your normal, that's how you think of the world. I had to get a little older before I realized there were large houses, small houses, and people with no houses at all. It was an eye-opener. But I still hold to the premise that wherever you are loved is what makes a house a home. And I had great parents. I always wanted siblings, but it didn't happen, and now the only one left is me. I was thirty-two when David and I got married, and we both decided children weren't on the agenda, so my family ends with me."

Bettina broke of a piece of her cookie and then stared at it, lost in thought before she spoke.

"I had a brother. He died in Afghanistan. I got married at eighteen. I was in my second year of college."

"Seriously?" Pauline said.

Bettina shrugged. "I graduated high school at sixteen. I had a very high IQ and a low opinion of myself. I married Gary Vale, a young doctor in residency at a big hospital in Kansas City, Missouri, and at his urging, dropped out of college and had two babies by the time I was twenty-two. My parents have been gone for about twelve years now. I have my children, who have continued to disappointment me in their adult years. Or... maybe I'm the one who disappointed them. Who knows?"

Janie reached across the table and gave Bettina's hand a quick squeeze.

"They're the ones who are going to be sorry. Do they know you've moved?"

She frowned. "No, and I'm not going to tell them, either. They have my number. If they want to know anything about me, they can call, and I may or may not answer."

Pauline was sitting quietly, listening while mentally comparing her life to theirs.

"We are all so different, and yet we all wound up attracted to the same man. How did that happen?" she said.

"We don't know what he was really like," Janie said. "*He* conformed himself to suit us so we would be sucked into his con. Never forget that, sugar."

Pauline let the words sink in. "I never thought of it like that, but you're right. And I'm also remembering that he never wanted to talk about himself—where he grew up, or anything like that."

Bettina leaned forward. "What if his parents are still alive somewhere?"

Janie shrugged. "I lived with him ten years, and if they were alive, they did not communicate with each other. Personally, I don't think he ever had parents. I think the devil hatched him, then threw him out as a dud."

"I wonder if the devil took him back when he died," Gretchen muttered.

"The truth is likely the most obvious," Janie said. "He kept his story simple so he wouldn't get mixed up about what he told to which wife."

Bettina snorted. "I'll bet your right."

Janie was ready to change the subject and pointed out toward the rose garden.

"Look! There's a rabbit in the garden! I haven't seen one here in ages."

"Maybe he likes us," Pauline said.

Janie laughed. "Maybe he does," she said, then glanced at

the time.

"Gretchen is having her interview right now."

"It's for that receptionist job at the insurance company, right?" Pauline asked.

Bettina nodded. "We all know how orderly she is. She's already alphabetized the spice shelf and the pantry, and we've all seen her closet. She has blouses hanging together according to color, and the same with all her slacks. Her shoes are lined up so perfectly it looks like she freaking got on her knees and measured them. She's so organized. She'd be good at any job she gets."

Janie rolled her eyes. "Well, don't look in my closet. I'm just happy when everything is on a hangar."

They all burst out laughing, which sent the little rabbit scampering away.

"Well shoot. We scared the bunny," Pauline said.

"It will come back when we're inside and not so noisy," Janie said, and then glanced up at the sky. "Looks like we might be in for some weather tonight. Look at those clouds building up in the west."

"Ugh! I'm terrified of tornadoes," Bettina said.

Janie shrugged. "Anyone with a brain in their head should be afraid of them, but no worries. We have a full basement under this house. It even has beds and a half-bath. I've spent whole nights down there before. My father would take us down when it was stormy, and then they'd put me to bed. I'd just go back to asleep. I had it cleaned not too long ago, getting ready for storm season."

"Good to know," Bettina said. "It's that door off the kitchen, right?"

"Yes. Wanna see?" Janie asked.

"Sure, why not?" they said, and gathered up their things and went inside.

Janie turned on the lights at the head of the stairs and then descended.

"Use the handrail. The steps are a little steep," she said, as she led the way.

Pauline stopped at the bottom of the stairs, staring about in shock. "This place is huge."

"It's a footprint of the house above it, so, yes, it's big," Janie said. "As you can see, there are generations of junk down here. I used to roller skate here when I was little. Lots of concrete floor space. That sled on the wall was my father's when he was a boy. My grandfather used the work bench, but those are Dad's tools on it."

"I know nothing about tools and fixing things," Bettina said.

"I know how to fix some things. When I was still home, I used to help my dad," Janie said, and then pointed at the other end of the basement. "Down there are the beds and the half-bath. I put drop cloths over the beds to keep them as clean as possible for when we needed them."

"Wow, girl. This whole place is amazing. You have everything," Bettina said.

And then they all stopped, looked at each other, remembering what they'd lost.

"Not everything," Janie said. "Let's go back up. I want to check the weather."

They went back upstairs, turned on the TV to check the weather, and were relieved to learn there were no impending weather fronts strong enough to create tornadoes.

"I feel a need to bake," Pauline said. "It's calming to me, and this weather makes me antsy."

Bettina sighed. "I can't bake worth spit, but I can mix a good drink. I was working as a bartender in a hotel bar when I met David. That was after my divorce. But I wouldn't go back to that life. I should have stayed in college and gotten my teaching degree, but I didn't, and now here I am."

"How many college credits did you have when you quit?" Janie asked.

Bettina frowned. "Can't remember for sure, but I could probably finish my degree in a year or under."

"It's something to consider," Janie said.

"No money," Bettina said.

"So, what do you like to do?" Pauline asked.

Bettina sat a moment, and then smiled. "I love dogs. I would like to work for a groomer, but right now I'd settle for dog walking."

"It's good to work at something you like," Janie said, but she was still thinking about Pauline's claim to baking. "Hey, Pauline, what thing do you bake best?"

Pauline didn't hesitate. "Bourbon pecan pies."

"Holy shit, girl! Where have you been hiding that skill?" Bettina said.

"So, bake a pie," Janie said. "The kitchen is yours."

Pauline clapped her hands. "I'm excited. I will. I will."

They were still talking when they heard a key in the lock and looked at each other.

"Gretchen's back!" Bettina said, and then shouted. "We're in the kitchen!"

They sat, listening to her footsteps coming through the foyer, then through the dining room toward where they were sitting. When she walked in with a big grin on her face, they knew.

"I got the job! I start next Monday," she cried, and then did a little dance.

"Oh honey! You rock!" Janie said.

"Congratulations," Pauline cried.

"How much are they gonna pay you?" Bettina asked.

Janie shook her head. "Bettina, you just make my day. Leave it up to you to get down to the nitty-gritty."

Gretchen giggled. "Twenty-five hundred a month. Take home will be a little less. Last job I had was a bank teller after my first husband died. Then David didn't want me to keep working there, so I quit. This is a good start." And then she got a funny look on her face. "Well shit."

"What's wrong?" Janie asked.

"I just realized why David insisted I quit the bank. If I'd still been there, there was no way he could have hidden all his money transfers from me," she muttered.

"Ah... Yet another worm has emerged from his rotten life," Janie said.

"To hell with him," Pauline said. "I'm going to the store. Before I leave, do we have bourbon in the house?"

Gretchen blinked. "You really shouldn't drink and drive."

They laughed.

"What?" Gretchen asked.

"No worries," Janie said. "It's for a recipe. And yes, Pauline, there's bourbon in the liquor cabinet in the library. How much goes in each pie?"

"Just a couple of tablespoons," Pauline said.

"Then we're good," Janie said. "Shop away. I want pie for dessert tonight."

"Bourbon pecan pie sounds absolutely orgasmic," Bettina said.

"Well, that might put the vibrators out to pasture," Janie said.

"We'd be the first women in history to get fat on sex," Bettina said.

They shrieked, and then burst into laughter.

Pauline was still smiling when she left the house, and Gretchen went upstairs to change.

Bettina was fiddling with the cast on her finger.

"I need to see about getting this brace off my finger. I don't have a family doctor here, yet. What would you recommend?"

Janie paused, thinking before she answered. "Um... I think I would do one of those 24-hour emergency clinics for the brace, and you can decide on a doctor later."

"I'll go tomorrow," Bettina said.

"I'll text you the address for the one I use. I'm going to be in the office for a while. I have work to do," Janie said.

Bettina sighed. "I'm going to research and see how many dog-walking services there are in St. Louis. And, I'm just gonna say,

if I hadn't already wished David Logan to hell, I'd be doing it now."
She slapped the side of her leg in frustration, and then left the room.

Janie's eyes welled, then she set her jaw and headed to the office, swiping tears as she went.

The bourbon pecan pie was gone. They'd each had a piece, and then the last two pieces were eaten out of the pie dish, their forks dueling for bites between the four of them.

Gretchen groaned. "I have never eaten anything this good in my life."

Bettina licked her fork and sighed. "Better than sex, and it lasts a lot longer, too."

There was a long moment of silence, and then they looked at each other and rolled their eyes.

"Here's where he'd say, 'Oh, damn. Sorry hon. You're so hot I lost control'," Janie muttered.

Pauline snorted softly. "Two minutes tops, and he was done."

Gretchen sighed, her shoulder slumping where she sat.

"So, apparently he had one conversation and carried it with him like a backpack. Every time he hit a different house, he pulled out the same patter and ran through the spiel with all kinds of charm while waiting for us to simper and laugh. I am sick to my stomach, and it's not from too much pie."

Janie put her hand palm up in the middle of the table. "All for one..."

Bettina frowned. "Wait, what?"

But Pauline got it. She laid her hand over Janie's. "Come on, y'all."

They stacked their hands one upon the other.

"And one for all," Janie said.

"United we stand. Divided we fall," Pauline added.

"Who said that?" Gretchen asked.

"Alexander Dumas. It's a line from *The Three Musketeers*," Janie said.

Gretchen nodded. "Oh, that's right. I was trying to remember the origin. And we can do this if we do it together."

"Tonight, a pie. Tomorrow the world," Bettina said.

Their laughter filled the room where they were sitting, and what was leftover went into their hearts, filling up the sad places and the broken places. They went to bed in good spirits, full of sugar and laughter.

But then sleep came, and their good humor fell victim to the memories. They were all still wrestling with the shock of opening the door to the patrolmen, and dealing with various levels of sleeplessness and nightmares that came from being betrayed by the man in their beds.

Pauline woke up sobbing just after three a.m. and crept downstairs, only to find Janie sitting at the kitchen table with a cold drink in one hand and a box of tissues near the other. Janie's eyes were red-rimmed and swollen. When she looked up and saw Pauline she sighed.

"You, too?"

Pauline nodded.

"What's your poison?" Janie asked, pointing to her glass.

"I'll have whatever you're having," Pauline said.

Janie got up, took a liter of Dr. Pepper out of the frig, put a few ice cubes in a glass, and finished it off. It was still fizzing when she set it in front of Pauline.

"Thanks," Pauline said, and took a slow sip. "I always liked to feel that fizz on the tip of my nose when I was a kid," she said, and then reached for one of the tissues and wiped her eyes. "This is crazy. I hate him all day and dream about him all night."

A tear rolled down Janie's face unheeded. "Same. In the dreams, he's the man who made me laugh and made me believe I was a woman worth loving. And then he morphs into a vampire with fangs and drains my blood. I get the analogy. You know, he drained us of everything monetary, and the pain of the bite goes all the way to my heart."

"How long did you say you were married?" Pauline asked.

"A little over ten years. What about you?" she asked.

Pauline sighed. "Two years. Still in the honeymoon phase, I guess, but we dated a year before he proposed. I guess he needed another transfusion of money, and the only way he could get it was to marry me."

"I'm sorry," Janie said.

"Hell, I'm sorry for all of us," Pauline said. "Screw him and the lie he rode in on."

Janie looked up. "That would make a good bumper sticker."

Pauline blew her nose and then grinned. "There's a new job to add to my web design service. Creating my own bumper stickers, and the first one off the assembly line would read, EX-WIVES R US."

Janie sighed. "That would definitely catch on."

Pauline shrugged, and so they sat, sipping their drinks and trading mutual complaints until their glasses were empty.

"Feel better?" Janie asked.

"Yes, I do. Thanks," Pauline said.

"Glad for the company," Janie said. "Go to bed, sugar. I'll clean up here."

Pauline stood, then gave Janie a quick hug. "You are such a good person. I will never be able to thank you enough for opening up your home to me—to all of us. You saved us."

"And you all are saving me, so we're even," Janie said.

Pauline left Janie at the table. She didn't want to get up. She didn't want to go back to bed, but she also wasn't running from her truth. So, she cleaned up their glasses, then turned out the lights and went back to her room.

Tomorrow was Thursday, July 2. Just another day.

The next morning dawned gray and overcast, a continuation of the front Janie had seen moving in last night. It had yet to rain, but it was threatening.

Refusing to be deterred by the weather, Pauline drove Bettina to a 24-hour clinic to get her finger checked out. After a wait, and then a couple of x-rays to verify the healing, they removed the brace and pronounced Bettina good to go.

"It feels amazing to get that brace off, even if my finger does feel a little weird." Bettina said, wiggling her fingers as they got back in the car to go home. "Did you ever break a bone?"

Pauline nodded. "I broke my collarbone when I was a kid, but they just strapped me up and told me not to climb anymore trees until it was healed."

Bettina grinned. "You were a tomboy?"

"Yes. I was an outdoor kid. I grew up on my grandparents' farm. My mother had no part of my life. She dropped me off one summer at their house and never came back."

Bettina was horrified. "Oh my God. I'm so sorry!"

Pauline shrugged. "Everybody walks their own path. Hers was a path to disaster, but at least she didn't drag me along with her."

"I guess that's one way to look at it," Bettina said. "Anyway, the black eye is long gone, and now so is the brace. I'm finally free to job hunt!"

"Call Janie and tell her we're bringing a pizza home for lunch," Pauline said. "We'll pick one up on the way."

Bettina nodded and gave Janie a call. After that, they swung by the pizza place Janie recommended, went in and ordered the largest pepperoni pizza to go, and sat down to wait.

Outside, the clouds continued to gather. When they finally got their order and started home, the wind was changing.

"There's a storm coming," Pauline said, and accelerated, hoping to get back and inside before the rain hit.

Bettina gripped the pizza box a little tighter as they sped up. "This pizza smells amazing. This was a good idea."

"It sounded good to me, too," Pauline said. "We'll be home in just a few minutes. It should still be good and hot."

Bettina glanced at her. "You said home. Does Janie's house feel like home to you?"

Pauline shrugged. "I don't know what I'd call it, but it is a true blessing to me to be there. I feel safe. Becoming a widow—or whatever it is you call a woman who just *thought* she was married—left me completely alone in the world. I wake up every morning in a state of gratitude."

Bettina nodded and had to focus on something else so as not to cry.

"I feel the same. Janie is tiny, but her spirit is huge, and her generosity is beyond understanding. I am also grateful to be there."

"Yikes, there's are the first raindrops," Pauline said, and turned on the wipers.

"Yes, but we're almost there. There's the house."

Pauline swerved up into the drive and parked. They got out in haste, hurried up the front steps, and were barely beneath the verandah before the sky unloaded.

"Whoa. We made it!" Bettina said.

Pauline unlocked the door, then glanced back at the sky. It looked bad. She shivered as they hurried inside, locking the door behind her before following Bettina into the kitchen.

The table was already set, so they put the pizza box in the middle of it. Gretchen poured their drinks, and Janie set paper napkins at their places.

"This smells so good. Thank you!" Janie said, and then jumped at the clap of thunder above them.

"Are we in a storm warning area?" Bettina asked.

"Tornado watch," Gretchen said.

Pauline frowned. "At least we have an amazing storm shelter."

"And we have pizza," Janie said.

"And we have each other for company," Gretchen added. "When I think back to how many stormy nights I spent alone, and how many holidays I spent alone, I get pissed all over again."

"Take a bite of pizza. It'll take that bitter taste right out of your mouth," Bettina said.

"Ex-wives R Us," Pauline said, and took a big bite.

The pizza disappeared as fast as the Bourbon pecan pie had, and after the kitchen was cleaned up, they meandered off to their own resources.

Pauline was back at work in the red room, and Bettina was on-line, creating a new page on Facebook for a dog walking service. If nothing happened with it, she could always take it down, but it was what she wanted to do right now.

Gretchen was doing laundry to make sure all the clothes she'd wear to work were clean, and Janie was in the office, working on the books for her clients. Outside, the downpour continued, covering the city in a heavy gray curtain of rain.

It was after seven p.m. when Janie finally quit for the day. She was caught up with entries. It had been hours since pizza, but she didn't want to cook, and didn't know if the others had made dinner.

As she was going up the hall, she heard voices and laughter and friendly arguing coming from the kitchen. Now she knew where they were, just not what they were doing. And then she walked into the kitchen and froze in her tracks. They were playing cards and in various stages of disrobing. She took one look at them and burst out laughing.

"If that's strip poker, whatever you take off next, don't let it be a bra."

They erupted in giggles.

"You're one to talk," Gretchen said.

Janie smirked. "Yes, but mine are still tied down. Did you guys eat dinner?"

"We snacked earlier. Not real hungry," Bettina said.

"I'm making popcorn. Want some?" Janie asked.

"Ooh, yes! Sounds perfect!" Pauline said.

Soon, the smell of melting butter and popping corn filled the room. The deck of cards was put away, and the clothes were back on.

"How about movie night. We can watch the big screen TV in the living room," Janie said.

"Yes!" Bettina said. "You pick."

Janie frowned. "What if you don't like what I like?"

Gretchen threw popcorn at her. "Do you hear what you just said? We already loved the same man. And now we hate the same man. I think we can handle a movie."

Janie sighed. "That makes us sound like such dumb-asses."

"We're not dumb, we're just broke, and through no fault of our own. Now. Shut up and pick a good movie. Just make sure it's not a romance. I don't believe in that anymore," Bettina muttered.

"I have the perfect one," Janie said, and they followed her into the living room to the big-screen TV, picked a chair, and settled in with their bowls of popcorn and cold drinks.

She scanned through Netflix until she found it, then clicked *play*.

"Oh, I love this!" Gretchen said. "*Jumanji 2-The Next Level*. We get to look at Dwayne Johnson, and Kevin Hart and Jack Black are hilarious. It's a super cast."

"Don't forget Nick Jonas! We can't hate him. His only crime is being young and cute," Bettina said.

They settled in to watch, and it wasn't long before the old mansion was filled with the sound of laughter. It was the perfect way to end a rainy day.

The thunderstorm passed sometime during the night, and by the time they were up Friday morning, steam was already rising from the wet surfaces. Summer in Missouri was an unforgiving sauna.

Janie was in the living room, running the vacuum over the popcorn crumbles from last night, when she thought she heard the doorbell. She turned off the vacuum and went to the door. It was the mailman.

"Morning, Mrs. Logan. I have a certified letter for you. Sign here, please."

"Morning, Hank," Janie said, signed where he pointed.

Hank handed her the letter, plus the rest of her mail.

"Thanks," she said.

Hank nodded, then instead of hurrying away, paused.

"I haven't seen you to express my sympathies, but I am so sorry about everything you're going through. You are such a kind woman, and you don't deserve what happened."

The unexpected sympathy caught her by surprise, and all of a sudden, there was a lump in her throat.

"Thank you," she said.

He nodded, touching a finger to his cap as he left.

Janie closed the door, then carried the mail to the kitchen and began to sort out the girls' forwarded mail, making a little pile for each of them. Then she opened the certified letter. She'd seen the return address and guessed what it was, and she was right.

It was the life insurance check from David's employer. She looked at the amount, thinking it couldn't have come at a more opportune time, then went looking for the others. Pauline was on her way back up the staircase with a load of clean laundry when she caught up with her.

"Pauline, do you know where the others are?"

"Still upstairs," she said.

"Would you do me a favor and have everyone meet me downstairs at the kitchen table. We need to have a meeting."

"Sure thing," Pauline said. "We'll be right down."

Janie put up the vacuum and then headed for the kitchen.

A few minutes later, she heard them talking as they descended the staircase, and then the click of the footsteps as they crossed the foyer. The grandfather clock at the far end of the hall began to chime. It was ten a.m. She was just about to make their day. Then they walked into the kitchen in silence, their expressions tense.

"The mail came. Have a seat," Janie said, and then kept standing after they sat down and reached for their mail. "There's something I found out a while back that I need to share with you. I've waited until I had it in hand before I mentioned it, but it just came in the mail, so today is the big reveal."

Bettina frowned. "I am going to lose my shit if there's another wife."

"No, nothing like that. It's actually good news. When David was killed, I had to notify his boss, and before we hung up, he informed me that the company had life insurance policies on all of their reps, and it was double indemnity if the death was an accident. So, the fifty-thousand-dollar policy they had on him became a one hundred-thousand-dollar policy, and it came today."

"Oh my God," Gretchen whispered.

Janie saw the shock on their faces, and quickly explained. "It's in my name because I was the legal wife, but I am splitting it four ways. It doesn't come close to paying back what he stole from us, but it's sure a blessing now."

Pauline gasped.

Bettina's eyes welled.

"You don't have to do this," Gretchen said.

Janie frowned. "I know that, but I want to, and I'm going to. Now, I can either deposit it and write each of you a check, or you can all come with me to the bank, and we'll divvy it up there."

One by one, they got up without speaking, and wrapped their arms around her, holding her so tight it was hard to breathe.

"I'll go with you," Pauline said.

"So will I," Gretchen said.

Bettina nodded. "Me, too."

"Awesome," Janie said. "I'll get my purse."

The three went upstairs on the run as Janie went to her bedroom. She put on a little lipstick and fluffed her hair, changed her shoes, and by the time she got back, they were waiting for her in the hall.

Janie winked at them. "Okay, sister girls. Let's go do this."

They loaded up in her car, and away they went, riding in silence—still in shock from the unexpected gift.

Once they arrived at the bank, their anticipation was at an all-time high. The relief of this windfall was going to be the cushion all of them needed. But the moment they walked in together, they became the immediate focus of every employee there.

Janie had banked there all her adult life. Everyone who worked there knew her. The older employees had known her father before her, and in the last ten years, they'd come to know David, as well.

They were all also aware of his betrayal, and they'd heard rumors that the four wives were now living together, and the opinions as to the wisdom of that were rampant. However, in this stately institution, opinions would not be voiced, even though they could not help but notice how striking each woman was in her own right.

Janie bypassed the tellers and went straight to one of the officers sitting at a desk. The woman looked up, recognized Janie immediately, and came out from behind her desk with a smile on her face.

"Good morning, Mrs. Logan. It's good to see you."

"Good morning, Ellen. I want to introduce you to the ladies with me. This is Pauline Logan, Bettina Lee, and Gretchen Lowry. Girls, this is Ellen Arnold. If you ever decide to move your accounts, I highly recommend this bank, and this lady would be the ideal one to help you do it."

Ellen beamed. "Ladies, it's nice to meet you all. I'll get a couple more chairs here, and we'll be good to go." Then she pulled up two chairs from another location, and they were soon seated. "Now how can I help you?"

Janie laid the check on the desk.

"This came today from the company our husband worked for. One of their perks was a life insurance policy. It's made out to me because I was the only legal wife, but that's his fault, not ours. So, I want to divide it four ways. Twenty-five thousand to each of us. However the girls want their share delivered is what I need you to help me do. If they want cashier checks, or have their share transferred directly from my account to their banks, then we need to do that. Or if they want to open accounts here today in this bank, then I'd like your help with that. It will be their choices."

"I can certainly make that happen," Ellen said. "So ladies, which delivery would you prefer?"

"I'll open an account here and have my current bank transfer my money into this account later," Pauline said.

"I want to do the same," Bettina said.

"As do I," Gretchen added.

Ellen beamed. Three new customers for their branch was a good thing.

"Then let's begin," she said, and took the check. "First thing we're going to do is deposit the money in Janie's account and go from there."

The three wives sat, feeling the panic of their situation fading as their little nest eggs became reality, and the bond between the four of them grew even stronger.

It was almost noon when they left the bank, and as they piled into the car, Janie offered up a suggestion.

"Let's go somewhere for lunch to celebrate!"

Gretchen clapped her hands. "Awesome! Where are we going?"

"There are some great Italian restaurants here. How does that sound?" Janie asked.

"Yes!!! Love it," Bettina said.

"Sounds wonderful," Pauline added.

Janie drove through the winding streets until she arrived in an old part of the city called The Hill. A large portion of the original residents of the city had been Italian immigrants, and the culture was still alive and strong here. She took a turn onto Wilson Street and then drove until she came to a restaurant called Zia's on The Hill and parked.

"I hope you're hungry. The food is amazing, the servings are generous, and this is my treat."

"Oh, thank you! I love pasta of any kind," Gretchen said.

"Then we came to the right place," Janie said, grabbed her purse, and got out.

They walked inside single file then waited to be seated.

Four striking women walking into a crowded dining room causing a stir would not be unheard of. But because Janie was born and raised in St. Louis, and feisty little redheads were hard to forget, quite a few of the diners recognized her. Once they realized who she was and connected the gossip about her deceased husband's other wives living with her, the identities of the other three began falling into place.

As soon as they were seated, they opened their menus. At that point, Janie whispered.

"Girls, are your ears burning?"

They looked up.

"What?" Bettina said.

Gretchen shrugged. "Uh, are you referring to the fact that everybody is staring and talking about us?"

"Oh, good Lord," Pauline muttered.

"Let them look. They're not going to see anything but four

women having lunch," Janie muttered. "I'm going for baked penne with meatballs."

Bettina looked back at the menu. "I want to try this pasta and shrimp dish with oil and lemon."

"I'm choosing fettuccine Alfredo with shrimp," Gretchen said.

"Ooh, same pasta for me, but with chicken," Pauline said.

They sat for a moment, staring off into space and then all of a sudden, they looked back at each other as if they'd been caught in some kind of betrayal.

"Just say it. You know we're all thinking it," Bettina muttered.

"No," Janie said. "I'm not going to keep his memory alive by recounting what he liked to eat, like the damn bowtie pasta to which you are so subtly referring, or anything else about him. I want to forget he ever existed."

"I want to forget, too," Bettina said. "But right now, I can't. Every day something triggers a memory, and that memory still hurts. Even when I laugh, it hurts."

Janie sighed. "You're right. Today you're sad. And today, I'm mad. We're all a mess on any given day. Sorry, sweetie."

"Understood, and I'm sorry, too," Bettina said, and reached across the table to give Janie's hand a quick squeeze.

The moment passed, and then their waiter appeared, took orders for their drinks and a toasted ravioli appetizer for the table, and left. While they were waiting, Bettina's phone signaled a text. She glanced down to see who it was from and gasped.

"What? Is something wrong?" Pauline asked.

"No! Something is finally right! It's a response from the dog walking site I set up on Facebook yesterday. I think I have a customer! I'll respond after we get home, because I want details. I'm not taking jobs in bad parts of town."

"I can help you with that," Janie said. "I grew up here. I'll know if the area is reputable."

"Much appreciated," Bettina said.

They were still celebrating Bettina's good news when Gretchen saw the waiter coming with their appetizer and drinks. After that, they no longer cared how many people were eyeing them or what kind of jokes were being made of their lives. Their conversation had shifted to the finer points of dipping sauces as they dug into the toasted raviolis.

After the table was cleared and readied for the entrees, a couple walked past their table, and as they did, the woman recognized Janie and made a U-turn.

"Hey, Janie."

Janie looked up and smiled. "Brenda! Hello!" Then she quickly made introductions. "Girls, this is Brenda Busby. She owns Crowning Glory, the best hair salon in St. Louis, and my go-to for cuts." Then she went around the table, introducing the girls. "Brenda, this Pauline Lord, Gretchen Lowry, and Bettina Lee. We consider ourselves sister-wives."

Brenda smiled. "What gorgeous ladies! It's a pleasure to meet you. If you're ever in need, Janie has all my info." Then she put her hand on Janie's shoulder. "It's good to see you out and about. Enjoy your lunch."

"What a nice lady," Pauline said, as the stylist walked away.

"Yes, and good at what she does," Janie added.

But Janie's introductions had been overheard by other diners at nearby tables, and now the curiosity seekers assumptions had been confirmed. They were the bigamist's wives!

A short while later, the entrees arrived, and they immediately began eyeing each other's orders.

"That looks amazing," Gretchen said, pointing at Janie's baked penne and meatballs.

"Want a bite?" Janie offered.

Gretchen grinned. "Really? And you can have a taste of mine."

Suddenly, the four of them were giggling and pushing their plates into the center of the table so they could all have a bite of each other's food. In the middle of their tasting, a woman sitting at the table next to them looked over at her husband and rolled her eyes.

"Oh my God, Larry! Just look at them. I suppose when one's shares a husband, sharing food and lodging follows."

Larry frowned. He'd long ago accepted that his wife, Julia, was outspoken, but this was rude to the point of hurtful. He frowned and shook his head at her, but it was too late. Her caustic comment had been heard.

All four of the girls turned and stared at her, and then Bettina laid down her fork.

"Let it go," Janie said.

"Like hell," Bettina muttered, and then got up and walked over to the table, smiling with every step.

Now Julia was horrified, and just the tiniest bit afraid.

Bettina leaned over the table and lowered her voice. "We couldn't help but overhear your opinion of us, and we just wanted you to know what a cruel and judgmental ass we think you are. Do enjoy your food, and while you're at it, mind your own damn business."

Then she walked back to their table with her chin up, and her hips swaying. She sat back down, picked up her fork, and then looked at the girls.

"She sends her regards," Bettina said, and they burst out laughing.

Julia was mortified that they were laughing at her and leaned toward her husband to whisper. "Larry! I want to leave now!"

"When I'm finished," he said. "And let that be a lesson. Next time, keep your damn mouth shut."

Julia's eyes welled. "How could you say such a cruel thing to me?"

"You were cruel to them. If you dish it out, you have to be tough enough to take it. Now go apologize or go sit in the car. I'll be along shortly."

Julia flushed an angry red, grabbed her purse, and strode out of the restaurant with her nose in the air.

Larry signaled a waiter, who hurried to the table.

"Yes, sir?" the waiter asked.

"See the table where those four ladies are sitting?"

"Yes."

Larry handed the waiter a credit card. "Please put their meal on my tab and check me out. I need to leave."

"Yes, sir. Would you like me to box up your leftovers?" he asked.

Larry shook his head. "That's not necessary. I'm in something of a hurry, so if you could put a rush on it, I would appreciate it."

"Certainly," the waiter said, and hurried off to ring up the tab. He came back shortly, laid the bill on the table for the man to sign, along with the credit card.

Larry signed the credit card receipt, adding a generous tip for the waiter.

"Thank you, and when you tell them their tab is paid, give them my apologies, as well."

"Yes, sir," the waiter said.

Larry pocketed his card and got up to leave, as the waiter hurried over to the table where the girls were eating.

They hit pause on their conversation as the waiter stopped at their table.

"Ladies, the gentleman who's just leaving wanted me to express his sincere apologies, and he has paid for your lunch. Enjoy the rest of your meal, and I'll be right back to fill up your glasses."

The waiter left, and the girls all turned toward the door just in time to see a man turn and give them a thumbs up as he was leaving.

"That's her husband!" Bettina said.

"Oh, wow. That was so nice of him," Pauline said.

Bettina nodded. "Yes, it was. But he's still married to a bitch."

Janie grinned. "Tell it, girl. Don't hold back."

"Well, she is," Bettina muttered. "Somebody please pass the salt."

And just like that, the ugly part of their day had just been washed clean by the kind heart of a stranger.

About an hour later, they left the restaurant and headed home, all talked out and thinking about a nap.

It had been a good day. Surely the best day they'd all had since before their worlds came crashing down. They had money in the bank. Food in their bellies. And hope in their hearts.

As soon as they got home, Bettina went to get her laptop, and sent a reply to the woman who'd messaged her. A few minutes later, she received a response via Facebook Messenger, requesting to interview Bettina to see how she would interact with her dog, a Cavalier King Charles Spaniel, before making a decision. At that point, Bettina picked up her laptop, went to look for Janie, and found her in her office.

"I have a name and address," Bettina said. "Can you vet it for me?"

"Sure thing," Janie said.

Bettina turned the screen toward Janie so she could read it.

Janie saw the address, then pulled up a new screen on her computer and typed in the address. It came up with a picture of the house and a map of the city of St. Louis, with an arrow on the address. She enlarged the view, and then nodded.

"This is an upscale area, so that's good. Now it all comes down to you and the dog owner reaching a mutual agreement. Let me see... What's her name again?"

"Shelby Attilla. I looked her up on FB. She owns an upholstery company."

Janie's eyes widened. "I thought the name was familiar. Her company reupholstered the love seat in my bedroom a couple of years ago. Her husband, John Attilla, is a lawyer."

Bettina nodded. "Okay, then. I'm going to respond. Thanks, honey."

"You're welcome, and good luck," Janie added, as Bettina left the room.

Bettina went back to the kitchen, sat down at the table, and then took a deep breath before sending off her response.

Again, a response came quickly.

Are you free to come to my address today? I'm home, and I'd like to be here when you meet my little Loki.

Bettina glanced at the time. It was just after three p.m. Her hands were shaking as she typed her reply and hit send.

I can stop by around 4:00 p.m. today, if that works for you.

Another message popped up.

Perfect! See you soon.

Bettina entered the name, address, and phone number in her phone, then took off upstairs to change. Ten minutes later, she came flying back down the stairs and went straight to the office.

"Janie. I have a four o'clock interview. Do you think I'm dressed properly for a dog walker?"

Janie eyed the dark denim pants, the bright red knit shirt, and the running shoes Bettina wore, and gave her a thumbs up.

"You look perfect," she said. "Do you know how to get there?"

"I have OnStar GPS in my car. Wish me luck," she said.

"Luck, and you've got this," Janie said, then went back to work.

CHAPTER FOUR

Bettina dumped her purse in the passenger seat, put her cell phone on Blue Tooth, then started the car to cool it off. She already knew where a PetSmart was, so she backed out of the drive and sped away.

Once she arrived at the store, she jumped out on the run, and a few minutes later, returned with a bag full of dog treats and leashes. She opened one of the treat bags and grabbed an individual packet of treats and dropped it in her purse. Then she gave the address of her destination to the OnStar operator, and as soon as she had directions, she began following the prompts.

To say she was hopeful was putting it mildly. Seven years ago, she'd quit her bartending job because David hadn't thought it proper for a married woman to be doing that. Looking back, it made no sense, because she spent three weeks of every month alone. But he'd wound his way into her psyche to the point that she'd agreed and obeyed everything he suggested, wanting to please him. Was it a subconscious feeling of the fear of losing him, too? She'd lost her first husband to cheating and always wondered if she'd never been enough. Then she'd gone overboard with David and given up her autonomy, thinking it was the way to keep him. She'd never know for sure why she'd let it happen, but the lesson had been brutal. She'd never bow down again.

She was as prepared for this opportunity as she could be. She knew the going rate for dog walkers in St. Louis. She'd already signed up for personal liability insurance before she created her Facebook site. She also knew that it was her responsibility to provide treats, pooper bags, and leashes for the walks. What she had yet to learn was how she would access the dogs at each residence if the owners were at work, but if this interview was successful, she'd find out today.

It took almost thirty minutes to maneuver through traffic to get to the address, but as Janie mentioned, it was definitely upscale—older homes like Janie's that Bettina considered mansions.

And then she saw the house. The grounds were well cared for. The oblong, three-story brick structure had no verandahs—just a stoop and an ornate entry, a chimney rising high above the roof like a candle on a cake, and a portico on one side of the house for parking, as was common from the architecture of the era.

Bettina parked at the curb, then hurried up the long walkway to the front door and rang the bell. A few moments later, a woman in a simple dress-style uniform answered the door.

Bettina smiled at her and started talking.

"I'm Bettina Lee. Mrs. Attilla is expecting me."

"Yes, ma'am. This way please. Mrs. Attilla is in the library," she said, and escorted Bettina to a room just off the foyer. As soon as they crossed the threshold, the woman introduced her arrival. "Ma'am, Bettina Lee is here."

Shelby Attilla looked up, then stood and came toward Bettina with her hand outstretched.

"Thank you for coming," Shelby said. "Please have a seat," and gestured toward a chair opposite the sofa where she'd been sitting.

"Certainly," Bettina said, and then saw a beautiful little dog on the sofa beside Shelby. "Oh! A Tricolor Cavalier! He's beautiful. You said his name is Loki?"

Shelby was pleased that the woman knew her dog breeds.

"Well, it's not his registered name, but we call him Loki. Cavaliers aren't particularly athletic dogs, and he's going on five years old. They also aren't normally a long-lived breed, but we just adore him, so we're cautious about him and his care."

"We had a Ruby Cavalier when I was young. He was funny and sweet as anything and had us all trained."

Shelby laughed. "Yes, they do like their routines. Please, come sit beside us."

Bettina moved from her chair to the far end of the sofa. As soon as she sat down, the little dog immediately looked up at Shelby.

"It's okay, baby," Shelby said, and gave him a kiss on the top of his head. "This is Bettina. You know how you like your walks? Bettina likes walks, too."

Bettina offered her hand, palm side down, for the little dog to sniff, and began to talk to him in a soft, quiet voice.

"Good boy, Loki. You are such a handsome little man. Yes, you are." She looked up at Shelby and shook her head. "Those eyes. They speak volumes, do they not?"

Shelby nodded.

Bettina stroked the top of his head, and then scratched the back of his ears, while talking to Shelby.

"I carry little treats on walks," Bettina said, and slipped a small, unopened packet of them from her purse. "This is the brand, but if you prefer something different, I can always oblige. I also use my own leashes. Do you clip onto his collar, or do you use a harness to walk him?"

"The brand of treats is fine. He's had them before. We've always used the harness style. There's less stress on the neck area," Shelby said. "We put the harness on him, and then clip a leash to that."

Bettina nodded. "I want you to know that I carry personal liability insurance for this job. I will furnish the pooper bags, my own leashes, and I also carry water and little disposable bowls so they can drink. I would never let two animals drink from the same bowl, and if the weather is too hot, I will make sure they are not walking on hot concrete. I'll carry them before I'd let that happen. I charge $30.00 for a thirty-minute walk once a day. I do not intend to take multiple dogs for a walk together unless they belong to the same household. And, if you have preferences about not walking them in inclement weather, just let me know."

"All of that is reasonable, and no, we would not want Loki walked in rain or snow," Shelby said. "Do you have references?"

Bettina sighed. "I just recently moved here from Kansas City. The only person I know well enough to furnish a reference for me is Janie Logan. She has a bookkeeping business. I'm living in her home now."

Shelby nodded. "I know Janie." And then her eyes widened. "Oh wait! Are you... I mean, you both have the same last name. Are you family?"

"I'm not going to lie," Bettina said. "We were married to the same man."

Shelby expression softened. "Oh Lord. You're one of the wives. My dear! I am so sorry. I cannot imagine what you ladies have been through. I have so much admiration for you four taking charge of your own fate. And living together to limit expenses is genius. I don't know that it would have occurred to me to be so generous."

"Janie is our angel. We're all trying to regain financial security after what was stolen." Bettina blinked back tears, struggling to keep her voice from trembling. "If you are uncomfortable trusting me to—"

"Not at all," Shelby said. "Since I'm home today, do you have time to take a little walk with Loki and me? That way I can see how you handle him, and he will be more comfortable with you when you do it alone."

"Yes, of course," Bettina said. "I didn't bring my backpack with the water, but I do have leashes in the car."

"We'll use one of mine, today," Shelby said. "You can sit and keep Loki company while I change into my walking shoes."

"Yes, ma'am," Bettina said.

"Ma'am sounds so old. How about Shelby?" she said, and then gave Loki a pat on the head as she stood. "Stay, Loki. Mama will be right back."

The little dog's gaze stayed on Shelby's exit until Bettina began stroking his head again and gave him a little scratch beneath his chin. When she did, his eyes closed. She chuckled.

"You like that, don't you, boy?" she said, and gave him a couple more chin scratches, then scooted a little closer.

By the time Shelby came back carrying a harness, a leash, and a pooper bag, Loki was tucked against Bettina's leg with his chin on his paws, so lulled by the petting that he was almost asleep.

"Ah. . . A true dog whisperer," Shelby said, and jingled the leash. "Loki! Wanna go for a walk?"

The little dog's head came up, and he looked at Bettina. She grinned, picked him up, and set him down on the floor. He trotted up to where Shelby was standing.

Bettina laughed. "I'd say that was a resounding 'yes'."

Shelby put the halter on him, clipped on the leash, and they left the house by the front door with Loki leading the way.

"I let him set the pace, but he's bad to want to eat everything in sight, so you'll have to watch that," Shelby said.

Bettina was nodding and making mental notes as they went, but the day was beautiful, and the slight breeze made walking on the tree-lined streets a joy as Shelby kept up a running monologue.

"My husband, John, and I are at work five days a week. Barb is our housekeeper and will be the one who'll bring Loki to the door in his harness, and the one who'll take him on return. Just text me when he's home every time, and I'll Venmo the money directly to your account."

Bettina was nodding and paying attention to the route as they walked.

"This is a beautiful area of the city, although the area where Janie's home is located is beautiful as well. Her home is referred to as the Duvall Estate. It's fairly well known in the area. I think she's the third generation to have lived there."

"The grounds at her home are stunning," Bettina said. "Roses and flowering bushes, and all kinds of flower beds. She spends a lot of her down time outside puttering, as she says."

"I don't have a green thumb at all. What is growing on our property is due to someone else's skill. Certainly not mine," Shelby said.

All of a sudden, Bettina bolted forward, grabbed Loki by the harness, and dropped down on her knees and thrust her finger into the side of the little dog's mouth. Moments later, she dug out a toadstool and tossed it in the street.

"Oh, my Lord!" Shelby cried. "I didn't even see him do that."

"I was watching," Bettina said. "I think I'll shorten the leash so he doesn't have so much wandering room. He can still be the boss, but from a shorter distance."

Shelby got down on her knees and hugged Loki.

"You stinker!" she crooned, and opened his mouth to make sure it was all gone.

"What I pulled out was still intact," Bettina said, and pointed to the toadstool she'd tossed into the street.

Shelby stood. "Thank you. That was amazing, and you're hired. Can you start Monday? And, weather permitting, you would walk him Monday through Friday, around nine a.m.? That way you'll be finished before it gets too hot."

"Perfect!" Bettina said.

They finished the walk together and Bettina held the leash on the way back, shortening it enough that Loki did not have access to rambling.

As they reached the front door to the old mansion, Bettina got down on her knees, gave Loki a tiny treat, and stroked his little head. "You are such a good boy. I'll see you soon, okay?"

Then she got up and dusted off her hands and knees.

"Thank you for the opportunity, Shelby."

"No, thank you for good eyes and quick wit," Shelby said, then stood on the steps with Loki and watched until Bettina was in her car and out of sight.

Bettina was in great spirits when she got home. She walked into the house, then followed the sounds of voice until she found the girls in the kitchen in the middle of making cupcakes.

"Hi honey! How did it go?" Janie asked, as she looked up from the bowl of cake batter.

"You're not smiling like that for the hell of it, are you? You got your first client, didn't you?" Gretchen said.

"I did. Shelby Attilla has the most adorable little tri-color Cavalier King Charles Spaniel I have ever seen. His name is Loki, and I am already in love."

"Congrats, girl! As long as your new male-crush is a four-footed fur-baby, you should be fine," Pauline drawled.

Bettina grinned. "Ain't that the truth. So, are those chocolate cupcakes you're making?"

"Yes, they are," Janie said. "But we're still debating about frostings. Pauline likes chocolate on chocolate. Gretchen likes cream cheese frosting, and I'll eat chocolate cake with or without frostings."

"Do a cream cheese frosting with chocolate sprinkles, then you have some of both," Bettina said.

"Good call," Janie said. "Gretchen, I know I have cream cheese. Look and see if I have chocolate sprinkles."

"You do!" Gretchen said, and knew right where they were because she'd organized that shelf, as well.

Janie nodded. "Problem solved."

The baking proceeded, then after the cupcakes had cooled, they were frosted and sprinkled.

"About two of these and a glass of cold milk is all I want for dinner," Pauline said.

"Me, too," Bettina said.

Janie glanced at Gretchen, who had already peeled the foil away from a cupcake and was taking a bite.

When Gretchen realized they were all grinning at her, she blinked. "What?" she mumbled, talking around the bite in her mouth.

"Want milk with that?" Janie asked.

She nodded, her mouth still full of cake.

Pauline, ever the quiet one, suddenly teared up, and when they saw her, there was a mutual outcry.

"Honey! What's wrong?" Janie asked,

"Are you okay?" Bettina cried.

Surprised by Pauline's sudden show of sadness, Gretchen nearly choked, trying to swallow her bite as she handed Pauline a handful of tissues.

Pauline sat down at the table and began wiping her eyes.

"Nothing is wrong. It's just us... Being together... Being happy. I haven't had this sense of family since my grandparents died."

"Oh, bless your heart," Janie said, and handed her a cupcake. "Here's one to start on. Somebody break out the glasses and get the milk. We're not going to get booze drunk, but I can guarantee we're all gonna go to bed with a sugar high."

That night, Gretchen was in bed, full of cupcakes and milk, watching a movie when her cellphone rang. She glanced at Caller ID, started to let it go to voicemail, and then changed her mind and answered.

"What do you want?"

Her sister, Erin, gasped. "That's rude!"

"Want me to laugh at you, like you laughed at me?" Gretchen asked. "What do you want? I'm busy."

Erin sighed loudly. "Look. I'm sorry. I didn't think you'd be so touchy and offended."

"Touchy? About becoming a widow, a victim of a conman, and broke and homeless? *You* offended *me*," Gretchen said.

There was a moment of silence, and then the tone of Erin's voice shifted. "You mean... you really are homeless? I thought you were exaggerating."

"I'm not anymore, no thanks to you. And I start work at a new job on Monday," Gretchen said.

"Where are you?" Erin asked.

"With friends," Gretchen said.

"Well, I need an address," Erin snapped.

"No, ma'am. You don't need an address, because you aren't invited into my life anymore."

"But we're sisters!" Erin said.

"Were. You vacated the privilege when you laughed at my sorrow. When you made fun of my grief. Sometimes blood is not thicker than water. Go live your best life, Erin. I'm fine where I am."

Erin was still talking when Gretchen disconnected. When her phone rang again, she muted it, turned off the TV, and cried herself to sleep.

Saturday morning dawned on the Fourth of July, and the city was abuzz. The annual parade on Market Street was on the agenda, along with a fireworks display at the Arch after dark.

But the girls weren't buzzing about anything. Janie had a nightmare hangover, and Gretchen was in a mood, worrying about her new job. Bettina had fallen into a David mood and cried herself to sleep last night, and this morning, the inside of her eyelids felt like sandpaper.

Pauline was somber, remembering last year on this day she'd

been at the lake with David. She hated herself for missing him and hated him for what he'd done to her.

But they all made it down to breakfast together without taking their misery out on each other and were eating quietly and reading the local paper on their phones.

Janie knew about the parade, and now that they'd all read the headlines in the morning paper, so did the others. She hadn't attended that in person in years and wasn't in the mood to be 'on display' but didn't want to be the odd man out if they wanted to go.

Gretchen paused in the middle of reading.

"Good Lord. The high today is supposed to be over a hundred degrees. I know I'm not sticking my nose out today. Blondes like me do not always have more fun in this kind of weather. There's not enough sunscreen to keep me from cooking in that."

"Same," Bettina said. "I turn beet red, then blister and peel."

"I don't burn easily, but I do not enjoy that kind of heat," Pauline said.

Janie looked up. "Then that sounds like nobody cares to miss the parade."

Gretchen immediately felt guilty. "Oh, if you want to go, we can—"

Janie shook her head. "Honey, I live here, and I haven't gone to a Fourth of July parade since I graduated high school. And I don't even try to drive downtown after dark to watch fireworks at the river. It's madness. If you want to watch fireworks, just look out the east bedroom windows upstairs. You'll have a bird's-eye view."

"Are they allowed to shoot off fireworks here in the city?" Pauline asked.

"No. But that doesn't mean they don't. Every year, some idiot will still shoot off fireworks and set a roof on fire. If it's not their own, it's a neighbor's. Fortunately, this block, and the one behind me, no longer have families with young children, so the danger for that to happen here is next to zero."

Bettina took a sip of her coffee and then leaned back in her chair.

"That doesn't mean we can't celebrate the Fourth on our own."

"Doing what?" Gretchen asked.

Bettina shrugged. "Oh, I don't know... Like a picnic on the back verandah at noon? Watching fireworks from the air-conditioned comfort of my bedroom tonight, eating ice cream and cake to celebrate?"

"I would love that," Janie said. "I'll put some eggs on to boil. You can't have a picnic without deviled eggs."

"I'll run by KFC later and get a bucket of chicken and the ice cream for tonight," Bettina said.

"I'll make potato salad," Gretchen added.

"I'll bake the cake," Pauline said.

And just like that, the holiday of doing nothing but feeling sorry for themselves had been replaced by a day-long party. Excited by the plan, they began cleaning up their breakfast dishes, and then started prepping for the food they intended to make.

Being an only child, whose grandparents passed when she was so young she barely remembered them, Janie loved having all this going on in the kitchen at once. She put eggs on to boil, and then she and Bettina began helping Gretchen peel potatoes.

"I like pickles in my potato salad," Gretchen said. "Dill or sweet?"

"It's your potato salad. You make it the way you like it, and we'll eat it," Janie said.

Gretchen grinned. "This will be a potluck picnic. Everyone brings a dish that's an old family recipe, and we all get to taste the history of our people."

Bettina rolled her eyes. "My family was the one asked to bring paper plates and the liters of pop. So, I'll be getting Colonel Sanders to fry my chicken, and Ben and Jerry will be churning my ice cream."

They laughed.

"Pauline, what kind of cake are you going to make?" Janie asked.

"My grandmother's go-to recipe was a Mexican chocolate sheet cake. It's really good, and simple to make," she said.

"Then I"m definitely getting ice cream to go with it," Bettina said.

"Oh my gosh... We just ate breakfast, but just thinking about all this good stuff is already making me hungry," Gretchen said.

The morning passed in a flurry of cooking and washing up, and cooking some more, and then setting things back for later.

The potato salad was made and chilling in the refrigerator next to Janie's deviled eggs and pasta salad. The Mexican chocolate cake was cooling on the counter in a sheet pan. The chocolate icing with chopped pecans had been poured over the warm cake and was already setting up. By evening, it would be a decadent dessert. And just for fun, Pauline made some cinnamon sugar pinwheels out of a refrigerated can of crescent rolls for a noon-time sweet.

Bettina headed to the nearest KFC around eleven a.m. to get a bucket of extra-crispy chicken, leaving the others gathering up paper plates, napkins, and flatware to take outside. It was the happiest she had felt since before her world fell apart. She was sitting at a stop light when her cell phone rang. She saw who it was, and started not to answer, but the mother in her couldn't ignore it again, so she answered, and then put it on speaker so she could keep driving.

"Hello?"

"Mom, it's me, Joe. Patty is on the line, too. Don't hang up."

Bettina sighed. "What do you want?"

"We're in Kansas City. We got off a plane, rented a car, drove to your house to spend the holiday with you and it's empty! There's a freakin' 'For Lease' sign in the yard. Where the hell are you?" he said.

"Were you not listening when I told you two that I was going to lose everything?" she asked.

Patty was crying. "We didn't know you meant *this.*"

Bettina was suddenly furious. "Then what the hell else did you think I meant? No! Never mind. Don't answer that, because it doesn't matter, and I don't much like either one of you anymore."

"Mom! You don't mean that!" Joe cried.

"Yes, I do. I love you both, but I don't like the adults you have become. You haven't been to see me once in the years since David and I got married. I'm surprised you even found the house where I used to live."

"But we didn't like him," Patty said.

Bettina's heart hurt at how long they'd ostracized her, and she wasn't in the mood to pacify the whine in her daughter's voice.

"Oh, shut up, Patricia Ann. So that meant you couldn't be bothered with your own mother because she wasn't living her life to suit you?"

Joe interrupted without giving either one of them time to continue the fuss.

"Where are you? We came all this way to see you."

"Then I guess you're going to go all the way home without succeeding in your quest," Bettina said. "You should have called. I could have saved you a trip."

There was a long moment of silence. She could hear Patty crying, but then Patty had always cried when she didn't get her way, so this was nothing new.

Joe's voice broke. An indication of the emotions he, too, was struggling with.

"Does this mean you don't ever want to see us again?"

"I kind of forgot I had children, because you two seemed to forget I existed. I haven't seen either of you in over seven years. I don't even know what you look like anymore. You never called. I always had to call you. You conveniently forgot my birthday, and Mother's Day, even though I sent gifts for both of you on all the right occasions. And just because the worthless son-of-a-bitch I thought I was married to is dead now, doesn't change the fact that you took your spite out on me. I don't want to see your faces. You broke my heart."

"We at least deserve to know where you are. That you're not living on the streets somewhere," Joe said.

"You deserve nothing. You're both adults who I raised with all the love I had to give, and you turned into your selfish, soul-sucking father. I am in a wonderful home. I have a job beginning on Monday, and I have three other roommates."

Patty gasped. "You're living with strangers?"

"They aren't exactly strangers. In fact, we're almost family."

"Mom! Stop being so fucking secretive, and just tell us where you are!" Joe shouted.

"It isn't a secret. Thanks to the local media, practically everybody in this city knows who we are and where we live, and the fact that we're all living together."

"Who's we?" Patty cried.

"David's wives. All four of us. Living together, and making it work. And just so you don't feel like the assholes you are, your treatment of me isn't all that unique. As it has turned out, all of us have been treated like shit by friends and family, and side-show freaks by the media. Nobody cared what David did to us or saw us as victims. All of sudden, we were people to despise and ridicule. Go home. You have my phone number, and that's enough. And I'm serious. You aren't people I want to visit with right now. I'm on my way to get fried chicken for a picnic, and you're not invited."

Bettina had tears in her eyes as she disconnected, but this loss of a connection between her and her children began when she'd divorced their father and got a job bartending in a hotel. Marrying David Logan was just the icing on the cake of their discontent, and this was what she called 'tough love'.

They thought they could pick and choose when to have her in their lives, but that's not how Bettina rolled. Either they loved her, or they did not. And right now, she didn't think they cared for anyone but themselves.

By the time she got to the KFC drive-through, she had her emotions in check and was thinking about the girls waiting for her and the chicken. She still had to pick up the ice cream on the way home. After that, it was picnic on the porch and good times.

Picnic prep was in full swing. Janie got two American flags out of the attic and hung them in the flag holders on the back verandah.

Gretchen was running in and out of the house, putting a tablecloth over a folding table they'd set up, and carrying flatware and plates.

Pauline was dusting off the chairs, and at Janie's instructions, had turned on the big fans hanging from the ceiling of the verandah to stir the air above where they would sit.

Janie had her phone on Spotify and hooked up to a speaker to have music while they ate. She had her favorite playlists on shuffle, depending on her mood, and today it was a mishmash of country and rock blasting out into the air. Every time someone's favorite song came on, they began singing along with it, unabashed by forgetting words or being off-key.

Pauline had just taken her little cinnamon sugar rolls out of the oven, and they were cooling on a rack when Bettina returned.

"Chicken in the kitchen!" she said, as she came in carrying two bags, one with the chicken, the other with the ice cream, which she quickly put in the freezer.

"Then let's get food on the table," Janie said, and they began carrying out the dishes, Gretchen's potato salad, Janie's deviled eggs, and a colorful pasta salad. Pauline had a basket of hot rolls and butter, and Bettina carried the bucket of chicken.

They were laughing and talking as they put the food on the table, when Gretchen happened to look up and saw a woman standing at the fence, watching them. She waved, and after a moment, the woman waved back.

"Hey, Janie. Your neighbor looks lonely."

Janie turned around, saw Florence and sighed. "She's also nosy."

"Does she live alone?" Pauline asked.

"No, her son and his family live with her," Janie said. "They're probably downtown at the parade."

"Aw... Want to ask her to come eat with us?" Bettina said.

Janie sighed. "There's no guarantee she won't be rude."

"We're big girls," Gretchen said, then took off down the steps and loped across the yard to where the woman stood. She could see the surprise on the woman's face but didn't give her a chance to get nervous. "Hi! I'm Gretchen. Janie said your name is Florence."

"Um, yes, I'm Florence. I heard the music, and I wanted to see what—"

"Are you alone today?" Gretchen asked.

"Yes. My son took his family downtown for all the celebrations."

"Come eat with us!" Gretchen said. "We're having a picnic."

"Oh, I wouldn't want to intrude on—"

Gretchen knew Florence wanted to. She could see the longing in her eyes to be part of the fun.

"Don't be silly! It's just us girls. You'll fit right in! Come on. I'll meet you at the front door. We're just about to sit down."

Florence smiled shyly, smoothed down her hair, and nodded.

"Okay then. I believe I will."

"Awesome. So, let's go. Fried chicken is waiting."

Florence turned and made a beeline for her back door, as Gretchen headed back to the house on the run.

"So, what's the verdict?" Janie asked, as Gretchen came bounding up the steps.

"She's on her way," Gretchen said. "I'm letting her in the front door," she added, and ran into the house.

"Ooh, what fun," Bettina said. "I'll get another glass and plate. I love surprises. The party is getting bigger."

CHAPTER FIVE

Moments later, Gretchen came back outside with Florence at her side.

"Girls, this is Florence. Introduce yourselves."

Janie smiled. "Florence and I don't need an introduction, and welcome to the party."

"Hi, I'm Bettina."

"I'm Pauline."

Florence was in perfectly ironed slacks and a cotton shirt. They were wearing blouses and capri pants, or t-shirts and shorts. Two of them were barefoot, and none of them were wearing makeup. She couldn't help but notice how attractive they were.

"It's so sweet of you to invite me to your picnic," she said.

"Our pleasure," Janie said. "Take a seat, and what's your poison? Iced tea or lemonade? Oh... and the tea is unsweetened."

"I haven't had lemonade in ages, and it sounds so good. I'll have that," Florence said.

Pauline scooped ice into a glass from their ice chest, filled it with homemade lemonade, and set it at Florence's place, and then they all sat down. Just before they started to eat, Janie tapped her fork against her glass, and then picked it up.

"Ladies, a toast! We've gone from sad-ass to bad-ass. To friends and sisters of the heart!"

"Sisters of the heart!" they said, and lifted their glasses in unison.

After that, it was all about passing food and filling plates, with AC/DC blasting "Highway to Hell," a song that could have been their anthem.

"This is the best time this house and I have had in years," Janie said, as she served herself another deviled egg.

"True that for me," Bettina said. "Just think of all the weeks and holidays we spent alone."

Florence frowned. "What do you mean?"

Gretchen shrugged. "Think about it, honey. You're a man with four wives, strung out from one side of the state to the other. You can't be in four places at once, so you pick one location, and spin some big story to the wives in three other places as to why they're spending yet another holiday alone. Then you're so charming to all of them when you do see them, they blindly accept the bullshit."

Florence's eyes widened. "Oh my God! I never thought... I didn't realize the ramifications of..." And then she stopped and shook her head. "My hat's off to all of you, and my sincere sympathies for the tragedy and the travesty of your lives."

And in that moment, Janie knew Florence meant it.

"Well, you can bet the last piece of fried chicken in the bucket that it'll never happen again," Janie said. "Now, enough about that. Florence, what's your favorite memory of the Fourth of July?"

Florence's eyes lit up, and her little mouth pursed, like she was sucking air through a straw, and then she started talking.

"Nearly drowning when I was ten because my brother threw me in the pond to teach me to swim."

"Oh my God!" they said in unison!

"That wouldn't be my favorite memory," Gretchen said.

"Who saved you?" Bettina asked.

"A fourteen-year-old boy named Henry Lane. He was my brother's best friend."

Janie started smiling. "Your Henry?"

Florence chuckled. "Yes, my Henry, God rest his soul. I'd had a crush on him forever, and then after he saved me, his protective streak turned into love when we got older. So, that's why nearly drowning is my favorite memory of the Fourth."

"That is so sweet," Pauline said. "And speaking of sweets, I'm going to bring out the little cinnamon sugar buns."

"Oh, my Lord... I am so full, I don't know if I can eat another bite," Bettina said.

Pauline came back with a plate piled high with the little buns, and Bettina was the first to take one. She ate it in three bites.

"Yeah, that's how I diet, too," Gretchen said, and snagged one for herself.

They were sitting around the table, still telling stories from their childhood when Spotify shifted to a new song, and all of a sudden, the girls squealed and began a litany of comments.

"Yes!"

"My favorite!"

"Oh my God! I can't sit still and just listen!"

"Nobody like Queen!"

Florence waved her hand. "I'm older than you girls. I don't recognize this song. What is it?"

"It's Queen! The song is 'Somebody to Love'!" Janie said, and bounced up from her chair, grabbed a spoon for a microphone, and started dancing and singing with the song as she moved up and down the length of the verandah.

Bettina licked the potato salad off her spoon and joined her.

Gretchen stood up, threw her arms up into the air and started belting out the chorus, with Pauline right beside her.

Florence sat back in her chair, reveling in their abandon and the joy on their faces. In that moment, she knew if her hip wasn't so arthritic, and she knew the words to the song, she'd be dancing along with them. These women weren't bemoaning their fate. They were celebrating their own independence on Independence Day.

But once they were up, they danced and sang from one song into the next until sweat was running down their backs and beaded across their foreheads. Still, it didn't matter. When one song ended, their neighbors on the other side of the fence started clapping and shouting, "More, more, more!"

Janie took the lead on Bon Jovi's, "Livin' On a Prayer."

Bettina did the same on a Green Day song.

And Pauline rocked out on Nine Inch Nails.

It was all music from their youth.

And then it shifted to Chris Stapleton's bluesy, country song called, "You Should Probably Leave." By the time the Stapleton song was over, they were laughing.

"That's something we should have told He Who's Name Shall Not Be Mentioned," Bettina muttered, and they laughed even harder, because it was easier to laugh than it was to let go of the tears they still held inside.

"It's getting too hot for this, and I need to get the potato salad back in the refrigerator," Janie said.

Florence stood. "I ate my way from one end of this table to the other without having to cook a thing, but I'll sure help you clear the table," she said, and together, they began carrying food into the house.

While Janie put leftovers in the refrigerator, the others started clearing off the table. Before long, the only thing left as a reminder of the day were the two flags still flying from the porch.

They sent Florence home with leftovers for her supper, and a round of hugs for her company.

And all the way back to her house, Florence kept thinking of what amazing women they all were, and how horribly, terribly wrong she'd been.

It had been a life-changing day for Florence Lane.

And it had been a life-changing day for the residents of the Broke-Ass Women's Club, as well.

They'd hosted a party. With guests. Well, one guest. And they'd danced themselves into a whole new mindset. It was a good day, and it wasn't over yet.

As soon as the kitchen was clean and everything put back to rights, Bettina spoke up.

"I have an announcement to make."

They all stopped and turned around, giving her their full attention.

"I am full as a tick and going to take a nap so I'll be ready for fireworks tonight."

Gretchen grinned. "Fireworks as in the kind you and Johnny shoot off, or the kind that explode in the air?"

Janie frowned. "Johnny? Who's Johnny?"

Pauline giggled. "That's what Bettina named her vibrator."

Janie was stunned. "You named it?"

Bettina grinned and shrugged.

"Well yes, didn't you? Mine's Elvis" Pauline said.

"I named mine Justin, after an old boyfriend," Gretchen said.

Janie stared. "Why do I suddenly feel like I'm in middle school sex education, finding out that little boys' thingies get hard, and wondering if they break?"

They all laughed at her, but Janie didn't care.

"And that's a wrap," she said. "Have a nice nap."

"What are you going to do?" Pauline asked.

"I don't know. But after ten years of lonely nights with mine, I feel like a hooker, and should at least find out its name."

They were still chuckling as they went upstairs. She followed them to the foot of the stairs and heard them begin calling out to each other as they went into their rooms.

"Good night, John Boy!"

"Good night, Elvis."

"Good night, Justin."

She grinned, and then walked the long hallway to her room, kicked off her shoes, and fell belly down on her bed. She was so tired, and happier than she'd been in years.

Even after the girls woke up from their naps, they stayed in their rooms, reading and watching TV, except for Pauline, who went to the red room to work. Her client was in a hurry for his website, but he kept changing the design and what he wanted to add, which slowed the process.

Finally, she had sent him an email with an itemized quote for the cost of all of the changes and was curious to see if he'd responded. And he had. When she read his response, she laughed.

"Holy crap, Pauline. Wait! That's five thousand dollars I don't have. What can we do?"

She was shaking her head as she responded.

We can go back to the original design for the original price, or you're going to have to give up some things to get others. It's up to you to decide what is most important for your business. Artsy design, or the easy to follow, informational links you want prospective customers to have. I am sending you a list of the costs for each link you want to install, and I think it should be your choice as to what you want to give up, and what you can't live without. Let me know ASAP, or we won't make your timeline.

Pauline hit send, and then switched back to the file on her second client and went to work on it. She loved the creativity of this job and the privacy of getting to do it at home. No coping with office politics. No boss to answer to. Just the skills she had and a good eye for design.

She worked until it was nearing sundown, then saved everything and got up, stretching her long legs before heading downstairs. It had been so long since the picnic that she was getting hungry, but she was saving her appetite for cake and ice cream.

They broke out the Mexican Chocolate cake and ice cream just after sundown, then took their servings up to Bettina's bedroom, pulled back the curtains, and lined up on the edge of her bed to watch fireworks through the bank of windows. And when it was over, they took their dirty dishes downstairs and hugged each other goodnight.

"This has been our best day yet," Janie said. "Thank you for coming to live with me."

"Ditto, and thank you," Pauline said.

"Ditto twice," Bettina said.

"Ditto thrice," Gretchen said, and then grinned. "Okay, that was a little Downton Abbey, but what can I say. I'm a fan."

Monday morning was a day of new beginnings at the Broke-Ass Women's Club.

Gretchen was up before daylight, excited for her first day on the new job, and Bettina was right behind her. They were dressed and in the kitchen having breakfast when Janie came in, still in her pajamas. Her hair was a tangle of red curls, and she was barefoot.

"Honey! Are you sick?" Gretchen asked.

"No. I just couldn't get to sleep last night, so I got up and began filing all of the first of the month reports for my clients. I'm still not done."

"Oh Lord!" Bettina said. "I think I've done something when my checkbook balances."

Janie didn't comment. Bettina put on a big show about being an air-headed blonde, but Janie suspected it was all an act. She made herself a cup of coffee, then turned around and offered a toast.

"Big day for both of you," she said. "Make it great!"

"You, too!" Bettina said. "Go crunch those numbers."

Janie gave them a thumbs up and left the room.

"She's just so darn cute," Gretchen said.

Bettina sighed. "If I looked as good without makeup as she does, I'd never wear it. She looks about twelve."

"Oh, you wouldn't leave the house without makeup, and you know it," Gretchen said. "And neither would I."

They acknowledged the truth with a nod and finished eating.

Gretchen left first. Her day was from eight to five.

Bettina left in plenty of time to get to the Attilla residence by nine.

Janie was finally dressed and at work in her office, and Pauline at work in her office upstairs.

The house was quiet, and all was right in their world.

Gretchen walked into the insurance agency with her chin up

and confidence in her step. Juana Gilbert, the lady who was retiring, was staying on a week to get Gretchen trained for the receptionist job she'd held for the last fifteen years.

When she saw Gretchen enter, she stood.

"Good morning, Gretchen. That shade of blue looks lovely on you. Follow me and I'll show you the breakroom and your own personal locker to stow your purse and stuff."

On the way, they stopped in at the boss's office.

"Morning, Sarah. Gretchen is here, and I'm showing her around," Juana said.

Sarah Biggers looked up from her computer.

"Morning, Gretchen, and welcome. Juana will get you settled in, and we're really glad to have you."

"Thank you, Mrs. Biggers," Gretchen said.

"No formalities here. I'm Sarah. And then there's Charlie and Lisa, the other agents who work out of this office. You'll meet them later."

"Yes, ma'am," Gretchen said.

A short while later, Gretchen was at her desk with Juana at her side, going over the computer programs the office used and learning how to access information and documents.

Gretchen was familiar with the programs, which gave her more confidence, because God knows she needed it. There were few perks that came with a receptionist job, but for her, the biggest one was having a female for a boss. Having to answer to a man right now would not be in her best interests or his.

Bettina arrived at the Attilla residence with a spray can of mace in a little holster belted around her waist, bottled water, doggy bowls, treats, pooper bags in her backpack, and a leash in her hand. She was as prepared as she knew how to be and wanted this to work.

She rang the bell, and a few moments later, Barb, the housekeeper, opened the door. Loki was at her heels, already wearing his harness.

"Good morning," Barb said. "Loki is ready for his walk."

"I see that," Bettina said, and stepped over the threshold to clip on the leash. She got down on her knees and gave Loki a quick pet. "Hello, pretty boy! Wanna go for a walk?"

The little dog licked her fingers, his feathery tail wagging back and forth as she stood.

"Okay, Barb. We're off. I have the house phone for a contact number in case of emergency, is that right?"

"Yes," Barb said. "See you in a bit."

Bettina nodded and waved, then took off toward the sidewalk to retrace the route she'd taken with Shelby and with Loki on a much shorter leash.

The day was already warm, and a breeze would have been appreciated. Leaves hung limply from the branches, without the impetus to rustle.

Loki was prancing, his tail arched and flowing like a show pony. He sniffed at a beetle crossing his path, and Bettina saw it.

"No, sir! We do not eat bugs."

The little dog paused and looked back at her.

She grinned. "Yes, I'm talking to you. No bugs."

He yapped. She laughed, and the walk continued past elegant homes and properties that ranged more into mansions and estates than just big houses with back yards.

Although the neighborhood was classy, Loki was less impressed. His focus was on the man and dog across the street, and on a butterfly, and a squirrel scolding from high up in a tree as they passed.

He sniffed bushes, and peed on fire hydrants, and trotted at his own little pace. Fifteen minutes had passed before he found a spot to poop, and then there was the business of bagging it. All the while, Bettina talked to him. Once she was finished, she gave him a little treat, and then poured some water in a bowl and waited while he drank.

"My goodness... So thirsty," she murmured as Loki lapped and lapped until his little chin whiskers and the long hair on the tips of his ears were dripping wet. Finally, he stopped drinking and looked up.

"All done?" Bettina asked.

Loki yapped.

She dumped out the water and put the used bowl in her backpack.

"It's time to go home, buddy. Are you ready? Let's go!"

When they reached the street corner, Bettina took a turn to the right and headed back in the direction of the Attilla property, dumping the bag of poop in a public trash can at the next street corner.

Loki's little tongue was hanging out as they went, but the sidewalks were all shade, so she knew his feet would not be burning.

The traffic in the area was fairly busy, and she paid little attention to it until a car came up behind them and honked. When she turned to look, she saw a woman driving past. Her window was partly down to accommodate the dog with its head hanging out of the window. She waved back, smiling to herself at the joy on that dog's face. Tongue hanging out, ears flapping, living its best life.

Loki yapped at the dog, and then it was gone.

"Little tough guy. This is your neighborhood, and you're telling him all about it, aren't you?" Bettina said.

Loki's little tail was wagging, but he kept on plodding, still nosing everything in his path until finally they were within sight of the residence. The little dog had slowed down considerably, and she could tell that he was tired. When they came out from under the shade and out into the sun, she paused.

"Hold on a minute, buddy," she said, and leaned over to feel the sidewalk. It burned her hand, which was a sign it was going to burn his little feet, too. "Whoa! That's too hot for you, little man," and scooped him up into her arms.

Loki licked her chin and then went limp, resting in the crook of her arm as she carried him the rest of the way home.

She rang the doorbell, and when Barb came to the door and saw Bettina holding him, she looked upset.

"Is he okay? Did something happen?" she asked.

"No, he's fine. But when we came out of the shade into the sunlight, I felt like the sidewalk was too hot for his feet, so I carried him." Then she gave him a quick hug. "See you tomorrow, buddy," she said, unclipped her leash from his harness and watched him trot inside.

"Thank you for being so considerate of him," Barb said.

"He's a love. Have a nice day," Bettina said, and jogged back to her car, ready to get in and turn on the air conditioning.

Once inside, she sat a few moments letting the car cool off as she sent a text to Shelby Attilla that said the walk was over, and she then drove away.

Janie was in her office posting invoices and paying bills for a floral shop called Flowers by Baxter. Baxter Williams had been her client for almost eleven years, so she was familiar with every company the florist dealt with. Wholesale flower companies. Companies they ordered vases and baskets from. The companies that supplied floral foam, and floral picks, and ribbon.

Baxter always received the invoices at his office, stamped them "To Pay," and got them to her. She had authorization to submit electronic payments on his behalf and was working through the current stack when she came across an invoice that didn't look right. The only info on it was two gross, but no mention of what the items were, and with money due to a company called Moffitt and Sons, to the tune of nearly five hundred dollars. That was a lot of money for floral supplies. She assumed whoever had created the invoice from the other company had accidentally omitted the rest of the info.

As she was looking at it, it dawned on her that there had been an invoice similar to this in last month's lot, and maybe even one before, but for far less money. Curious, she pulled up last month's records, scanned the paid invoices, and found it. One invoice from Moffitt and Sons for two dozen, without mention of the items, for just over one hundred dollars. She went back one month farther, and found another invoice denoting floral supplies, with forty-six dollars being owed to the same company. All three invoices had been stamped To Pay, but she couldn't imagine Baxter not denoting what they were for, even if the company had omitted the information.

Curious, she Googled Moffitt and Sons and got a hit on a tool and die company in Chicago, and another hit on a plumbing business in New Mexico. Then she tried finding it through floral supplies and got nothing. All she had was a bank routing number and an account number to send the payment.

She kept telling herself Baxter Williams knew what he was doing, because he was a stickler for details, but she couldn't, in good conscience, let it go without checking. So she reached for the phone on her desk and called the shop.

"Good morning. Flowers by Baxter. How can I help you?"

"Devyn, this is Janie Logan. Is Baxter around? I have a bookkeeping question."

"He's in his office. Give me a second to transfer the call," she said.

Janie waited, and then the call was picked up.

"This is Baxter."

"Hi, Baxter. This is Janie. I have a quick question about one of your invoices."

"Oh, sure thing. What's up?" he asked.

"I am entering invoices to be paid, and I came across one that's a little puzzling. You have it stamped To Pay, but it's a new company to me. Moffitt and Sons. The invoice is for almost five hundred dollars, but it doesn't say what for. All it says is '2 gross'. I thought it was strange that you'd let that pass, and then remembered a similar invoice last month to the same company for just over a hundred dollars, and then I went back the third month, and there was another one for just a little under fifty dollars. I paid those two without thinking, because they were in the lot you'd given to me and stamped To Pay, like all the others. But this last one was a huge jump in cost, and I still don't know what it's for. Does any of this ring a bell?"

"That can't be right. I do all the ordering, and I never heard of Moffitt and Sons. Are you sure it's mine?"

"I'm looking right at it. Yes, it came in with the rest of your invoices, and this is the third month from the same company. The address on the invoice is Kansas City, Kansas, but there's no listing for anything like that on the web. Wait. Let me get screen shots of all three, and I'll text them to you, okay?"

"Yes! Please!" Baxter said. "I'll get right back to you as soon as I see them."

"Okay," Janie said, and hung up. Then she grabbed her cell phone, took a shot of all three invoices, sent them, and put the most recent one aside as she continued entering the others.

Within minutes, her phone rang, and she could tell by the sound of his voice when she answered that he was upset.

"Janie! It's me. Whatever you do, do not pay this. I don't know what's going on, but this is not a valid invoice. I never heard of this company. It does not come up on Google. I may have an employee issue here, but that's not your problem. Thank you so much for catching this! If you don't mind, I'm going to run by your house and pick it up, and can you make copies of the other two invoices for me, as well? I don't have them in my files. I want the evidence in my hand when I confront the scammer," he said.

"Of course, and I'm so sorry, Baxter. I'm here all day. Come by at your convenience," she said.

"Thank you. I'll be there within the hour," he said, and disconnected.

Janie hit Save on what she'd been doing, then went back into her computer files and copied the other two invoices before leaving the office.

She was walking up the hall toward the kitchen to get something to drink when Bettina came in the front door.

"Hey, girl. You have a nice glow. Want something cold to drink?" Janie asked.

Bettina rolled her eyes. "I'm not glowing. I'm sweating like a pig. It's really getting hot outside, and I'd love a Coke, or whatever's on hand," she said. After following Janie into the kitchen, she went outside to dump trash from her backpack before coming inside to wash up.

"I trust your walk went well?" Janie asked, as she poured up two glasses of Pepsi.

"It did. I know this isn't a big paying job right now, but I can build on it, and I do love it," Bettina said.

"That's what matters," Janie said.

Bettina nodded, then took a long drink.

"Yum. That hits the spot. I'm going to my room to get my laptop. I want to see if I have any new dog walking messages on my Facebook page."

"Okay," Janie said. "I'm waiting on a client to come by to pick up some paperwork."

Bettina took her drink and her backpack, then left the room.

Janie took the invoice and her drink into the living room and kicked back in the recliner to wait for Baxter.

About forty minutes later, she was still waiting and watching TV when she saw a car come flying down the street. The driver suddenly hit the brakes, backed up, and turned up into Janie's drive so fast she heard the tires spinning.

She saw a woman get out and run toward her house. When she began ringing the doorbell, and then knocking in loud, rapid succession, Janie frowned, put the invoices in the coffee table drawer, and went to the door.

There was a thirty-something blonde with turquoise-tipped hair, wearing jeans, sandals, and a white lab coat standing on her doorstep. Without introducing herself, she started talking.

"Hi! Baxter sent me to pick up the invoices!"

Janie frowned. "I'm sorry. I don't know you."

She frowned. "That doesn't matter. Baxter sent me. Where are they?" she said, and started to walk inside.

In that moment, Janie was wishing she hadn't opened the door. This didn't feel right. Baxter would have told her if he was sending someone else.

"Just stop right there," Janie said. "Nobody invited you inside, and Baxter would not have sent a total stranger to my house without first letting me know."

All of a sudden, the woman leaped, and within seconds Janie was flat on her back with the woman sitting on her. Her hands were around Janie's neck, and she was still shouting, "Where are they? Where are they?"

In that moment, Janie knew it was fight or die. Still gasping for air, she dug her fingernails into the woman's cheeks and raked them down her face. Shocked by the pain, the woman loosened her hold, giving Janie time to catch her breath. As she did, she began kicking and screaming "Help! Help!"

The woman grabbed Janie again, choking her and slamming her head against the floor as she kept shouting, "Where are they?".

They were making so much noise that neither of them heard the sound of footsteps on the stairs. By the time the intruder realized they were in her face, it was too late to react.

One moment, the intruder had been straddling Janie's waist, and the next thing, blood was spurting from her mouth and nose, and she was flat on her back with an Amazon of a woman holding her down.

Pauline's hand was throbbing, but she ignored the pain as she rolled the woman belly down, pinning her arms behind her back, and smashing her cheek against the floor.

"I've got her," she shouted. "Call 9-1-1!"

Bettina had pulled Janie into a sitting position against the wall and was still down on her knees beside her as she made the call.

"They're on the way," Bettina said, and then dropped her phone back in her pocket and cupped Janie's face. "Honey! Honey! Are you all right?"

Janie was crying and shaking so hard, she didn't have breath enough to speak, and just kept nodding her head.

Bettina ran for the kitchen and came back with a couple of wet cloths to wipe the blood from Janie's face.

"What happened? Do you know her?" Bettina asked.

"No. I was expecting one of my clients. I don't know who she is," Janie said.

The woman was beginning to rally and thrashed beneath Pauline's hold.

"You broke by doze! I can't breeve."

"Shut up. You're not gonna die," Pauline said, and tightened her hold on the woman's hair.

Then another car pulled up, and Pauline saw a man get out and start running toward the house.

"Here comes another one!" she shouted.

Janie looked out the door. "No. That's Baxter. My client."

Baxter came inside on the run, saw the woman on the floor, and gasped in disbelief.

"Phoebe? What the hell?"

But Phoebe wasn't talking.

Then Baxter saw Janie, ran to her, and knelt down, horrified by the blood all over her, and the cut on her forehead. "Janie! My dear! Are you all right? What happened here? Why is Phoebe here?"

"I don't know her, or why she's here," Janie said. "She just showed up at the door in a panic, telling me you'd sent her to pick up the invoices. I doubted her story, and when I did, she attacked me."

"Oh my God," Baxter said, and looked over his shoulder. "She must have overheard our phone conversation. Now I know who's been stealing from me, because coming here gave her away. But her presence here leads me to believe she has an accomplice. She's only worked for me for three months and would have no way of knowing who does my books, or where to find you without being told. She had the beginnings of a nice little fraud scheme in progress, and I think slipping in a fake invoice three months ago, for such a small amount, was her way of testing the system to see if she could get paid. When it worked, she tried a larger amount the second month and got that money, too. So she went for an even bigger one, and that's when you caught it. I'm so sorry that you were hurt. I'm just sick that this has involved you."

"Not your fault," Janie mumbled, but she couldn't stop shaking.

Bettina finally had the blood wiped off Janie's face, and then folded the other wet cloth and pressed it against the cut on her forehead.

"Can you hold this tight enough to stop the bleeding?" she asked.

Janie's hands were still shaking, but she propped an elbow on her knee and pressed the cloth against the cut.

At that point, the police pulled up at the curb, sirens blaring.

When they saw all the cars and the door standing wide open, they came into the house with their weapons drawn, then took one look at the situation, holstered their guns, and pulled out cuffs.

"This is the woman who attacked Janie. She's all yours," Pauline said, and got up, shaking her hand, trying to get the feeling back in it.

CHAPTER SIX

The police cuffed Phoebe, and when they stood her up, blood dripped down her face and onto her clothes.

"Dey broke by doze," Phoebe moaned.

An officer stepped forward. "I'm Officer Giraldi. Who called the police?"

Bettina raised her hand. "I did."

"Do all of you live here?" he asked.

Janie staggered as she stood, still holding the bloody cloth against the cut on her forehead.

"Not all. I'm Janie Logan. This is my home. Bettina Lee and Pauline Logan also live here. I have a bookkeeping service in my home. I was expecting Mr. Williams, who is a client. But then the doorbell rang, and when I answered, that woman—who is a stranger to me—pushed her way into my house and attacked me. Bettina and Pauline saved me."

"We heard Janie screaming and came running," Bettina said. "The woman was sitting on Janie and had her hands around her throat, choking her. Pauline punched the crazy bitch and took her down. We will be filing assault charges against her."

Giraldi eyed Pauline, thinking she was sure tougher than she appeared, and hid a smile at Bettina's "crazy bitch" comment as he continued to take notes of their statements.

Baxter picked up the story. "I'm Baxter Williams of Flowers by Baxter. Janie is my accountant. She called me this morning, alerting me to some suspicious invoices from my shop. I immediately suspected an employee was trying to defraud me. I wanted to see these fake invoices for myself, and a short while after our call, I left the shop to come here, only to walk in on this. This woman is Phoebe Riggs, an employee of mine. She's only worked for me for three months. I didn't know who was involved in the fraud until now. Phoebe has given herself away by trying to get the invoices back before I saw them. But she would have had no way of knowing about my bookkeeper, or where she lived. So, now I'm suspecting she had an accomplice. I will be filing charges against Phoebe, and as soon as I root out her accomplice, I'll add a name to those charges."

Giraldi was still making notes. "I'll need written statements from all of you and your contact information." He pointed to Baxter. "You first, sir."

Baxter rattled off his name, the name of his business, and his phone number. And then Giraldi went down the line, getting the women's names and contact info, and then Baxter gave him Phoebe's name.

"I have Phoebe's contact info in my office at work. I can text it to you when I get back," Baxter said.

"That'll work," Giraldi said, and then the blast of another siren was added to the chaos as an ambulance rolled up to the curb to pick up Phoebe, who'd been cuffed, informed of her rights, and was officially under arrest.

An officer cuffed her to the Gurney, then followed behind the ambulance to E.R.

Janie pointed to the coffee table. "Bettina, the invoices are in the drawer. Would you please give them to Baxter?" she said, and then the room started to spin. She backed up against the wall to keep from falling and slowly slid back down to the floor.

Pauline rushed toward her. "What's wrong?"

"I'm dizzy," Janie said.

"There's another ambulance on the way," Officer Giraldi said. It should be here at any moment. Which car belongs to the Riggs woman? We'll have it towed from the property."

Baxter pointed it out, and Giraldi called in to the station to have them dispatch a tow truck to the residence. He squatted down beside Janie and lightly checked her pulse.

"Am I dead?" Janie muttered.

He smiled. "No, ma'am. Not even close. I'm sorry you were hurt, but help's on the way."

At that point, the other ambulance arrived, sirens blaring.

By now, every person in the neighborhood was standing in their front yard, watching. But when they saw Janie being wheeled out on a Gurney, their curiosity turned to dismay.

Florence was standing on her porch next door, and when she

saw Janie being put into the back of the ambulance, she came running toward the house, only to be stopped by an officer standing
guard at the door.

"What happened? What happened? These girls are my neighbors!" she cried.

Pauline heard her and came outside.

"We're okay, Florence. There was an intruder here, but the police have her in custody. Janie can tell you all about it when she
comes back. I promise."

"Are we in danger?" Florence asked.

And then Baxter spoke up as he was leaving.

"No, ma'am, you are not in danger. The intruder was an employee I fired. Janie got involved only because she's my bookkeeper.
The woman has been arrested. You're all safe." Then he turned to
Giraldi. "Officer, am I free to leave? I need to get back to my shop to
continue my investigation before the accomplice finds out Phoebe
has been arrested."

"Yes. If we have further questions, we know where to find you,"
Giraldi said.

Baxter sighed. "Ladies, my sincere apologies for this. But it will
not go unpunished. I promise," he said, and then he got in his car
and drove away.

Florence went home, and Giraldi left, taking the other officers
with him.

Finally, the house was theirs again. The girls took one look at
each other and then hugged.

"Oh, my God. Can you believe that just happened?" Pauline said.

Bettina noticed Pauline was favoring her hand and reached for
it, then frowned at the swelling. "You need to get ice on that."

"Not yet. One of us needs to go to the hospital and be with
Janie. And the other one should clean up this blood. It looks like
we butchered a hog in here."

"I'll do the cleaning," Bettina said. "You get an ice pack and take
it with you to ER. Call if you need me."

"Okay," Pauline said, and then paused. "Didn't they say they
were taking her to SSM Health?"

"Yes, and I think there's an actual ice pack in the big deep freeze
in the utility room. Get it out and take it with you. I'll have this
mess cleaned up by the time you get back."

Pauline ran upstairs to get her purse, found the ice pack in the
deep freeze, and took off out the door. She jumped in her car, entered the hospital address in her GPS, folded the ice pack over her
hand, and drove away.

It was becoming apparent to Janie that Phoebe had banged her head against the floor harder than she'd first thought. It was pounding with every heartbeat, and her vision was blurry. The shriek of the siren screamed inside her head, and she kept mumbling, "Turn it off," to the EMTs.

They didn't know what she was talking about and kept reassuring her they were on the way to ER, and that they were almost there. When the sirens stopped on their arrival, she breathed a sigh of relief.

But the relief was short-lived. The hustle of getting her out of the ambulance and wheeling her into ER exposed her to a whole other set of flashing lights—which turned out to be the fluorescent lights in the ceiling above, as they moved her quickly into an exam bay. The doctor and nurses awaiting her arrival were all talking at once as they moved her from the Gurney to the exam bed.

Motion made her nauseous, but it dissipated when they quit moving her around. The EMTs were talking to the doctor, giving him an update on her stats as well as her mental confusion in the ambulance, and then a nurse began cutting off her clothes. When she cut the bra apart between the cups, Janie winced, accepting the inevitable as her boobs took advantage of their freedom.

Then a man loomed into her line of vision. He had a kind face and a gentle voice.

"I'm Doctor Rollins. Can you tell me your name?"

"Janie Logan."

"Do you remember what happened?" he asked.

"Yes. A stranger pushed her way into my home and attacked me."

"How did you get this cut on your forehead?" he asked.

"I don't know. Maybe from the ring she was wearing. She knocked me backward onto the floor and then jumped on me... choking me."

The doctor had already noticed the marks on her neck that were beginning to bruise. He slid his hand beneath her head to feel for blood and felt a huge knot instead.

"Get me a portable x-ray in here, STAT," he said, and began pressing his fingers against her stomach.

"Does this hurt?" he asked. "How about here? And here?"

"No," Janie said.

"You have significant bruising on your ribs."

Janie frowned. "I'm not very big. She was. And she was sitting on top of me. And just for the record, I wasn't confused in the ambulance. The noise of the sirens was making my head hurt worse.

When I kept telling them to turn it off, I was referring to the sirens."

He smiled. "Duly noted," and continued his examination, including cleaning the cut on her forehead.

A few minutes later, they wheeled in the portable x-ray, took pictures of her head and the area of her bruising. As they were rolling the machine out of the room, Pauline appeared, her purse over her shoulder and the ice pack wrapped around her hand.

"I'm family," she said, and went straight to the foot of the bed.

Janie had been holding it together until she saw Pauline. The comfort of a familiar face sent tears rolling.

Doctor Rollins glanced up, then noted the ice pack on the woman's hand and frowned.

"Are you injured, too?"

"Not really. It's been a while since I sucker punched an intruder. It's just sore, so I'm icing it."

Janie frowned. "What if you broke it?"

"Only I didn't," Pauline said, removed her hand from the ice pack and wiggled all the fingers and moved her wrist up and down to prove it.

Doctor Rollins reached for her hand, felt of all the bones and joints, and then turned back to Janie.

"Nurse, bring a tray please. We need to glue this cut on her head."

The nurse left the room, returning shortly with everything Rollins had asked for. Once he'd finished, he put a small bandage on her forehead, and then patted Janie's arm.

"I'm going to go check the x-rays. I'll be back shortly." He nodded at the nurse, and then left the exam room.

The nurse moved to Janie's side and readjusted the sheet over her body. "Are you warm enough? Would you like a blanket?"

"Yes. It's chilly in here," Janie said.

The nurse exited the room, leaving Janie and Pauline alone. Pauline pulled up a chair beside the bed, dumped her things on it, then leaned over and gave Janie a hug, before smoothing flyaway red curls from her forehead.

"You scared us to death," she said.

"I was scared for myself," Janie said. "Thank God you two came to my rescue. All the way here, I kept remembering before... and how often I had to take myself to the doctor when I was sick. I came home to an empty house afterward to nurse myself back to health. If this had happened before you came to live with me, I'd be dead." Then she sighed as tears rolled again. "How did we fool ourselves into believing we had a husband?"

Pauline shrugged. "Because we didn't want to be alone?"

More tears rolled. "But that's just it! We *were* alone. All the time.

Except for five or six days a month. Then we heaped praise and adulation on the bastard for just showing up."

"When you put it like that, we were a little pathetic, weren't we?" Pauline muttered, and then patted Janie's hand. "Who knew being a bookkeeper could be dangerous?"

"Not me," Janie muttered.

And then the nurse came back with a heated blanket and put it on Janie.

"Feel better?" she asked.

"Yes, thank you," Janie said.

"This is your call button," the nurse said, as she pulled it down from a hook on the bed and laid it beside Janie's pillow. "Just buzz us if you need something," and then she was gone.

"What's happening at home?" Janie asked.

"I suspect the neighbors have all gone back inside. They were all in their yards on both sides of the street for quite a while. Florence had a melt-down when she saw them bringing you out of the house on a Gurney. We assured her you would fill her in on the details when you came home, and Bettina is cleaning up blood."

Janie frowned. "Good Lord."

"None of it matters because you're okay," Pauline said. "You don't need to talk. Just lie back and close your eyes. I'm not going anywhere until I can take you with me."

"Then I'll be going home naked, because they cut my clothes off me," Janie said, then reached for Pauline's hand.

Pauline clasped with her uninjured hand and left the swollen one beneath the ice pack.

By the time Bettina had the blood cleaned up, she was sick to her stomach. Part of it was adrenaline crashing, and part of it was thinking how close they'd come to losing Janie. Finally, she allowed herself to feel the panic of everything that had happened and sat down at the kitchen table and cried.

She was still crying when her cell phone rang. When she saw it was from Pauline, she sucked up her emotional meltdown and answered.

"Hey, honey, how's Janie?"

"Okay, I think. She's resting, and we're both waiting for the doctor to return. He went to check on X-rays, but we need a favor."

"Name it," Bettina said.

"They cut Janie's clothes off her in the ER. Can you go to her room and get underwear and clothes and bring them here, please? We're hoping he's going to let her come home, but at any rate, whenever she's released, she's going to need a bra and panties, along with some easy to get on and off clothes."

"Of course!" Bettina said.

"Have you called Gretchen?" Pauline asked.

Bettina sighed. "No. I hated to upset her on her first day at work."

"If we're not home before she gets off work, she's going to wonder where we are," Pauline said.

Bettina checked the time. "You're right. Maybe I'll call her on the way to the hospital."

"I think we should," Pauline said. "One for all and all for one, you know?"

"Absolutely. See you soon."

Bettina pocketed her phone and headed down the hall on the run. It didn't take long to gather up what she needed, stuff it all in a tote bag, and grab her purse and car keys. Next, she headed out the door, locking it as she went. She sent Gretchen a text, asking her to call when she could, and drove away.

Gretchen was in her element.

There were things to file, and things to organize.

Messages to take and messages to deliver.

She knew the office closed from twelve noon to one p.m. for lunch, but she'd brought her lunch from home, and took advantage of the breakroom and quiet of the office to eat. She didn't have money to waste on daily lunches and had no desire to go out and dine on her own. When the others came back from lunch, she was already at her desk with a stack of messages for each agent.

Sarah Biggers, Gretchen's boss, was talking on her cell phone as she walked in. Gretchen handed over her messages as she passed and went back to work.

The other two agents came back together. Gretchen glanced up.

"Lisa, you had a couple of calls while you were out. These are the numbers to call back. Charlie, you had three. These are your call back numbers."

"Thanks, Gretchen," Lisa said.

Charlie took them with a nod, reading the top one as he headed down the hall to his office.

And then Juana called in, panicked. "Gretchen, I have a flat! I'm sitting in the parking lot of the restaurant waiting for roadside service. I'll get back as soon as I can, but in the meantime, ask Sarah for help if you get stumped."

"Oh, bless your heart," Gretchen said. "No worries. I'll be fine."

And she was. She had the appointment calendar in front of her, and she already knew how to funnel through walk-in clients. The rest of it was simple. After visiting with a woman this morning who was waiting to talk to Charlie about insuring a house she was flipping, the idea of selling houses took root. She could study for her real estate license at night and work this job during the day.

Juana finally returned, red-faced from the heat, and a bit frazzled from the stress. She began apologizing as she walked in the door.

"I'm so sorry. This was just unforgiveable, and on your first day at work. Are you okay?"

Gretchen got up. "I'm fine. You, however, look like you could do with something cold to drink. Sit, and I'll get you some water."

"You don't have to wait on me," Juana said.

"I know, but I'm happy to do it. Just take a deep breath and relax. I'll be right back," Gretchen said, and headed for the breakroom. She got a bottle of water from the refrigerator, brought it back to Juana, and was just about to sit back down at her desk when she got a text.

When she realized it was Bettina, she looked up.

"Excuse me, but this is family." She quickly pulled up the text, read it, and knew within moments that something was wrong. She sighed, and then stood. "I'm going to the breakroom to return this call. My family knows this was my first day on a new job, and they would never tell me to call home unless something has happened."

"I hope it's nothing, but I'll cover for you," Juana said.

Gretchen was already making the call as she headed back to the breakroom. The phone had barely begun to ring when Bettina picked up.

"Gretchen! I'm so sorry to bother you at work, but we didn't want you to come home to an empty house and not know where the hell everyone was."

Gretchen's heart skipped a beat. "Oh, my God. You're scaring me! What's wrong?"

And then she began explaining. "Janie was attacked today—in the foyer of our house. It's a long, involved story, but the woman who attacked her has been arrested and taken to jail."

Gretchen gasped. "Oh, my God! Please tell me she's going to be okay!"

"I'm pretty sure she is. But she was talking and standing up throughout the investigation, and then on the verge of passing out.

Probably a concussion. We're just hoping that's all."

Gretchen groaned. "I'm sick. Just sick about this. She's so little. What can I do?"

"Oh hell, girl, I don't know. I already mopped up the blood."

Gretchen gasped. "Blood? There was blood?"

"Yes. Janie's forehead was cut, but she got her licks in, too. She dug holes in the bitch's face with her nails, then Pauline punched her and broke her nose."

Gretchen's voice started to shake. "Good Lord! Should I come to the hospital after I get off work?"

"If they admit her, I'll let you know. Otherwise just assume we're coming home with her. I'll figure something out for dinner."

"Okay," Gretchen said. "I'll pick up something for dessert. Tell her I'm so sorry, and that I send my love."

"Will do, honey. I'm really sorry to have called you at work, but we're family, and we all deserve to know what's happening. Okay?"

"Yes, okay, and thank you for letting me know," Gretchen said. She disconnected, put her phone back in her pocket, then ran into the bathroom and threw up. It took a few more minutes to calm down before she went back, but the stricken expression on her face was apparent the moment Juana saw her.

"Gretchen? Are you okay?"

Gretchen was carrying a bottle of water with both hands as she slid into the chair behind her desk.

"A member of my family was attacked in our home today. I don't know all the details, but the intruder was a stranger who's been arrested. Janie is in ER. She was hurt, and she's so little. Barely five feet tall. I just can't imagine anyone hurting her like that. Thank God there were other family members at home who heard her screaming."

"Oh, my God! I'm so sorry," Juana said.

Gretchen nodded, then took a drink of water and sat for a few seconds, staring off into space. Then the office phone rang, and every emotion she felt was put aside.

"Biggers Insurance Agency. How may I direct your call?"

"This is Maris Roland returning Lisa Beal's call."

"One moment please," Gretchen said, and rang Lisa's office. When Lisa picked up, Gretchen spoke. "Maris Roland on line two for you."

"Thank you, Gretchen," Lisa said, and picked up the call.

Gretchen returned the receiver and turned back to her computer, trying to remember what she'd been doing.

Janie's eyes were closed when Doctor Rollins and his nurse came back into the room.

Rollins glanced at Pauline.

"Is she asleep?"

Janie's eyes popped open and answered for herself. "No, she's not asleep. She's just wishing her headache to the pits of hell. So, what's the verdict?"

He walked back to the side of her bed, pulled out an Ophthalmoscope, and began checking her eyes again before answering.

"Well, you have a hard head, which is good. We don't see any swelling in the brain, and your ribs are intact. You do have a mild concussion, and the best treatment for that is rest for about twenty-four to forty-eight hours. That rest includes mental and physical rest. If symptoms persist after that, or you get suddenly worse, you need to come back immediately."

"Can I go home?" Janie asked.

"Yes, providing you're not alone."

"She's not going to be alone," Pauline said. "What can she have for the pain?"

"Over the counter pain meds will work. I'll send a paper with directives," he said.

"In the meantime, if you could spare a couple of aspirin here, I would appreciate it. Otherwise, the ride home is going to be a hoot," Janie said.

At that point, Bettina arrived with the tote bag of clothes.

"Another family member?" Doctor Rollins asked.

"Yes, I'm another family member," Bettina said.

"Just in the nick of time, girl. I get to go home and now I won't be going buck naked," Janie said.

"I'll get your paperwork ready," Rollins said.

"What about the pain meds?" Pauline asked.

He glanced at her and then nodded. "They'll bring them to you shortly."

"Can she get dressed?" Bettina asked.

"Don't let her stand up on her own. You can help her dress, but don't turn loose of her. It's going to take time for the dizziness to pass," he said, and then left the exam room.

Bettina set the tote bag on the bed and began pulling out the clothing.

"Oh, Gretchen was properly horrified and sends her love," she said.

Janie sighed. "I was properly horrified, too. Never knew paying bills for a client could take such a wrong turn. And look where it got me."

"Close the door," Pauline said, and then also pulled the curtain closed around Janie's bed.

Between her and Bettina, they got Janie dressed, and then put her back on the bed and pulled up the covers.

"Just rest, honey," Pauline said. "Knowing hospitals, this is going to take a while."

"Then I'm going to go back home," Bettina said. "Is there anything I need to get for you? Do you have enough pain meds at home? Are you sick at your stomach? I can pick up something for that."

"I have everything I need at home, and that includes all of you. I already said this to Pauline, but I'm going to repeat it for you. If you two hadn't been home today, I think that woman would have killed me. You both saved my life, and I will never forget it."

Bettina hugged her.

"I don't think I've ever been so scared. I'm pretty sure I peed my pants when Pauline punched her in the face."

"Oh Lord. Thanks for the information," Pauline said.

Janie laughed, and then grabbed her head and groaned. "Ow. No funnies until my head quits hurting, please."

Bettina shrugged. She wasn't one for hiding the truth about anything.

"Anyway, I'm going to go home and change my pants. I'll see you there," she said, and gave Janie a quick kiss on the cheek. "I'm leaving the door open so they won't forget you're in here," she added, and pushed it against the wall as she left.

Baxter Williams walked back into his shop with a look on his face that gave every employee in the building serious pause. And when he stopped at the door and locked it, then turned the OPEN sign to CLOSED, they froze.

"Everyone! In my office! Now!" he said, and watched as all six of them stopped what they were doing and scurried down the hall to his office with him on their heels.

As soon as they were inside, he shut that door, too, and then pointed.

"Sit on the sofa. Sit on a chair. Or sit on the floor. But sit down now!"

They dropped.

"Phoebe has been arrested. She went to Janie Logan's residence today and attacked her, trying to get back the false invoices she's been slipping into the shop invoices to defraud me of money. Two of them slipped past me during the past three months, but Janie caught this last one and called me. After that, it was only a matter of figuring out who'd been doing it."

Baxter watched every face in the room as he paused for effect. The levels of shock and disbelief looked real. But he wasn't through.

"However, it appears Phoebe overheard our phone call and took off out of here like she was on fire. She wanted to get the false invoice Janie caught. But here's the rub. She's only worked here three months. She had no idea that Janie Logan does my books, or where she lived. But most of you do. So, I know for a fact she had an accomplice, because one of you had to give her that information. And guess who started talking to save her own ass?"

Nate Roberts bolted up from his chair.

"She's lying. We don't even get along. Why would I do—"

Baxter wiped his hand across his face.

"You're as stupid as she is. She gave herself away by going after Janie, and you just gave yourself way by denying something she never said."

Nate's mouth opened, his eyes widened, and Baxter could tell he was thinking about running.

"You lied!" Nate cried.

"And you helped her steal," Baxter said. "Who's in the most trouble here?" Then he picked up the phone and got Officer Giraldi's card out of his pocket and called him.

The rest of his staff was in shock. One of the women got up and stood against the door to the office so that Nate couldn't run, while the rest of them moved to the other side of the room, getting as far away from him as possible.

As soon as Baxter delivered his message, he hung up.

"Devyn, would you please bring me a roll of floral tape," he asked.

"Yes, sir," she said and bolted out of the room on the run, returning moments later with the roll.

Baxter took it, then pointed at Nate. "Turn around."

Nate bristled. "You're not a cop. I don't have to—"

Baxter grabbed Nate by the arm, spun him around, and yanked his arm so high behind his back that he was begging.

"You're breaking my arm! Stop! Stop!" Nate cried.

But Baxter just grabbed Nate's other arm and began wrapping the floral tape around both of his wrists until he was cuffed in a wreath of sticky green. Then he sat him down in the corner of the room and stood over him.

"The rest of you please go back to work, and someone unlock

the front door and turn the OPEN sign back around. The police should be here shortly."

"Yes sir," they said, and left the room in silence, too shocked to speak.

"Why did you do it, Nate? You've been with me for a good four years. I thought better of you," Baxter said.

Nate wouldn't look up and wouldn't talk.

"Whatever," Baxter said. "I'll find out the truth and then we'll all know. Phoebe is the kind who'll betray her own brother to save her ass."

Nate's head came up, and the look in his eyes was pure horror.

Baxter gasped. "You two are related, aren't you? *Are* you her brother, for real?"

Nate nodded, then leaned his head against the wall and started crying.

"Was this her idea?" Baxter asked.

Nate nodded.

"And you just went along with it because you're related? Without any thought of loyalty to your employer? Never mind the fact that it was illegal."

"I didn't want nothin' to do with it. But Phoebe is mean. She always was. She stamped the fake invoices and slipped them in with the ones you'd already vetted. And when they came back, I removed the fake one from the stack. You weren't supposed to ever know it had been there. But then Janie caught on, and called, and Phoebe heard you. That's when she made me tell her where Mrs. Logan lived."

"Made you how?" Baxter asked.

"She said she'd make me sorry if I didn't tell her. I was afraid of what she'd do, so I told."

"And it nearly got Mrs. Logan killed," Baxter said.

Nate's head came up. "What?"

"Phoebe was choking her and beating her head against the floor when Janie's roommates stepped her. They took Janie to ER. I don't know her condition. But you can imagine how disgusted and dismayed I am that she got hurt because of people who worked for me."

"I'm sorry," Nate said, and started bawling. "I didn't think she would hurt anyone like that."

"Bullshit," Baxter said. "You were afraid of her enough to help her commit fraud. And yet you thought that tiny little wisp of a woman would be safe around Phoebe? You make me sick. Both of you."

Then the sounds of sirens announced the arrival of the police.

"It appears your ride is here. Oh... and you're fired."

CHAPTER SEVEN

Bettina sent a text to Gretchen, letting her know they were bringing Janie home, then drove away from the hospital, rattled to the core. When she'd wiped the blood off Janie's face, she'd also wiped away her makeup, and lying in that hospital bed, Janie had looked like a little girl. They'd glued the cut on her forehead, which was good. It hadn't required stitches. But it had reminded them, once again, how quickly life could end.

She stopped at a local supermarket and went back to their deli to pick up some food, finally settling on chicken salad to make sandwiches, and broccoli cheese soup for four, then headed home.

Pauline took her melted icepack and her purse and left to bring the car around. Heat slapped her in the face as she jogged across the parking lot to the car. She reclined the passenger seat, then drove to the ER entrance, parking in one lane of the breezeway to watch for them to bring Janie out.

As soon as she saw them, she got out to help the orderly get Janie into the car, then buckled her in while eyeing the pain on Janie's face.

"Are you okay, honey? Do you need the seat adjusted a little?"

"I'm good, but I'm going to keep my eyes closed on the ride home."

"You don't need to talk, either," Pauline said. "We'll be home soon, and then you can lie down where it's cool and quiet."

Janie reached for Pauline's arm. "Thank you."

Pauline just shook her head. "You don't thank me. This is what family is for," she said, then she got in the car and drove away.

The aftermath of the trauma and then the adrenaline crash were catching up with Janie. It hurt to swallow. It hurt to turn her head. It hurt to take deep breaths. She felt like she'd been trampled and didn't know how to react to the shock of what had happened.

Phoebe Riggs had done more than physically hurt Janie. She'd destroyed the illusion of safety in which Janie lived. Her house had always been the refuge during sad times and bad times. It had withstood blizzards and tornadoes, torrential rains and flooding over three generations of Duvalls, and then one crazy woman's appearance had revealed a flaw in Janie's thinking. Once a door is open, anyone or anything could come inside—even the devil in disguise.

She was going to get a Ring doorbell installed to insure no more surprises.

By the time Pauline got her home, Janie was trembling from the pain.

Pauline called Bettina for help, and together, they got Janie in the house and down the hall to her room.

"Bless your heart," Pauline said, as she pulled back the covers on Janie's bed and then eased her down on the mattress. "Do you want to change into a nightgown, or just lie down with your shoes off?"

"Just lie down," Janie said, and eased back onto the pillow and closed her eyes. "I have to rest for a bit."

"What if you need to go to the bathroom?" Bettina said.

Janie waved her hand. "Bring me my phone. I'll call for help. I promise."

"Do you know where it is?" Pauline asked.

"It was on the end table in the living room when I went to answer the door. It should still be there."

"Be right back," Pauline said, and ran up the hall to the living room, found it right where Janie said it would be, and hurried back. "Got it," she said, and laid it on the table beside the bed.

"Thank you," Janie said. "Go on, both of you. I swear I'm not moving until my head quits pounding."

Bettina dashed into the bathroom, and came back with a cold wet washcloth, and laid it on Janie's forehead.

"Feels good," Janie mumbled, and pulled the covers up under her chin.

"Please don't get up by yourself," Pauline said.

Janie sighed. "I won't. I promise."

The girls looked at each other, and then reluctantly left the room.

Gretchen got a text, letting her know Janie had been released.

When the office hours ended, she stopped at a bakery on her way home and got four strawberry Napoleons for dessert. Maybe something sweet would taste good if nothing else tempted her.

She kept hitting red lights all the way back and began wondering if the Universe was trying to tell her to slow down. To calm down. Because all she could think about was how close they'd come to losing Janie—like they'd lost David. One minute he was alive and breathing, and then life for him had ended. If Bettina and Pauline had not been home, the same thing might have happened to her.

She took a deep breath, and then exhaled slowly, trying to settle the knot in her stomach. It didn't help. The trauma of their lives had taken on a whole new level of fear. The "what if" fear.

She knew "what if" better than most. She'd buried two husbands now, and she was only forty-three years old. She'd only known Janie for a few months, but in that short length of time, she'd become so dear to Gretchen that the thought of losing her, too, was horrifying.

By the time the light turned green, tears were rolling. The intrusion into their safe haven had happened. Janie was alive, but Gretchen was coming to realize how false her sense of security had been.

She cried enough to ease the knot in her stomach, then reminded herself to suck it up. The last thing they needed at home was for her to walk in looking like her best friend had died—even if it had nearly happened.

By the time she pulled up into the driveway, her tears were gone and so was the shock of the news. Her mother used to say, "And this, too, shall pass." She was holding that as a given.

She grabbed her things, including the box with the strawberry Napoleons, and got out. But once inside, walking through the foyer took on a whole new meaning. She couldn't help but look to see if all the blood was gone, then shuddered thinking about it. She put the desserts in the refrigerator, then went to see if Janie was awake.

As she neared the bedroom, she heard voices, and realized it was coming from a television. The door was ajar, and so she slowly pushed it inward, peeked in, and saw Janie propped up on pillows, watching TV.

"Hey, honey. Can I come in?" Gretchen asked.

Janie waved her in. "How did your first day at work go?"

Gretchen walked in, eased down on the side of the bed, and took Janie by the hand.

"My day was good. I am so sorry yours was the day from hell."

Janie rolled her eyes. "Girl, you have no idea. But it's over. The nut is behind bars, and I'm pressing charges. My client is pressing charges, too, and then she'll be on a prison bus to nowhere."

"Are you in pain?" Gretchen asked.

"Yup," Janie said, and pulled up the t-shirt she was wearing to show Gretchen the bruises on her body.

"Oh, my God," Gretchen said, and then noticed the bruises on Janie's neck, as well. "Your neck!"

"She was choking me, and the knot on the back of my head is hell to sleep on. But I'll bet she hurts worse than me, because I dug furrows down her face with my nails, and Pauline punched her out and broke her nose, then held her down until the police came. It's a shame it wasn't caught on camera. I'm pretty sure it would have been the cat fight of the year. All we needed was the mud pit."

Gretchen shook her head. "I don't know how you can joke about nearly dying."

"I guess because I didn't?" Janie said.

"It would happen when I wasn't here to help."

Janie frowned. "You are helping. You're all working now, and that's keeping all of us afloat. Be proud of yourself for landing a job."

"Yes, okay, I'll accept that, but just so you know, I brought home strawberry Napoleons for dessert tonight. I hope you feel good enough to enjoy yours."

"Are you kidding? I might not get much dinner down, but I always feel good enough for dessert," Janie said.

Gretchen nodded. "I'm going to change clothes and see what's happening for dinner. Do you need anything before I go?"

"I'm not allowed to get up and walk around on my own until the dizzy spells pass. Would you help me get to the bathroom and back?"

"I sure will."

Janie threw back the covers, swung her legs off the side of the bed, then grabbed Gretchen's arm when the room started to spin.

"Whoops. Wait a sec until the merry-go-round stops."

"You just say when," Gretchen said.

A few moments later, Janie tightened her grip and stood up. "I'm okay now."

Gretchen steadied her as they went into the bathroom. A couple of minutes later, she walked her back to the bed, then tucked her in.

"How do we know when you need help?" Gretchen asked.

Janie pointed to her phone. "I have all of you on speed dial. If it's me calling, I probably need to pee."

"Are you going to feel like eating dinner?"

"I haven't eaten since breakfast, so yes, please," Janie said.

"Okay then. I'll tell the girls. I'm going to change. Do you want to eat in here or at the table?"

"The table. I want my life back, even if it has to happen in increments."

About an hour later, the girls had just sat down to eat when the doorbell rang.

"I've still got one good hand to punch with. I'll get it," Pauline said, and got up from the table.

"Lord," Janie muttered. "Somebody go with her. I don't want her getting side-swiped, too."

"I'll go," Gretchen said, and hurried after her.

But they both came back only moments later, with Gretchen carrying an enormous arrangement of cut flowers.

"For Janie," Paulie said, and set them on the island.

"Oh my gosh! I'll bet Baxter sent them," she said, and when they handed her the card that came with them, she opened it and read it aloud.

"My heartfelt apologies for what happened, and my lifelong gratitude for rooting out criminals in my midst. The accomplice was identified and is also in jail. Get well soon, dear friend. Oh...and your 'sisters' are amazing."

"Yay, us, and that's a huge arrangement!" Bettina said. "When they start putting gladiolas and lilies in bouquets, I know they're either going to a banquet or a funeral."

"It came far too close to the latter to suit me," Janie said. "We can put it on the table in the foyer later," she said, and picked up her soup spoon. "Whoever thought of soup, good call," she said.

"Want a sandwich?" Bettina asked.

"Maybe a half," Janie said, as they settled in to eat.

Gretchen filled them in on what her job was going to be like and kept the idea of studying for a real estate license to herself for the time being.

"I got two more calls for dog walking, but I'm not responding until Janie gives me the okay on addresses," Bettina said.

"Just give me the names and addresses, and I'll check them out for you," Janie said.

"We can do it tomorrow after you've rested," Bettina said.

"All I have to do is look at a map. That's not going to matter," Janie said.

Bettina nodded. "Okay, if you're sure. But we'll do it later. I'm starving, and these chicken salad sandwiches are delicious."

"Did you make it?" Gretchen asked.

Bettina laughed. "You know better than that. It's compliments of our favorite deli, and so is the soup."

"I don't care where it came from, it's all so good," Janie said.

"Wait until you see dessert," Gretchen said, and when they'd finished the soup and sandwiches, Gretchen pulled out the strawberry Napoleons.

Janie ate what she could but was already wearing out.

Finally, she held up a hand.

"Somebody save me from myself and take this food away. I need to go lie down."

"I'll walk you back," Pauline said.

"We'll clean up, and then I'll bring my laptop so you can vet the new possible clients," Bettina said.

"Sounds good," Janie said, and leaned on Pauline as she returned to her room.

After getting Janie settled, Pauline handed her the TV remote and refilled her water glass.

"Call if you need me," she said.

"I will, and thank all of you for today," Janie said.

Pauline just shook her head. "Girl, that's part of my prayer every night—thanking *you* for taking care of us. Get some rest. You've had one hell of a day."

"Hopefully, tomorrow will be better," Janie said, and turned on the television, then closed her eyes.

Bettina showed up about fifteen minutes later, and after checking out the names and addresses, Janie voiced her opinion.

"The first address is in a decent area. I'm not so sure about the second one, so once you see it, you'll have to make your own decisions. Now it's all up to whether you get along with the dogs and people," Janie said.

"That comes with the first meet. Thanks, sugar. I'm going to contact them and set up interviews," Bettina said, and went back to her bedroom to respond to the queries.

By bedtime, she'd set up interviews tomorrow with Dave Peterson and his rescue dog, Tinkerbelle, and with Ronda Bailey and her yellow lab, Buttercup. She was excited for more business, even if it was going to mean being on the go all morning. But first she had to walk Loki.

By the time night fell, Baxter's bouquet was on the table in the foyer, the kitchen was clean, and Janie had been put to bed like a baby.

Later, Gretchen came downstairs in her PJs and slipped into Janie's bedroom, carrying her pillow and a blanket.

Janie was hurting too much to sleep, and when she saw Gretchen coming in, she rolled over.

"What's happening?"

"I'm sleeping on your day bed," Gretchen said. "I don't want you alone at night until you're better. So, if you need to get up, or need something for pain, just say my name. I'm a light sleeper."

Janie's eyes welled. "Oh, honey. You don't have to do that."

"I know, but I want to," Gretchen said. "Have you taken any pain meds since we brought you back from dinner?"

"No."

"Then I'm getting you some. You have to stay ahead of the pain, not wait for it to hit again," Gretchen said, and went into Janie's bathroom to get water. She came back and shook out two pain pills into her hand.

Janie downed the pills, then chased them with the water.

"Thank you. So much," Janie said.

"Welcome, sugar. Now lie back and close your eyes. Hopefully the pills will kick in soon, and you'll get a little easier."

Janie did as she was told, listening as Gretchen settled herself onto the daybed, and then wrapped up in the blanket. She heard her sigh, and felt a such a sense of comfort, knowing she wasn't going through this night alone.

But when sleep finally pulled Janie under, David was in her dreams. Calling to tell her he wasn't going to make it home for his birthday.

Calling her to tell her there was an emergency at work, that he was having to cover another rep's territory.

Calling her to tell her to be careful.

Calling her to tell her he was sorry.

In the dream, he quit calling and she wondered why, then forgot he existed.

After that, her rest was uninterrupted until Gretchen's alarm went off on her phone, jarring her awake. She woke up and rolled over just in time to see Gretchen reaching for her phone to shut it off.

"I'm so sorry," Gretchen said. "Can I help you to the bathroom before I go upstairs to get ready for work?"

"Yes, please," Janie said, and after coming back from the bathroom, dutifully took two more pain pills before laying back down.

"As soon as I get dressed, if the others aren't up, I'll get you some coffee and toast," Gretchen said.

"You just feed yourself and go to work. Pauline is here all day. I'll eat when she does."

"You sure?"

"Absolutely," Janie said. "And thank you for staying with me last night."

Gretchen gave her a thumbs up. "See you when I get home this evening. Be good to yourself."

"I will," Janie said, and then rolled over and closed her eyes.

As she did, David's face appeared, and then faded. She didn't want to dream about him again. She didn't want to even think about him and guessed the trauma of yesterday had triggered the shock and trauma of the day he died.

Whatever.

She'd chosen him, and he'd chosen his own path. The only good thing to come out of it were his wives, who'd become more of a family to her in a few short months than he had in the past ten years.

Whatever, again.

Even though Pauline worked from home, she had still set her alarm last night because she wanted to be up to check on Janie. She dressed quickly, pulled her hair back into a ponytail, and took off downstairs.

Gretchen was already gone, and Bettina was getting ready to leave when Pauline entered the kitchen.

"Have any of you checked on Janie?" she asked. "She didn't call me last night."

"Gretchen slept on the day bed in her room last night," Bettina said. "I poked my head in the door to check on her, and she had gone back to sleep."

"I never thought to do that," Pauline said.

"I think Gretchen is still feeling bad for not being here when it all happened and just wanted to do her part to help. I accept that. Janie has done so much for us, that we all want to return the favor. And FYI—it will be after lunch before I come home. After I walk Loki, and I have two more prospective clients to interview."

"Congrats," Pauline said. "Be safe."

"I will. See you later."

"Later," Pauline echoed, and then hurried down the hall to Janie's room.

The door was ajar. She peeked in, saw Janie reclining in her bed watching TV, and walked in.

"Good morning, sunshine. How do you feel this morning?" she asked.

Janie turned off the TV. "Better than when I went to bed, for sure. I'm dying for a cup of coffee. Want to help me out of bed so I can wash up?"

"You bet. Easy does it," Pauline said, and steadied her as she stood. "Are you still feeling dizzy?"

"Not much," Janie said, and Pauline helped her to the bathroom, then walked with her up the hall to the kitchen.

"You sit, and I'll make breakfast for the both of us. What sounds good to you?"

"Honestly, just toast and coffee."

"That's easy," Pauline said. "Coming right up."

Janie was quiet as they ate, and Pauline sensed there was more to her silence than a headache.

"What's wrong?" she finally asked.

Janie sighed. "I had dreams last night."

Pauline frowned. "Let me guess. About David, right?"

Red curls bounced as Janie nodded, and when she looked up, her eyes were teary.

"I guess my subconscious is my nemesis."

"Well, you were hurting physically, and when you slept, you just retrieved emotional pain to go with it," Pauline said. "We can be mad as hell about what he did to us, but we don't have the luxury of getting to being mad *at* him, because he's gone."

Janie nodded. "When I got that call, and then found out what he'd done, the shockwaves of that revelation wiped out the grief."

"That's how we all felt. Tricked. Lied to. And ashamed," Pauline said. "So, don't feel guilty about being sad. It's just a lingering emotion, okay?"

"Okay," Janie said, then pushed back her plate and took a last sip of coffee. As she did, her cellphone rang. She glanced at the caller. "It's a client."

"Don't mind me. I'm going to clean up," Pauline said.

Janie nodded, then answered. "Hello, Daryl. This is Janie."

"Janie! I just read the morning paper and saw the story about what happened to you! Are you all right? Are you home?"

Janie stifled a groan. "It's in the paper?"

"Yes! Is there anything I can do for you?" Daryl asked. "Just say the word, and I'll happily volunteer."

Janie sighed. "That's so generous of you, but I'm not alone, and I'm going to be fine."

"Okay then, but I want to commend you on catching onto the fake invoice scam. Baxter Williams praised you loud and long when they interviewed him. I feel fortunate to have you as my bookkeeper."

"Thank you, Daryl. That means a lot."

"Take care," he said, and hung up.

Janie laid down the phone. "I guess we made the paper again. Did anyone bring it in this morning?"

"Not that I know of," Pauline said. "I'll go check," and came back carrying it a couple of minutes later, then handed it to Janie. "Here you go."

Janie quickly unfolded it, then breathed a sigh of relief.

"At least we're not the headline this time. But we did make the front page."

Pauline grinned. "And our notoriety is less shocking than before."

"Oh God, don't remind me," Janie said, and quickly scanned the story.

"It says here Baxter even rooted out the accomplice. An employee named Nate Roberts. I know Nate. Oh wow! It appears he was her brother, and they're both in jail awaiting arraignment." Then she looked up in horror. "Oh no! What if they bond out?"

"Don't worry," Pauline said. "You're no longer a target. She didn't want you. Just what you had. Baxter and the law now have possession and knowledge of what she's done. If she does anything, she'll skip bail and leave the state. Besides. I'm still here," Pauline said, then raised both her arms and flexed her muscles.

"You are indeed a warrior. How's your hand?" Janie asked.

"Stiff, but healing. I'm bossy, too, and I think you've been up long enough. Back to bed rest for you. Do you want to shower and change before I go to work?"

"If you have time to spare," Janie said.

"I have all day to work. I want to know you're comfy first," Pauline said.

Gretchen was at her desk with Juana beside her, still coaching her on her new duties, when Sarah came out of her office.

"Gretchen! I just saw a story in the paper about two employees at a local flower shop being arrested for fraud, and the story states that before the arrests, one of the employees attacked Janie Logan in her home. Isn't that where you live?"

Gretchen looked up. "Yes. I got a call about it just after lunch yesterday."

"Why didn't you say something?" Sarah asked.

Gretchen shrugged. "It was my first day on the job, and truthfully, I was in such a state of shock, I didn't know what to do. Everything was over with by the time they called me, and they were bringing Janie home, so..."

"Well, good Lord! If you have family emergencies, all you have to do is let someone know. We'll cope. Family comes first, girl," Sarah said.

"Duly noted," Gretchen said.

"Is Janie all right?" Sarah asked.

"I think she's going to be. She has a concussion, a cut on her forehead, and she's bruised up pretty badly. She's not allowed to get up on her own yet because she's still dizzy, but I slept on the daybed in her room last night."

"Please give her our wishes for a swift recovery," Sarah said.

"I will, and thank you for your concern," Gretchen said.

Sarah went back into her office, and they went back to work.

Bettina arrived at the Attilla home to get Loki. Barb answered the door with the little dog in tow. He yapped when he saw Bettina and began wagging his tail.

"He sure likes you," Barb said, as Bettina knelt to clip her leash onto Loki's harness.

"I like him, too," Bettina said, and kissed his little face before she stood. "Okay, we're off. See you soon."

The air felt thick and sultry. Even though the horizon was mostly clear, it felt like storm weather, and Bettina kept an eye on the sky as they walked. The little dog kicked into trot when he sniffed something interesting, as if he was in a hurry to explore it, and then slowed back into a walk when his discovery phase was over. He was such a little character, and so animated with his responses to Bettina's voice and commands, that his antics often made her laugh.

By the time he finally decided on a place to poop, Bettina had fished a leaf out of his mouth and a straw from someone's soft drink that had been dropped in the grass. She gave him a drink of water, and then turned at the next street corner to head back home.

As they were walking, her phone signaled a text. It was from Pauline.

St. Louis and surrounding area in tornado watch. Storm front predicted to hit around noon. Be careful.

"Oh crap," Bettina said, and responded with a Thumbs Up emoji to let her know the message had been received.

Then her attention was pulled back to Loki, who'd stopped to bark at a squirrel scolding him from high up in a tree.

"Come on, buddy. Mr. Squirrel does not welcome your company, and it's time to go home."

Loki looked up at Bettina and barked again.

"I know, but he doesn't want to play. Now move, mister," she said, and gave the leash a tug, leaving Loki no room to argue.

Still watching the sky, she soon had him back at the house, rang the doorbell, then knelt to give him a little treat and a pat on the head.

A few moments later, Barb opened the door.

"If you don't already know, we're predicted to have some thunderstorms in around noon," she said.

"I just got a text about it," Bettina said, as she unhooked her leash.

Loki trotted inside, yapping as he went. "He saw a squirrel. He's probably tattling on me because I wouldn't let him stay and bark at it."

Barb grinned. "That sounds about right. Stay safe today," she said, and closed the door.

Bettina hurried to her car, put the address of her first interview into her GPS, and drove away.

CHAPTER EIGHT

The address was in a less exclusive part of St. Louis, but still nice housing. Bettina located the house easily, while noticing the apartment building on the far corner of the block. There was more city traffic here, and this was closer to the main drag, but it was nothing that put her off.

The lady's name was Ronda Bailey. She and her husband, Mike, owned a body shop in the industrial part of the city. They had a yellow Lab named Buttercup, and that's all she knew. Now it was time to meet the family.

The house was a white, two-story Victorian with a widow's walk on the dark green roof, and green window boxes overflowing with colorful pansies and petunias. It looked like something out of a storybook.

She parked in the driveway, then hurried up the front steps and rang the doorbell. Inside, a dog began to bark, and then she heard it charge the door in a frenzy. She frowned, but before she could process the idea of walking an aggressive dog like that, the door swung inward, and a tall, skinny blonde in yoga pants and a slouchy, over-sized t-shirt was in the doorway.

She didn't say hello. She didn't inquire about anything or try to silence her manic dog. Her gaze went straight to Gretchen's boobs, while her dog shot out of the house and was now out on the porch, circling Bettina and still barking.

Bettina frowned, waiting for the woman to call off her dog, but since she just kept staring, Bettina spoke first.

"I'm Bettina, the dog walker."

"You don't look like I thought you would," Ronda Bailey said.

Bettina frowned. *What the hell was she supposed to say to that?* She chose not to answer.

At that point, Ronda's focus suddenly shifted to the dog. She grabbed it by the collar and gave it a yank.

"Buttercup! Shut the hell up!" she said, and put the dog inside. She closed the door, then stayed on the porch with Bettina, while the dog continued to bark.

Bettina blinked. "Uh... is your dog trained to commands?"

"She isn't trained to anything," Ronda muttered.

"But she's trained to a leash, right? I mean, you walk her on a regular basis?"

"Not really. Mike walks her in the evenings and on weekends. She's his dog. He just clips a leash on her and holds on. I guess you could say she walks him."

Bettina's frown deepened. "I'm sorry. I'm a dog walker, not a trainer. I don't want to be responsible for a dog that doesn't understand commands, but thank you for your time," she said, and began walking down the steps.

"Wait! You mean you're telling me no?" Ronda shouted.

"Yes, I'm telling you no," Bettina said, and kept walking.

The woman cursed, then slammed the door behind her as she stomped back into the house.

Bettina felt like running as she went back to her car. That was less than productive, but in no way did she want anything to do with a big dog with a tendency to run amuck.

She entered the next address of David Peterson into her GPS and drove away. She had no idea what size the dog, Tinkerbelle, was, but she wasn't going to be fooled into assuming it was a little one just because of the name.

She was going to be almost an hour early for the appointment and didn't know whether to kill time or call and see if he was available now. But after knowing the weather was changing, the thought of delaying didn't seem like a good idea. She decided to at least drive by the address to get a feeling for the area. This was the one Janie hadn't been sure about. And, since she had plenty of time, she stopped at a fast-food drive-through to get something to drink.

After doing that, she got back into traffic and followed the prompts on her GPS, sipping her cold Coke as she went. And the closer she got to her destination, the less comfortable she felt about it. She was well aware of good and bad people in all levels of social structures. She'd just left a perfectly lovely neighborhood and home inhabited by a total bitch, so she didn't want to judge this person only on the area in which he lived.

When she arrived at Peterson's address, she drove past it slowly, eyeing the neatly mowed yard, the fenced-in backyard, and the old, ranch-style house, then drove through the surrounding neighborhood to get a feel for the place in which she'd be walking Tinkerbelle. It wasn't posh, but it also didn't set off any alarms, so she pulled over at a curb, made the call, and then waited for someone to answer. It rang so many times she expected it to go to voicemail, and then finally, a man answered, and in an abrupt, raspy voice.

"Hello?"

"Mr. Peterson, this is Bettina Lee—the lady you called about dog walking. My last appointment ended sooner than expected, and I was wondering if it would be okay for me to come by now since I'm already in the area?"

Again, he left her waiting for an answer so long that she thought he'd hung up.

"Mr. Peterson? Hello? Are you still there?" Bettina said, and thought she heard him sigh.

"Yes, I'm here," he said. "I was just wondering if this was a good idea after all."

She frowned. "Oh. Okay. If you've changed your mind, then—"

"No," he said. "It's fine. You can come."

"Thank you. I'll be there in a few minutes," Bettina said, and then put the car in gear and turned right at the next corner to get back to his house.

She was trying not to read too much into his less than enthusiastic response, even as she was pulling up into his driveway. Then she grabbed her purse and palmed her keys as she strode up to the porch and rang the bell, which again, set a dog to barking. Then she heard a muffled command, and the dog hushed. That was a plus. She was all set for a positive meeting until David Peterson opened the door.

Within the space of three seconds, she saw boxes of stuff lined up against every wall, a small fuzzy dog that couldn't walk four steps without stopping to scratch, a man who smelled like he hadn't bathed in a year, and the odor of rotting food. Then she caught movement on top of the boxes against the wall to her left.

The man's eyes narrowed nervously as he read her reaction.

Hers widened as a rat crawled out of a box above the man's head.

"Sir, you don't need a dog walker. You need help. Is there someone I can call for you?"

"You don't want the job?" he asked.

"No. Just no," she said, then turned around and walked back to her car and drove away.

She couldn't get the smell out of her nose and kept taking sips of her cold drink to calm the nausea in her belly. This day was becoming a huge disappointment. The dog walking business was proving far more difficult than she'd thought. And she was mad. She felt sorry for dogs being with people who weren't taking proper care of them, but their lives, and the paths they were on, had nothing to do with hers.

It was nearly eleven o'clock. The sky was already darker, and the wind was rising. All she wanted now was just to get home to the girls and the safety of their house. And if need be, to the basement beneath it.

Pauline had just signed off on a website after the satisfaction of the client had been obtained, and after receiving the payment, notified him it was live. She was thirty-three hundred dollars to the good and had one other client in line. It was a big job, and would take at least a month, maybe more. But today was a good day.

She stretched as she stood, felt her pocket to make sure she had her phone, and then started downstairs to check on Janie, when a rumble of thunder sounded in the distance.

Her first thought was for Bettina, hoping she wasn't out in the middle of the approaching storm, and then hurried to Janie's room.

Her door was open, and she was dressed and watching a local weather bulletin when Pauline walked into the room.

Pauline sat down on the bed beside her to watch.

"It's going to get ugly today, isn't it?" she asked.

"It sure looks like it," Janie said. "Have you heard from Bettina?"

"No. I was just about to ask you the same thing. Do you think we should call her?"

"I sent her a text earlier this morning about the weather, and she responded, so I know she read it."

"Okay then. How about some lunch?" Pauline asked.

"Do we have anything to make sandwiches?" Janie asked.

"We have a couple of kinds of lunchmeat, cheese, and all kinds of condiments."

"Let's do that. If the storm gets bad and we're trying to cook, the power could go off," Janie said.

"Oh, good call," Pauline said. "Do you need to make a pit stop before we leave your room?"

"I already did," Janie said.

Pauline frowned. "Janie..."

Janie waved off the warning. "My head barely hurts, and I'm not a bit dizzy."

"Whatever," Pauline muttered. "You're still holding onto me to get to the kitchen."

Janie grinned. "Yes, ma'am," she said, and turned off the TV as she got up.

They were on their way down the hall when they heard the front door open, then close with a bang, and then Bettina came storming through the foyer toward the stairs.

"Is everything okay?" Janie asked.

"I have to take a shower! I'll explain later," she yelled, and ran up the stairs.

"That's bound to be a good story," Pauline said.

"You know it," Janie said. "So, three sandwiches instead of two." And then thunder rolled again, this time much closer, as rain began splattering against the west windows.

They turned on the TV in the kitchen to keep an eye on weather bulletins, and Janie sat at the table as Pauline went to make sandwiches.

"I finished a website this morning," Pauline said. "One happy client down. One more to go. I'm hoping for some new business, too, since I jazzed up my own design website."

"Congrats, girl! You amaze me at being able to do all that," Janie said. "How did you ever get started at it?"

Pauline paused and looked up. "After my first husband split on me, and we divorced, I spent a lot of damn days alone. So, I went to a technical college, learned the basics, and then taught myself the rest of it. It seemed easy. I guess I have a head for the technology. Then, as fate would have it, I spent the majority of my second marriage alone, too, and here I am."

"Well, good for you, honey. And I'm not evoking the ghost that still haunts us by remarking upon him," Janie muttered.

Pauline winked. "Ham or salami? Mayo or mustard? Lettuce, tomato, pickles?"

"If we have onion, I would love a salami sandwich with mustard and onion," Janie said.

"We have onion," Pauline said, and got it out of the refrigerator.

A few minutes later, Pauline carried their plates to the table.

"I'm leaving everything on the island for Bettina," she said, and then seconds later, they heard her coming down the stairs as fast as she'd gone up. "And here she comes."

Rain was coming down in sheets now, sluicing off roofs and windows alike, and the constant beep of updated weather bulletins was in the background as Bettina entered the kitchen.

"Thanks for leaving everything out for me," she said, and began making her own sandwich.

"What happened to you?" Janie asked.

Bettina was licking mayo off her thumb as she looked up. "The better question might be, 'what didn't happen'? I didn't get any new clients," she said, then tossed a handful of chips onto her plate and carried it to the table.

"I'm sorry," Pauline said.

"Oh Lord! I'm the one who turned both of them down," she said, then took a bite, rolling her eyes as she chewed. "I love peppered salami."

Janie frowned. "Did I steer you wrong on the neighborhoods?"

Bettina popped a chip in her mouth then chewed and swallowed.

"The neighborhoods were fine. The problem was the dogs and the people. The dog at the first place was a big lab. It was aggressive and never stopped barking at me. The woman never told it to quit. She just kept staring at my boobs, then told me I didn't look like what she expected."

Pauline laughed. "What the hell is a dog walker supposed to look like?"

Bettina nodded. "Exactly my thought. Anyway, long story short, the dog had never been trained to a command or to walk on a leash. I told her I wasn't a dog trainer and turned down the job. Made her so mad she shouted at me, slammed the door, and went back to the crazy, barking dog."

"Good grief!" Janie said.

Bettina nodded. "As for the last place I went... That's why I came home and showered. When the man came to the door, I saw boxes from floor to ceiling everywhere, with only a single, narrow aisle to get from one room to another. A serious hoarder. There was a rat on top of a box, and a little fuzzy dog that couldn't walk for having to stop and scratch. The man didn't look like he'd bathed in a year, and the house smelled like rotting food. It was run or puke on his shoes."

Pauline gasped. "Oh, my God! What did you say?"

"I told him he didn't need a dog walker, he needed help. And then I asked him if there was someone I could call. You know what he said? 'So, you don't want the job?'" I just said 'no,' and ran. So, that was my day. How was yours?"

"Well, Janie got dressed on her own, and took herself to the bathroom while I was upstairs. And I finished a website for a client," Pauline said.

"And now here we are, eating salami sandwiches and hoping we don't blow away," Janie added.

Bettina shifted focus. "Janie! So, you're feeling better?"

"Quite a bit," Janie said.

"Awesome! And Pauline, congrats on finishing a job. As for me, I'm rewording my ad on my dog walking page."

"How so?" Janie asked.

Bettina waved her finger in the air and began counting off the items. "I'm adding a condition to my services. I don't take on un-vaccinated dogs, or filthy dogs, or dogs with fleas or skin diseases. I don't take aggressive dogs, or dogs that have not learned to obey basic commands or that have not been trained to a leash. That should weed out anymore of this crap. Otherwise, I'm going to have to move on to a different job search for myself. And the next time someone tells me I don't look like a dog walker, I'm going to tell them they don't resemble the jackass they are acting like, either. So, there's that."

Pauline and Janie burst out laughing.

"Well, I am," Bettina muttered.

A few minutes later, Pauline got a text.

"It's from Gretchen. She says they have access to a storm shelter, and not to worry about her, and for us to stay safe and she loves us."

Pauline replied to the text, and then she and Bettina began clearing off the table, leaving Janie with the cookie jar and a refill on her drink.

They had everything cleaned up and put away and were in the living room watching television to keep an eye on the weather bulletins running in a scrawl at the bottom of the screen.

Bettina brought her laptop into the room with her and had already added the wording she wanted to her dog walking site. She read it back to them to see what they thought.

"I think you've just weeded out a whole bunch of problems," Janie said.

Pauline grinned. "You missed your calling. You would have made a really good trial lawyer. Your summation skills are beyond reproach."

Bettina grinned. "I would have made a terrible lawyer. I don't like to follow rules, even though I always wanted to teach. But I'm still bothered by that poor man. His living conditions are horrible. Hoarding can be a symptom of mental health issues. I feel like I should call someone."

"I know someone who works in social services," Janie said. "I could give you his number if you do want to call about him."

"Yes, I think I do," Bettina said. "In fact, the longer I've thought about it, the more I feel as if he was reaching out for help and using my dog walking as an excuse. I don't think he was ever sincere in hiring me. He just wanted me to see him. You know?"

"That's very intuitive of you," Pauline said.

"I'm going to my office to get Mike's number," Janie said, and when Pauline jumped up to go with her, she rolled her eyes. "I feel so important. Like I'm some famous person who goes nowhere without her bodyguards."

"Just shut up," Pauline said. "You didn't see what we saw—you flat on your back getting the life choked out of you."

Janie sighed. "You're right. I'm sorry for griping. And I do have an appointment scheduled to add a Ring doorbell. No more surprises, right?"

"You're forgiven," Pauline said, and winked.

Janie wrote down the info, then gave it to Bettina.

"Thanks. I'm going to the kitchen to make the call. Keep an eye on the weather for me. My ears are popping, and that's not a good sign," Bettina said.

Pauline frowned. "What do popping ears have to do with storms?"

"Barometric pressure falls when storms approach. It increases the atmospheric pressure, but I never knew anyone who predicted storms because their ears popped," Janie said.

"I guess we'll know soon enough if she's on point," Pauline said, and turned the volume back up on the TV while Bettina was at the kitchen table, on the phone with Mike Halford from Social Services.

"Mr. Halford, my name is Bettina Lee. Janie Logan gave me your name and number as someone who might be able to help me."

"Ah, yes! I know Janie. What can I do for you?" Mike asked.

Bettina began explaining how she'd met Dave Peterson, and what she'd seen, and then ended with what she'd just said to the girls.

"I feel like he is expecting me to report him, because he needs help and is either afraid to pull the trigger on himself or doesn't know who to reach out to. But his situation is dire. I cannot stress enough the level of degradation in which he and that poor little dog are living."

"Whether he wants you to report him or not is beside the point. It's imperative to get him help and get rid of that kind of debris. It fosters rats and all manner of varmints that carry diseases that can spread beyond his property."

"Ugh. I didn't even consider that," Bettina said.

"I really appreciate you caring enough to report this," Mike said.

"I don't want to get him in trouble with the law. But I think his health is in danger. He doesn't look well, and neither does the dog," Bettina said.

"I understand. We'll check in with him. If it's as bad as you reported, one look is all it will take to create a case file for him. After that, we can get him help."

"Okay. I feel better for having called," Bettina said.

"Thank you again, and give Janie my best," Mike said.

"Yes, sir, I will," Bettina said.

She dropped her phone in her pocket and went back to the living room.

"Well, I did it," she said, as she plopped down on the sofa beside Janie. "And Mike sends his best."

"He's a good person. He'll do right by that man," Janie said.

And then two things began happening at once. A weather alert started beeping on the television, and the tornado sirens began going off in the city.

"Oh boy," Janie muttered. "We need to get to the basement."

They left the room quickly, with Janie between them, and turned on the light before starting down the stairs.

"Janie, I'm going down first, then you get behind me and hold onto my shoulders to steady yourself. Bettina will be right behind you. That way if you feel weak or stumble, we'll stop your fall," Pauline said.

Janie wasn't in any position to argue. When Pauline started down, she was right behind her, holding on. Bettina shut the door and followed. As soon as they were down, they headed for the beds and chairs at the far corner of the basement.

Bettina pulled the dust cover off one bed, settled Janie on it first, and then they sat down beside her. Even though they were below ground, they could hear the storm winds rising until the scream within was like a banshee, and behind the wail, it began to rain, then hail.

Pauline jumped at the sound. "Oh my God! Your poor flowers."

Janie was in the middle of the bed and staring up at the small basement windows, watching debris spinning about within the air.

And then they jumped at what sounded like distant gunshots.

"The trees. Those are trees," Janie moaned.

Pauline scooted closer and put her arm around Janie's shoulders, as Bettina started to shake.

"This is bad, isn't it?" Bettina whispered.

"But we're safe, and that's all that matters," Pauline said.

Janie slumped. "I know. Let go of expectations and deal with the consequences later."

As the finality of what she'd just said sank in, they linked hands and held on, listening to the storm playing hell over their heads.

The moment the tornado sirens began sounding, Sarah Biggers jumped up from her desk and ran, shouting at Charles and Lisa to get to the storage room. But they were already running in that direction as Sarah headed to the front office to get Juana and Gretchen.

"Come with me!" Sarah shouted.

Gretchen had her purse over her shoulder and was on Juana's heels as they followed Sarah into the back room to the aboveground storm shelter. Gretchen was the last one inside, and the moment she crossed the threshold, Sarah pulled the door shut and locked it down.

There were two long benches inside the eight-person shelter, and everyone quickly chose a side and sat.

Lisa was in a corner, trembling in terror.

"Oh, my God! Just listen to that wind!"

Charles was sitting between her and Juana, and trying to be brave, but he was as anxious as the rest of them.

Gretchen was on the opposite side of the shelter beside Sarah and holding her purse against her chest like a shield. She was grateful the power was still on, because she had something of a problem with claustrophobia.

"I hope this is not the day I die," she muttered. "I'm still too mad at David to have to face him right now."

Sarah gave her hand a quick squeeze. "I don't know whether to commiserate or laugh about what you just said."

Gretchen rolled her eyes. "It's best we laugh, because I'm absolutely certain God does not want that kind of discord up there."

Charles frowned. "I'm sorry. Are you saying you've recently lost someone you loved?"

Gretchen looked up. "If I say, 'a bigamist with four wives', would that ring a bell for you?"

Charles blinked. "Oh. Wait! Are you saying you're one of the wives?"

She nodded, then leaned back and closed her eyes. She had assumed they already knew, but it didn't matter. The more they knew, the less she had to worry about having to explain herself.

"I'm so sorry," Charles said.

She looked up, her eyes blazing in sudden anger.

"Don't be sorry for me. We nuked what was left of him and told the funeral home to dump his ashes." Their mutual gasps of shock were so intense that Gretchen felt the air shift within the enclosure. She shrugged. "It's best not to make enemies of people you sleep with. They tend to take it personally."

Sarah chuckled. "All four of you are to be commended for how you're dealing with the devastation. I can't spend an hour with my own mother-in-law without wanting to tear out my hair, or hers, and yet all four of you are living together, and I assume making it work."

Gretchen tightened her hold on her purse. "Janie Logan, the only legal wife among us, gave us an invitation we couldn't refuse. We would have all been destitute and homeless, but for her."

There was a long moment of silence, followed by a horrendous crash. Lisa screamed. Gretchen froze. And Charles fell off the bench.

Sarah gasped. "Oh, my God! What was that?"

Juana started praying.

Charles dragged himself up and sat back down.

"Well, that was embarrassing. It just startled me, I guess. I haven't fallen out of a chair since I was six, when I grabbed for the tablecloth and took half of the Thanksgiving dinner with me as I went."

They laughed, but their amusement was short-lived when the power flickered and went off, leaving them sitting in the dark.

"Oh, shit," Gretchen moaned, as her heart began to pound. She broke out in a cold sweat and quickly lowered her head to keep from passing out.

All of a sudden, there was light in the darkness as the others began pulling out their cell phones. Using the light from their screens to turn on the flashlight features, they saw Gretchen with her head between her knees.

Sarah reached for her. "Are you sick?"

"No. Just afraid of the dark. God, please let this storm be over," she mumbled.

"We have light. Open your eyes," Sarah said.

Gretchen looked up, saw all the cell phones in their hands, and shuddered.

"Shit. That just got real."

"Lisa is terrified. Charles fell out of his seat. I'm afraid the building will be gone when this is over, and Juana is still praying. You're allowed to be afraid, too," Sarah said.

"Many thanks," Gretchen said, then dug her phone out of her purse and held it, just in case more light was needed.

It felt like forever, but within fifteen minutes, they could tell the storm was passing from the sounds of a dying wind. Still, none of them made a move until they heard the all-clear siren.

"That's what we've been waiting for. Let's go see what's left of the place," Charles said.

Sarah unlocked the door, but when she tried to push it open, it would only open a few inches.

"Something's blocking it," she said.

"Here, let me," Charles said, and stepped forward, put his shoulder against the door, and pushed.

It gave way a few inches, and he pushed again, and again, until the opening was wide enough for them to emerge. A metal storage cabinet had fallen over, dumping the contents out onto the floor and partially blocking their exit Rain was pouring in from above.

"Damn it, Sarah. Part of the roof is missing," Charles said.

"I don't care if I get wet. I need out," Gretchen said.

They came out one by one into the storage room, carefully making their way through all the cans and bottles on the floor, and then opened the door leading out into the hall.

"Oh, thank God! The roof held in here. Everything appears to be sound. Check your office windows to see if any of them are broken," Sarah said, and headed up front. The shatter-proof glass of their front door was sound, but when they looked out into the parking lot, they saw the vehicles that had been hammered by the hail.

Gretchen spotted her car, and except for the hail dents, the windows appeared to be sound. There was debris in the parking lot, but the surrounding buildings were still standing, so she guessed the storm had carried debris from somewhere else and dropped it here as it passed.

Her stomach knotted as she thought of home and the girls.

Please God let them be okay, and let our house be standing.

"Okay," Sarah said. "I need to call my husband and get him on the job to get the hole in the roof covered up. I know you're all worried sick about your homes and families. Go home. I'll let you know when it's safe to come back to work. And be careful driving. You may have to take some backroads to get there."

Gretchen went to the breakroom to get her things and met Juana coming out on the run and in tears.

"You did good, today, Juana. Thank you for praying us all to safety."

"My husband is not answering the phone," she said.

"That doesn't mean he's hurt. He might just be tending to business," Gretchen said. "Drive safe. You won't help him if you get into a wreck."

"Yes, yes, you're right, and thank you," Juana said, and bolted out of the room.

Gretchen had no signal on her phone, either, so she slung her tote bag over her shoulder on top of her purse, palmed her keys, and headed out of the building into the rain.

The power was still off inside the house when the all-clear sirens sounded, but there were enough windows in the basement to light the way back to the stairs. Pauline aimed a flashlight on the steps as they emerged into the kitchen.

"I'll go up into the attic and check the roof," Bettina said.

"Here, you'll need the flashlight," Pauline said.

Bettina grabbed it and took off upstairs.

"I'm going to do a run through the downstairs to make sure we don't have any broken windows," Pauline said. "Will you please stay in the kitchen until we get back?"

"And do what?" Janie said.

Pauline set the cookie jar in front of her.

Janie groaned. "I feel so useless."

"Someone has to eat them. Better you than me," Pauline said, then took a cold bottle of pop from the fridge and unscrewed the lid for Janie. "There. Now save us from ourselves. I won't be long."

"You are so full of shit," Janie muttered, and then turned to the kitchen window. She was afraid to look out, but she needed to know what kind of damage the grounds had suffered.

The shrubs looked beaten by the wind, but she knew they would recover. She'd lost a couple of large limbs from her trees, but they were still standing, and so was the fencing. Every bush that had been blooming had been denuded of its blossoms, but they would grow more. She was grateful for what had been spared and could finally breathe easier.

She sat down, fished a cookie out of the cookie jar, and took a bite while listening to the sounds of running footsteps both upstairs and down, quietly grateful for their presence in her life.

A few minutes later, both girls returned with good reports.

"No broken windows," they both said.

"And no obvious water leaks in the attic," Bettina added.

"All we need now is for Gretchen to walk in the door, and the power to come back on," Janie said.

"I'll call her," Pauline said, but the call went to voicemail.

"It doesn't have to mean anything," Bettina said. "The power is out. Maybe some cell towers were hit. That could explain the spotty phone service."

They nodded in agreement as they sat, picking at their cookies and pretending they weren't worried. But the longer they waited, the more phone calls they made that went unanswered.

They'd reached the point of panic and moved themselves into the living room so they could watch for her car to come up the drive, and then they ran out of anything to talk about. The worry they felt turned to panic, then to the unspoken fear that something could have happened to her. Something bad.

"I will not lose another someone I love. God won't let that happen," Janie muttered.

Pauline got up and walked out of the room.

Bettina slid closer to Janie, until their shoulders were touching.

"The city might be in shambles for all we know, but that doesn't mean she's not okay," she said.

Janie sighed. "Yes. You're right. Communication is the first thing to go when this kind of shit hits the fan."

They sat motionless as the sky cleared. The sun came out and started moving shadows across the floor as a reminder that, whatever else was happening, come nightfall, it was going to get dark.

Finally, Pauline came back. Her eyes were swollen and red-rimmed as she reclaimed her seat. And the moment she sat down, the lights flickered, and they had power again.

"Well, if your stately presence was all it took to get our power back, you should have come back sooner," Bettina drawled.

They all looked at each other, and then burst out laughing, because crying together was getting old. Then they settled in to keeping watch, and it felt like time stood still.

CHAPTER NINE

Gretchen drove slowly trying to get to the other side of town, but it wasn't easy. Sightseers in cars clogged streets just to check out storm damage, while others were like her, just trying to get home.

There were trees down on main thoroughfares and side streets, and trees had come down on the cars parked beneath them. Power poles that had bent to the power of the wind leaned and metal buildings had lost their roofs.

But the farther she drove, the more convinced she was that the tornado had not come down, and that the damage she was seeing was from the wind velocity as it passed overhead.

Twice she started down a street only to see it blocked by debris and fallen limbs and had to turn around and look for another way. Then, without knowing the city well enough to find the back streets that would get her home, she got lost, and gave up on GPS because it could not predict the clear routes she needed.

She kept trying her cellphone, hoping to get a signal, but to no avail, and over an hour later, was still driving in the downpour, unable to find her way to the historic district.

She'd been turned back twice by electric companies dealing with hot power lines lying in the streets, and once by the fire department pulling a wrecked car off a broken fire hydrant so they could shut off the gush of water shooting up into the air. Her frustration was elevated by her fear for the girls, and without the ability to call and check on them, it made everything worse.

Then, when she found herself blocked again, she laid her head on the steering wheel and burst into tears.

Suddenly, there was a knock at her window. She looked up and saw a fireman. She rolled down her window, oblivious to the rain that immediately blew in.

"Ma'am? Are you okay? Are you hurt?" he asked.

Rain was falling on her face now, blurring the tracks of the tears.

"I'm not hurt. I'm trying to get home, and everywhere I turn, a street is blocked. I don't know the city well enough to find secondary routes, and my cell has no signal. I'm lost, and I'm scared, and I don't know if my family is okay."

He shifted where he was standing to block off the rain coming in her window.

"Exactly where is your house located?"

"In the historic district," she said, and gave him the address.

He hesitated a few moments, thinking, and then asked.

"Do you have pen and paper?"

She nodded.

"Write down these directions. We've already been up that way, and a lot of streets should be cleared enough to allow you to pass."

She grabbed a notebook and a pen from her tote bag and quickly took down his directions.

"Thank you. Thank you so much," she said.

He smiled. "You're welcome," and started to walk away when Gretchen called out.

"Wait! What's your name?"

He paused, then turned. "John. My name is John."

"So, John, what station do you belong to?"

"Engine House 22. Why?" he asked.

Gretchen was trying not to cry again. "I just wanted to know where the angels in this city stay," she said.

He grinned. "Yes, ma'am."

She waved, then rolled up her window and turned her car around to begin following his directions.

It took fifteen minutes before she found familiar territory, and then another ten to get home. But the relief of seeing that big, beautiful house still standing in the rain, and everybody's car there but hers, was all it took for her to burst into tears again.

She parked, grabbed her things, and got out, running toward the house. She had barely reached the verandah before the front door flew open, and all three girls spilled out of the house. Ignoring the fact that she was soaked to the skin, they wrapped her up in their arms.

"We were so worried!" Janie said.

"We called and called, but you never answered," Bettina cried.

"Are you okay?" Pauline asked.

Gretchen couldn't stop crying. "I've been trying to get home for hours. I was so worried about all of you and didn't have a cell signal. Trees are down. Power lines are down. Streets are blocked off. I've been lost so many times, I didn't even know which direction I was driving. But I'm okay now. I'm home."

They dragged her into the house, then Bettina followed her upstairs, while Pauline and Janie went back into the kitchen to make coffee. Gretchen was soaked and besides needing dry clothes, she needed something warm inside her.

A few minutes later, they were downstairs again, and all the girls were seated around the kitchen table, just like they'd done on the day they'd first met.

"What happened at your work? Where did you take shelter?" Janie asked.

Gretchen's voice was shaking. Even the retelling of what happened had the ability to rattle her again.

"Sarah has a large above-ground storm shelter in the back room. We were all in it. The wind was terrible. Something hit the building hard and scared us into thinking it was caving in. Then a few minutes later, the power went out. I don't think I've mentioned it before, but I have claustrophobia, and I'm afraid of the dark."

"Oh, my God," Bettina said. "What did you do?"

"I closed my eyes and put my head between my knees to keep from passing out. Then Sarah told me to look up, and they'd turned on the flashlight features on in their cellphones. We sat like that until the all-clear siren sounded, then couldn't get out because something had fallen in the storm and blocked the door."

"You must have been so scared," Janie said.

Gretchen nodded, and then burst into tears. "Shit. I'm sorry I'm crying. That's all we do, isn't it? I know it feels like that's all I've done ever since that damn phone call that ended life as we knew it."

Pauline frowned. "Never apologize to us for admitting how you feel! All four of us are walking wounded. We just have the kind wounds that don't show. We were worried sick. All of us. And now we're so grateful you're here sitting at this table. Understand?"

Gretchen wiped her eyes. "If it hadn't been for a fireman named John from Engine House 22, who took the time out of what he was doing to give me directions to get home, I'd still be out there lost and driving around."

"That's awesome!" Janie said. "We need to do something special for him and the men at his station."

"I could make some Bourbon Pecan Pies for them," Pauline offered.

"Oh, my God! Would you?" Gretchen asked. "That would be wonderful! I'll help in any way I can."

"Well, now that you mention Bourbon, I was already traumatized by my morning before you went missing, and after all this, I think a shot of Bourbon might be in order. And I'll pony up for a new bottle before you need to bake," Bettina said.

"I'll have to pass. I'm still taking pain pills," Janie said.

"I'll drink yours, too," Bettina said. "I'm not over the hoarder."

"I'll get the Bourbon," Pauline said, and left the room, heading for the library.

"What hoarder?" Gretchen asked.

"Oh, allow me," Bettina said, and started recounting her morning, beginning with the woman and the crazy dog, and ending with the hoarder and the rat, and then calling social services about him.

Gretchen shuddered. "You have more guts than I do."

Bettina frowned. "I think we're all pretty equal when it comes to guts. We married the same crook and lived to tell the tale."

Silence followed the declaration until Pauline came back with the booze, poured out three shots, and a shot of Pepsi for Janie.

"To us!" Pauline said, and downed her shot in one gulp.

"And to hell with tornadoes," Bettina added, as she knocked back her shot like a pro.

"I haven't eaten since breakfast, and I don't do much drinking. So, if I get weird, just chalk it up to what's left of this day," Gretchen said, and swallowed her shot like medicine.

Janie was wary of amping up the dull ache in her head by tossing back a cold drink and chose to sip until it was gone. But when all four shots had disappeared, they turned the glasses upside down with a thunk, looked at each other, and grinned.

Then Janie pointed toward the utility room.

"There is a frozen pizza in the deep freeze. Somebody turn on the oven. We don't want Gretchen getting weird."

After that, the trauma of the day began to fade.

The girls were doing what they did best.

Taking care of business.

And taking care of each other.

Later that night, Bettina got a text from Shelby Attilla telling her it wasn't safe to dog walk, and that she'd let her know when the streets were clear in her area. Now Bettina didn't have to set an alarm to get up early, and Gretchen already knew she wasn't going back to work until further notice.

For the interim, the girls were back where they'd started. All under the same roof, waiting for the other shoe to fall. And it didn't take long.

Neither snow nor rain, nor heat or gloom of night—or a tornado—stopped the St. Louis Post Office from delivering the mail.

Janie had just gotten it out of the mailbox on the front porch and was on her way to the kitchen with it. It was two days since the storm. The house cleaners had been here yesterday, and she was moving slowly about the house, reveling in her ability to stand upright without the constant feeling of being spun into outer space, and the Ring doorbell had been installed.

Someone was doing laundry, because she could hear the washing machine changing cycles, and she could also hear the tree-trimmers out back, sawing up the fallen limbs with their chainsaws.

She poured herself a cup of coffee, then sat at the table and began sorting mail.

Gretchen came in with an empty laundry basket, dropped it off in the utility room, and sat down with Janie.

"That's your stack," Janie said, pointing to a few pieces of mail to her right.

Gretchen glanced through them, laid aside the bills that needed to be paid, and then tossed the rest.

"Will we ever get through paying off his debts?" she muttered.

Janie looked up. "Do you have many?"

"Just one credit card, but he had it maxed."

"Same, so technically, he had four credit cards for himself, at four different homes," Janie muttered. "Did he explain it was his work expenses?"

Gretchen nodded.

"And did you ever look at it, or question the purchases?" Janie asked.

"No."

"Same. We were idiots," Janie said.

There was no denying the obvious. Gretchen nodded again.

Janie finished sorting the lot, then began opening her mail and setting aside bills to be paid and letters to be answered. Pauline and Bettina walked in just as she picked up one long, legal-size envelope with the return address of a Dallas, Texas law firm.

"Mail call," Bettina said, and picked up her stack, while Pauline took the stack that was left.

Janie frowned. "A letter from a lawyer in Texas. What fresh hell might this be?" Then she tore into the envelope, scanned the letter inside it, and stood up with a shriek. "Oh, hell, no!"

The girls jumped.

"What's wrong?" Gretchen asked.

"Somebody named Rachel Edwards has hired herself a lawyer, claiming she's David Logan's only child and demanding a share of the estate, including this house!"

They looked at each other in stunned silence, and then Janie's eyes narrowed.

"She's either pulling a con, or she might actually be his kid. Crooked and dumb run deep in DNA." Janie tapped the papers the lawyer had sent. "So, she wants his shit? I think we should give it to her. I'm going to start photocopying every bill I've paid on his behalf, and then get the amounts on the money he embezzled through forgery from my saving account. I want a total from each one of you of the debt he left you with and exactly how much money he stole from each one of you. We are going to present her with the amount of debt he owes, and if the funeral home still has his ashes, she's going to get those, too. I'll get my lawyer on this and have him send an itemized invoice of his debt and inquire as to how she intends to begin paying that back. She thinks he owned this property. She's got another think coming. But that tells me she's done her research. She knows where we're living, and she wants in the door. "

They stared at Janie for a moment, and then Bettina grinned.

"You make a formidable enemy. I am in awe."

"I'm going to my office," Janie said, and stomped out of the room.

"I guess we'd better get those figures together for Janie," Pauline said, and one by one, they dispersed until the room was empty, and the only sound to be heard was the washing machine on spin cycle, a little off balance, and dancing across the floor.

Rachel Edwards was in her late twenties, but she looked like the life she'd lived—hard and worn out. Her life had been on the skids for a while, and there were times when she wondered what she'd be doing now if she hadn't dropped out of high school at seventeen.

She was five years old when her mother hooked up with David Logan. He'd lived with them until after her tenth birthday. He and her mother ran scams and cons all over the country, staying just ahead of the law. Then one day, Rachel woke up, and David had been gone. Her mother told her never to mention his name again, and so she hadn't. Then she'd forgotten that he'd existed.

Until she saw a story on the news about a man killed in an accident. His death had revealed him as a bigamist with four wives. She thought nothing of it until a day or so later when she saw it again on other programming and caught the name: David Logan. Then she saw his photo, and nearly fell out of her shoes. As she lived and breathed, it appeared Daddy Dave was no longer a part of this world.

She was sorry that he'd died, but she had to give it to him for pulling off such a monumental scheme. Four wives! In different parts of the same state. And even more remarkable to her was that he'd been holding down a real job to cover his ass.

She hadn't thought much more about it until she saw photos of the four women. They appeared to be upscale from the women he'd known before, and that's when it hit her. He'd married them for their money.

Out of curiosity, she did Google searches on them and didn't find out anything of note, other than the only legal wife lived in St. Louis, Missouri, and that her name was Janelle Duvall Logan.

During the ensuing weeks, she shifted her focus to that name and found an address. Then she did a Google search on Zillow for the same location, and when she saw the mansion sitting on that property, the hair stood up on the back of her neck.

"Whoa! You struck gold there, didn't you?" she muttered.

And that's when she got the idea to make a claim on his estate. According to the obituary she'd found, he'd been cremated, and she remembered him telling a story about being on his own from the age of eighteen. He'd also claimed he'd never had family, so she wouldn't have to produce DNA to prove her legitimacy, because there was no one to compare it to.

What she did need was to prove he'd been part of her childhood. So, she began digging through her mother's old pictures until she found more than a half-dozen photos of her as a child standing at David's side. One with her, her mom, and David at the beach in Galveston, and a couple beside a Christmas tree. There was even one of her helping him wash his car out on their driveway. It was right after he'd come to live with them, so she couldn't have been more than six. The absence of him with her as a baby could be explained away as losing belongings in a fire.

The next part of her scheme required money, because she needed to hire a lawyer. Her boyfriend was as broke as she was, so she fell back on her old standby and went to working the streets, spending day and night hooking up with johns to pad her bank account.

Then one morning, she came home and discovered her boyfriend was gone. She didn't care. He'd just been a warm body to fuck, and she had more than enough of that already. The downside of needing lawyer money was that the johns were meaner now than they used to be. But she rose to the occasion, and as soon as she had enough for a retainer, she found herself a lawyer and presented her request. The lawyer wasn't on anyone's A-list, but he was legal, and perfectly happy to take her money and her case.

Three days later, she received a text from the lawyer's office. Her letter had been sent. Now it was all about waiting to see what kind of a fire it would light.

Rachel thought she was sitting pretty until that same night, a tornado went through St. Louis, and then she panicked. What if her big dreams had been blown away with the fancy house and the woman in it? But wait! Rachel took a deep breath and considered the second-best option. The house could be gone, but the land would still be there. At least she could file on the property as the only surviving heir and sell.

She had no idea that all four of the wives were in residence together, and she also did not know the level of fury she had unleashed. But she was about to find out.

It took the entire day for Janie to get all the information together, and then she made an appointment with her lawyer.

The next day, Bettina went back to dog walking, and Gretchen took Janie to her lawyer's office. It was the first time Janie had been out of the house to see the storm damage, and she realized again how grateful she was to have escaped with only a few downed limbs.

"Are you worried about this claim?" Gretchen asked, as she backed out of the drive and drove out of the neighborhood, heading toward the courthouse.

Janie was vehement. "No, and hell no. Even if she is his kid, he owned nothing, and all that was mine before I ever met him is still in my name only. If he hadn't died in that wreck, he'd be in prison. As it is, all she's going to get is a big dose of his reality."

Gretchen sighed. "I hope you're right. I half-expected another wife might come out of the woodwork, but I never thought about kids. He didn't like them and didn't want any."

"I know. I never really thought about raising a family. And then he didn't want any, and he was gone all the time, so I saw no need to consider it," Janie said, and then leaned forward and pointed. "Take a right turn here. His office is halfway down that street. The building with the burgundy awning out front."

"Ah. . . Yep, I see it," Gretchen said, and pulled into the parking lot adjacent to the building. "I'll wait for you here."

"Come in with me," Janie said. "It'll be more comfortable in the waiting room."

"Okay. If you're sure," Gretchen said.

Janie frowned. "Of course I'm sure. You're not some drug runner the family's trying to hide. You're my sister wife, remember?"

Gretchen rolled her eyes. "And to think, I used to make fun of that TV show. Oh well, at least they knew what they were getting into when they married the dude. We somehow missed that option."

They got out of the car and went inside.

The secretary looked up from her desk.

"Good morning, Janie. You're looking well. Have you fully recovered from that horrible attack?"

"Morning, Fran, and yes, for the most part. I'm still sporting bruises, but the worst has passed. I don't believe you've met Gretchen, though. Gretchen, this is Fran Langley, James' right-hand lady. Fran, this is Gretchen Lowry."

Gretchen smiled. "I'm one of the wives. It's a pleasure to meet you."

Fran grinned. "James is expecting you, Janie. I'll let him know you're here."

"Thanks," Janie said.

Gretchen pointed. "I'll be over here when you're ready to leave."

"Thanks, honey," Janie said, and then looked up as James Bedford opened the door to his office and came out to meet her.

"Come in, come in," James said, and escorted her back into his office.

As soon as she was seated, he reclaimed his chair behind his desk. "It's good to see you up and around. You certainly had a scare with that intruder in your home."

"You have no idea," Janie said. "Weird day, for sure."

James nodded. "Now. What's the big mess you said you were bringing to me?"

Janie pulled the letter from Rachel Edward's lawyer out of a folder and handed it over.

"I got this in the mail yesterday."

He read it without comment and then looked up.

"Tell me what your thoughts are," he asked.

"That it's a scam, for a number of reasons. She's demanding a share of his estate, which says she knows nothing about him or his life, and only knows what I have. He didn't even own a car. The car he died in belonged to the company he worked for. As you know, we always filed separate income taxes because of my business, and nothing I owned previous to our marriage was ever put in his name. The only joint account we had was the checking account. And after his death, I discovered it was nearly empty. He did not own any of the other houses he was living in with his other wives. They were all rentals or leased. He had no property. So even if she was his child, which he never mentioned in the ten years we were married, there's nothing for her to claim. Am I right?"

Nathan nodded. "Since she's an adult, the social security child support she might have drawn after his death would have only been available to her until her eighteenth birthday, so she can't claim that. And if he owned nothing, then she has nothing to claim. She has no legal right to anything else."

"That's what I thought," Janie said. "So, rather than challenge her claim and drag this through the court just to prove she's running a scam, what if we turned the tables on her and basically accept her claim, send her an itemized list of his debts, and of the money he stole and embezzled from all four of us? We can ask her what kind of a schedule she would like to set up to begin reparations for what he stole?"

Nathan blinked. "Wow. That might be a first for me. Sending back a payment due bill to someone claiming to be an heir to an estate."

"It's not illegal to send a bill," Janie said.

"No. No, it's not," James said.

"And, in the letter, tell her we don't need DNA for proof of her connection to David. If she claims him, then his debts are her responsibility. She can set up a payment plan through her lawyer, and he'll notify us of the date each month that we can expect to be reimbursed. Also, remind her that since the other three wives were never legally his, then they are not responsible for his debts. So, she will owe money to them as well. But just so you know, we've all been making payments on his maxed-out credit cards. Also make sure she and her lawyer understand that he owned nothing. Not any part of my property or my business, and that we filed income tax separately. I owe nothing to any of his long-lost relatives."

James nodded. "Yes. I can do that. I'll get the letter worked up today and get it out in the mail."

She pushed the file folder across the desk.

"This is a detailed invoice of monies stolen or embezzled from each of us, as well as monies owed to his personal credit cards. None of which, by the way, were available for us to use, because we'd been given to understand that all expenses on them were work related."

"Can I keep this file?" he asked.

"Yes. They're copies. I have the original set at home in my safe."

"Excellent. So, she struck a match, and you're about to blow out her little bonfire before it ever gets a chance to breathe and grow."

"That's the plan," Janie said.

"I like it," he said. "I'll let you know when the letter goes out, and when I hear back from the lawyer, you'll be the first to know."

"Thank you, James. I appreciate this, and I appreciate how considerate you've been with me through this whole bigamy mess."

"Of course. Now go home and let go of the worry. No matter how loud this Rachel Edwards gets, noise will get her nowhere in a court of law."

He walked Janie out into the reception area, nodded cordially to Gretchen, and went back into his office.

"Ready to go?" Gretchen asked.

"Yes, please," Janie said.

"It was a pleasure to meet you, Gretchen. Have a nice day, ladies," Fran said.

They exited the office and walked into the sunshine. Janie filled Gretchen in on all the details as they drove home, and as they pulled into the drive, Bettina drove up behind them.

They went inside together, talking nonstop and ready to get on with the day.

"Was your lawyer on board with your plan?" Bettina asked.

"Yes. He'll send my response back to the lawyer in Dallas, and then we'll have to wait and see how long it takes for Rachel Edwards and her claim to David Logan to disappear."

Bettina gave her a high five and went upstairs to get her laptop. She'd seen the alerts from her dog walking page on Facebook, but texting at length on a phone got on her last nerve. She was on her way to her room when she heard Pauline start laughing. Curious, she followed the sound to the red room, which had become Pauline's office, to see what was going on.

The door was open, and Pauline was at her desk.

"Hey, girl. I heard you laughing. What's funny?" Bettina said.

The smile was still on Pauline's face as she turned around. "Look at this email. It's from a client who runs a members only gym. He's trying to build his membership, so he's updating his website, and has decided to have one day a week open to the public. People will pay a nominal fee for that day and have access to part of the facilities, but not all. His plan is that if more people see what he has to offer, they might sign up for private membership. But this is what he sent me."

Bettina moved closer to look over Pauline's shoulder at the email on the screen.

Pauline, I love what you're doing, but I want to make sure that PUBIC ACCESS on Wednesdays is the first thing they see. Maybe the lettering would be in a different font, or a larger font, or maybe the wording would be in red... or a bright flashing yellow... I don't know. You're the expert. I just want them to see PUBIC and come running.

"Oh, my gawd," Bettina said, and then burst out laughing. "They'll *come* for sure... whether it's running or not."

Pauline giggled. Bettina's bawdy humor was priceless.

"Back to work, girl! Fix that man up. I have to go communicate with dog people," she said.

"Good luck," Pauline said.

"Yup. I'm sure I'll need it," Bettina said, and went to her room, while Janie and Gretchen were getting settled in for the day.

Because of the days when she'd been ordered on bed rest, Janie was still behind on bookkeeping. So, she grabbed a bottle of pop from the refrigerator and headed to her office.

Gretchen was at a loss as to what to do and wandered off through the house before winding up in the living room. She was staring at the fireplace and then at the bookshelves on either side of the mantel. Not only were they out of alphabetical order, but they weren't sorted into fiction and non-fiction.

Within minutes, she had kicked off her shoes and was at the shelves, sorting and alphabetizing books.

She thought about the fireman named John and wanted to make sure when they took the pies, that it was on a shift he was working. So, she stopped what she was doing, got a phone number for that engine house, and called.

Within minutes, she found out that he would be on a twenty-four-hour shift tomorrow, and then off two days. She also found out there were less than a dozen men, counting the captain, at the station, so she was guessing about five pecan pies would suffice.

Later that evening, she approached Pauline about baking while they were cleaning up the dinner dishes.

"Are you still willing to make those Bourbon pecan pies?" Gretchen asked.

"Sure. When do you want to deliver them?"

"Well, the fireman who helped me is on shift starting tomorrow.

So, if we baked five in the morning and let them cool a bit, we could deliver them early afternoon."

"Works for me," Pauline said. "I'm excited to get to bake again."

"I'll help," Gretchen said. "And I really appreciate you offering to do this."

"He helped get you home. The least I can do is bake a pie."

CHAPTER TEN

Early the next morning, Pauline began making dough for the crusts. Once it was done, she sectioned it up into six equal pieces and began rolling them out into circles, putting each one in a disposable pie pan, then into the refrigerator to chill while she mixed up the fillings.

"You made six crusts," Gretchen said.

"One is for us," Pauline said.

"Oh, yum!" Gretchen said, and promptly became the sous chef and dishwasher, doing whatever Pauline wanted or needed and keeping baking utensils washed up for reuse.

When Janie showed up, they were in full assembly line mode. She paused in the doorway, thinking how wonderful it was to wake up to this.

"Don't mind me," she said, as she slipped behind them to get a cup of coffee, and a bowl and spoon for cereal.

"She's making an extra one for us," Gretchen said.

"I'm not gonna cry about that. I smelled this goodness all the way from the stairs," Bettina said, as she walked into the kitchen.

"When are you going to deliver them?" Janie asked.

"Sometime this afternoon... As soon as they've cooled enough to transport," Gretchen said. "Want to come with?"

"Yes! Absolutely!" Bettina said.

"I will, too," Janie said.

"Good," Gretchen said. "We're delivering five pies to the station."

Then the oven timer went off.

"First two done!" Pauline said, as she took them out and put them on a cooling rack. She went back to mixing up the filling for the next two crusts.

Janie groaned. "Here I am eating a bowl of cold cereal, and there sits the most gorgeous pie ever!"

"It's the 'better than sex' pie, remember?" Bettina said.

"We remember. That pie was so good, Elvis, Johnny, and Justin could have never come close to that sugar ecstasy," Gretchen said, referring to the vibrators they'd named that David had given them as wedding presents. "Hey, Janie. Did you ever name yours?"

"No. Mine's in the witness protection program, and I don't have security clearance."

Laughter exploded within the room, as Janie wiggled her eyebrows and took another bite of cereal.

Pauline got the filling mixed up for two more pies, filled the chilled crusts and slid them into the oven, then she set the timer.

"Two more in baking, and two to go," she said.

"Oh... As of today, I have three new possible clients," Bettina said, as she poured frosted rice cereal pops into her bowl. "They're all in the Attilla neighborhood. I think Shelby Attilla has been bragging. At any rate, I'm going to meet the dogs and owners right after I walk Loki."

"Awesome," Janie said. "Fingers crossed."

Bettina nodded as she picked up the milk carton with both hands and began slowly pouring milk into her bowl.

Gretchen was watching, curious about the precise, pencil-thin pour going into the side of the bowl.

"Why do you always put milk into a bowl like that?" she asked.

Bettina looked up. "Like what?"

"You pour that milk like it's being rationed," she said.

"Oh. It's not that. I don't like soggy cereal, and I don't want it to float. So, I just pour a little bit of milk and eat from the bottom first, then pour a little more until it's all gone. It used to drive David nuts."

Janie sighed. "I snore. He complained about it all the time. Even bought me some of those little strips to put on my nose before going to bed, then didn't want to look at me after I had one on my nose."

Gretchen frowned. "That's mean. I know you snore. I slept in your room with you, remember? But it's a cute little snore. The habit I had that he didn't like was clipping my toenails in bed while we were watching TV."

"I've got all of you beat," Pauline said. "I was a half-inch taller than him. He absolutely hated it when I wore heels."

"You're right. You win," Bettina said.

"He was a shallow man. It has taken all four of us putting our life experiences with him together before we could see who he was," Janie muttered.

"And even with that, who was he really?" Pauline muttered.

Janie shrugged. "We may not ever know who he was, but we know what he was made of."

"What's that?" Gretchen asked.

"One hundred percent, authentic, bullshit," Janie said.

"Amen to that," the girls echoed.

As soon as Bettina finished eating, she took her dishes to the sink.

"Happy baking, y'all. I'll be back in plenty of time to help deliver pies," she said, and grabbed her things and hurried out the door.

"I'm going to work," Janie said, and left the pie baking duo on their own.

Bettina was on her way across town when her cellphone rang. She didn't recognize the number, but since she had a business now, she answered under the assumption that it could be a potential client and put it on speaker.

"Hello?"

"Bettina Lee, this is Mike Halford from Social Services. I wanted to give you a little update on the hoarder you reported."

Bettina's stomach knotted. "I'm almost afraid to hear it."

"No, no, don't be. It was the best thing you could have ever done for that man. I won't go into details, because they're pretty horrific, but the State Health Department is working with us getting the house emptied out. The little dog has been to a vet and is now with a foster family. The man is in hospice. He has cancer. He's dying and he knew it. You were right in believing he was desperate for help. He was afraid he'd pass away in the house, and there'd be no one to take care of Tinkerbelle."

Tears welled. "Oh, my God. Bless his heart. Bless his heart," Bettina said.

"He asked us if the dog walker lady was the one who turned him in. When we told him it was, he wanted you to know how grateful he was, and to thank you. So... That's why I called. Your instincts were on point. You did a good thing," Mike said.

"Thank you for letting me know, but why didn't he just call for help?" she asked.

"People with emotional problems have trouble communicating. I think he couldn't face the questioning and guilt. He wanted help.

He just didn't know how to go about getting it."

"That's the saddest thing," she said.

"Sad is part of my job, but I want to thank you, too. You helped. Far too many people look away," he said, and disconnected.

She grabbed a handful of tissues and started wiping her eyes. She didn't cry pretty and didn't want to advertise it. By the time she arrived to get Loki, she had her emotions under control. She got out, pausing long enough to get everything she needed, then hurried to the door and rang the bell.

Barb answered the door a few moments later with Loki at her heels.

"Morning, honey!" Barb said. "He's raring to go."

Bettina clipped her leash on Lokie's harness. "Then let's get this party started, buddy. What do you say?"

Loki took off out the door at a trot.

"He's so ready to go with you that he doesn't even wave good-bye," Barb said, and laughed at her own joke as she closed the door.

Bettina felt better just being outside with this little dog. He was such a charmer and had a funny personality. But she didn't trust him for one second. His curiosity and penchant for wanting to eat everything in sight kept her on her toes.

By now, people in the neighborhood had caught on to the fact that Bettina was the dog walker, and some of them had begun sitting out on their front porches just so they could wave as she and Loki passed by.

One older woman, in particular, liked to work her flower beds early in the morning before it got too hot, and she always paused long enough to call out a greeting. Today was no exception.

Bettina noticed that she was deadheading rose bushes, but when she saw them coming up the sidewalk, she stopped and waved.

"Good morning! And good morning to your fine gentleman!" she said.

Loki barked once, as if to say hello, and Bettina called out. "Your roses are beautiful," and waved as they passed her by.

A sprinkler system was on in the yard a couple of houses down, and Bettina knew they were going to get wet. But it was too warm to care, and it might even feel good.

Loki wasn't too keen on water in his face and trotted through the shower at a quicker pace, forcing Bettina to run to keep up.

They took a turn at the next corner and headed west. The entire street for blocks was lined with old growth oaks and elms. It was Bettina's favorite part of the walk, because it was all in the shade.

The same little squirrel in the same big oak tree seemed to be waiting for Loki to appear, because the moment they passed beneath it, she heard it start scolding. Loki ran to the tree, barking back in canine retaliation, and the fuss was on. It took a couple of treats to redirect the little dog's attention, and they moved on.

A couple of minutes later, she saw his nose to the ground, and then he paused. She didn't know what he'd found, but she knew it was already in his mouth, so she bolted forward. She dropped to her knees beside him and immediately poked her finger in the side of his mouth to get it open.

"Spit it out you little garbage disposal," she said, and when she got his mouth open, fished out a red plastic cap from a soda bottle. She put it in her pocket. "No, sir," she said, and gave his little head a smooch.

He looked up, his little tongue out, panting from the heat and the exertion of not wanting to give up his goody, then licked her chin.

Bettina rolled her eyes. "You are such a little charmer. Thank you for the kisses, but that is not your toy."

She got up, brushed off the knees of her blue jeans, and their journey continued. Loki poked around beneath bushes, sniffing at the bases of trees, until he finally did his business, then drank half a bowl of the water she poured out for him. But instead of taking off again, he sat down and started licking one foot.

Bettina frowned.

"Oh, baby, what did you do?" she muttered, picked him up and carried him to a nearby bench, and then sat down and began looking at his foot.

Almost immediately, she saw something stuck between his toes, but when she tried to spread them apart to get to it, he cried.

"Oh, I'm sorry, baby, but I need to look," she said, and moved slower and gentler until she got the toes apart enough to see what looked like a small thorn—probably from that last bush he'd prowled under.

She tied his leash to the arm of the bench, then took off her backpack, pulled out a little first aid kit, and dug until she found the tweezers she knew were there, and then she very carefully pulled out the thorn.

He cried again and licked her hand after it was out.

"Poor baby. I'm sorry it hurt, but it's gone now. All gone," she said. She poured disinfectant between his toes, then gave him a little treat for being so good, before packing everything up.

As she was shouldering her backpack, a teenage boy came out of the house across the street and jogged over to where they'd been sitting.

"Ma'am, is everything all right? I saw you looking at his paw."

Bettina looked up. "That's so sweet of you. He had a thorn between his toes, but I got it out. He's okay now."

"If he's not okay to walk, I can drive you home," he offered.

"Thank you, but we're fine, and we're not far from his home."

"He's not your dog?" the boy asked.

"No. I'm his dog walker," Bettina said.

"Oh. Wow. My Gran has a poodle. She's been looking for someone to walk it. Do you take new customers?"

"I do," she said, and then pulled a business card out of her backpack and gave it to him. "You can have her call me if she's interested. I have a Facebook page with all of my info."

"Thanks," he said. "I will."

"Thanks for checking on us," Bettina said.

"Yeah sure, no problem," he said, and after giving Loki's head a quick scratch, he loped back across the street and went into his house.

Bettina shouldered her backpack again, untied Loki's leash, and put him down on the sidewalk.

"Are you good to go?" she asked. "Ready to go home?"

Loki yapped, and took off at a little trot, but on a much shorter leash. Bettina wasn't giving him another inch. He'd done enough damage for one day.

She was fifteen minutes later than usual bringing him home, and she could tell Barb had been concerned.

"Sorry we're a little late," Bettina said. "He got a sticker between his toes, and we had to stop and get it out. Tell Shelby it's his right front paw. I poured some disinfectant on it, and I'm sure it will be fine, but it won't hurt to take a look when she gets home."

"Oh my!" Barb said. "Poor little guy. Thank goodness you pay attention. That could have worked its way up into his foot and gotten infected."

"Yes, ma'am," Bettina said. "I'll see you tomorrow."

She hurried back to her car, sent Shelby a text that Loki was home, and then took off to visit with prospective new clients.

She met Aaron Carter and a little Yorkie named Bruce.

Then drove to Sherry Lawrence's residence and met her little rescue dog Charlotte.

Her last appointment was with Frieda Turnbull to meet her terrier named Puppy.

They all fit Bettina's requests and requirements, were used to being walked, and had enough training to be manageable. And they were delightful little fur-babies.

Satisfied with taking them on as new clients, she left them with a timeline of when she'd be coming by to walk them. It was just after twelve when she headed home, and her guess had been correct.

Shelby Attilla had been bragging about her dog walker. Word of mouth advertising was a wonderful thing.

She pulled up at the house about thirty minutes later, saw the pies sitting on racks all over the island, and hurried upstairs and then down the hall to where Pauline was working.

"I'm back. I'm going to clean up. Give me twenty minutes," Bettina said.

"Great. Did you have a good day?" Pauline asked.

"I did. I have three new clients. All small dogs with good manners."

"Congrats," Pauline said. "I'll go tell the girls to start boxing up pies."

"I'll meet you downstairs," Bettina said, and ran back to her room, stripped, and jumped in the shower. A short while later, she came out of her room with her purse on her shoulder and took off down the stairs.

The girls were in the kitchen with the pies.

"I'm ready!" she said.

Janie looked up. "Congratulations on your new clients."

Bettina smiled. "Thanks. It's an ego boost for sure."

"Everyone, grab some pies and follow me," Gretchen said.

They filed out of the house with the boxes, carrying them like ring bearers walking down the aisle of a church, and piled into Gretchen's SUV.

Pauline was in front with a boxed pie between her feet and one in her lap. Bettina and Janie were in the back seat holding pies, with one in the seat between them.

"Do you know how to get to Station 22?" Janie asked.

"I have the address in my GPS," Gretchen said, and drove through the portico and circled back out onto the street.

"Does the Captain know we're coming," Pauline asked.

Gretchen nodded. "I called him this morning and asked. If they're not out on a call, it will be fine. If they are, there will still be someone at the station to receive the pies. But I hope they're there so you can meet John. He was such a sweetheart to help me get home."

"Does he know we're coming?" Janie asked.

Gretchen shook her head. "I asked the captain not to tell him. I kind of wanted it to be a surprise."

"Fun stuff," Bettina said. "Do I look okay?"

They all turned and looked at her. Even Gretchen, who was driving, glanced up in the rearview mirror.

"Please tell me you have no interest in flirting today," Gretchen muttered.

Bettina frowned. "Hell no, to the flirting. But I'm still a woman. And I still want to look good enough that some man wishes he was mine."

They burst out laughing and rode the rest of the way to the fire station in an upbeat mood.

"We're here," Gretchen said, as she pulled up into the long drive leading to the station house. She reached for her phone. "Let me give the captain a call. He's going to have the guys all come outside. Even though I'm thanking John personally, they're all included in the thank you for what they did to help during rescue and clean-up after the storm."

"This is so fun," Pauline said.

"They're going to freak out over your pies," Janie added.

Gretchen was on the phone, talking, and then turned to the girls as soon as she disconnected.

"Okay, we get out now. Give me a second, and you can hand me two boxes. Then you guys get the rest."

After a little bit of juggling, the four women were lined up in front of Gretchen's SUV holding the pies, watching as a dozen men came piling out of the station, with an older man beside them.

"Welcome, ladies. I'm Captain Rizzo. Which one of you is Gretchen?"

"That would be me, sir," Gretchen said.

Rizzo nodded and turned to his men. "Hey John! Do you recognize this lady?"

Gretchen rolled her eyes as a young man with blonde hair stepped out of the crowd.

"Don't ask him that," Gretchen said. "The only time we met, I was crying my eyes out." Then she shifted focus. "John, I'm the woman who got lost the day of the storm, remember? You gave me directions to get home again."

Recognition dawned, as he smiled. "Yes, ma'am! I do remember."

"Good, because I'd hate to think Pauline made all these Bourbon Pecan Pies for nothing."

"Those are for us?" John said.

"Yes, for you and all the crew, as a measure of our thanks and appreciation for all you did that day after the storm. These girls are the family I was trying to get home to. The redhead is Janie Logan. The other blonde is Bettina Lee. The tall one with dark hair is Pauline Lord, our baker extraordinaire, and I'm Gretchen Lowry. Come get your pies," Gretchen said.

The men swarmed them, thanking them for the pies, and thanking Pauline for baking them.

"It's my pleasure," Pauline said. "I love to bake."

"And we love to eat," they echoed. "You can bake for us anytime."

"Thank you for all this," John said.

"You're so welcome, and thank you for helping me find the way home," Gretchen said.

"If these taste as good as they smell, I can't wait," Captain Rizzo said.

"Enjoy, and thank you again," Gretchen said. "It's been a pleasure to meet you."

"The pleasure is all ours," Rizzo said. "Drive safe going home."

The girls got back in the car and then watched the firemen going back into the station house.

"I wonder how long it will take a dozen men to eat five pies?" Pauline said.

"A lot less time than it took you to bake them, that's for sure," Gretchen said. "And I owe you for the effort."

Pauline sighed. "You don't owe me anything. We're family, remember?"

"Every day of my life, and I am grateful," Gretchen said.

CHAPTER ELEVEN

The rest of the week passed without a disaster. Not even a problem reared its ugly head. It was as if the Universe was finally giving the girls a break.

But back in Dallas, Rachel Edwards was impatiently biding her time, waiting to hear from her lawyer. Surely Janelle Logan had received the letter by now, and most certainly had contacted her own lawyer. Still, Rachel couldn't help but worry, wondering if they'd already set a private investigator looking into her life. Wondering if they were actively trying to disprove her claim. Wondering what she should be doing to cover her ass.

Then she woke up Monday morning to a text from her lawyer, asking if she could come to his office before noon. She fired back an affirmative answer and jumped into the shower. It was finally happening!!

She did a little happy dance as she got dressed and didn't even get pissed at the roach that ran across the kitchen counter while she was making herself a Pop Tart, convinced this life and all that came with it was going to be behind her. No more turning tricks. No more back-alley, one-room apartments. No more fly-by-night boyfriends. She was moving up in the world.

Her car had quit running months ago, so she took an Uber to the lawyer's office and walked in with her shoulders back and her chin up.

"I'm Rachel Edwards. Mr. Wainwright is expecting me," she said.

"I'll let him know you're here," his secretary said, and buzzed his office. "Rachel Edwards to see you."

Rachel heard his reply. "Send her in," and when the secretary nodded, she let herself into his office.

"Good morning, Miss Edwards. Have a seat."

Rachel was smiling as she sat down. "I assume you have some news for me."

Wainwright looked up, then sighed. "Yes, ma'am. I have news, but it's not what you were expecting."

Rachel's gut knotted. "Well, I didn't expect she'd buckle under without a fight."

Wainwright shook his head. "Oh, she's not fighting anything. But your assumption that your father owned any part of her property was wrong. All of that belongs to his widow. His name is on nothing but a marriage license. Mrs. Logan has replied with a complete inventory of what he owned, which was nothing. She also sent a complete invoice of what he owed on four credit cards, which are all maxed out. And there's a bill from each of the four wives explaining what he forged and how much he embezzled from each of them. They are willing to give you time to set up payment plans to reimburse them for what your father stole, and to remind you that if he had not died in the wreck, he would be in prison. Without saying the actual words, it is obvious that they hold extreme levels of hate for the man, and that anyone related to him, they consider tainted from the same blood. You are also to be informed that McAllister Funeral Home in St. Louis, Missouri may still have his ashes if you want to claim them, because all four wives rejected them."

Rachel was hyperventilating and didn't know it. All of a sudden, she felt like she was floating. The last time she'd felt like this, she'd taken a big hit of Ecstasy and was having herself one hell of a ride. But there were no drugs in her system. Just shock and a sudden urge to hide.

"I... don't know what to. I wasn't expecting... This isn't what..."

Wainwright nodded. "Yes, ma'am. I understand. How do you want me to reply?"

Rachel shuddered. Swallowing the bile rising in her throat, she looked out the window over Wainwright's shoulder without actually looking him in the eyes.

"Tell them I am rescinding any claims on his estate," she said.

Wainwright nodded. "I can do that. But you should know that if they want to get ugly about this, they might try to take you to court to try and get his debts repaid through you. It probably wouldn't work, but it could be a long and expensive fight for you before their claims against you are rejected."

"Oh, my God," Rachel mumbled. "I have to go now."

She got up, staggered slightly, and walked out without

looking back.

Wainwright shook his head, and then buzzed his secretary. "Lavelle, will you come in my office. I need to send a letter."

Rachel was out on the sidewalk and walking in the wrong direction before she came to enough to realize it, then she sat on a bench beneath some trees near the courthouse and called an Uber.

It took twenty minutes for her ride to show up, and by the time she got home, she was in hysterics. She needed to get the hell out of Dallas before they sent someone to find her, so she headed for the refrigerator, dug through the freezer section until she got to a large plastic tub of Country Crock margarine, and pulled it out.

Only it wasn't full of margarine. It was the repository for all the money she had left in the world. Less than five hundred dollars between her and homeless. She needed to rethink her goals in life. For a party girl, the thought finding herself a working man and settling down was more appealing than it used to be. Even if she had to learn to cook and squirt out a couple of kids to satisfy her wifely duties, she was willing.

She needed not to be found and then have to confess that she'd filed false claims against an estate. She also needed not to be found and dunned for Daddy Dave's final con.

She had a TV she could pawn. She could sell her old car that wouldn't run. She had enough to sell that would get her the money needed to disappear, and the first thing she did was carry her small flat-screen TV down the block to the pawn shop. She walked out a hundred dollars to the good.

After that, she called a couple of guys she knew who bought junkers to repair and resell, and she sold her car for four hundred dollars. Watching them haul it off that evening was the final step in making a quick exit.

She'd already priced a trip from Dallas to Salem, Oregon on Amtrak. Two hundred and fifty-two bucks for an eighty-six-hour train ride and changing trains and luggage mid-journey. It sounded like a long, hard trip, but it beat a bus ride all to hell.

Tomorrow morning, she'd be on that train, hoping she could outrun the biggest mistake of her life.

And while Rachel was making peace with her decision to leave Dallas tomorrow, life for the girls was moving past the tornado.

The next morning, as Rachel was boarding Amtrak for Salem, Oregon, Gretchen was on her way back to work.

She showed up at the insurance agency with lunch from home and a big smile on her face. She already knew Juana wouldn't be there. She'd only agreed to one week, and the storm took a chunk out of the plan. But Gretchen was ready to be in charge of something. After months of feeling like her legs had been cut out from under her, it felt good to know she was on the job and knew exactly what to do.

Her boss, Sarah, was already there when she arrived and met her at the desk.

"Welcome back, Gretchen. This is a key to the front door so that you can open the office if I'm not here. If you have questions, you know where to find me. Otherwise, you're riding herd on the appointments and the phone now."

"Thank you," Gretchen said, and promptly put the key on her key ring. "And, I have a question about the appointments that were scheduled before we shut down. Have they been rescheduled, or do I need to reach out and let everyone know we're back in business?"

Sarah blinked. "Oh, my God. I completely forgot about that. Then the answer is no, they weren't rescheduled, and yes, please, give them a call and reschedule at their convenience. Just give us all the new schedule when you've finished, and then we'll work the new calls in around them."

"Will do," Gretchen said, and began digging out the appointment book.

Sarah sighed. "I suspect you're going to be worth your weight in gold around here. Are you always this organized?

Gretchen nodded. "It's a blessing and a curse. Ask the girls. The spice shelf in our kitchen is alphabetized. So is the pantry. All the plates and dishes are stacked in an orderly fashion, and the cutlery is in place in the drawers. The clothes in my closet are sorted and arranged according to color and what they are. I can't help myself, and fortunately, they don't seem to mind."

Sarah laughed out loud. "You think you can do anything with Charles's office? It looks like it belongs to a teenage boy with a penchant for baseball."

"I wouldn't want to intrude in his space," Gretchen said. "And St. Louis does have their own major league baseball team, so I'm sure all of his clients understand."

"I suppose," Sarah said. "But his office looks like my son's room, and he's twelve."

Gretchen grinned, and then Charles walked in carrying a Starbucks cup in one hand and his briefcase in another.

"Morning everybody! It's good to be back, isn't it?" he said.

"Yes, it is," Sarah said, and then winked at Gretchen as Charles disappeared down the hall.

A few minutes later, Lisa arrived with a box of fresh doughnuts.

"Just a little welcome back to all of us," she said, as she sailed past Gretchen's desk. "They'll be in the breakroom. Help yourself."

"Thank you," Gretchen said. "They smell wonderful. I will," and went back to the roster of names she had before her, still phoning clients to reschedule appointments.

It took a little over two hours to contact all of them, but she'd done it, and the ensuing week was going to be busy, which is just how she liked it.

Bettina was busy, too, and it was just how *she* liked it.

She'd already walked Loki, and then Aaron Carter's little Yorkie. So far, the morning couldn't be going any better. Bruce, the Yorkie was bitty, and while she gave him the full thirty-minute walk, they didn't cover nearly as much territory as she did with Loki.

Also, Bruce was minus the urge to taste all the trash on the sidewalks and trotted like a little prince with his ears up and his nose in a constant state of sniff. Genetics were a bitch, because his tongue didn't exactly fit in his little mouth, but it didn't seem to bother Bruce, or his ability to take a drink when Bettina paused to give him water. She'd returned him to Aaron in a timely fashion. He was as pleased to see Bruce, as Bruce was to get home.

The heat of the day was amping up to downright discomfort, and she still had two to go. With thirty minutes to get to her next appointment. Bettina took a side-trip to get something cold to drink, and then headed for Sherry Lawrence's house to walk her rescue dog, Charlotte.

Charlotte was what Sherry called a Heinz 57 dog—a mix of a little bit of everything. A pretty little brown and white, short-hair with black nails, a heart-shaped black nose, and little black lips, it was the only dog Bettina had ever seen that could pass for full-on Goth.

She arrived, parked her car on the street beneath a shade tree, then got out and restocked her backpack before heading to the door. She heard the dog bark when she rang the doorbell, and then moments later, Sherry, who was in her mid-fifties, answered the door in cutoff shorts and an old Dallas Cowboys t-shirt, with Charlotte at her heels.

"Good morning!" she said. "Charlotte is ready to go."

"And I'm ready for Charlotte," Bettina said, as she clipped a leash on the little dog's collar. "We'll see you later. Charlotte! Wanna go for a walk?"

Charlotte pranced out of the door like the little princess she was, and off they went.

It soon became apparent to Bettina that Charlotte was a neighborhood favorite. Everyone they passed seemed to recognize and greet her, leaving Bettina to introduce herself. While the job itself was repetitive—walking, watching dogs sniff, watching dogs pee on everything, and finally pooping—it was the dogs that made the job a delight.

Each one had its own unique personality.

A little shy. Or very vocal.

Or over-eager at the sight of birds and squirrels.

The downside was weather, and right now, it kept getting hotter. By the time Bettina got Charlotte home, her shirt was sticking to her back.

"She is a delight," Bettina said. "She had two little treats and a bowl of water, and she's ready to find a cool spot to take a nap."

"Thank you," Sherry said.

"You're welcome." Then Bettina patted Charlotte's head. "Bye, sweet girl. I'll see you tomorrow," and headed to her car.

Once she was inside, she jacked the air conditioning up as cold as it would go, turned the fan on blast, and just sat there with her eyes closed until the sweat had dried on her brow. Only then did she put the car in gear and drive away.

The last stop was at Frieda Turnbull's house to walk a little Jack Russell terrier named Puppy. A landscape crew was at the property, mowing and weeding when she arrived, so she parked in the street, grabbed a leash and her backpack, and then headed for the door.

She rang the doorbell, then waited, but Frieda didn't answer, so she rang it again. That's when heard yapping. Moments later, Frieda opened the door, a little breathless, and with an apology.

"Oh, my Lord... How long have you been standing here? I'm so sorry. I'm a little bit hard of hearing, and with all this yard work going on, I didn't hear the doorbell. But I did hear Puppy. She's good to alert me to stuff."

"It's okay," Bettina said. "I only rang twice." Then she clipped the leash on Puppy's pink collar and gave her a quick pat. "Wanna go for a walk?"

Puppy's little ears came up, and her tail began to wag.

"I think she's ready," Frieda said. "Have a good walk, and I'll see you soon."

"Yes, ma'am," Bettina said, and off they went with Puppy moving out in front, testing the length of the leash before she backed herself off a bit to slack the tension.

Bettina liked this dog's attitude. She trotted with a bounce, and when her tail wagged, it tended to rotate like helicopter rotors, rather than wag back and forth.

Unique. That was the right word for Puppy. She was unique.

They walked the route Bettina had been shown during her interview and was again grateful for the old growth shade trees along the sidewalks. Puppy had her own route for sniffing. Every fire plug, every other tree, and most bushes.

When they passed houses with other dogs, even though Bettina couldn't see the dogs, she knew they must be out in the back yards, because they would start barking, and Puppy would yip back, as if in greeting. And then the barking would stop.

Nearly thirty minutes later, they were on their way back when they passed by a large, two-story red brick with a perfectly manicured landscape, and a privacy fence in the back yard just visible from the street. Suddenly, a dog with a loud, savage bark began sounding off. It was obvious it didn't want them in his space.

The little terrier suddenly stopped and came back to Bettina on the run.

"Well baby, bless your heart," she said, and picked her up.

The little dog was trembling in fear, which made Bettina wonder if she'd had issues with that dog before, or if she just sensed the danger. At any rate, she hurried past the house, and when they were far enough away, she put Puppy back down and walked her the rest of the way home.

As she was returning her to Frieda, she mentioned what had happened.

"We couldn't see it, but the dog's bark sounded vicious. It scared Puppy to the point of coming back to me to be picked up. I carried her out of the area before I put her down again."

"Oh no! Poor baby," Frieda said. "I know which house you're talking about. It belongs to Rance and Lisa Lavin. To my knowledge, they never had a dog before. Either they have a new dog, or maybe guests with a dog. I hope those guests leave soon. I don't like Puppy being frightened like that."

"I didn't like it either. We can easily take a different route tomorrow and bypass that block altogether," Bettina said.

"That's a good idea. Thank you," Frieda said. "So, we'll see you tomorrow?"

"Yes," Bettina said, and then impulsively knelt and gave Puppy a hug. "I'm sorry you were scared, baby. We won't go that way again, okay?"

Bettina got a lick on the chin for her trouble and felt better about it as she walked away. When she finally headed home, it was with relief.

She'd just made a hundred and twenty dollars for a half day's work. That was going to total out to six hundred dollars for a five-day week, and twenty-four hundred dollars a month.

At Janie's urging, she was keeping track of the gas she bought, and the mileage used during her work. And she was keeping all of the receipts for her dog walking purchases. It was such a relief to know she was going to be solvent and participating in the financial aspects of their home. She could buy groceries. She could help pay a bill. And maybe someday, she'd be free of the debt of David Logan's bad choices.

When Bettina finally got home, she checked her phone to make sure all the clients had paid her, and they had. Tonight, Janie was going to show her how to upload QuickBooks to her laptop and give her a brief lesson on how to use it so she could do her own book-keeping. But for now, all she wanted was to shower and eat. So, she grabbed her backpack and headed for the house.

The blast of cool air as she walked in the door was as welcome as a lover's kiss. She inhaled slowly, feeling the stress of the day falling away, and went straight through to the kitchen to throw away the trash from her backpack, and recycle the water bottles she'd emptied. Then she replenished the pack so it would be ready for tomorrow and left it in the corner of the pantry.

As she paused at the foot of the stairs, she heard Janie on the phone with a client. She backtracked to the office to let Janie know she was home, stepped into the doorway, and waved.

Janie gave her a thumbs up, and then Bettina did an about face and went upstairs. A shower and a change of clothes later, she headed for the kitchen. After making a sandwich and adding a scoop of potato salad to her plate, she sat down and began going through the mail Janie had left there for her as she ate. Most of it was sorting through junk mail, David's credit card bill, and a reminder from the DMV to renew the license tag for her car. Nothing drastic. Nothing unexpected, which was always a plus. She pushed it aside and began eating. Without the noise of TV for background. Without bothering to find something to read. Just grateful for the blessing of this house and feeding her hunger.

A few moments later, Janie came in.

"Hey, Miss Bee, I was on the phone with a client. It's hot as a two-dollar pistol out there today. I'll bet you feel sapped."

Bettina smiled. She'd never had a nickname before, and she liked it.

"That's okay. I didn't have anything to say. I just wanted you to know I was home."

Janie made herself a cold drink and sat down at the table with her.

"I like having people coming and going here, and it's comforting to know where everyone is," she said.

"I know what you mean," Bettina said. "Knowing there's someone who cares enough about you to worry if you're late is a comfort to me, too."

Janie heard her, but she was also sensing something else was bothering her.

"Is something wrong?" she finally asked.

Bettina was surprised by Janie's perception of her mood.

"Not really. It's just been one of those days when unexpected things happen that leave you feeling off center. You know?

"Want to talk about it?" Janie asked.

"I stopped to take a break," Pauline said, as she walked into the kitchen. "What happened? Talk about what?"

Bettina glanced up, absently thinking how great Pauline looked, no matter what she was wearing. Today she was all long legs in skinny jeans, and wearing a tank top showing the defined muscles in her bare arms that had given her the strength to punch out Janie's attacker.

"Oh, I just had an off-putting morning," she said. "I was on my way to my first appointment when I got a call from Mike Halford, the guy from Social Services. He's the man I reported the hoarder to."

"I didn't know you'd reported him," Pauline said.

Bettina sighed. "Well, I did. I felt like there was a bigger issue going on, and I asked Janie how to go about reporting his situation. She gave me the name of a man she knew in Social Services, and so I called him. Today, he called back with an update."

"What did he say?" Janie asked.

Bettina's eyes welled as she pushed her plate aside.

"In short, the man, in his way, had been asking for help. Mike said the State Health Department was in the act of clearing out the house of all the garbage. The little dog, Tinkerbelle, was taken to a vet and is now in foster care, and the man, Dave Peterman, is in hospice. He has stage-four cancer. He was dying, and he knew it. His sole purpose for calling me was hoping I'd report him. He was afraid he'd die in the house, and there'd be no one to take care of Tinkerbelle, or even know she was there. He asked Mike if the lady dog walker was the one who reported him, and Mike said yes. He sent me a personal message, via Mike, thanking me. He wanted to be rescued. He just didn't know how to go about it."

Janie gasped. "Oh, my God, honey. Your instincts were right."

"That's so sad," Pauline said. "Thank goodness you were astute enough to realize there was more to the call than the obvious."

Bettina nodded. "I know I'll never forget him. Even in his darkest days, and knowing he was dying, that man still had more love and responsibility in him for that little dog than David Logan had for all of us."

"That gives me shivers," Pauline muttered.

"Anyway... Everyone is being taken care of, which is what matters," Bettina said, and then trashed her leftovers and put her dishes in the dishwasher. "I need to go to the DMV and renew my car tag. I could look up some locations, but Janie has become my own personal GPS. My Alexa. My Siri. So sister girl, where should I go to do this?"

Janie grinned. "Happy to oblige. I use Olivette License Agency. I'll text you the address, so you'll have it in your phone. It's been in business longer than I've been alive."

"How do you remember addresses like that?" Pauline asked.

Janie laughed. "Numbers is how I roll."

"And I appreciate your overflowing font of knowledge," Bettina said. "Is there a grocery list to fill? Or prescriptions to pick up somewhere before I come back?"

"Oh, yes. A grocery list," Janie said. "And there's money in the jar."

Bettina grabbed the list and the grocery money and headed out the door, while Janie and Pauline went back to work.

Bettina jumped in the car, drove straight to the tag agency, and went inside. The place was busy. Some people were sitting in chairs along a wall, while others were standing in different lines for different services. Once she figured out which window she needed to go to, she got in line.

A couple of minutes later, she got a text from Janie asking her to add coffee creamer to the list. She sent back a thumbs-up emoji and then for lack of anything better to do, checked her dog-walking site on Facebook to see if there were any questions or new requests.

There were so many people talking at once that it all began sounding like radio static. Just constant chatter in undertones too soft to be understood. Then, in a momentary lull, she heard clearly heard two women's voices.

"Bigamist... Saw her photo in the paper. I know it's her," and the other say, "Brainless blonde. What do you expect?"

The skin crawled on the back of Bettina's neck. But the line kept moving and she was telling herself to ignore it, ignore it, ignore it. But then they laughed out loud, and she turned around so fast she caught them staring straight at her.

The startled expressions on their faces gave them away. They knew from the look on Bettina's face that she'd heard them, and that she was pissed. Both women lifted their chins and stared back, but Bettina just kept staring them down, refusing to be the first one to look away.

The line kept moving, and Bettina moved with it, walking backward, her gaze still locked on their faces. Suddenly, she pointed a finger straight at them so fast they both jumped, as if she'd been pointing a gun. Only then did they duck their heads and look away.

"That's what I thought," Bettina muttered, and rolled her eyes, then pivoted, walked up to the counter, handed the clerk her paperwork, and did what she had come there to do.

She had the new sticker for her car tag and the paperwork in hand as she started for the door, then paused right in front of them. Two middle-aged harpies in clothes reeking of weed. Dyed black hair with white roots showing and makeup to the point of clownlike to hide the sores they'd picked on their faces.

"Shit for brains examples of humanity. Take a bath. Both of you. You reek," she said, and then sailed out the door and drove to the supermarket in a state of rage.

"I hate you, David Logan. Fucking worthless piece of shit husband you pretended to be. How is it possible that you're dead, and yet you're still messing with my life?"

And then she reached the supermarket and went inside.

It was the elevator music playing softly in the background, and the blessed air conditioning set on "blizzard" that finally cooled her down. After that, she began filling the list and adding extras now and then that she knew were needed.

Bettina was a woman without a lot of patience and with a "take no prisoners" mindset. By the time she got to the checkout lane, she'd flushed her thoughts of that incident and those women like shit down a toilet.

It was time to go home.

It was mid-afternoon at the insurance agency when the door opened, and a tall, good-looking man walked in, looked at Gretchen with surprise, and blurted out, "You're not Juana!"

"Yes. I know," Gretchen said. "Can I help you?"

He flashed a big, cheesy smile.

Gretchen did not reciprocate.

"I'm Van Ellis, Charles's brother. I need to talk to him."

"He has a client with him at the moment. Have a seat," she said.

"I'd rather talk to you," Van said, and leaned against her desk with his arms folded.

Gretchen sighed. She didn't want to be rude to family members of people she worked with, but this guy was already getting on her nerves.

"You can talk from any one of those chairs," she said.

He laughed, as if what she'd said was the funniest thing he'd ever heard, but he did back off and sit down.

"Well, since you're not Juana, if I may ask, what is your name?"

"Gretchen Lowry," she said, and turned back to her computer, but she knew he was staring, and it made her uncomfortable.

"Has anyone ever told you how much you look like Reese Witherspoon?"

Gretchen was horrified. That's what David had always said. Irked, she pretended she didn't know who that was.

"Look like who?"

"You know... The actress, Reese Witherspoon!" he said.

"Oh. Her. No. I can't say that they have," and pulled up another email.

"Are you married?" Van asked.

She stopped typing, turned, and looked him straight in the eyes.

"Your choice of conversational subject matter is entirely too personal. There are several magazines there at your elbow. Feel free to choose one to entertain yourself until your brother is free."

He blinked, then his face flushed.

"My apologies," he muttered.

Gretchen nodded, then went back to work.

A few moments later, Charles appeared with his client.

"Let me know if you have any further questions," he said to her.

"I will, Charles, and thank you," the lady said, and left the building.

Charles turned toward his brother, smiling.

"Hey bro! What brings you here?"

"Do you have a minute to talk?" Van asked.

"Sure! Come on back," Charles said, and then glanced at Gretchen. "Hey, Gretchen. This is my brother, Van. Van, this is Gretchen Lowry. She replaced Juana, who retired."

"He already introduced himself," Gretchen said, and then the phone rang, and she was tending to business when they left the lobby.

Van said nothing, and Charles sensed tension.

"Come on back," he said, and led the way into his office. The minute the door was shut, he frowned at Van. "What did you do?"

Van was instantly defensive. "I didn't do anything. I was just being friendly... making chitchat."

Charles's eyes narrowed. "Don't bullshit me, brother. I know you too well. Did you hit on her?"

Van shrugged. "Not really. I asked her if she was married, because if she was, I wouldn't want to be 'that guy', who didn't care if they were married or not. I have my own set of limits, you know. "

"Jesus, Van. Her husband recently passed."

"Oops," Van said.

"Oops doesn't begin to cover your *faux pas*. Her deceased husband was that bigamist who was all over the news a few months back? She's one of his wives. He robbed her of everything she owned. He did it to all four of the women, and I'm pretty sure the last thing any of those women want to deal with is another fast-talking man."

Van paled. "Well, hell."

Charles sighed. "Exactly. Now, why are we having this conversation?"

Van slumped into a chair. "I'm going to trade cars and wanted to know how much higher my insurance would be if I went from a sedan to a sports car."

"I can help you with that," Charles said. "What kind of car are you thinking about getting?"

The conversation then shifted from Van's social *faux pas* to cars, and the moment passed for Van.

But not for Gretchen. She was angry that she'd felt so defensive, but it was all because she'd immediately seen him as a predator, and that was David's fault. She wasn't old, and she wasn't dead. There was nothing wrong with some guy hitting on her. Yes, he'd gotten too personal, but her feelings were so raw that she didn't know how to deflect without being insulted. Maybe time would heal that, but she was a long way from being there.

A short while later, Sarah came up to the front desk and immediately noticed Gretchen's ready smile was missing.

"Everything okay?" she asked.

"Yes," Gretchen said. "Do you want that stuff to go in the mail?"

"Yes, please," Sarah said, and laid the stack of envelopes she was holding into a wire basket on Gretchen's desk. She glanced at her again, then thought better of pushing the issue and went back to her office.

When Charles and his brother finally came out, Gretchen was

in the breakroom getting a bottle of water. She heard them walking up the hall and waited as they said goodbye to each other before she came out. She met Charles on his way back to his office and could tell by the look on Charles's face that he knew his brother had gotten out of line, but she didn't want him apologizing for something he didn't do.

Then he opened his mouth, and she knew he was going to do it anyway.

"Hey, Gretchen..."

"Nope," she said, and kept walking.

Charles sighed. *Damn it, Van. Look what you did.* Then he shrugged it off and went back to work.

Gretchen was at her desk when the mailman came by, delivered their incoming mail, and picked up the outgoing. They had a couple of walk-ins later in the afternoon, along with the rest of the day's appointments. When it was finally quitting time, Gretchen was the first one out the door.

Sarah came up front and was surprised she was already gone.

"Hey, what happened here today that I don't know about?" she asked.

Lisa shrugged.

Charles frowned. "Van was here. Made an ass of himself and hit on Gretchen. She didn't say much, but she didn't take it well. I tried to talk to her about it after Van left, and she cut me short with a 'Nope', like she didn't want to discuss it, so I let it go."

"Crap," Sarah said. "Well, maybe she will have worked through whatever it was that bothered her about it by tomorrow."

"She's pretty. Why would she be offended about being flirted with?" Lisa asked.

Sarah frowned. "You're not even married Lisa, let alone ever been widowed, so I'm not going to try and explain how broken she must be feeling. And Gretchen has been widowed twice now. I can't speak for how she feels about it, but I can promise you, being married to someone who victimized you will put a really big chip on your shoulder."

"That's harsh," Lisa said. "I didn't know she'd been widowed twice. I feel bad for blowing off her attitude. I'm sorry."

Sarah nodded. "Personal business needs to stay personal."

"Yes, ma'am," Lisa said. "I'm going home. Got a date."

"Have fun," Charles said. "I'm taking the family for spaghetti tonight."

Sarah groaned. "That sounds good, but I'm too tired to go out. The hubs is grilling tonight. I want food at home with my feet up. You guys head out. I'll lock up."

CHAPTER TWELVE

Gretchen hadn't run away from anything in her entire life. She'd always faced trouble head-on. But when her workday was over, she ran. Without saying goodbye to anyone. Without acknowledging that she was upset. And now she felt like a coward. By the time she pulled up in the drive and got out, she was on the verge of tears.

Then the sound of laughter and the scent of dinner cooking washed over her, and all the angst she'd been feeling disappeared. This house and these women were her safe place to fall. Swallowing past the lump in her throat, she called out.

"I'm home!"

Within seconds she was swarmed.

"It's party night," Janie said, and handed her a stuffed mushroom on a napkin.

Bettina handed her a cocktail.

And Pauline hugged her.

Gretchen laughed. "What are we celebrating?"

"Us!" Janie said.

"I'll drink to that," Gretchen said, and took a sip of her drink. "Yum! This is amazing. What is it?"

"A Miss Bee special," Janie said.

"Who's Miss Bee?" Gretchen said.

Bettina held up her hand. "Me! B is for Bettina, the best mixologist behind a bar you'll ever meet!"

"All the better to hurry back down," Gretchen said, holding her food and drink. "And I'm taking these with me while I change."

"Hurry back," Pauline said. "Dinner is nearly ready."

Gretchen popped the little mushroom in her mouth and headed upstairs, chiding herself for letting a man with a little brain and a big ego upset her to the point of tears. The incident today had been nothing more than a milestone moment in the life of a widow. Being reminded that she hadn't died with David had been a shock. She'd let herself feel guilty for being attractive. And angry that someone noticed it and stepped over a line. But in the grand scheme of life, Van Ellis meant nothing.

She changed quickly, switching work clothes for shorts and a shirt, and her dress shoes for sandals, sipping on her drink as she went. By the time she came back down, she was relaxed and happy.

To her surprise, the dining room table had been set for a meal, and the crystal chandelier was doing a grand imitation of a Disco ball by refracting light all over the ceiling. A small plate of the appetizers had been moved from the kitchen to the dining room, along with veggie crudités and dill dip grandly displayed on an ornate serving tray.

"Wow! This is like dining under the stars!" Gretchen said, as Janie walked in carrying a steamy baking dish straight from the oven and put it on a hot pad. "Is that smothered chicken?"

"Yes, in mushroom sauce," Janie said. "It's something my mother used to make for Sunday dinners."

Gretchen sighed. "Mine did, too! I love this and haven't had it in years!' Pauline came in with a large bowl of tossed salad, and Bettina was carrying two side dishes. Pauline followed with a pitcher of tea to fill up the glasses, and then they sat.

Plates were passed and filled.

The Broke-Ass Women's Club was in session.

"Janie, this chicken is amazing," Gretchen said.

"Thank you. I don't cook nearly enough, and I should, because I enjoy it. Seems like I'm always home with my nose in numbers. Tell me what went on in your world today."

Gretchen rolled her eyes. "I got hit on, and it took me by surprise."

"As I keep saying, we're not the ones who died," Bettina muttered, and poked a bite of chicken into her mouth.

"What did you do?" Pauline asked.

Gretchen sighed. "I did not handle it well. It sort of scared me, and then I sulled up like a pissed-off possum."

"Made you feel like you were cheating, didn't it?" Janie asked.

The girls looked up from their plates, surprised by her comment. Janie had never let on to any of them that she felt this vulnerable. She was their rock.

"Yes!" Gretchen said. "Has that happened to you?"

"Nobody's made an actual pass at me, but I see them looking...

considering their chances. And since the mere thought of getting involved with another man makes me sick to my stomach, I immediately resent their assumptions," Janie said.

"It took me a while to get over it," Gretchen said. "I know he offended me, and that was enough."

"You stand your ground, girl," Pauline said. "Just because we're flying solo now doesn't mean we don't know how to fly alone."

"Ooh, that's bumper sticker worthy," Janie said.

"It's too long for a bumper sticker. Maybe a flag," Pauline said.

Janie grinned. "Always the pragmatic one."

Gretchen quickly shifted the conversation.

"Hey, Bettina. This was your first day with your three other clients. How did it go?"

"Good. I have the cutest Yorkie named Bruce. A little rescue dog named Charlotte, and a Jack Russell terrier named Puppy. She's a sweetheart. Oh, I'm seconding Gretchen. This chicken is delicious."

"There's plenty if anyone wants seconds," Janie said.

Never one to be shy, Bettina picked up her plate. "Yes, please."

Janie put another piece of chicken on her plate, along with some more mushroom gravy.

"Moochaz grasscias," Bettina said.

"I didn't know you spoke Spanish," Pauline said.

Bettina snorted. "Did you not hear that appalling accent? I don't speak Spanish. I barely do intelligent English. I was just showing off."

The room echoed from their laughter. They kept trading stories throughout the meal, and again after the table was cleared. Then they carried dessert and coffee outside to the back verandah to watch the sunset.

"Best way to greet the night is with cake," Pauline said.

"I'll eat to that," Janie said, and curled her feet up beneath her, settling into an old wicker chair with blue gingham pillows.

Almost immediately, Gretchen spotted Florence, the next-door neighbor, on the back deck of her house.

"Oh, look! There's Florence!" Gretchen said. "I'm going to see if she wants to have dessert with us."

"Good idea," Janie said, as Gretchen took off toward the fence.

"Hey Florence! What are you doing?" Gretchen asked.

"Oh, just watching the sunset."

"Are you alone?" Gretchen asked.

"Yes, my family went to play miniature golf."

"Come have cake and coffee with us," Gretchen said.

Florence smiled. "I'd love to."

"Great," Gretchen said. "You know the drill. I'll meet you at the front door," she said, then headed back to the house on the run.

"Is she coming?" Janie asked.

"Yep. I'm going to let her in right now," Gretchen said.

"I'll get her cake and coffee," Pauline said, and followed her inside.

Moments later, Florence came outside carrying a dessert plate with a piece of coconut cream cake. Pauline was behind her, carrying her coffee.

The smile on her face was evidence of her delight as she sat down in a chair beside them.

"Thank you, girls," she said, took a bite of cake, and rolled her eyes. "Oh, my word! This is so good."

"Pauline made it," Janie said.

"You are an amazing baker," Florence said.

Pauline smiled. "I'm pleased you like it."

Then they all picked up their forks and their cake plates and turned toward the West as they ate. The sun was already below the treetops, and the evening sky was beginning to explode into a vast array of oranges and purples.

"Just look at that," Florence said.

"Magnificent," Janie said.

"God's sure showin' off," Bettina said, and licked her fork.

Gretchen sighed. She didn't have words for how all this made her feel, but it was certainly making up for the funk she'd brought home with her.

Pauline was silent, but there were tears in her eyes. None of them knew, and she wasn't going to talk about it, but when David had been home, they'd often watched the sunset together. She used to think he was special, but not anymore. Knowing their marriage hadn't been real had broken a part of her that would never going to heal.

And so they sat, eating and drinking, and telling stories about life that made them laugh. No one wanted to cry. Tonight was too special for tears.

Pauline walked Florence home, and then locked up when she came back inside.

Janie was in the kitchen emptying the coffee pot and putting the dessert dishes into the dishwasher. As soon as it was loaded, she started it up.

"Need any help?" Pauline asked.

Janie smiled as she looked up.

"No. I've got it. You go on up, honey. See you in the morning."

Pauline nodded but didn't move. From where she stood, the light over Janie's head made it look like she was wearing a halo. And it fit. Never in her life had she ever met anyone more likely to be an earth angel than Janie Logan. Such a mighty force within this tiny woman.

And then Pauline blinked, and the halo was gone.

"Night, Janie. See you in the morning."

"Sleep well," Janie said, and then hung up the wet dishcloth and turned out the lights.

Rachel Edwards was in her Amtrak roomette, on her way to Oregon, getting ready to go to bed. Lulled by the motion and the sound of the train, she was exhausted, mentally and physically.

Since her trip was so long, she'd splurged for the private room, which included meals and a bathroom and shower. As tiny as it was, it was also the nicest, cleanest place she'd ever in her life slept in, and since she didn't know what was ahead of her in Salem, she decided to take advantage of the little luxury while she could.

She had spotty access to WiFi, but when she could, she kept searching online for jobs in Salem, and for the cheapest places to stay, all with the continuing hope that those four wives would not come looking for her.

As she crawled into her bunk for the night, she thought about her childhood and her life on the road with David and her mom. They'd always been on the move. Looking back, she guessed it was because they, too, were on the run from either the law or people they'd conned.

She sighed, accepting that the apple had not fallen far from the tree, and then closed her eyes and fell into a deep, dreamless sleep.

As she dressed the next morning, she looked out the window at the passing scenery, trying to figure out where she was, and then decided it didn't matter, because the closer she got to Salem, the farther away she was from the trouble she'd unleashed.

The rest of the week unrolled without drama for Janie and the girls, which eased the energy in the house.

Bettina changed her walking route for Puppy and got one more dog to walk. The teenager, who'd come to see if they needed help the day Loki got the thorn in his paw, was good on his word. He had mentioned her to his grandmother, after all, and now she was walking Pinky the poodle, which made five dogs a day, and she wasn't getting home until mid-afternoon.

Janie took on a new client, and Pauline was putting the finishing touches on the gym owner who'd wanted PUBIC ACCESS written in big red letters on his website. Even though she had corrected the spelling, it still made her laugh just thinking of the shock value that would have generated.

Gretchen went to work every day with a better understanding of how to deal with her own emotions and made peace with the fact that being a woman with big boobs and a pretty face, it was a given she would get hit on.

And for all of them, it felt as if the chaos caused from David's death was ending and their lives were finally settling into safe routines.

After almost four days on the road, Rachel Edwards reached Salem, Oregon. She gathered up her luggage, hailed a cab, and was driven to the room she'd reserved at a nearby motel.

It wasn't the Hilton, but it was a room, and she wasn't on the streets. Her immediate plan was simple, and one she had no worries about finding. She was aiming for a waitress job where the tips were good.

In her mind, she'd escaped.

It was time to start over.

It was mid-afternoon of Pauline's birthday.

Janie was getting ready to run errands when her phone rang. The moment she saw it was James Halford, she dropped everything and answered.

"Hello?"

"Hello, Janie. We finally received a reply from Rachel Edwards' lawyer. She has withdrawn the claim. Everything has been dropped and cleared in the court."

"Thank God," Janie said. "One less hassle to have to deal with, and I hope it is the last. Thank you so much."

"You're welcome. I'll send you a final bill on this issue, and we'll call it closed."

"That will be one bill I won't mind paying," she said. "Have a good day, and thanks for letting me know."

"Absolutely," James said, and disconnected.

Janie breathed a quick sigh of relief. One more bad memory from David Logan's past had been wiped clean, so she picked her up things again and headed out, anxious to get everything done. Thunderheads were building on the horizon. Hopefully it would just be wind and rain, but this was storm season, and nothing was guaranteed.

Her first stop was at the pharmacy to pick up toiletries, and some Godiva chocolates for Pauline. Pauline hadn't told any of them it was her birthday, but Janie made it her business months ago to find out the dates of all their birthdays. Parties were fun, and getting a year older deserved a celebration, especially in this, the Year of Broke-Ass Women.

As soon as she was finished at the pharmacy, she headed to a local deli to pick up party food, and then to the bakery to pick up the cake she'd ordered. Her last stop was at Flowers by Baxter to get the birthday bouquet. She glanced at the clock on the dash as she got out. It was nearing quitting time for most businesses, and she wanted to get home before five o'clock traffic.

Baxter saw her come in, and went to meet her, giving her a kiss on the cheek and a quick hug.

"Janie, darling! It's so good to see you. I have your bouquet ready, and what fun! A surprise party. What do you think? Is this okay?" he asked, knowing full well she was going to rave, because all of his work was amazing.

"Okay? It's gorgeous," Janie said. "Blue is her favorite color, and those blue Dutch Irises are stunning."

"I'll carry it to the car for you," Baxter said, and swooped it up from the counter. He picked up a cardboard box, too.

"Wait, I need to pay for it first," Janie said.

"You don't owe me a thing. This is on the house."

Janie beamed. "That's so sweet of you, Baxter. I'll be sure to let her know of your generosity!"

"My pleasure," Baxter said, then settled the box in the car seat and put the arrangement in the box. "This will help you get it home safely. Have fun," he said, and went back inside.

Janie drove away with one hand on the box to keep it from sliding and breathed a sigh of relief when she finally pulled up and parked beneath the portico. Bettina was home, and Gretchen would be, soon. So she grabbed the sack from the pharmacy and slipped inside.

Bettina was in the kitchen when Janie came in.

"Is Pauline still upstairs?" Janie asked.

Bettina nodded.

"Good. Come help me carry stuff in," she said.

They were walking down the front steps when Gretchen pulled up and parked.

"Yay! Just in time," Janie said. "If you'll carry the cake box, and Bettina gets the bouquet, I'll get the big bag from the deli."

"This is going to be so much fun," Gretchen said, as they piled into the house and went straight to the kitchen. They began getting things out of bags and boxes, and setting everything in place, anxious to get everything in place before Pauline appeared.

Janie signed a birthday card and laid it on top of the box of chocolates. Bettina had bought her a jar of bath salts, and Gretchen had her a pair of soft, fuzzy socks, because Pauline was always complaining of cold feet.

They arranged the gifts around the flowers, then laid out party food beside the birthday cake.

"Did you get candles?" Bettina asked.

"There's a fancy one in the pantry," Janie said. "It looks like the Eiffel Tower. It's in a little box."

"How stinkin' cute is this?" Gretchen said, as she put the candle on the cake. "Why the Eiffel Tower?"

"Who doesn't want to go to Paris?" Janie said.

Bettina giggled. "Right?" Then she lowered her voice. "Do we know how old she's gonna be?"

Janie shrugged. "She's the last and youngest wife, and it doesn't matter. What does matter is that this has been the year from hell, and we're all still here."

"Amen to that, sister," Gretchen said. "I'm going to go change out of my work clothes. Want me to bring Pauline down with me?"

"Yes!" Janie said.

"I'll hurry," Gretchen said, and took off upstairs.

Less than ten minutes later, Janie heard footsteps and voices.

"Here they come!" she said.

Bettina lined up behind the island with Janie, waiting for them to walk in, and when they did, all three of the girls shouted, "HAPPY BIRTHDAY!!! SURPRISE! SURPRISE!"

Pauline gasped, and then started grinning.

"Oh, my God! You scared the crap out of me! What have you done?"

"We are throwing a surprise birthday party for you!" Janie said. "We have flowers and presents, food and a birthday cake!"

"I can't believe this! I thought I was going to let this one pass without notice!"

"No way!" Janie said. "This is the year for surviving shit. Not ignoring it!"

"Amen to that!" Bettina said.

"Open your presents!" Gretchen said. "I'm starving."

The girls watched in quiet delight as they stood around the island, while Pauline cried over the cards, opened the gifts, and then thanked them profusely.

"This is wonderful! I haven't had a birthday like this since my grandparents died. Thank you from the bottom of my heart."

"You're welcome!" Janie said. "And now we eat before Gretchen passes out from starvation."

They piled their plates full of goodies, and carried them to the table, talking as they went.

"Well, girls, I finally heard back from my lawyer today. David's fake daughter called off her claim. Nothing like debt to end pipe dreams," Janie said.

"Good," Bettina said. "I hope she has nightmares about collection agencies for the rest of her life."

"I enrolled online today to take classes to get a real estate license," Gretchen said, and popped a stuffed olive in her mouth.

"Oh, my gosh! That's wonderful!" Pauline said.

Gretchen shrugged. "I got to thinking, I need a job that will provide me with a decent living where I can still be my own boss. Sitting in the insurance agency, listing to customers talking about buying and selling their houses, and getting insurance to cover remodels, is what made me think of it. And the more I thought, the more I liked the idea."

"I'm proud of you," Bettina said. "I love dogs, but I've already realized being a dog walker is not a career. It's a job. I want to finish my degree. I'm looking into taking online classes from one of the colleges here."

Janie sat quietly, watching the girls faces, and remembering how defeated they'd all been when they'd first met at the funeral home.

"You should all be so proud of yourselves. We lost our footing this year in the worst possible way, but nobody threw up their hands and quit. And now look where you are. Working and planning for the futures you want."

"But Janie, none of this would be happening if it hadn't been for you. We were drowning, and you saved us," Pauline said."You gave us sanctuary and time."

Bettina nodded. "Yes, you did. And I hope you know you're also stuck with us for the rest of your life. I've lost all the family I care to lose in this life, and I'm not quitting on you. Ever."

"Broke-Ass Women's Club, or whatever you want to call us, I call you sister," Gretchen said.

Tears rolled down Janie's face, but she was laughing.

"I am perfectly happy being stuck with all of you forever—if that's what you want. And I also want some more cold shrimp and cocktail sauce. Now no more of this making me cry business. We still have food to eat, and we also have to set the Eiffel Tower on fire before we can cut cake."

That night, Pauline sat on the side of her bed, brushing her long dark hair and eyeing the bouquet she'd carried to her room, along with the gifts and the cards, and felt such peace.

From the moment she'd learned that her mother was never coming back for her, she'd grieved the abandonment. Even though her grandparents had loved her and raised her as their own, the hole in her heart had never filled.

Her first husband had been worthless, but she'd wanted so badly to be loved that she'd married him anyway and suffered the consequences. Being abandoned meant she was unworthy of love, and when he'd left, she assumed again it was because she wasn't worth loving. David's lies and betrayal had only made it worse. Nothing and no one had ever filled that emptiness within her.

Until now.

These women had become family—sisters in the truest sense of the word.

She laid the hairbrush aside, and then wound her hair up and clipped it to the top of her head, grabbed the jar of bath salts Gretchen had given her, and headed for the bathtub. She was ending this most perfect day with a most perfect soak in lavender scented bath salts and thanking God for putting her in this place.

Gretchen was online in her bedroom, already going through the prerequisites for becoming a realtor, more than ready to open her mind to something new. She was envisioning the real estate office that would be hers one day, and the sign over the door.

Four Sisters Realty.

She was so going to rock that job.

Bettina was kicked back on her bed, going through info about the local colleges, and trying to figure out how to get her old transcript from Kansas State University.

Janie was in the tub and up to her chin in bubbles. Today had been a positive day from beginning to end, but she was tired, and a long, hot soak in a jetted tub was always good for what ailed you.

She leaned against the little pillow beneath her neck as the jets of water pummeled her body, thinking of how drastically her life had changed, and even though it had taken a death for her to see it, changed for the better.

Life had kicked them in the gut, and they'd kicked back with a vengeance.

CHAPTER THIRTEEN

Months passed and life with it.

Gretchen was studying to take a test for her realtor's license.

Bettina was enrolled in online classes at Maryville University and working toward finishing her degree.

It was October, and last night's rain had left a chill in the morning air.

Bettina was dressed for the weather with her hair pulled back at the nape of her neck, wearing jeans, a long-sleeved shirt, and a quilted jacket. She loved all the dogs she walked, but she was partial to Loki. He was a charmer, and she was looking forward to their walk as she drove to the Attilla property.

A short while later, she arrived at the house, grabbed her backpack, holstered her can of Mace, and took a leash with her as she got out, strode up the steps, and rang the doorbell.

Barb came to the door with Loki at her heels.

"Morning, Bettina! I hope you're ready for Loki. He's been to the door twice this morning, so I know he was looking for you."

Bettina laughed and knelt down to clip her leash on Loki's harness and give him a quick pet.

"We do have ourselves a good time," Bettina said. "And it's a nice, cool morning, so the walk itself will be pleasant. See you soon."

The housekeeper went back inside and closed the door as Bettina took off with Loki in the lead, as always, his little tail bobbing with every bouncy step he took.

The leaves on the trees were turning—some the color of cocky cardinals, some sunflower yellow, and some tangerine orange, leaving the dark evergreen trees more noticeable now than they'd ever been in the summer. Fallen leaves were rife upon the brown grass, making Loki's forays into the bushes even more fun to explore, and making Bettina's job of keeping things out of his little mouth that much more difficult.

They'd done the tour, pooped the poop, and had a drink and a treat, and were making their way home when Bettina heard someone shout. She pulled up on Loki's leash to stop him, and then turned around to see what was happening. When she did, her heart stopped.

A huge dog was running toward them without making a sound. No growling. No barking. Just steel-eyed intent on an attack, and at that moment, Bettina knew there was a chance neither she nor Loki would live through this.

She was screaming for help as she ran for Loki and swept him up in her arms. The moment she had him, she pulled the Mace from the holster, spun, and aimed.

The dog was only seconds away, and she was still screaming and shouting for help. Loki was barking and whining, and she held onto him with both arms to keep him from leaping out of her grip.

The dog growled as it leaped, and when it was in the air, she sprayed the mace full force in its face. It yelped as it hit her, and they all went down in a tumble.

The mace had momentarily blinded the dog, but it hadn't stopped it. Now it was in a frenzy of rage and pain, snapping, snarling, and biting.

Loki was crying and yipping, and Bettina could feel the big dog's teeth in her legs. She was kicking and rolling, still holding onto Loki as she sprayed the dog one more time, and then rolled over, curled her body up on top of Loki and prayed to be saved.

All of a sudden, there were voices all around her, shouting at the dog, and then the weight of it was off her body, and she could hear people running. Someone else was at her side, touching her head, then her back.

"The police and an ambulance have been called. Can you sit up. I need to see how bad you're hurt," a woman said.

Bettina rolled over, still holding Loki, and that's when they saw the little dog she'd sheltered beneath her.

"Oh, my God. Bless your heart. Bless your heart."

Bettina sat up with Loki clutched against her breasts. Her eyes were burning from the Mace, and Loki was whining and rubbing his face against her jacket.

"My backpack. Water. I need water."

The woman tore into the backpack, pulled out two bottles of

water and opened them. Bettina sloshed her own eyes with water so she could see what she was doing, and then sat Loki in her lap and began washing his little eyes and face, over and over, until he quit whining and collapsed against her, trembling in every muscle.

"I'm Carol Benning. I need to look at your legs, honey. You're bleeding."

Bettina nodded and put her face against Loki's head as the woman pulled aside the ripped fabric and poured some water on the cuts and puncture wounds. It only made them burn worse. At that point, Bettina grabbed her phone and called Shelby. It rang a couple of times before she picked up, and Bettina could hear the concern in Shelby's voice.

"Hello? Bettina? Is something wrong?

"Yes. We're about a block and a half away from your house. We just got attacked by a big dog. Loki wasn't bitten, but when I maced the dog, we both got a dose of it, too. I can't walk. I need you to come get him and take him to the vet to make sure his eyes and lungs are okay. We're on Oak Street."

"Oh, my God! Honey! Were you bitten?"

"Yes. But I'll be okay. Just come get the baby."

The line went dead in Bettina's ear, and then she called Janie.

"Hello? Bettina? Is something wrong?" Janie asked.

"Loki and I were attacked. Big dog. Can you come get me? I can't walk."

"Oh, Jesus," Janie muttered. "Where are you? Where's the dog?"

"Some people stopped to help me and ran it off. We're on Oak Street, about a block and a half away from the Attilla property. I'm bleeding. Police were called."

"Pauline and I were running errands, and we're not very far away. We'll be there in minutes." Janie said, and the line went dead.

Bettina put her phone back in her jacket pocket and then cuddled Loki close, talking and petting as she continued to flush his eyes, until he finally quit shaking.

Now more people were gathering, and Bettina could hear the Benning family telling the crowd around them what had happened, and that one of their sons had caught the attack on video.

And then suddenly, Shelby Attilla was pushing through the crowd. She took one look at Bettina and Loki and burst into tears.

"Oh, sweetheart. You are so hurt," Shelby said, as she knelt beside Bettina, and then scooped Loki up in her arms.

"But I'm not dead," Bettina said.

And then Carol Benning spoke up.

"We saw the whole thing happening from a block away and got here as quick as we could. My husband and sons beat the dog off her, and it ran away. She saved your little dog by covering it with her body."

Shelby just kept shaking her head in disbelief. "You sacrificed yourself to keep him safe!"

And then in the midst of the crowd, the police arrived and began assessing what had happened. They got Bettina's statement, but all she could tell them was that it was a big reddish-brown dog with short hair.

Then they heard the story from the Bennings, including having a video. But once they realized the Bennings had been driving a convertible, giving them a clear line of sight to video the attack, they knew they'd lucked out and called Animal Control to assist in hunting it down. Mr. Benning and his sons showed the police the direction in which the dog had run off and sent the video to the officer's phone to help them identify the dog.

But Bettina was frantic about Loki's welfare.

"Shelby, please get Loki to the vet. It took forever for him to quit shaking, and I know his eyes are still burning because mine are." And then she saw Janie and Pauline pushing their way through the crowd. "See. My sisters are here now. I'll be fine."

Shelby nodded. "Okay, but I'll be in touch. We love you dearly for saving Loki. I'll call you later to make sure you're okay," and then she took off through the crowd with her little dog in her arms as Janie and Pauline dropped to their knees beside Bettina.

Bettina kept trying to focus, to tell them how grateful she was for the simple sights of their faces, but she was still locked into the attack, shaking from the pain and trying not to scream.

The girls were in shock, seeing the visible evidence of what she'd endured. There was blood everywhere. Her jeans had been ripped to shreds, leaving her wounds painfully visible.

"Oh honey... Dear God! I am so sorry. Where's the ambulance?" Janie said, as she wrapped her arms around Bettina's shoulders.

"I don't know. They called for one," she said, and buried her face against Janie's neck.

"I hear sirens now," Pauline said, as she smoothed Bettina's hair away from her face. "Oh no! Your jacket is torn, too. Did it bite your back and arms, too?"

"I don't know. I just hurt all over," Bettina said, and then burst into tears. "I thought I was going to die. Carol and her family saved me," she said, and pointed to the woman sitting at her feet.

At that point, Carol began explaining it again.

"Thank you so much," Pauline said, and got the woman's info, then gave her an email, asking for her to send them a copy of the video.

When the police came back to question Bettina further, Janie added her info to the mix.

"I'm Janie Logan, one of Bettina's next of kin. Would you please put me down as the contact person to be notified when this dog is found? And will we be given the name and info of the owners?"

"If we can find it, it will all be on the incident report," the officer said. "You can call the precinct and request a copy."

"Thank you," Janie said, and then the ambulance arrived, and the EMTs moved everyone away so they could get to Bettina.

Bettina reached in her pocket and handed her phone and car keys to Pauline.

"Will you drive it home for me? And I have my dog walking clients' numbers in a group on my phone. Please let them know I won't be there today. They're going to be wondering what happened."

"Of course," Pauline said, and took the phone and the keys as the EMTs began assessing Bettina's wounds. Then they loaded her up into the ambulance and headed for the hospital, while Janie and Pauline headed to the Attilla property to get Bettina's car.

As Janie was driving, Pauline sent a text to the dog walking group to let them know what had happened, and that Bettina would contact them later as to when walks could resume.

"I can't believe this just happened," Janie said. "It had to be terrifying."

Pauline nodded. "Thank God those people witnessed it and saved her. Now if the police and animal control can only locate that dog and owner, we'll be able to file charges against them."

"Including loss of income," Janie said.

Pauline sighed. "I can't help but wonder how this is going to impact her dog-walking job."

"I know how I would feel, but I'm kind of afraid of dogs anyway, so this would end my dog-walking days. Oh, here's her car," Janie said, and she pulled up behind it.

Pauline grabbed her things and got out.

"Meet you at the ER," Janie said.

"The same one they took you to?" Pauline asked.

"Yes," Janie said, and reached for her phone to call Gretchen while Pauline was getting in the car.

The call was ringing as she drove off, with Pauline right behind her.

Gretchen was going through emails when her cell phone rang.

She saw Janie's name come up on Caller ID and answered.

"Hey, Janie. What's up?"

"Bettina is in an ambulance on the way to ER. She was attacked by a loose dog while she was walking Loki."

Gretchen felt the blood draining from her face. "Oh, my God. How bad is she hurt?"

"Bad enough. Pauline and I are on the way to the ER now."

"Where did they take her?" Gretchen asked.

"To SSM Health, the same hospital where they took me," Janie said.

"I'll find it," Gretchen said. "I'll see you soon."

"Okay, but there's no need to speed. Her life is not in danger. She's just really hurt."

"Understood," Gretchen said, and disconnected, then took off down the hall to Sarah's office. The door was open, and Sarah was at her computer when Gretchen knocked, then walked in.

"Sarah, Janie just called me. Bettina was just attacked by a dog as she was dog-walking this morning. She's on her way to ER, and I need to go. As soon as I see her and know if she's going to be okay, I'll be back to finish out the day."

Sarah shuddered. "My honest-to-God worst fear. I am afraid to go walking in my own neighborhood because of that. I'm so sorry. Yes, of course you must go. Switch the office calls to my phone, and I'll tend to business until you get back."

"Thank you," Gretchen said, and headed for the breakroom to get her things. She stopped back by her desk long enough to log out of her computer, and switch the calls, then she was gone.

The police were on the hunt, as was Animal Control. With a vicious dog on the loose, there would likely be other victims unless it was found. They had called in multiple units to patrol the area, all looking for a large, reddish-brown, short-hair. They knew it had been sprayed with Mace, so it would likely be exhibiting recognizable behaviors, like whining and drooling, excessive licking, and for certain showing signs of irritated eyes and mouth.

And then they lucked out.

The St. Louis Police Department received a call from an angry dog owner named Tony Watts, stating someone had Maced his dog and he wanted to file a report. Realizing the call had come from an area near where the search was taking place, the information was quickly relayed to the searchers. Within minutes, multiple patrol cars descended upon the complainant's address.

A couple of officers went to the door, rang the bell, and were soon greeted by a big, middle-aged man with a shock of graying hair. He was red-faced and furious until he saw police and a van from Animal Control pulling up in his drive.

"Tony Watts?" an officer asked.

His frown deepened. "Yes, I'm Tony Watts? What the hell is all this?"

"You reported your dog had been Maced. Will you please bring the dog to the door?"

"It's hurt, dammit! What is Animal Control doing here?"

"We're searching for a dog who just attacked a woman. She Maced it as it was attacking her and the small dog she was walking. She is seriously injured. We need you to bring your dog to the door for identification."

Watt's eyes widened. "I don't think my—"

"We have video of the entire attack from passersby who stopped to help and ultimately saved her. So, if you want to clear your dog of the attack, then show us what it looks like."

"Fuck," Watts muttered, and then turned around and yelled. "Darrin! Bring Judge to the door."

A few moments later, a teenage boy came into view, with a big reddish-brown dog on a leash.

"Me and Mom are just getting ready to take him to the vet," he said.

But Tony Watts was beginning to realize that might not happen.

The officers looked at the dog. It matched the look of the one in the video, and it had all the symptoms, right down to the red, watering eyes and mouth. It was whining in pain and slobbering profusely.

"What breed of dog is this?" one asked.

"It's a Rhodesian Ridgeback," Watts said. "Damn good guard dog."

"It's also the dog we've been looking for," the officer said, and waved at the Animal Control officers to come forward.

"I don't believe you!" Watts said. "Show me the video."

And so they did, and the look on Tony Watt's face went from shock to horror in seconds.

"Oh, my God," he muttered. "I don't know how this happened. Judge has been in the back yard all morning."

Then his son, Darrin, ducked his head. "Not all morning, Dad. I guess I didn't latch the gate securely when I took out the trash. I didn't know he was gone until about thirty minutes ago, when I saw him come running toward the house. I just shut him back up in the yard and then saw something was wrong with him afterward. That's when I told you."

The officer pointed at the dog. "Animal Control will be taking it into custody now. You need to provide them with verification of vaccinations, and whatever medical treatment the dog needs, it will get. But do not assume you'll get him back. He tried to kill a woman. We'll need your information for the victim. At a minimum, you will be responsible for her medical bills. And she is free to file a civil suit against you, too."

Tony Watts was speechless, then turned on his son. "Look what your carelessness caused."

And then the officer contradicted him. "No, sir. Having a dog this unpredictable and aggressive is what caused the incident. Otherwise, it would have just been a loose dog complaint."

Tony Watts frowned, then looked away. There was no arguing with the truth.

The boy was wild-eyed and already in a panic. "I'm sorry, Dad."

"I'm sorry, too," Watts said, watching in disbelief as two officers from Animal Control led their dog to a van and drove away.

As soon as the needed information had been received, the police were gone, and Tony Watts was on the phone with his lawyer, verifying the extent of his liability.

Bettina was on an exam table in ER, stripped of her clothing, and mostly covered with a sheet, except for where the bite marks were. Between shock and the adrenaline crash, she still couldn't stop shaking. They were flushing out the puncture wounds, and cleaning up the gashes on her arm, and on both legs. The teeth marks on her back were minimal thanks to the quilted jacket she'd been wearing and were little more than scratches. The trauma team talked to her the entire time they were working, knowing that the simple act of answering their questions would help her focus on something besides the pain.

Bettina kept watching the door, and when Pauline and Janie finally walked in, the relief she felt was immediate.

"These are my sisters," Bettina said.

The doctor eyed the women and frowned. It wouldn't be the first time someone tried to pass friends off as family just to get into ER.

"You don't look alike," he said.

"Maybe not, but we were all scammed by, and married to, the same man at the same time. So, that has to count for something," Janie snapped.

His eyebrows rose, then he grinned.

"Point taken. Just stay out of the way."

Bettina saw the fire in Janie's eyes and relaxed. Going through shit like this alone was one thing. But having her sisters' backup was all she needed. And when they began deadening all the areas on the front and backs of her legs they were about to sew up, Bettina just closed her eyes and kept thinking, *Having babies hurts worse. Having babies hurts worse.*

As Gretchen was leaving the agency, she was remembering they'd cut the clothes off Janie when she'd been attacked, so she headed home first to get some clothes for Bettina, just in case.

She went in the house on the run, bolted up the stairs to Bettina's room, and went for the loosest, most comfortable things Bettina wore—pajamas, a bathrobe, and slippers. She stuffed them all in a bag, then headed for the hospital.

This whole incident was a horrible reminder of how random life was, and how quickly it could end. While she'd been at the agency blithely answering phones and emails and directing clients to the proper offices, Bettina had been fighting for her life, and none of them had known it. It was as random and unexpected as David's death. The blessing here was that Bettina had survived. She shed a few tears, then sucked it up and kept driving. Dwelling on old wounds and unfounded fears solved nothing.

By the time she reached the hospital and drove around to the ER entrance, she was hoping to walk in on Bettina fussing with doctors and ordering everyone around.

But when she walked into the room carrying the sack with the clothes, and saw Bettina, then the bloody wounds on her body, and the doctor shooting her up to deaden the pain so they could suture the gashes. She nearly went to her knees. It was all she could do to speak.

"Hey, Miss Bee. I'm here, too," she said.

Bettina opened her eyes, and when she saw Gretchen, fresh tears welled. "Hey, girl. I'm a mess, aren't I?"

"You are always a mess. It's why we love you," Gretchen said. "You will heal from this, just like we're healing from the load of shit we've been wading through all year. Be tough, sister. We've got your back."

The doctor laid a hand on Bettina's shoulder. "We'll give the shots a couple of minutes to work, and then suture the gashes on the front of your legs before turning you over to do the ones on the backs of your legs."

"Then can I go home? "I don't have insurance. I can't afford hospital care."

The doctor hesitated. "I would release you on contingency. You're not going to be able to care for yourself at first, but if you have someone who can come stay with—"

"She lives with us," Janie said. "We'll take care of her."

He eyed the women, and then nodded. "I don't doubt that for a moment."

By the time they'd finished with stitches and bandages, Bettina had been given a shot for tetanus, a shot of antibiotics to ward off infection, a list on wound care, a bag of gauze pads and tape, and a prescription for pain meds. She was ready to be released. They got her dressed, then waited for the release papers before finally loading her up in Janie's car with the front seat reclined and her safely buckled in.

Pauline went to get the prescription filled. Gretchen went back to work, and Janie and Bettina headed home.

"Are you okay? Not hurting too much?" Janie asked, as she pulled out of the parking lot and back into traffic.

"For now, I'm good pain-wise, but I don't know if I'll ever be able to go for a walk on a city street again," Bettina said.

Janie frowned. She'd been afraid of this.

"I can't begin to say I understand what you went through. But how you feel, is how you feel. And if this job is no longer feasible then it's not the end of the world. You're alive, and you have a world of other choices, so don't even dwell on what if. Not now. You just need to get yourself healed."

Bettina closed her eyes, lulled by the comforting words, and the fact that she was still breathing.

Once they reached the house, Janie helped her out of the car.

"Let's get you upstairs and into bed before the pain meds wear off," she said.

"I can walk. I just feel stiff," Bettina said.

"And you're going to be sore and in pain for some days, but you are allowed to proceed at your own pace. We'll get you comfy, and Pauline will be here with the pain meds later. Then she'll be upstairs with you during the day, so you won't have to think about going up and down the stairs to eat until you feel like it. Can I get you anything? Something to drink?"

Bettina shook her head. "The thought of food kind of turns my stomach. But I would like something cold to drink. My throat is sore and dry—probably from all that screaming."

Janie hurt just thinking about it and hugged her again. "It breaks my heart that this happened."

"Me, too," Bettina said. "All I want to do right now is lie down."

Janie steadied her as they went up the stairs, and then took her into her bedroom and pulled back the covers.

"One good thing. Today was cleaning day, but the crew has come and gone. It smells all lemony clean, and they won't be here to bother you," she said.

"I wouldn't even care," Bettina said, as she took off her bathrobe, stepped out of her slippers, and eased herself down onto the bed. "Lord, it feels good to be home."

Janie covered her up, brushed a stray lock of hair off her forehead, and then patted her arm.

"I'm going down to get you something to drink, and I'm also going to bring up a little plate of cheese and crackers. You need not to take pain pills on an empty stomach."

Bettina nodded. "Does Pauline still have my phone?"

"Yes," Janie said. "I'll remind her to bring it to you when she gets back, but if you're wanting to call your children, you can use my phone right now."

"I'm not telling them anything. All they do is blame me for whatever is happening."

Janie frowned. "I'm so sorry. That must be the hardest thing."

"My body will heal long before what they did to me will," she said, and closed her eyes.

Janie sighed. "I'll be right back."

Bettina shifted to a more comfortable position and closed her eyes, remembering her life before David... Before the bartending job.

Remembering her ex-husband, Gary, and how much they'd loved each other. Remembering their children as babies, and the utter joy she'd felt in being their mother. She had rejoiced in their first words and first steps, and taught them how to feed themselves, and what it meant to play fair, and be honest. She'd been the soccer mom. The mom sitting in the stands at football games and watching her daughter excel in drama class. She'd been so proud of them and their accomplishments and happy in her life.

Until betrayal.

The utter shock of finding out Gary had had an affair with her best friend, Ellie, had broken her heart. But after the divorce, when her children had chosen the nicer house and the parent with more money over her, it had destroyed her. She'd lost faith in herself.

She'd come in last place as a wife and as a parent, and David Logan had finished her off by dotting the I and crossing the T on the idiot she'd believed herself to be.

Until now.

She was still kicking because today she'd fought back.

It was empowering.

She'd fought to stay alive and to keep Loki alive, and she'd done it.

If God was the one who'd sent the Benning family down Oak Street today, she was grateful for the angels they'd become.

She heard Janie come back into her room, but her eyes were too heavy to open, and so she slept.

Janie left the food and a bottle of water on the bedside table, and Pauline came up later, left Bettina's phone and the prescription bottle of pain pills beside it, and tiptoed out.

Sleep was the best thing Bettina could do for herself right now.

Gretchen got back to work while everyone was still at lunch, so she let herself back into the office, went to get her sack lunch, and took it to her desk to eat. The food had no taste, but she was already light-headed from the shock and the sight of Bettina's wounds. She knew she'd never make it through the rest of the day without something in her stomach.

When she was finished, she dumped the rest in the trash, got a bottle of pop from the refrigerator, and was on the phone with one of Lisa's clients when Lisa came in the door.

Lisa waved, as Gretchen covered the mouthpiece. "This call's for you. It's Ray Morgan."

"Thanks, Gretchen. Put it through to my office," Lisa said, and hurried down the hall.

"One moment, Mr. Morgan, and I'll transfer your call," Gretchen said, made the transfer, and then hung up just as Sarah and Charles walked in.

"Oh, you're back!" Sarah said, as they both paused at Gretchen's desk. "How's Bettina?"

"Full of stitches and puncture wounds, but she's alive. The girls were getting ready to take her home when I left." Then she shuddered. "When you think of being bitten by a dog, you automatically think... punctures, right? That dog didn't just bite. It was trying to kill. I quit counting stitches at forty-six."

Charles frowned. "That's horrible. Did they find the dog? Do they know who it belongs to?"

"I don't know," Gretchen said. "The last info we had was that police and Animal Control were looking for it."

Sarah shuddered. "Like I told you before... my worst nightmare. I hope they find the owners and make them pay."

"We'll make sure of that, if they find them," Gretchen said.

"She has our sympathies and prayers for healing," Sarah said. "And keep us updated. I need to know for my own sanity that a dog like that has been found and taken off the streets."

"I will," Gretchen said.

It was late afternoon.

Janie heated chicken noodle soup for Bettina, put it in a big mug, and took it and a spoon up to her, then began filling her in on everything she'd found out while she was eating.

"This tastes good," Bettina said, as her phone dinged again beside her. "The only people who have my phone number in this whole town besides y'all are my five clients. They've already sent condolences, and now they're on round two of asking if they can help."

"I would expect no less from them," Janie said. "You've had the day from hell. I do have a bit of news. I had a copy of the incident report faxed to my office. The police did find the dog and its owners, and get this. The owner made a police report about someone Macing his dog. That's how they found it so quickly. Animal Control confiscated it. The courts will decide what happens to it, but that's on them. We have the name and address of the owners now."

Bettina took another sip of broth, and then leaned back.

"How do I go about this?" she asked.

"My advice would be go through a lawyer. Thinking they're going to get the pants sued off them holds far more weight in getting people to do the right thing," Janie said.

Bettina frowned. "I'm not out to bankrupt anyone. But I do expect my medical bills to be paid for, and something for pain and suffering and loss of wages. I think that's only fair. I might ask John Attilla. Since he's Loki's owner, and all."

"Good idea," Janie said. "Basically, he would just be drafting and sending the letter with your demands. Now finish your soup. Are you starting to hurt more?"

Bettina's eyes welled. "Yes. Trying not to think about it."

"As soon as we get some food in you, you can take something for pain."

Bettina sat up a little straighter in bed, started spooning noodles into her mouth, and sipping more broth until the mug was empty.

"That's better," Janie said, and shook two pills out into Bettina's hand and handed her the bottle of water beside her bed. "Down the hatch, then lie back and wait for it to kick in before you get too feisty."

Bettina rolled her eyes as she downed the pills and eased back onto her pillow.

"No worries. All my feisty got chewed up and spit out today."

Janie kept eyeing Bettina closely as she straightened her covers. Pain was visible on her face, and she was so pale she didn't even look like herself.

"The wind is coming up," Janie said. "I'll turn up the thermostat some when I leave, but are you warm enough right now? I have plenty of blankets. I can put another one on your bed."

"No need," Bettina said. "I'm warm and full of good soup."

"Okay, then I'm going back downstairs. Pauline will be in and out to check on you, and you have your phone. Call me if you need something, and I'll bring it right up."

"I will," Bettina said, and closed her eyes.

Janie retrieved the empty mug and spoon and turned off the overhead lights in the room as she left, leaving on only a lamp beside the bed and the lights on in the adjoining bathroom.

Bettina kept hearing the intermittent dings from texts and calls that she let go to voicemail. She wasn't up to talking to anyone about what had happened. She'd answer them later.

CHAPTER FOURTEEN

Later that night, the girls helped Bettina downstairs into the warmth of the kitchen to eat. Afterward, when they all moved into the living room by the fireplace to watch TV, Pauline moved the recliner a little closer to the fire for her, and once she was seated with her feet up, they covered her with a soft, fuzzy blanket, then settled in to watch the evening news and weather.

It had begun raining as they were cleaning up after dinner, and they wanted to find out if it was going to get cold enough overnight to freeze. Janie had already winterized the house and all the outside water faucets, but it would matter for Gretchen's drive to work in the morning if the streets were slick.

Janie and Gretchen were curled up on the sofa. Pauline was sitting in a big leather easy chair leafing through the paper, and Bettina was dozing in the recliner when a newscaster came onscreen, announcing the lead-in for upcoming news.

"Local dog walker viciously attacked by loose dog. Deemed a hero for saving the little dog she was walking. Stay tuned for details."

"Oh wow, Miss Bee. You made the evening news!" Janie said.

"Yay me," Bettina said, but sat up so she could watch.

Pauline frowned. "I know you don't want to hear this, but think how grateful the Attilla family is tonight."

Bettina sighed. "Oh, I know. Shelby has texted me three times. Once to tell me Loki is okay. Once to ask about my condition, and then ask if there was anything I needed."

At that point, the commercials ended, and the two newscasters began talking, warning viewers the film clip they were about to air had violent scenes and might be difficult to watch, and then the Benning video was on the screen, and all they could do was watch in horrified silence as the event unfolded.

All of a sudden, Bettina pointed. "See the old man on that porch in the distance? I heard someone shout out a warning, but never knew who it was. It's what made me turn around, otherwise this could have had a different ending. It must have been him," Bettina said.

When it reached the point where Bettina was Macing the dog as it knocked her down, Gretchen gasped and clapped her hands over her mouth.

Bettina closed her eyes. She already remembered it enough without having the added images of her desperation locked into her memory.

Janie and Pauline were in tears all the way through it, then when the newscasters began talking about the dog being taken by Animal Control, and the owners unavailable for comment, Janie took note.

"Unavailable for comment, my ass. Watching that might not have been such a good idea. Are you okay?" Janie asked.

Bettina rolled her eyes. "As okay as I can be considering my experience as a chew toy. I officially reject the idea of ever doing it again. It fucking hurts."

They blinked, and then burst out laughing.

"You cursed," Gretchen said.

"But with restraint," Bettina said.

Janie giggled. "I'd say *fuck* is a pretty aggressive word."

Bettina winced as she shifted to a more comfortable position. "Today is not a day to remind me of social mores."

"We're so sorry," Pauline said. "You say 'fuck' all you want. You've earned the right to be pissy."

Their laughter was tense and a little apologetic for giving in to humor at such a dire time, but it shifted the vibe from Bettina-meets-Kujo to something lighter.

Nearly an hour passed, and they were debating on watching a movie on the big screen TV, or going their separate ways for the evening, when the doorbell rang.

Janie grabbed her phone and checked the Ring app. It was their neighbor. She got up and went to the door. Janie opened it to find Florence's son, Carter Lane, on the doorstep with a bouquet of flowers.

"Hi, Janie. We all saw the newscast earlier in the evening about what happened to Bettina, and we're so sorry. These are for her with our best wishes. Sorry they're from the supermarket, but Mom insisted on bringing them tonight, and she's down with a head cold, so she likely won't be over until she's better, but she sends her love to all."

"That's so thoughtful," Janie said. "Tell her Bettina said thanks, and we're wishing her a swift recovery."

"Will do," Carter said. "Goodnight."

Janie locked the doors then carried the flowers back into the living room and put them in Bettina's lap.

"These are for you from Florence and her family."

"Oh, they're beautiful," Bettina said. "Roses in winter. How special."

"I'll put them in water for you. Would you like them carried up to your room?" Pauline said.

"Please," Bettina said, and handed them over.

"Are you warm enough," Gretchen asked. "I can make you some hot chocolate."

"Sounds good," Bettina said.

"I'll have some, too. Want me to help?" Janie asked.

"No need. I'll make some for all of us," Gretchen said. "Pauline can help me carry it back."

Janie sat down on a footstool near Bettina's chair, then pulled back the blanket and gently eased up the legs of her pajamas up to check the bandages.

The fact that there was no fresh blood visible was reassuring, so she eased them back down.

"Looks okay, but how bad are you hurting?" Janie asked.

"On a scale of one to ten, I'm about a seven," Bettina said, blinking back tears.

"Do you want to go up to your room now? We don't have to do all this movie stuff together," Janie asked.

"Not yet. The movie will be a good distraction."

Janie leaned over and kissed her on the forehead.

"I'm so sorry, sweetie. But since you are such a kick-ass heroine, how about a movie with a kick-ass female in the lead?"

Bettina nodded, so she began scanning Netflix and Prime for something to watch.

Pauline took the roses up to Bettina's room, and then helped Gretchen carry in the mugs of hot chocolate. They settled into their seats, and when Janie hit Play, and the opening credits of *Mulan* appeared, they cradled the warm mugs in their hands and began watching the story of a young woman from a world long ago, in a land far away, become a legend among her people.

Rain began to splatter against the windows, but the warmth of their drinks and the heat from the fireplace warded off the night chill.

Bettina was emotionally exhausted by the time the movie was over.

They had helped her up to her room, tending her like she was their baby. Brushing her hair and tying it back from her face—helping change her into clean pajamas and giving her medicine, until she was in so much pain it hurt to breathe.

"Would someone please put my phone on the charger, leave a light on in the bathroom, and say prayers that I'll be able to sleep?" she asked.

"Consider it done," Janie said, as she put the phone on the charger, then went into the bathroom and turned on the nightlight.

"I'm leaving your door open and my door open tonight," Pauline said. "If you need anything, just call out. I'll hear you."

Gretchen got the extra blanket from the foot of the bed and spread it over Bettina's covers.

"We've got your back," Janie said. "All you have to do is rest and get well."

Bettina closed her eyes, desperate for them to leave. She didn't want to talk. She couldn't focus on the words. She was empty of everything but pain.

And then they left. She heard the murmur of voices in the hall but didn't have the energy to care what they were saying. She was just waiting for the pain pills to pull her under.

Tony Watts couldn't sleep. His wife, Kay, was upstairs, angry and worried they were going to be sued for so much money that they'd lose everything. He kept reassuring her that their liability insurance would cover the victim's medical bills and demands, and at the same time, accepted it was their fault.

Looking back, if he had just given in to Kay's desire for a Yorkie three years ago, none of this would be happening. He was the one who'd wanted a big dog—one that would be a companion for their son, Darrin. But as it turned out, the really cute puppy had grown into a very large, very aggressive dog. And this had happened.

He stared into the fire, trying not to think of Judge being put down and of the Lee woman's suffering. They'd said on the news report that she had over sixty stitches and many puncture wounds. They'd all watched the video in horrified silence and heard her screams during the attack.

He scrubbed his hands across his face, then got up and walked to the windows overlooking the front of their property. It was still raining, and the house was cold. Either he went to bed, turned up the heat, or got shit-faced drunk.

Age and reason shifted his focus from the latter to the first. He'd go to bed. Everything always looked brighter on a new day.

It was ten p.m. when Rachel Edwards let herself into her apartment, then locked the door behind her. She smelled like the diner where she worked—grease, fish, and stale coffee. This wasn't the "starting over" dream she'd had when she left Dallas, but it was better than fucking strangers, and the fry cook at the diner liked her—as in, flirted and hit on her every day.

He was fifteen years older than her, but he was divorced with no kids, had a good car, and his own place. Every day when she went to work, she played him like the hunter she was, and him the little fish swimming around a worm. She was just waiting for the fish to bite so she could set the hook.

She emptied her pockets, counted out her tips, and then stuffed the money in the oatmeal container she used for a stash and pushed it to the back of the pantry.

The apartment was chilly, so she turned up the heat and headed for her bedroom, stripping as she went, and dumping her work clothes in the hamper. After a shampoo and a shower, she towel-dried her hair, put on old sweats and a long-sleeved t-shirt, and went back to the kitchen.

A bowl of cold cereal later, she felt better, and turned on the TV to unwind a little before going to bed. Tomorrow was her day off, so she got to sleep in.

She'd long since let go on the fear of being chased down for money, but that stunt had taught her a lesson. She wasn't smart enough to pull a con, and she liked Oregon and her job was fine. Maybe because it was so far away from who she'd been. She'd dodged a bullet and didn't want back in that war. Whoever those women were who'd married Daddy Dave, they must have had their own set of issues. If they hadn't, they wouldn't have married him.

Daddy Dave was history.

The scam she'd tried to run was history.

Oregon was her future, and so was the fry cook.

He just didn't know it yet—but he would when she set the hook and reeled him in.

Bettina was dreaming.

In the dream, she was running with Loki in her arms, knowing there was a monster on her heels. No matter how fast she ran, she couldn't lose it. She could feel the heat of its breath, and the pull on her clothing when its teeth caught in the fabric. Loki was whining and yipping in a frantic little "save me" sound when the monster's teeth finally caught, tearing through her clothes into her flesh. She was screaming when the sound of her own voice woke her. That hadn't been a dream. That part was real.

She sat up in bed, her heart pounding as she peered into the shadows for signs of the monster, and then suddenly, her overhead lights were on, and Pauline was running toward her bed.

"Oh God, I am so sorry," Bettina mumbled. "I think I was dreaming."

Pauline sat down at the foot of the bed. "It's okay. I just came to make sure you're okay."

Then Gretchen came into the room, and they heard Janie coming up the stairs.

Bettina glanced at the clock. It was just after three in the morning, and she'd gotten everyone out of bed.

"I'm so sorry. It was just a bad dream," she said.

"Well, this is one night I won't have to get up to pee before dawn," Gretchen said. "I'm pretty sure you scared it out of me before my feet hit the floor."

They laughed, and the mood shifted from fear and tension to humor. They were pros at laughing at themselves.

"Everyone go back to bed. I've got this," Pauline said.

The other two gave her a hug and went back to their rooms.

"Now that we're awake, I'm going to make a pit stop before I try going back to sleep," Bettina said, and threw back the covers.

But when she went to get up, she was so stiff and sore she could barely swing her legs of the side of the bed.

"Shit, shit, shit," Bettina muttered. "This hurts so much."

"Let me help," Pauline said.

"It's just pain. I can withstand pain. I cannot withstand being helpless. I can do it," Bettina said.

Pauline saw the fire in her eyes and stepped back.

"Just because you're mad at the situation, doesn't mean you get to be mad at me," she said.

Bettina wilted. "I'm sorry. I am a horrible patient. Always have been. I'm mad that my good job is over. I'm frustrated, and I hurt. A lot. But none of that is your fault."

"I know," Pauline said. "Now, do you want help or are you hoping to make things worse?"

Bettina blinked, and then threw back her head and laughed.

"Jeeze... That's what I was doing, wasn't it? *Mea culpa*, sister. From time to time, I have a subconscious need to be an asshole. Yes, and thank you for the help."

Pauline grinned and held out her hand. Bettina grabbed it and held on as Pauline pulled her up. The muscles in Bettina's legs were so sore from the attack and the stitches that she could barely pick up her feet, so she scooted herself into the bathroom and closed the door.

After she came out, Pauline helped her back to bed, pulled up the covers, and then patted her shoulder.

"Try to get some rest. We love you dearly. We're so sorry this happened. And anytime you feel the need to be an asshole, give us a heads up, so we can duck before you let fly."

Bettina grinned. "I'll keep that in mind. Thank you for everything."

"You're welcome," Pauline said, then turned out the lights before returning to her room.

Bettina was already in the kitchen the next morning when Janie came in to make coffee.

"Hey girl! You made it downstairs on your own! Good for you!"

"I reminded myself that pain won't kill me. Nothing on me is broken. I'm not going to tear stitches out just walking, so I just have to get over it."

Janie saw the pain in her eyes, guessed she hadn't slept well, and just hugged her.

"Would pancakes make your world a little better today?" she asked.

Bettina leaned into Janie's hug.

"You make my world a little better every day, but the pancakes would be tasty, too."

"Give me a few minutes to make batter, and it shall be done," Janie said, and got down a large bowl and began measuring ingredients.

She hadn't intended to do anything but make toast and coffee before going to the office, but family took precedence over work.

Gretchen came in all dressed for the office and gave Bettina a quick hug then topped off her coffee before pouring a cup for herself.

"I'm making pancakes. Get another plate down if you want some."

"I never refuse pancakes," Gretchen said, and did as Janie

asked, then got out butter and syrup and put them on the table.

Pauline walked in just as Janie was taking the first stack to the table for Bettina.

"Pancakes. I made enough batter for all of us," Janie said.

Within a few minutes, they were all at the table, enjoying the unexpected treat and bragging on Bettina's fortitude in getting herself downstairs. Gretchen finished, then made her lunch and left for work.

There were a few moments of silence, and then as if on cue, they all looked up at the same time.

Bettina sighed. Her shoulders slumped.

"Yes, I had a bad night. Nightmares. It was to be expected. I had them after David was killed, and this too, shall pass. I have to change the dressings. I can't see the backs of my legs well enough to know if they're okay, so I'll need a little help with that. I'm supposed to watch for infection."

"I'll help, honey," Pauline said. "I work upstairs, and I don't need total silence to do my job. If you want to spend the day with me in my office, you can. It is the spare bedroom, after all."

Bettina nodded. "I'll be fine but thank you for the offer."

Janie took a sip of her coffee, then leaned forward.

"Just a little heads up. I was online this morning. Someone uploaded the video of your attack onto social media. I haven't checked, but I'm betting it winds up on a lot of other sites, too, which means your children are likely to see it."

"Shit," Bettina said. "I suppose it's to be expected, but if the first words out of their mouths are about how awful I am for not telling them, instead of asking me how I am and how I feel, I'm hanging up."

Pauline frowned. "Will they really do that?"

Bettina shrugged. "So far, that's all they've done. I never said anything about it before, but they called me July 4th. They'd flown into Kansas City to spend the holiday with me and freaked out when they saw the house where I'd been living was empty, and there was a For Lease sign in the yard. The first thing they did was attack me for not letting them know where I was. I reminded them that they had not once, in all the years David and I were married, called or visited, and that just because they didn't like him, didn't mean they were supposed to quit on me."

"I'm so sorry," Janie said.

"So am I, but I'm over it," Bettina said. "I also reminded them that I'd said I was going to wind up homeless, and you know what my daughter said? I didn't think you meant it."

"You could have given them this address," Janie said.

"Yes, I know. But what I'm saying is… I'm their mother, and they abandoned me. Now they're grown, and I owe them nothing. Not explanations. Not excuses. Not reasons. I love them. But I am not someone to be played with. I do not have to have their approval before they decide to accept me as their mother again. I did nothing to shame them. They shamed themselves."

"Lord. There's a gold-plated reason for never giving birth," Pauline said.

"I admire your fortitude and your attitude," Janie said. "You are teaching your children a lesson right now—that life isn't forever. And once trust is broken, it is never the same."

"Thank you for understanding, and for the heads up about the video on social media. I never dreamed an innocent job like dog walking would ever take a turn like this."

"None of that is your fault. Look at me," Janie said. "I'm a simple bookkeeper, working alone for the last twenty-something years at an oh-so-safe and insignificant little job—until I opened a door to a stranger and nearly died," Janie said, and then laughed.

"Well, that wasn't a bit funny either," Pauline said.

"That's because you nearly broke your hand punching out my attacker," Janie said. "And I will forever regret not witnessing that punch."

"I saw it," Bettina said. "There was lift-off behind that punch. One minute the bitch was straddling you, and the next she was flying through the air backwards. Pauline is a badass."

They laughed again, lifting them all out of a funk and into the reality of life.

By noon, Bettina had showered, and with Pauline's help, changed her bandages and taken her meds. She called Shelby about the possibility of asking John to represent her, and John had immediately called her back. After a discussion to outline the details, he was sending a letter informing Tony Watts of Bettina's claims, and now it was a wait and see. Either Watts would agree and pay up or contest it, and then she would sue him. But as John pointed out, the whole thing was cut and dried. He couldn't claim innocence. He would get the police report of the attack and the police report Watts made about someone Macing his dog. They had the Bennings as witnesses, and their video to prove it, which left Tony Watts with no options.

Bettina's son, Joe, was the one who saw the video first. He'd gotten up early to check numbers on the stock exchange for a client who wanted to liquidate a large number of shares. He was still at the computer, drinking his morning coffee, when he got a text from his dad. It was the video.

Knowing that was his mother, fighting for her life while protecting that little dog, shattered him. He watched it over and over and over, hearing her screams until he was in tears and shaking, then went online and read the story in detail in the St. Louis newspapers. And when he was finished, there was no denying that if those people had not showed up to help her, she would have died.

He knew Patty hadn't seen it, or she would have been calling him in hysterics. He also knew that if his mother had wanted them to know, she would have called.

This horrible chasm that was between them now was all their fault. They'd turned their backs on her from the day of their parents' divorce. Back then, he and Patty had still been in school and selfish as hell. They hadn't wanted to move with their mother and change schools. They wouldn't be living in their upper class neighborhood or going on all the cool holiday trips. And their dad had had them convinced she was everything but a hooker.

And when she'd gone to work as a bartender in a hotel, which was a perfectly respectable job, their dad had made it sound like she was turning tricks instead of mixing drinks. They'd known better. But it was the excuse they'd needed to keep their lives intact, and to hell with their mother's fate.

He was as ashamed, and sad... As sad as he'd ever been in his life. He sent the video to Patty in a text, with the message...

This is Mom. She's alive, no thanks to us.

And then waited.

Patty Vale was already at work at the bank when she got Joe's text, and as soon as she got to a stopping point, she hit save on her computer then got up to take a quick break.

She locked the bathroom door and then put down the lid on the toilet to use as a seat and sat down to read. She saw the words he'd written, and sighed, wondering what other drama had occurred in their mother's life, and then she saw the video and went into shock.

Like Joe, she watched it over and over, unaware of the tears rolling down her face until someone knocked on the bathroom door.

She jumped, then burst out of the room sobbing, the phone clutched in her hand like it was the last lifeline to her mother.

Her boss came out of the office, frowning.

"Patty! What on earth?" he said.

"My mother! This is my mother!" she cried, and thrust the phone in his face.

He glanced at the video that was still playing, then gasped.

"I saw this on the news this morning. It's terrible. Is she alive?"

"Yes, but I don't know how bad she was hurt. I need to go home."

"Yes, of course," he said. "If you need a couple of days off, just call me."

She nodded, grabbed her things from her desk, and ran out of the office all the way to the parking garage to get to her car. She needed to call Joe.

Joe's phone began to ring, and then Patty's face popped up on caller ID.

"Hell of a mess, isn't this?" he said when he answered.

"It's horrible. It's awful. Oh, Joe. Her screams. I will hear them in my head until the day I die. How bad is it?"

And so he began to tell her what he'd learned, which was far less than what they wanted to know, and ended with the situation they'd put themselves in.

"She was released from the hospital, so she's home, somewhere in St. Louis, living with David's other wives, whoever they are. The last time we called her, she made it plain what she thought of how we'd treated her, and—"

"But Joe! That's not fair! We said we were sorry. We want to—"

Joe interrupted. "Stop. Just stop, Patty. Listen to what you're saying. *We* said. *We* want. We never asked her what she thought. What she wanted. She was the one who was wronged. Dad cheated on her—with her best friend—and then dumped Mom to marry her. And then Mom winds up with a dishonest, cheating husband again. We turned our backs on her for the nice address and Dad's deep pockets... And without conscience, lived with the woman who betrayed her."

Patty was sobbing so hard, he could barely understand her, but he got the gist of it. They had to find a way to make things right, and he didn't disagree.

"I'll start calling her. And you call, too. But not together. We're not going to gang up on her again. Understand?"

"Understood," Patty said.

CHAPTER FIFTEEN

Bettina was having a hard day.

Between the pain and defeat she felt, she'd skipped lunch to stay in bed. All she wanted to do was sleep this nightmare away. Being physically attacked had somehow released the grief she'd buried.

Yes, she'd cried when David died, but it had quickly turned to anger once she'd learned of the deceit, denying her a widow's grief. Now, it was all coming up, and she felt like she was coming undone.

She was dozing—somewhere between dreams and oblivion—when it began to rain. The sound of it hitting the roof and blowing against the windows made her shiver. She pulled the covers up a little closer around her neck as she listened to it pour. The heavens had unleashed. Maybe God was crying with her.

A short while later, she heard footsteps coming up the stairs and glanced at the clock. It was nearing three p.m. She closed her eyes, unwilling to talk. The footsteps stopped outside her door and then moved away. Likely Pauline checking in on her.

She sighed. They were all being so sweet and so good to her. She should feel blessed, but the truth was, she was angry, so angry at life for everything that had happened. The dog attack wasn't the issue. It had just ripped away the scab from the wound of her children's harsh words. She'd done nothing wrong, and yet she'd become a pariah.

It would be a cold day in hell before she ever looked at another man in a romantic way. She grabbed her phone and put it on mute, then cried herself to sleep.

Joe Vale was in his home office. He couldn't concentrate and had finally given up pretending to work. He had to reach out. He needed to hear his mother's voice to know she was okay, so he called her—three times with no answer—before finally leaving her a message.

"Momma, I just saw the video of you being attacked by that dog. OMG... I'm so sorry. Please call me back. I need to know how bad you're hurt. If there's anything I can do. If you'll let me come see you. I will hear your screams in my sleep for the rest of my life. Please, Mom... Just call, even if all you have to say is how much you hate me. I just need to hear your voice. I love you."

Then he dropped the phone into his pocket and stared at the wall above the computer screen. Watching that video was like watching her being murdered. But for the grace of God, it might have been so. He was afraid—afraid that he and Patty had created such a toxic environment for her that they would never see her again.

Patty Vale called her mother, and when it went to voicemail, she immediately left a message.

"Mommy, I know you got hurt. Joe showed me the video of the attack. I know you hate me, but I don't hate you. I just hate myself for what I did to you. I was a selfish bitch when I was younger, and I'm obviously no better now, or I wouldn't have been so ugly to you. I'm not asking for forgiveness. I just need to hear your voice—to know that you're going to be okay. I want to come see you, but I understand I've lost the right to assume I would be welcome, and that's on me. I love you, Mommy. Please call. Tell me what I can do for you. I will do anything to help you get better. I thought I was watching you die. It was a slap-in-the-face moment I will never forget. I don't want to lose you. I love you."

And then she laid down on the bed with the phone beneath her hand and cried until her eyes were so swollen she couldn't see.

Bettina woke, glanced at the time, and sighed. It was just a few minutes past five p.m. Gretchen would be home any minute.

She rolled over onto her back, threw the covers aside, and sat up on the side of the bed before reaching for her pain pills. She shook a couple out into her hand, then remembered she hadn't eaten anything since her toast and coffee this morning. She set them back down on the end table beside her bed.

It was time to rejoin the living.

She glanced out the window as she made her way to the bathroom. It was still raining. What a cold, miserable day.

When she came out, she grabbed her bathrobe and put it on over her pajamas, slid her feet into her slippers, then dropped the pain pills in one of the pockets. Getting dressed was out of the question, but there was also no need. As soon as she ate, she was coming back to bed.

Day two of getting eaten alive was worse than day one. Everything throbbed—muscles, the bites, the places that had stitches. She could only imagine how the rest of the week would play out. She opened the door to her room just as Pauline was leaving her office.

Pauline saw her and jogged to catch up.

"Hey, Miss Bee, are you ready for something to eat?"

Bettina nodded.

"So am I. Let's go see what we can do about that," Pauline said, and held onto her all the way down the stairs, not turning loose until Bettina was seated in a chair.

Janie stood at the stove, adding salt to a pot of something she had simmering.

"What smells so good?" Pauline asked.

"This weather feels like soup day. It's vegetable beef, and cornbread is in the oven. I love soup and cornbread," Janie said, and then glanced at Bettina. She was pale and listless, and staring blankly through the windows to the rain coming down.

Janie frowned, then poured Bettina a cup of coffee and carried a little plate of appetizers to the table.

"Just a little cream cheese concoction I made, and some of your favorite crackers. Help yourself. The cornbread will be done soon."

Bettina blinked, refocused on the plate before her, took a cracker, and popped it into her mouth, chewed, and swallowed.

"This is so good. What all is in this cheese spread?" Bettina asked.

"Umm, it's a combination of cream cheese, minced onion, red bell pepper, jalapenos, and a little bit of seasoned salt," Janie said.

"I love it," Bettina said, and took a second one.

After a couple of sips of coffee, she took the pain pills from her pocket and downed them, then leaned back in the chair and sighed. The pain pills were going to help her physical pain, but this house, these women, and their friendship were the medicines she needed most.

As she sat listening to Pauline and Janie's chatter, she heard the front door open, then close. The last member of the Broke-Ass Women's Club was in attendance.

Gretchen called out from the foyer. "I'm home!"

They heard her run up the stairs and then a door slammed a few moments later.

"I'll bet she's soaked to the skin," Pauline said.

"Hot soup and cornbread will fix that," Janie said. "Let's get the table set."

Pauline got down plates and soup bowls, as Janie took the cornbread out of the oven. A few minutes later, Gretchen was back, wearing sweats and her still damp hair pulled up in a ponytail.

"I got soaked," she said, as she entered the kitchen. "A gust of wind caught my umbrella as I was running to my car. I had a Mary Poppins moment and thought I was about to fly, and then the damn thing turned inside out and drowned me instead."

They laughed, Bettina included, and when she did, the sound rolled through her like a caress. More good medicine for what ailed her.

"Bless your heart. This hot soup will fix you right up," Janie said, and began ladling it into bowls.

Soon, they were all sitting around the table, talking about their days.

Gretchen noticed Bettina was unusually quiet and guessed the shock of the attack had worn off and reality was setting in. It hurt her heart to see her friend so despondent, and she decided to change the subject from work, since Bettina's job had come to such a horrible end.

"I got another phone call from my sister, Erin, today, and you cannot guess what it was about. Thanksgiving and Christmas! She wanted to know about my holiday plans. You know why I'm shocked? Because we haven't spent a holiday together in fifteen years. At least."

Janie glanced up. "You're more than welcome to invite her to dinner."

"No, thank you," Gretchen said.

"Then why would she do that now?" Pauline asked.

Gretchen snorted. "Because she's curious about all of you. And where I'm at. And what we're doing. She's eight years younger than I am, and we've never been close. But she was still my sister, you know? Then my first husband died. She was in Europe on holiday and couldn't be bothered to come home. When she returned some weeks later, all she wanted to talk about was her trip. I was blindsided by her lack of compassion. When I married David, she came to the wedding, then told me in private that I could have done better, and I never saw her again. Yes, we speak on the phone now and then, but they are duty calls. When all this happened with David, it was her 'I told you so' attitude that ended whatever there'd been between us. You know the old saying... "You can't pick your family, but you can pick your friends?"

"Wow, she's a real keeper, isn't she?" Pauline said. "Suddenly I don't feel so bad at being an only child."

Gretchen shrugged. "Love is wonderful. And love hurts. But family can break your heart faster than anyone else."

Bettina stayed silent, but she was thinking about her kids. She'd muted her phone this morning, and it was somewhere in her bed. She hadn't looked for it and wasn't sure she wanted to. But by the time they'd finished eating, the pain in her legs was beginning to abate. She'd check messages when she went back up.

Janie was clearing the table, when she suddenly stopped.

"Oh! Miss Bee, I forgot to tell you. You received two floral arrangements, and a beautifully wrapped gift via a delivery service while you were sleeping. I put the gift and one of the bouquets on the dining room table, and the other bouquet is in the hall. If you want them in your room, say the word, and we'll carry them up for you. I left the cards with the flowers, so I don't know who sent them, but I'm guessing some of your little doggies send their best wishes."

"Really? I want to go see," Bettina said, and eased up from the table.

"We all want to see," Pauline said, and they followed her first to the hall table and the arrangement of fall flowers.

Bettina removed the card, and then smiled. "It's from Bruce, my little Yorkie, and his owner Aaron Carter. Look. Aaron signed it, and so did Bruce."

They all saw the little paw print Aaron had drawn on the get-well card, alongside his own name.

"That's adorable!" Gretchen said.

Bettina pocketed the card and then went into the dining room to yet another arrangement, this time in colors of orange, reds and yellows—the same colors as the leaves on the trees.

"Aw, these are from Sherry Lawrence and her little dog, Charlotte."

"That's quite a gift box!" Gretchen said, eyeing the silver foil wrapping paper and the Tiffany blue bow.

Janie pulled out a chair. "Here, Miss Bee. You're still too pale for my liking. Maybe you should sit down to open this."

Bettina didn't argue. But when she sat down and read the gift card, she burst into tears.

"Oh, honey! What's wrong?" Janie said.

"It's from Loki. It says, 'With kisses and licks, for saving my life'."

Now they were all teary-eyed and quiet as they watched her remove the wrapping paper, then take the lid.

Bettina smiled. "It's a figurine that looks just like Loki. And there's a card around his neck."

As she set the figurine down to remove the card, Janie suspected it was more than just a cute figurine. She picked it up and turned it over.

"Girl, this isn't just a figurine. It's a Royal Doulton figurine. You might need to insure it."

Bettina's eyes widened. "Good grief. I've never owned anything that needed to be insured but a car." Then she opened the card and pulled out a check from John and Shelby Attilla, along with a written note. "Good Lord! It's a check for five thousand dollars!" Bettina said, and then picked up the note and read it aloud.

This is what we paid for Loki when we bought him. He is a family treasure, and you have given him a second chance at life. We will never be able to fully repay you for what you did for us... and for Loki. We wish you swift healing. All our love, John and Shelby. P.S. John has volunteered his services to you, pro bono.

"This is so unexpected, and so generous," Bettina said, and reached for the figurine, holding it against her chest like she'd so often held Loki in her arms.

"I'm sure going to miss that little guy."

"And life goes on," Pauline said, as she gave her a hug.

Bettina nodded. "Yes... Mine included, for which I am so grateful. I think I want to go lie back down now. I'm removing my dog walking service from Facebook and telling my clients I'm retiring from the job."

"If that's how you feel, then that's a good call," Pauline said.

"Do you want any of the flowers taken up to your room? Janie asked.

Bettina nodded. "The ones in the hall, from Bruce. It's the right size for my room. You can put this larger one wherever you like."

"I'll help you up the stairs," Pauline said.

"And I'll bring the flowers, and then come back and help Janie clean up," Gretchen said.

Bettina put the figurine on a bookshelf next to her bed and the check in her purse, while Gretchen placed the flowers on the small desk between her windows so Bettina could see them from her bed.

"Thank you both for helping me get settled. I'm comfortable and mobile enough to get myself to the bathroom and back. Go help

Janie clean up and thank her for dinner. It was perfect for this cold, rainy weather."

"Will do," they said.

"I'll check in on you before I go to bed," Pauline said, and if you want anything in the meantime, just call."

"I will," Bettina said, and then pulled back the covers to get in and saw the corner of her phone beneath one of the pillows.

She reached for it, took it off Mute, and then realized she had more unanswered messages and began going through the texts.

Frieda Turnbull, Puppy's owner, was having dinner delivered to them tomorrow evening at six p.m., with gratitude for her service, and Pinky the poodle's owner had sent her a one-hundred-dollar parting gift via Venmo.

She read the rest of the texts and started to put the phone down when she noticed she had two voicemails, as well.

She hit play on the first one, and immediately recognized her son's voice. She heard the tremor, and the utter sadness, in the words and felt as if she was coming undone.

She played it twice, and then went to the last voicemail, knowing before she ever heard a word, that it would be Patty. She had to play it multiple times to decipher everything her daughter was saying, because she was crying so hard, she had to stop and take a breath between sentences before she could continue. When it was over, she laid the phone aside, too emotional to call them back, and so angry that it took being mauled by a dog to elicit their sympathy. She'd waited a long time for them to remember she was *their* mother first. They could wait another night for her response.

Rachel Edwards had misread the fry cook's intentions by a mile. He didn't want to marry her. He just wanted to fuck her. For free.

Rachel had just given Pete, the fry cook, a blow job and was lying nude on her bed, watching him get dressed, while playing out the fantasy life she was imagining with him.

"You know what, Petey?"

Pete Welty glanced back at Rachel as he reached for his belt and grinned.

"I know lots of things," he said.

Rachel giggled. "I was just thinking how nice it will be when we finally get a place of our own."

He laughed.

"There is no us. You're always good for a fuck. But nobody ever said this was a permanent situation."

Rachel felt the blood actually drain from her face. She was shocked, and then enraged so fast it made her head spin. Before she thought, she leaped up from the bed and laid a slap on the side of his face that sent him reeling.

"How dare you talk to me like that?"

Pete saw red, doubled up his fist and hit her.

She screamed and turned to reach for her phone when he slapped it out of her hand and hit her again, and again, without saying a word. She was begging him to stop, but he didn't hear anything but the roar inside his head.

He kept hitting her... long after she'd gone silent. Long after she was motionless at his feet, and then he left her lying on her bedroom floor in a spreading pool of blood.

Bill Riley was Rachel's boss.

When Rachel didn't show up for work the next morning, he called, but she never answered. Everyone in the cafe knew Pete and Rachel had been seeing each other, so Riley went into the kitchen to talk Pete.

"Hey, Pete. Rachel didn't show. Do you know if she's sick or something?"

Pete was flipping eggs over easy and laying bacon strips on the grill, and never looked up as he answered.

"She was fine yesterday when she left work. I haven't talked to her since," Pete said.

Riley frowned. He knew better, because he'd seen her getting into Pete's car after work. And then he noticed the bruised and bloody knuckles on Pete's right hand.

"What happened to your hand?" he asked.

Pete never hesitated. "Oh... I was changing a flat. My hand slipped, and I jammed it against the wheel. Hurt like hell."

Riley didn't buy the story, but he let it slide and walked away.

But the next day, it was Pete who did not show up for work, and he wasn't answering his phone.

That's when Bill Riley called the police and asked them to do a welfare check at Rachel Edward's apartment.

A couple of hours later, he got a call that confirmed his worst fears. Rachel Edwards had been beaten to death. He told the detectives what he knew about Pete, gave them his last known address, and then went to his office and pulled up the website for the local paper and put two notices in the Help Wanted section for a waitress and a fry cook.

Life went on for Bill Riley.

Pete Welty was on the run.

But like Daddy David, Rachel Edwards' life had come to a sad and tragic end, with no one to mourn her passing.

The next night, the girls at the Broke-Ass Women's Club had dinner delivered to their house from Tigin's Irish Pub, compliments of Frieda Turnbull. Shepherd's pie and bread pudding with hard sauce was a hit, but they were all suffering carbohydrate stupors.

"Oh, my Lord. I am stuffed," Gretchen said, as Pauline was gathering up all the to-go containers to carry out to the garbage.

"So am I," Janie said. "The food was amazing. I couldn't stop eating, and now I feel like a bear ready for hibernation. I'm going to have to sleep this off to be able to move."

"I'll be sure and let Frieda know it was a hit when I send the thank you note," Bettina said.

"Tell her thank you from all of us," Pauline said, and headed out the back door with the trash bag in her hands.

"I'm going to watch a little TV by the fire," Janie said. "Anyone interested is welcome to join me."

"I have some calls to return, and then I think I'll do the TV thing up in my room," Bettina said.

"Need any help?" Gretchen asked.

"No. I've got this," Bettina said. "Sweet dreams to all. I'll see you man-yawna."

They laughed.

"Still throwing around that Spanish you don't know?" Gretchen said.

Bettina grinned. "Such as it is. It means tomorrow," she said, and left the room. It was time to respond to her children's calls.

Her steps were slow as she left the room, and the stitches felt like they were drawing up and shrinking into her flesh, but she kept moving through the foyer, then up the stairs.

She was gritting her teeth to keep from crying by the time she got to her room and closed the door. Once she got to her bed, she reached for pain meds. She hadn't had any since early this morning and was regretting that decision. She took the prescribed dosage, then kicked off her slippers, tossed her bathrobe at the foot of the bed, and eased in between the covers.

Her phone was beside the lamp, but she needed this throbbing to ease before she called. So, she began running through different mental scenarios of what to say. But in the end, she just sent Joe a text.

I'll talk to you both, but only on a conference call. I don't feel like reliving this twice. You call. I'll answer.

Then she turned on the TV and settled in to wait.

Less than five minutes later, her phone rang. It was her son. She hit Mute on the TV remote, let her phone ring three times, and then picked up.

"Hello."

"Mom! Thank you for returning my call. Patty is on the line, too," Joe said.

"Mommy, I'm here, too. How badly were you hurt? Are you going to be okay?" Patty asked.

"I have severe wounds. The attack was shocking, and frightening, and so far, still excruciating, but the physical wounds will heal."

"I'm so sorry," Joe said. "I watched that video over and over. I heard your screams. I can't bear to know what you went through to stay alive."

Bettina heard the regret and sorrow in their voices, but they didn't get a pass.

"What that dog did to me was just tear my flesh. That pain is nothing to what you two have done to my heart. I am your mother, and you threw me away. I've had to live with that. And now that I nearly died, you suddenly get a conscience? Do you see the irony? I've been sick many times alone. I grieved the loss of my home and my first husband alone, and then to have my children turn away from me, too? Because I didn't have enough money to satisfy your greedy needs? Because status meant more to you than love? And then the shit I just went through with David, and all you both did was belittle me for wanting to be happy again? So, you can certainly see why I am not impressed with your sudden concern."

Patty was sobbing, and she could hear Joe crying. But they were listening.

"I have no excuse," Joe said. "It's all true. I accept every sin of omission. I accept my omission of compassion. I accept what a low-life son I am to you. And I'm hoping, no... begging for another chance. To do better. To be better. To be your son in an honorable way. As I watched how fiercely you fought to stay alive, it hit me that this is what you've been doing all along. Just fighting to stay alive on your own terms."

Patty took a quick breath and jumped in.

"Mom... Mommy, please give me a chance. If I could start over from the day of the divorce, I would, but I can't go back. I can't change what I've said, or what I've done... and not done. I can't change anything of the past, but I will spend the rest of my life making it up to you, if you'll let me."

Bettina was listening, and silent—silent so long they both panicked, thinking she'd hung up.

"Mom! Are you there?"

"Hello? Mommy, are you there?"

"I'm still here, which is more than either one of you deserve. I don't trust either one of you, because I don't know the cold, hateful people you became, and so, time will tell, won't it? Thank you for calling to check on my welfare. But right now, I don't have even the first notion of what either one of you might say or do that would reassure me you're sincere. So, let's just leave it at that for now."

"May we come see you?" Patty asked. "Help take care of you?"

"No. I'm not ready to see either one of you. I am safe in this big, wonderful home. We all walked the same ugly road to get here, and here, we take care of each other. There's no discord in this home, and I'm not going to be the one to introduce it. You stay where you are... for now. But do one thing for me."

"Anything, Mom. Anything," they echoed.

"Take a look at your father. A good look. Listen closely at who he speaks of with disdain, and who he laughs at. If you pay attention, you will see his truth... and hear the lies. You'll see who he values and why—and the shortcuts he's willing to take to get what he wants. You don't need confrontations. Just look at your idol. Look for his feet of clay."

Then she ended the call and turned off the lamp, leaving the room lit only by the television screen. The show was still on Mute, giving her a whole other perspective of the story playing out.

Their expressions became the words she couldn't hear. Mouths wide open were either screams or silent laughter. Doors slamming that made no sound. Night turning into day. Moving crowds on city streets without audio to provide a background, made her think of ants—thousands of frantic ants in constant motion. It was the reverse of the phone call she'd just had. She'd heard her children's voices—heard them choking on their own tears. Their pleas for forgiveness had cut straight to her soul. But she hadn't seen their faces, or expressions. She remembered her sweet babies and the children they'd been. And what they'd turned into without her. She wanted to believe they were sincere, but at this point, she wasn't strong enough to bear another heartbreak if they were not.

After talking to his mother, Joe called his dad to thank him for sending the video, but it was Ellie who answered.

"Hello, Joey darling. How have you been?"

Joe frowned. "Uh... fine. I was trying to call Dad. Did I ring you by mistake?"

She giggled. "Oh no! He's just refreshing my drink, and when I saw it was you, I answered his phone. Hang on, here he comes. Gary, darling. It's Joe."

And then Joe heard his dad's voice.

"Hey, son."

"Hi, Dad. I just called to thank you for sending the video."

"Oh... That. Yes, well, it was sent on impulse. Not because I thought it was my business."

Joe frowned. "I would think the mother of your children would always be on your radar."

"Yes, of course. But you're both adults now, so I don't feel like you need to be protected from her anymore."

Joe flinched. Protected? From what? What had his mother said about feet of clay?

"She's going to be fine. Thanks for asking," Joe snapped.

"Good to know. Ellie and I had a bit of a laugh over the video, after all. The irony of going from street walker to dog walker, and then this happening. She never did have the sense to make good choices," Gary said.

Joe felt the heat rolling up his neck as he flushed in anger. Laughing about that happening to anyone was appalling, but his mother had been fighting for her life, and they knew her. Very well. He felt an immediate need to defend her.

"You speak of her as if she's stupid. Surely you haven't forgotten how smart Mom is. She graduated high school before her sixteenth birthday and was close to graduating college by nineteen, right before I was born. And she chose to marry you, so... Oh, wait. You're absolutely right," Joe said.

Gary laughed. "I'm always right."

"I'm glad she married you, or neither Patty or I would have been born, but she could have made a better choice in husbands. And her choice of a best friend was just as faulty. You. Ellie. I mean... She never saw that coming. Anyway, thanks for sending me the video."

Gary was in shock and moving into full blown rage at what his son had just said, and snapped back.

"Sounds like she's really playing you for a sucker. Laying out quite the pity party."

"Oh, hell no! Mom doesn't play games, and you know it. Actually, she's pretty fed up with men and family in general. She wants nothing to do with Patty or me. She doesn't trust us. She says we turned into very cold, ugly versions of you. She doesn't want to talk to us. She doesn't want to see us. So, you're not always right, Dad. Sometimes you're way the hell off the mark," Joe said, and disconnected.

Gary blinked.

His son had hung up on him.

"Is everything all right?" Ellie asked.

Gary shrugged. "Of course. Just Joe being Joe. You know how he is. After all, he is Bettina's son, too, and she could be maddening."

Ellie glanced at the high color on Gary's face and wisely changed the subject.

CHAPTER SIXTEEN

After the phone call from her children, Bettina slept better than she had in years. She didn't know what would come of it, but Patty had called her Mommy, and Joe had called her Momma. That was from their childhood. Not the aftermath of her divorce. Maybe they hadn't forgotten everything good about her after all.

The next morning, Bettina managed to get the bandages changed, by herself, and get dressed for the day. She might still be on bed rest, but she didn't want to spend the day in pajamas again.

She had breakfast alone in the kitchen, which was fine with her. She was tired of being coddled. She'd already emailed her professor to let him know she'd been injured, and that as soon as she was able, would catch up on a couple of lessons she'd missed turning in. His reply was positive, telling her that he'd seen the video for himself, and to take the time she needed to get her work in without worry of late papers lowering her grade.

After breakfast, she took her laptop to the living room, turned on the gas fireplace, then settled into the recliner. Part of her felt like she'd given up again. But she had to accept the reality of what had happened, too. So what if another door had closed in her life.

If John Attilla came through for her and got the lost wages she'd asked for as part of her settlement from the dog owners, she intended to enroll as a full-time student next semester, attend daily classes, and finish the degree she'd started so many years ago.

Satisfied that it was the smartest decision, she leaned back in the recliner, pulled the blanket up to her waist, and closed her eyes.

The next day, Janie took Bettina to a doctor for a follow-up on her injuries. The doctor changed the dressings, told her everything was healing normally, and to come back in another week to get stitches removed.

To celebrate the good news, they went through a drive-through on the way back, and got burgers and fries, then headed home.

"Maybe we should let Pauline know we're bringing lunch," Janie said.

"I'll text her," Bettina said, and reached for her phone to send the message. "Done."

Pauline was going through email, searching for a reply from a current client so she could proceed with the project, when she noticed an email from a contest she'd entered months ago, before David's death.

It was a contest honoring website designers, both independent and corporate. She'd entered it on a whim, submitting a web design she'd done for a museum. She hadn't thought much of it when she saw the mail. Likely a "thank you for entering" notice, and that would be the end of that. Then she scanned the brief message.

"Oh, my God! No way!" she cried, and read it again, just to make sure she hadn't misunderstood.

It was the real deal!

Her web design had won a national award.

She printed out the email and then went straight to the contest site to see it, and there it was! Her design! Her name! Her excitement kept building as she printed that page as well. Talk about adding cachet to her personal webpage! This would definitely help bring in new clients.

She was on her way downstairs with the printouts when she got a text from Bettina. She and Janie were on their way home with burgers and fries! She couldn't wait to share her good news!

Gretchen was in a funk. Today would have been her and David's wedding anniversary, and she was struggling, uncertain of how she was supposed to feel.

In her head, she was pissed.

But in her heart, she missed the man he had presented himself to be, which was the basic cause of her funk.

What the hell was wrong with her? She should not have an ounce of empathy left for him—liar and thief that he was. Maybe it wasn't him she was sad about. Maybe it was herself.

She'd left home without telling anyone goodbye and had to make herself go to work rather than call in sick, which was how she felt. She'd given no one in the office even a hint of her disposition, but she didn't have a fuck left to give, and when lunch time rolled around, she headed down the hall to Sarah's office.

"Hey Sarah, I'm going out for lunch today."

"Okay. No problem. We'll lock up as always. Have a nice lunch," Sarah said.

"You, too," Gretchen said, and stopped in the breakroom to grab her coat and purse, then headed out the door.

She made herself walk, although she felt like running as she headed for her car, but there was nowhere to run. Wherever she was, heartbreak went with her.

The day was brisk. The cold air was the slap in the face she needed to get out of her head. It was like cleaning out cobwebs in a hidden corner of a room. The sun was out, but the sky was more gray than blue, a sure sign the weather was going to change.

She jumped into the car and made it all the way out of the parking lot before she realized she was crying. And then there was no stopping the angry tears, and the only person she had to yell at was herself, so she did.

"For the love of God, Gretchen! This day is a fake! You can't have an anniversary if there was never a marriage. Get the hell over it."

Then she wiped her eyes, blew her nose, and laughed at herself for all the drama as she headed to her favorite bakery. She was going to eat dessert for lunch, take a walk, and find something to be happy about.

It took ten minutes to get to the bakery, and another ten to pick out what she wanted. Then she drove to a little park a short distance from work. She got out carrying her purse, a bag with her three snickerdoodles, and a bottle of water, then began walking until she came to a bench and sat down.

Her eyes were burning. Her nose was runny, both from the cold and her tears. She could smell the cookies and knew how good they were going to taste, but she didn't open the bag. She just sat, staring off into space, wondering how long it was going to take to get past this horrible, awful, feeling.

She was watching a couple of birds flitting from tree to ground and back up again when she heard what sounded like a faint cry. Thinking it was a hawk, she glanced up, but saw nothing. Then she heard it again—a little louder now. Loud enough to know she was hearing a child crying, not a bird. She stood up then turned around, searching the trees and the grounds behind her, thinking someone might be hurt, but saw nothing. The cries were intermittent, but louder, and she began moving into the park toward the sounds—afraid of what she might find—but knowing she couldn't ignore them. As she walked around a curve on the path, she caught sight of something yellow beneath a large bush and hastened her step. When she reached the bush, she gasped, and then dropped to her knees.

It was a child, hardly more than a toddler, crouched beneath the bushes, almost hidden from sight. His face was scratched, and there were streaks of dried blood and tears on his face and neck. He had bits of dried grass and leaves in his hair and was wearing a little sweatshirt and jeans, but no coat, and he was noticeably shivering.

Gretchen immediately looked around for signs of an adult, and saw no one, then took off her coat and wrapped him up in it and pulled him to her.

"Hi, sweetheart. My name is Gretchen. What's your name?"

"Billy," he said, and melted into her warmth.

"Where's your mother?"

"I want my Mommy," he said, and tears began to roll.

"Do you know where she is?" Gretchen asked.

"I want Mommy," he cried, and broke out into sobs.

"Okay, sweetheart. Don't worry. You're not lost anymore, because I found you, and now we're going to find your Mommy, okay?"

She made a quick call to 9-1-1, with Billy still crying in her arms.

"9-1-1. What is your emergency?"

"I'm in Forest Park, on the path near that big gazebo. I just found a lost child. He's very young. He's been lost a while, I think, because his little face is scratched up, but the blood is dried. I'm afraid he's hypothermic. He had no coat and is shivering uncontrollably. I have him wrapped up in my coat right now, but he needs an ambulance, for sure."

"How old is he?" the dispatcher asked.

"I'm guessing about three, maybe a little younger. He said his name is Billy."

"Where exactly did you find him?" the dispatcher asked.

"Under some bushes. He has brown hair and blue eyes, and he's wearing a yellow sweatshirt and blue jeans."

"Just stay where you are," the 9-1-1 operator said. "Police are on the way."

"Yes, ma'am," Gretchen said.

Relieved that help was on the way, Gretchen just sat down on the path, still holding him in her arms and thought of her cookies and the bottle of water.

"Are you thirsty?" she asked, and took the lid off the bottle and held it up.

He reached for the bottle with both hands and pulled it toward his little mouth.

"Oops, let me help you," she said, and gave him little sips until he seemed satisfied, and then she took a cookie out of the bag and began breaking little pieces off for him to eat.

And so they sat, with Billy eating the little bits of cookie, and Gretchen praying for the sound of sirens.

It felt like forever, but it was less than five minutes before a half-dozen officers came running up the path toward them.

The little boy pointed. "Daddy!" he cried.

Gretchen gasped. The uniforms. Maybe his father was a cop.

And then the officers took him out of her arms and helped her up, all talking at once, wanting to know where and how she found him, and that they'd been looking for him for hours.

Then one of them introduced himself.

"I'm Officer Crandall. I'll be needing your name and address."

"I'm Gretchen Lowry," she said, and gave him her home address, as well as where she worked. "I came to the park to eat lunch. I know it's a little late in the year for all that, but I wanted some time alone and a little fresh air. I was sitting on a bench a few yards back when I heard cries. I followed the sounds. He was under these bushes. He said his name was Billy and wanted Mommy. When he saw all of you coming, he pointed at you and said, 'Daddy'."

"His name is Billy Royal. His dad is a policeman. His mother was carjacked this morning after taking her daughter to school. They threw her out of the car and sped off, not knowing Billy was in the back seat. I guess once they saw him, they dumped him and kept going."

And then Gretchen looked up, and saw a tall, dark-haired officer running toward them with a frantic look on his face.

Crandall sighed. "That's Sean Royal, Billy's father."

"Daddy," the little boy said, and held out his arms.

Moments later, Sean Royal was holding his son and crying. Then he turned to Gretchen.

"Are you the one who found him?" he asked.

"Yes. I gave him water and most of a snickerdoodle. I hope that's okay."

"It's very okay, and thank you! Thank you from the bottom of my heart. You're the angel we prayed for. The ambulance is here. We have to go."

Gretchen watched them leaving and was about to turn around to pick up her things when Officer Crandall walked up with her coat, held it while she slipped it on, then picked up her things.

"Allow me to walk you back to your car," he said.

"You don't have to," Gretchen said.

"Yes, ma'am, I do, and I consider it an honor."

Gretchen nodded, as she put her purse over her shoulder, and started back up the path with the officer beside her, carrying the bag with the cookies, and the bottle of water.

"His wife... Was she hurt?" Gretchen asked.

"She has abrasions on her face, and it broke her arm when they threw her out of the car, but she'll heal. And now that she has her baby back, she'll be fine."

"Have you caught the carjackers?" Gretchen asked.

"Not yet, but we will. It was all caught on security cams. We've identified them. All we have to do is find them."

Gretchen nodded, thinking now of the repercussions of being the one who found the boy.

"Officer Crandall, I would consider it a huge favor if my name was not mentioned when you announce that the boy has been found."

Crandall frowned. "May I ask why? Do you have something to hide?"

Gretchen sighed. "It's not that. It's just that I've already been in the papers and on the news enough this year to last a lifetime, and I really don't want to go through any of that again. I'm one of the four women who was married, or thought she was married, to the bigamist who was killed in a car accident earlier this year. I live with his other wives now because he left three of us penniless and homeless. Janie Logan, the legal wife, offered us a place to stay. We're working, trying to get back on our feet. One of us made the news a couple of months back by being attacked in our home, and another of us, who was working as a dog-walker, was recently the victim of a vicious dog attack. She nearly died. We've had the year from hell, and all we want is to live our lives under the media radar. All this will do is drag up 'the bigamist's wives' shit again."

Crandall was stunned. "I worked that intruder incident at Janie Logan's residence. The old Duvall property, right? I didn't see you there."

"I was at work. I work for Sarah Biggers at her insurance agency."

"I'll talk to our Sergeant and the guys to make sure they don't mention your name, and I'm sorry for your troubles."

"Thank you," Gretchen said, and then began slowing down. "That's my car." She got the remote out of her purse and unlocked the door.

Crandall opened the door for her, waited until she was seated inside, then handed her the cookies and water.

"Thank you," Gretchen said.

"No, ma'am. Thank you. You know... Some days on this job just suck. And then there are the days when you know you're right where you're supposed to be. Today, this was you. For whatever reason, you were in the right place when you were needed most. God bless."

Then he thumped the top of her car, turned, and walked away.

Gretchen glanced at the time. She was going to be a little bit late, but it no longer mattered. She started her car and after she backed away from the curb, finally got a cookie out of the bag, and ate it as she drove. Today was never going to be about her anniversary again. It was forever going to be the day she helped Billy Royal find home.

She said nothing about it when she went back to the office, but as she was walking into the breakroom to put her up things, Sarah walked in behind her.

"Hey, Gretchen. You have some bits of grass and leaves on the back of your pants."

"Ah... I went to the park. I guess the bench I sat on was dirty. Thanks. I'll brush it off," she said, and went into the bathroom to clean up.

Unaware of Gretchen's drama, the girls were finishing up their lunch of burgers and fries, celebrating Pauline's good news. They had the television on in the kitchen for the noon news and weather and were debating as to whether they needed to make a trip to the supermarket before rain set in, when programming was interrupted for a Breaking News bulletin.

"Oh! It's about that little boy who went missing during that carjacking this morning. Turn it up!" Pauline said.

Janie grabbed the remote and upped the volume.

"St. Louis PD has just announced Billy Royal, the missing three-year-old who was abducted this morning during a carjacking, has

been found safe. He was spotted by a citizen in Taylor Park and is
being treated for hypothermia. His parents thank the public for all
the tips and reports, and the alert citizen who found their little boy."

"Oh, what wonderful news," Bettina said. "Losing a child is every parent's worst nightmare. I can only imagine how terrified they have been!"

"I'm guessing the carjackers didn't know the boy was in the backseat until they were driving away, but why the hell did they leave him in that park? There are ponds and woods all over the place. He could have died of drowning or exposure before he was found," Janie said.

"Well, thanks to the alert citizen, whoever he or she may be, this story has a happy ending," Pauline said.

There were people coming and going from the insurance agency all afternoon. Some were kept waiting in the outer office with Gretchen until someone was free to help them. Most of them spent their wait time on their phones, except for the ones who sat and stared at Gretchen as she worked, but today, she was oblivious.

She could still feel that little boy shivering in her arms and remembering the look in his tear-filled eyes when she'd wrapped him up in her coat. Knowing what he'd been through, she could only imagine how confused and afraid he'd been. And how he'd leaned against her as he ate, soothed by a stranger's warmth and the sweet-sugar taste of cookie melting on his tongue.

She couldn't get over the randomness of leaving the office for lunch. She'd never done that. Not once since she began working there. But today, on the anniversary of the day David Lowry had sworn everlasting love to her and said "I do," she'd broken her routine. Today, because she was sick to her stomach angry at a dead man, she'd saved a little boy's life.

She saw the pattern—how one little rock thrown into the ocean can cause ripples forever.

If David hadn't died.

If he hadn't left her penniless.

If Janie Logan had not invited them into her home.

If she'd never gotten the job at the insurance agency.

If this hadn't been her anniversary.

If she hadn't been so angry, she would never have left the office.

Or bought the cookies.

Or gone to the park.

They might never have found Billy Royal until it was too late. One rock... A million ripples... It was nothing short of a miracle.

Hours later, Gretchen left work in a daze. She was mentally exhausted and still locked into the drama of her day as she headed home.

Six o'clock in October was after sundown. The porch light was on as she pulled up beneath the portico, lighting her way up the steps. She let herself in, locking the door behind her, and then paused in the foyer, listening to the chatter and laughter coming from the kitchen. She squeezed her eyes shut so tight that tears welled in the corners, and then she took a deep breath and called out.

"I'm home!"

Pauline came running, alight with an energy, that Gretchen imagined she could feel, and handed her a glass of ruby-red wine.

"Hi honey! Go get comfy. We're celebrating me tonight. I won a website award, and I made a bourbon pecan pie for dessert."

Gretchen smiled as she took the wine. "Oh, my God! How exciting! Congratulations. Give me a few to get changed, and I'll be right down."'

She took a quick sip of the wine, then set it on the bottom step and ran up. She traded her work clothes for pink sweats, then put her hair up in a ponytail before running back down. She retrieved her wine and took another quick sip as she headed for the kitchen. She paused in the doorway, seeing the three women who'd come to mean more to her than her own blood kin, and then sighed.

She was home.

"What smells so good?" she asked, as she headed for the charcuterie board, snagged a cold peeled shrimp dressed with the tiniest sprig of fresh dill, and popped it into her mouth.

"Glazed pork tenderloin, baby potatoes, and fresh asparagus," Janie said.

Gretchen gave her a thumbs up as she chewed and swallowed the shrimp.

"Girl, tell me about your award," she said, and picked up another shrimp as Pauline began to explain.

They sat down to dinner, still talking about their days and Bettina's checkup with her doctor, and all the while, Gretchen listened, and laughed, and commented, but said nothing about what had happened. It still seemed a bit surreal and talking about it felt like bragging.

And then the doorbell rang.

"Who in the world?" Janie muttered, and got up.

They sat, listening, heard surprise in her voice, and then the sound of multiple footsteps coming toward the kitchen.

All of a sudden, Janie appeared, followed by a half-dozen uniformed policemen, one of whom was Sean Royal.

Gretchen sighed.

The cat was out of the bag.

"Gretchen, these officers want to speak with you. What on earth have you done?"

Gretchen smiled as she stood. "Nothing illegal, I assure you." And then she shifted focus. "Officers, I'm afraid you're a little late for dinner."

Sean Royal stepped forward. "Mrs. Logan, you may or may not remember these men. They were the first on scene with you. Officer Crandall here informed us of your wish to remain anonymous, and we not only honored that, but understand it. However, I was so rushed when we met, that I did not properly extend the gratitude you so richly deserve. Billy is alive thanks to you."

Gretchen sighed. "How is he? He was so cold. I had no idea how long he'd been there without a coat, and then I heard the report they aired about his condition."

"He suffered some hypothermia, but he's home. Both he and his mother are on bed rest, and my house is full of so many family members tonight, I'll likely have no place to sleep. My wife, Terrie, sends you love from the bottom of her heart, and I second it. I spoke to our Captain. He wanted to give you a medal, but I explained your wish to remain anonymous," Sean said.

"I don't need a medal. I didn't do anything extraordinary except go to lunch. But what none of you know is that I never go out to lunch from work. I always bring it from home. But today, for no particular reason, I just felt the need to go out, and so I went to the park with a bag of cookies and sat on a bench feeling sorry for myself because today would have been my wedding anniversary—except the sorry bastard I thought was my husband, was not—and he was dead. So, I didn't even have anyone to be mad at. And then I heard a child crying, and you know the rest. After all of you left, I kept thinking how nothing is random. The Universe knows what's happening, and what's needed, even when we do not. So, believe me, my reward—my blessing—was your son in my lap, wrapped up in my coat, eating my cookies."

"Jesus, Mary, and Joseph," Sean whispered. "You were the angel we prayed for. Thank you."

Gretchen smiled. "You are so welcome. I hope you catch the

carjackers soon."

"We already have one in custody, and a warrant out for the other one's arrest. We'll find him, too," Sean said, then finally looked past Gretchen to the other women at the table.

Gretchen turned. "Where are my manners? I want all of you to meet my family. This is Janie Logan, and this fine house we're living in is hers. This is Bettina Lee, dog-walker extraordinaire, who just fought off a beast of a dog, saved herself, and lived to tell the tale. And this brilliant lady is Pauline Lord. We've been having ourselves a little celebration tonight because she just won a prestigious award for one of the websites she designed. Girls, this is Sean Royal, the husband of the woman who was carjacked this morning, and the father of Billy Royal, the little boy who was in the car when it was stolen."

"You found him and said nothing to us! You nut! You don't get to remain anonymous here!" Bettina shrieked, then blushed when everyone burst out laughing at her remark.

"Ladies, it's a pleasure. You are, without doubt, the most remarkable women it has ever been my pleasure to meet," Sean said. "We'll be leaving now to let you finish your celebration. And don't worry, your secret is safe with us."

"I'll see you out," Janie said, and walked them back to the door. As she was watching them piling into three different police cars, she noticed at least three neighbors at their windows watching, and sighed. "We'll be notorious here forever," she muttered, and closed the door.

By the time she got back to the kitchen, the girls were grilling Gretchen for details.

"Why didn't you tell us it was your anniversary?" Bettina said.

"Well, you were still asleep when I left. What did you want me to do? Run into your room screaming, 'It's the anniversary of the day I married a thief,' and then run off to work?"

Bettina frowned. "Well, no. Now that you put it like that. But girl! We've eaten a whole meal without you saying a word about finding the little boy."

"This is Pauline's night," Gretchen said. "Besides, it felt like bragging or something. Anyway, I would have said something sooner or later."

"Why did you want to stay anonymous?" Pauline asked.

"I know why," Janie said. "Because the moment someone realized she was one of the wives of the dead bigamist, they'd forget about Billy Royal, and turn our lives upside down again. I saw at least three different neighbors peeking through the curtains as the police left the house. God knows what they'll make of that." And then she giggled. "And you know what? Since you all came to live here, it has been the most exciting and eventful my life has ever been. I was trying to come to terms with growing old in this house alone, and then there was you. Never, never, never be ashamed of who you are—who *we* are. Hear me? I'm proud of all of us for surviving the bastard."

Gretchen nodded. "You nailed it. Anyway, now that's all settled, how about that pie?"

Their laughter echoed, and the house sent it back, as if it was laughing with them.

CHAPTER SEVENTEEN

Bettina's stitches were removed a week later, and the counseling sessions she'd been attending for the trauma came to an end at the same time. She was officially released from doctor's care.

There were places on her legs that were still tender, but the relief of having the stitches out and not having to go back to counseling was a relief. As far as Bettina was concerned, her counselor, Marilyn Corning, had veered too far off the path of her having been mauled by a dog, to focusing on her being the victim of a bigamist and trying to get her to see them both as attacks.

She'd finally called the counselor on it.

"Look, Marilyn, the only similarities of those two instances are that I never saw either of them coming until it was too late. But the positive aspect for me is that I survived both. You can't talk me out of resenting my dead ex any more than you can convince me to lose my fear of dogs, because the actions of a liar and a mean dog have changed me. I'm not fine yet, but I will be. Thank you for your help. I think we're done here."

Marilyn Corning had been a counselor for over twenty-three years. She'd known from the moment Bettina Lee walked into her office, that the woman was one of a kind. There was no artifice about her, nor was there any pretense about her in denying any of what had happened to her life.

At first, Marilyn thought Bettina seemed to be dealing with it all by being angry and shutting down. Only Bettina proved Marilyn wrong. Bettina wasn't an angry woman with a chip on her shoulder, but she was a wise and wary one. Two entirely different things. And so, she ended their last session with a smile and a handshake and sent Bettina on her way.

At that point, Bettina notified John Attila that her medical treatments had ended, and to proceed with her claims. That's when they hit Tony Watts with her demands.

It was nearing Thanksgiving when they received word from Watts' lawyer that Tony Watts had agreed to all of Bettina's requests and had also offered his sincere apologies for her pain and suffering to the tune of one hundred thousand dollars, plus all medical bills paid.

She accepted.

She didn't want to know what had happened to their dog, but suspected that, since the attack was so brutal and unprovoked, the authorities probably had put the dog down. And for that, she felt no guilt. She hadn't raised it. She hadn't turned it into the beast it became. She was just grateful she had survived it.

But as the holidays drew nearer, the girls began to admit they were all struggling with celebrating Thanksgiving and Christmas. David was dead. Gretchen and Bettina, who still had families, were ostracized from them. They weren't in the mood for pretending it was a joyous celebration, and they'd called a meeting amongst the four of them to discuss it.

Janie began the discussion with her usual honesty.

"Look. I was married to David for ten years, and I didn't spend even half of those holidays with him. I baked a turkey on Thanksgiving. I put up a tree on Christmas. And I told myself we'd celebrate when he showed up," Janie said. "But I've been alone for a long, long, time. If this doesn't feel right to any of you, then we'll let it pass without an issue."

"Maybe we've been trying too hard to be okay," Pauline said. "I know I don't share my sad or angry times. I just bury them and keep going, Traditionally, I know these holidays usually revolve around family gatherings, but when you don't have family, they are the worst."

Bettina held up her hand. "And then there's me. I have family who doesn't want me. And we all had the same lying, cheating bastard in our beds. You three are who I'm thankful for. I don't need to eat turkey to prove that, but I'm good with whatever you all decide."

Gretchen sighed. "I have a sister. She's a failure in the context of family. But I think sitting around here on Thanksgiving Day and feeling sorry for ourselves is the worst thing we can do. We don't have to call it a celebration. It can be a milestone. Our first Thanksgiving as members of the Broke-Ass Women's Club. We make a reservation somewhere. We go out to a nice meal at noon. And we raise a glass to ourselves, and be thankful for Janie, who saved us."

Janie's eyes welled. "If that's what you want, then I'll make reservations today. They'll fill up fast. Just tell me if we're going the traditional route or something else."

They all looked at each other.

"Gobble gobble?" Bettina asked.

They grinned and nodded.

"Traditional. Turkey and dressing, with all the sides, and pumpkin pie," Bettina said. "Meeting adjourned."

Thanksgiving Day arrived, bringing cold wind and rain with it.

Bettina always needed her morning coffee before she could shift to conversation mode and entered the kitchen with that one thing in mind.

Janie was making toast. Gretchen was at the table reading the paper on her iPad, and Pauline was stirring honey into a cup of tea.

"Ugh. What dismal weather," Bettina said, as she took a cup from the cabinet.

Janie nodded. "Agreed."

"However, it's just cold and wet. Not enough to deter me from turkey and dressing," Pauline said.

"Right! Neither snow nor rain nor heat nor gloom of night... Etcetera, etcetera," Gretchen added.

Bettina snorted. "We're not delivering the mail. We're just going out to eat turkey."

Janie grinned. "Everyone, just leave Miss Bee alone long enough for that first cup of coffee to hit her veins, and she'll be fine."

Bettina carried her coffee to the table, and when Janie handed her a little plate with a piece of toast, she sighed.

"Sorry I'm in bitch mode. I don't know what's wrong with me."

"Same thing that's wrong with all of us," Pauline said. "We're still on the 'feel sorry for ourselves train', and I, for one, am sick of the ride."

Bettina took a quick sip of her coffee, and then reached across the table to give Pauline's hand a quick squeeze.

"You're right. I'll volunteer to throw you off the train, if you'll be so kind as to give me a swift kick in the pants every time I start bitching."

"Deal," Pauline said, and then glanced up at Janie. "What time is our reservation again?"

"Eleven-thirty."

"Good," Pauline said. "That gives me plenty of time."

"Time for what?" Gretchen asked.

"To dress up like I'm going to walk a runway. It has always been my practice that when I feel like shit, I go overboard in making myself look good. It's how I fake it 'til I make it," Pauline said.

"Damn, that's a good one," Bettina said. "Where were you when I was growing up?"

"Probably still out on the farm cleaning cow shit off my shoes," Pauline said.

As they laughed, the sound diluted and dispersed the dark mood they'd brought with them, and the morning passed.

Later, they left the house, dressed fit to kill as Pauline had said, and carried that attitude all the way to the restaurant.

After Janie pulled into the parking lot and parked, she turned around.

"Okay, we're here, and today, we don't give a shit what looks we get, or what we overhear people saying, or anything. We aren't criminals, and we are not victims. Not anymore."

"Yes, ma'am," they said, and then got out and went inside, sat in the lobby waiting for their names to be called, and entered the dining room with their heads up, their shoulders back, envisioning themselves on a catwalk, as they followed their hostess to the table.

It was a day for thanksgiving, and they were, by God, going to be grateful if it killed them.

If they turned heads, they didn't notice. They ordered wine with their meals, and when the food came and the sommelier had decanted and poured the sparkling Chardonnay, Pauline picked up her glass.

"A toast to Janie. Today, I am most thankful for her."

"To Janie!" the others echoed.

Janie sat, absorbing their presence and the friendship they shared.

"To all of us," she said, and the clink of crystal, glass to glass, confirmed the toast.

They ate their way through the feast while keeping up a constant chatter, and when coffee and pumpkin pie arrived, they were still telling stories of who they'd been as children, and the people who'd raised them.

They left the restaurant in the same manner in which they'd arrived, looking neither here nor there, but straight out of the dining area and out the door, heads up, hips swaying just enough to remind themselves they were still women of consequence.

It was the Saturday after Thanksgiving.

The girls had just finished breakfast, still sitting around the table finishing their coffee and playing catch-up on each other's news, when they began talking about Christmas.

"Okay. One holiday down. One to go. Do we cook dinner here, or do we go out to eat like we did for Thanksgiving?"

"I say dinner here," Pauline said. "And I also think decorating the house a little for the upcoming holiday would be good."

"I always hold a Christmas Tea a week before Christmas," Janie said. "So, we'll definitely be decorating!"

"What kind of tea?" Pauline asked.

"It's basically a come and go party for all my clients. And now this year, we'll be adding names to the invitation list. The people Gretchen works with, Bettina's ex-clients, if she wishes, and any local customers Pauline has picked up. It's just appetizers, eggnog, and Christmas punch. Nothing alcoholic."

"Oh, how fun!" Gretchen said. "I love festive things, and I need a little festivity in my life these days."

"What's wrong with your V-man, Justin?" Bettina asked.

"Dead batteries," Gretchen said.

"Well, the David we shared is dead, too, but you can revive Justin with new batteries. David darling is well past that," Pauline drawled.

Janie got up from the table and went into the utility room.

"Was it something I said?" Pauline asked.

They heard drawers opening and cabinet doors banging, and then Janie came back, plopped a brand-new package of long-lasting D batteries in front of Gretchen, and sat back down.

"There's your festivities," Janie said. "In the meantime, let's go prowling in the attic. You'll need coats and shoes, and old gloves if you have any, because it's likely cold as all get out up there, but it's also where a thousand years of holiday decorations are stored. We can at least bring down a wreath to hang on the door."

Gretchen grinned. "Justin thanks you for your consideration, but a thousand years' worth? Are you sure?"

Janie smiled. "Well, something like that. Are you game?"

"Whither thou goest, and all that," Pauline said. "I'll meet you in the upper hall. I'm going to get a coat and change my shoes."

"I'm in," Gretchen said.

"You know I'm not missing a party," Bettina said.

"Splendid!" Janie said. "I'll meet you upstairs."

They dispersed to get dressed, and fifteen minutes later, they were on their way up the attic stairs to the third floor.

A blast of cold air met them at the door as well as aimlessly floating dust motes.

"Lord, it's cold up here," Janie said, and shut the door behind them after they were in.

"I can see your words," Gretchen said.

Janie exhaled and then watched the warmth of her breath turn into a cloud in front of her face.

"What am I saying?" she asked.

Gretchen shrugged. "Don't know. I can't read smoke signals."

They laughed, shivering where they stood.

"I still can't get over how massive this place is," Pauline said. "How do you know where to look?"

Janie turned and pointed. "Duvalls have always been a little OCD about things. I think that's why being an accountant came so easily to me. Numbers don't vary. Things have an order. And we like things in their place. As you can see, there are old paintings and artsy things over there. Furniture is stored at both ends for balance. Daddy always said if we didn't, one day, the attic might just collapse on the heavy side."

Bettina laughed. "I like how your Daddy thought. That's priceless."

Janie smiled, thinking of him. "He was a witty man and very sweet. There are a couple of generations of china up here, too. But we came here for decor, didn't we? So, see that old Christmas wreath on the wall? That tells me where all things Christmas are stored."

"And the fake skeleton in the corner behind those boxes is Halloween?" Gretchen asked.

Janie nodded. "And that picture hanging on the East wall of the overflowing cornucopia is where Thanksgiving things are stored. My accounting records of past clients are here. Not everything is on computer. And now that I think about it, there may be some old things of David's still stored up here. Ugh. I never even thought of that when I got rid of his stuff."

Within seconds they all turned and looked at each other, and then out at the vastness of the attic before them.

Janie saw the looks on their faces and knew Christmas decor had just taken a back seat to their need for answers.

"It was ten years ago, but I do remember helping him carry some of his things up here. Want to help me look?"

They nodded.

"What do we look for?" Pauline asked. "Trunks? Boxes? Suitcases?"

"Boxes. There weren't many. Maybe a couple."

"Were they marked in any way?" Gretchen asked.

Janie frowned. "I'm not sure, but I know his name was on them, and they were marked 'Personal'. Oh... And they were taped shut." She walked out into the middle of the open space, slowly turning as she tried to think if there was something about where they'd put them to remind her.

And then she glanced toward a small window overlooking the back gardens, and a wave of anguish washed through her, remembering how he'd walked up behind her at the window, slid his arms around her waist, and then pulled her down to where the sunlight had thrown a blanket of light onto the floor, and made love to her there. She thought she'd seen love in his eyes. How desperately wrong she had been.

She turned around, unaware there were tears rolling down her face.

"They'll be somewhere around here. Maybe even under one of those packing quilts."

They saw the tears, and even though they didn't know why, they understood, surrounding her, holding her without words until she'd quit shaking.

"We don't have to do this," Gretchen said.

Janie sighed. "Yes, we do. I don't want him back, and I damn sure don't want the ghost of him hiding in my attic with what's left of his earthly belongings. And like you said. Maybe there are answers we need to know."

So, they began the search. Moving dust covers and old packing quilts. Shifting trunks and boxes.

Gretchen found the first one.

"Here!" she said. "There's one here."

"Unless he moved them over the years, the other one is nearby. They were all together," Janie said, and then to her shock, they found five.

"He added boxes!" Janie said. "I never knew!"

They stood over them, staring at his name written in thick black slashes on every box, and the three that he'd added were numbered, as well. #1. #2. and #3.

"What do we do now?" Pauline asked.

Janie turned and pointed at the door.

"Get a couple of those dollies. We'll take everything downstairs to the living room and go through them there. No need to freeze ourselves up here any longer than necessary. We can get Christmas stuff another day."

Within a few minutes, they had five boxes stacked on two dollies and took them to the living room. Pauline flipped the switch on the gas fireplace, and within moments it was blazing. They piled their coats on a chair, then unloaded the boxes in front of the fireplace.

"We need a knife to open these," Bettina said, and headed for the kitchen.

"Let's go through each box together, that way we'll all see the same things at the same time," Janie said, and when Bettina came back, they cut the packing tape on all of them.

"Where do we start?" Pauline asked.

Janie frowned. "I think with the two he brought here with him. That will be the past we know nothing about. And then we'll go, 1, 2, and 3 on the other boxes, in that order."

They chose a box, sat in a circle near the fireplace, and opened it. The first thing on top was a small box full of photos. Old ones. Group shots of a bunch of little boys standing on the steps of a huge gray building.

"Maysville Boys Home. I think we just got our first clue. As we suspected all along, David Logan had no family," Janie said, and began passing around the pictures.

Pauline gasped.

"What? Gretchen asked.

"What if. . . in a sick, twisted way, he made us his family. Yes, he stole from us, and lied to us, and conned us six ways to Sunday, but he didn't walk out on us, did he? What if that's why he kept adding wives. So that wherever the job took him, he was never alone?"

They sat, staring at each other for a few moments, and then Bettina snorted.

"I'm not buying it. We weren't family. We were chess pieces, and he was the player, moving us and our money around his game board until life smacked him down. I refuse to feel sorry for the son-of-a-bitch."

Pauline eyed the anger in Bettina's eyes and then grinned.

"Sorry. I wasn't fishing for sympathy for him. I was trying to make sense of the whole debacle. I just can't get over what a dumbass he was for doing it."

"Anyway, back to the box," Janie said, and kept pulling out more pictures.

As the photos progressed and the same group of boys aged, they finally recognized his face. Handsome even then, and already a head taller than most.

There was a high school diploma from a school in Ohio.

And then things that meant nothing to them, but things that he'd kept. A seashell. A woman's necklace. Old postcards. A summons to appear in court. An old car title. A 1988 car tag from Alaska.

The last thing in the bottom of the box was an unused condom, still in its packet.

Bettina rolled her eyes. "Oh, the irony," she muttered, as they dumped everything back into the empty box. "This one's ready for the trash. I can't wait to see what's next."

The second box was more revealing. Years of income tax papers with his aliases.

"At least the didn't leave us indebted to the IRS," Gretchen muttered.

Then notebooks with names and dollar amounts beside them. It didn't take a genius to figure out the comments. They referred to the cons he was running, and the people he was scamming.

"Somehow, I don't feel quite as stupid anymore," Gretchen said. "He was a pro in his field, and we were putty in his hands."

They went through the contents quickly. It was old news, and this was a new day. They stacked that box against the wall with the other one and pulled out #1.

The first thing on top was a picture of Bettina.

"Well, shit. Given that I am the first illegal wife, how much do you want to bet that #2 is Gretchen, and #3 is Pauline?" she said.

"Then let's see," Janie said. "Girls, go claim your boxes and see if Miss Bee is right." And she was.

Janie sighed.

"Why wouldn't there be a box for Janie," Pauline asked.

"Because I'm the legal one," Janie said. "No lies. No scams involved. Go ahead and go through your own stuff. Share what you want, but do not feel obligated."

They each began digging through their boxes, and for the first time, saw the true cunning of the man, and how cleverly he had conned them. Part of the time they were cursing. Part of the time what they found brought tears, and part of the time they were in shock at how intricately he had planned and thought out his every move by making sure they were still within his driving area, but never too close to get caught out with one wife by any of the others. With every revelation, their disgust grew at how easily they'd been duped.

Bettina was all the way to the bottom of her box when she found a small notebook. The first things she saw when she opened it were two old checks made out to David Lee and signed by Gary Vale. In that moment, her heart stopped. She couldn't believe what she was seeing.

"What the fuck!" she muttered.

"What's wrong!" Janie asked.

"I don't know! There are two checks made out to David from my ex-husband, Gary. One for five thousand dollars, and another for twenty thousand dollars. They don't appear to have been cashed."

"David never actually cashed checks," Janie said. "Mobile banking, remember? He loved that. Taking a photo of the check on his phone and sending it direct to the bank. He did all of his business and banking on his phone and laptop."

"Look at the dates. Do they mean anything to you?" Gretchen asked.

Bettina glanced back at the checks, and then froze. The hair on the back of her neck stood up, and she began frantically going through the notebook. The more pages she turned, and the more notes she read, the more enraged she became, until she was shaking.

Suddenly she was on her feet and shouting, waving the checks in one hand, and the notebook in the other.

"Oh my God! You will not fucking believe this! The date on the smaller check! It's the date David proposed. The day we got engaged. The date on the larger check is the day we were married. According to what David had written in the notebook, Gary paid him to marry me to end his alimony payments."

Janie gasped. "You aren't serious?"

"How did they even meet?" Gretchen asked.

Bettina rolled her eyes. "That's easy. Gary is a doctor. David was a pharmaceutical rep. I guess you might say they met on the job. And this answers a big question I've had ever since that day at the funeral home when we first met, and I found out that all three of you had assets he'd wanted, while I didn't have any. I kept wondering why he'd still married me. I didn't have shit. I tried to tell myself that maybe it was love, when in truth, I'd just been sold off to the highest bidder. If David wasn't dead, I'd kill him, and it's a good thing for Gary he's a long way away, or I'd be on his doorstop with a gun."

Then she flopped down in the nearest chair and started sobbing.

Shock rolled through the girls in waves, and then they were surrounding her, and hugging her, and holding her while she cried. There was nothing more to explain. She'd said it all.

She cried until her eyes were so swollen, it hurt to blink. That's when she wiped her eyes, blew her nose, and stood up.

"I am going to my room. He's not going to get away with this. I am going to make Gary Vale sorry he was ever born."

They heard her going upstairs, and then looked at each other in dismay.

"Going through this stuff might have been a bad decision," Janie said.

"Hell, no!" Gretchen said. "It answers questions. And answers end the 'what ifs'. For the first time since I found out what he'd done, I feel free... Like I've been released from the guilt of being angry at a dead man. And I'm with Bettina. If he wasn't already dead, he'd be looking over his shoulder for the rest of his life."

Pauline kept glancing toward the door.

"Do you think we should go see if she's okay?"

Janie shook her head. "No. She needs to take this all in and figure out what she's going to do about it. And you *know* she'll never let this slide. Gary Vale did a terrible thing, and his day is coming. And knowing Miss Bee, Gary Vale won't know what hit him."

The girls were right.

Bettina had cried away the shock and hurt. All that was left was an ever-growing rage, and the determination to show him for the lowlife he was.

Her head was spinning with scenarios, all of which would get her thrown in jail. And then it hit her. She grabbed her laptop, pulled up Google, and began researching the features on her iPhone.

After a few minutes, she uploaded a Rev Call app on her phone, re-read through the instructions on her laptop, and then laid the checks and the notebook on the little desk in front of her, glanced at the time, and did something she swore she'd never do again.

She sent a text to her ex.

Call me. Talk to me now, or you'll be talking to my lawyer.

Then she looked up and out the windows into the gray skies and the blowing wind of this cold November day and waited.

Gary Vale was at the breakfast table, finishing his last cup of coffee and listening to Ellie's plans for where they'd spend Christmas. She was aiming for a ski trip to Aspen.

"I don't want to go where it's cold," Gary said. "You know I hate winter weather. Let's do some place warmer... Maybe a beach somewhere, tropical waters and warm sand, for God's sake."

Ellie pouted. "But I love the après ski aspect so much. All the darling sweaters, fitted pants, and boots. Think roaring fires in the lodge and hot buttered rum!"

"You also look great in bikinis," Gary said, and winked.

She sighed. "But I had my heart set on—"

Before she could finish, Gary's phone signaled a text. He glanced at it, saw Bettina's name come up, and frowned.

"What the hell?"

"What's wrong? Who's it from?" Ellie asked.

"Bettina," he muttered.

They stared at each other, and then curiosity won.

"Well, rather than wonder what's on her mind, read the text and find out," Ellie suggested.

Gary shrugged, opened the text, and felt his stomach roll. "Crap."

"What does it say?" Ellie asked.

He turned the phone around and let her read it for herself.

Ellie gasped. "What does that mean?"

"Hell, if I know, but I'm about to find out," Gary said.

"I want to hear," Ellie said.

"I'll put it on speaker," Gary said, and made the call.

When Bettina answered on the second ring, she was screaming.

"You are a despicable excuse for humanity, Gary Vale. I found the checks!"

Gary grunted as if he'd been punched.

"What checks? I don't know what—"

Bettina interrupted. "Don't lie. I'm holding them in my hands as we speak. One made out to David Lee for five thousand dollars, dated the day he proposed. One made out to David Lee for twenty thousand more on the day of our wedding! You paid a stranger twenty-five thousand dollars to marry me, just to get out of alimony payments! You are a worthless piece of shit, Gary Vale. You sold me to a criminal without a fucking qualm. Whose idea was this? Yours or Ellie's? Oh, never mind! It doesn't even matter anymore. You sold me to a crook, then told lies about me to our children for years."

Gary glanced at Ellie. The red splotches on her face were evidence of the shock that they'd been found out.

"You said she'd never know!" Ellie hissed.

Gary covered his phone. "Shut it!" Then he started in on Bettina. "Are you drunk? Have you lost your mind? That's absurd! Yes, I did pay him some money, but for something else entirely. So, you can stuff your crazy suppositions up your ass and—"

Bettina interrupted again, shouting louder. "Bullshit! Shut up! Just shut up! You've already spouted enough lies about me to last a lifetime, and now you're going to listen! You can lie until the day you die, Gary Vale, but I am holding the proof. David loved mobile banking. He never physically cashed a check. He did the whole 'take a picture and hit send' thing, and then kept them. You did business with a crook. A conman. They always keep a little sump-em, sump-em back to hold over the people they scam, just in case a little blackmail is in order. It's all here in the notebook with the checks. The whole deal you made. You make me sick, Dr. Vale. First, do no harm. I guess I should be grateful you didn't just hire a hit man to take me out."

"What are you going to—" The line went dead in Gary's ear. He looked up at Ellie. "She hung up on me."

"Oh, my God! What are we going to do?" Ellie cried.

"Hell if I know," Gary mumbled, and stared out the windows overlooking the leafless trees and bushes into the cold, gray sky above.

Bettina listened to the recording, breathing a sigh of relief that she hadn't messed anything up, and then emailed it to herself.

Then she lined up the checks and the little notebook lying open to a page with Gary's name on it along with a tell-tale notation, and took photos of all of it, then sent them to herself in an email as well. Next, she saved everything into a file and began writing an email to Joe, copying Patty on it as well.

Found a box of David's belongings up in Janie's attic that were all about me. As it turns out, he and your father made a deal I knew nothing about. Your scum-sucking father paid David Lee—a conman—twenty-five thousand dollars to marry me to get out of paying alimony. You'll hear details in the recording of our conversation.

Needless to say, I am hurt and enraged beyond words. He better be glad there are so many miles between us.

Then she attached the recording and the photos and hit send.

Patty had just logged onto her laptop to check email when her mother's message popped up. She was so glad to see it that she immediately opened it, hoping it was her first gesture of forgiving them.

And then she read it.

It was shock—pure shock rolling at breakneck speed, hearing the recording of her parents' phone conversation—seeing the photos of the checks and the notebook. She couldn't believe their father had done it, even though she'd heard him admit it. The depth of his betrayal was right before her eyes, and she felt like the ground had just been cut out from under her.

She called Joe.

Joe was just getting out of the shower when he heard his phone ringing in the bedroom. He grabbed a towel and ran, picking up the call just before it went to voicemail.

"Hey, Sis! What's up?"

Patty's voice was trembling. "Have you checked your email this morning?"

"No, why?"

"Go do it, then call me back. Our world has just exploded," Patty said.

"What's wrong? Is it Dad? Is it Mom?" Joe asked.

"Everything, and both of them," she said, and hung up.

Now Joe was worried. Patty wasn't crying, but she sounded weird—like she was in shock. He dried off in seconds, pulled on sweatpants and a sweatshirt, and made a run for his office. The first thing he saw when he pulled up his email was the message from their mom, but after his sister's cryptic comments, he was dreading the contents.

And then he opened it, reading in disbelief until he heard his father's voice on the recording and saw the checks.

"Dad. You son-of-a-bitch."

Then he picked up his phone and called Patty.

Patty answered on the first ring.

"Joe! What the hell?"

"I am in shock," he mumbled.

"Same. All these years. All the innuendoes he made about Mom that we believed. All the snide remarks about the choices she made. And all the while, he'd set her up to fail. Right now, as a woman, I am so sad on her behalf that it hurts to breathe," Patty said.

"I'm about to call Dad. Want in on the conference call?" Joe said.

"Hell, yes."

"Give me a sec. I'll call you back, then Dad."

Patty waited, then when his call came in, she answered.

"I'm here."

"Calling him now," Joe said.

Moments later, they heard their father's voice.

"Hello, son. How are you this cold Saturday morning?"

"Sick to my stomach and about as shocked as I have ever been in my life," Joe said.

Then Patty pitched in. "Dad, it's me. You are a bastard. You betrayed us. I will never forgive you for what you did to Mom."

Gary froze.

Ellie walked in, saw the shock on Gary's face, and ran to him.

"What's wrong?" she cried.

"Holy shit. She told the kids," he whispered, and put the phone on speaker before he started talking.

"Look, Joe. You don't know the whole story. You can't believe everything she—"

"Shut the fuck up!" Joe yelled. "She recorded the phone call. We heard you. We heard her. We saw the checks. And the notebook. I don't know if you could be criminally charged for what you did, but you broke every law of morality. You disgust me!"

Gary was in a panic now. "Joe. Patty. You have to understand. I didn't know he was already married. I didn't—"

The moment Patty heard that, she jumped into the conversation.

"You didn't know and didn't care! He could have been a serial killer. An abusive maniac. A monster... and you still wouldn't have cared, because you were thinking about yourself. I thought you were a good man. And now it turns out the only monster our mother married was you! Mom wants nothing to do with us, and I want nothing to do with you. Ever again."

Gary couldn't believe this was happening.

"Please. Please. I love you. You two have to believe me. I can't bear you hating me. I never meant for—"

"Well, you damn sure didn't care if we hated our mother," Joe shouted. "And you've never done anything rash. Everything is always planned and executed accordingly. You got exactly what you wanted. You and Ellie. Was she part of this? Did you both conspire against Mom like this? Oh, who am I kidding? Of course, you did. Ellie got what she wanted, which was you. And you both got Mom out of your lives when you sold her to a crook. If Mom can't forgive us, then Patty and I are on our own."

Gary groaned. "No, no! Please don't say that! I can't lose you."

"You already have. You should be in prison for what you did," Patty said.

The line went dead, even as Gary was still begging. And when he realized they'd hung up, he dropped his head and burst into tears.

Ellie was in shock, and she was scared. She knew Gary. When the smoke from this conflagration finally cleared, he was going to lay the blame on her, because blaming someone else was how he coped with failure.

She walked out of the room, and the moment she was out of

Gary's sight, she grabbed her coat and purse and left the house. She needed to get to the bank. It was time to move a little more of their money into her private account. She'd been doing it for years as insurance against disaster, and the disaster she'd feared had finally hit. If ever there had been a "save herself first" situation, this was it.

Joe called Patty back.

"Now we call Mom, and pray she answers the phone."

"What do we say? How will we ever make her believe us again?"

"Just go with me on this," he said, then set up another conference call and rang Bettina's number.

Bettina was lying on her bed, staring out the windows.

The November sky was so gray and empty of light it looked like it was dying. Maybe it was just a reflection of how she felt, but rage had run its course. She felt used, abused, and defeated, and was trying to find something to hold onto that would make tomorrow matter. Then her phone rang.

She glanced at caller ID.

Joe.

Well, she'd sent the emails. She'd expected some kind of response, and this was likely it. She sat up, then reached for the phone.

"Hello."

"Mom? It's me. Patty is on the call. We're dumbfounded. Horrified on your behalf. Enraged at what Dad did. We are so sorry he did this to you, and we've already had it out with him. He no longer exists in my world."

"Or mine," Patty said.

She didn't comment, which made Joe anxious, but he kept talking. "So, if we're still on your hate list, then Patty and I are officially without family, because we will never claim kin to that man again."

"How you feel about that man has nothing to do with me," Bettina said. "I didn't send that to destroy him. I sent it to the both of you to defend myself, which I should never have had to do."

Joe felt sick. He heard something in her voice that he'd never heard before. Like she had already quit on everything.

"You're right, Mom. You're so right," he said. "But I want to ask you something. I think it might help us all come to terms with what has happened. Will you hear me out?"

Bettina saw something in the sky. A hawk—coming straight toward the house. Then when it swooped down and landed in a tree outside her window, she blinked. It felt like a message.

"I'm listening," she said.

Joe breathed a quick sigh of relief. "Thanks. There are a couple of things I need to know. When the police first notified you of David's death, were you shocked and sad? Pretty much in disbelief?"

Bettina frowned. She didn't know where he was going with this, but she'd promised to listen.

"Yes, that just about describes it."

"And then when they told you about his deceit, and you realized all the lies you'd been fed, and that you weren't the only victim, you got angry, right?"

"Anger is a mild word for how I felt, but yes. That's right."

"And in the ensuing days, you continued to discover you were the victim of a real conman, in more ways than one."

"Yes, that's true, too."

Joe took a deep breath and then exhaled slowly.

"So... I need you to understand that I think that's exactly what happened to me and Patty. I've been looking for his feet of clay like you asked, and now I see, they were visible all along. I'd just never noticed. To doubted. I think, like you, we were the victims of a con, only the conman was our father. We were stupid kids when you two divorced. When you moved out, Dad made sure to feed us the 'you've been abandoned' speech in every format he could come up with, until it began to feel real. He lied to us daily, and we believed it. We were stupid, but we were also being conned by someone we trusted, so the blinders were on. And then today, when you sent that email... Well, that was the police at *our* door, giving us the news that the dad we knew wasn't real, and telling us how deeply we'd been deceived."

"It's true, Mom. All of it," Patty said. "I can only imagine your shock and heartbreak. Finding out that Dad didn't give a damn about your life or safety, as long as he got out of paying alimony. It must have hurt all the way to your soul. I don't know if what he did was illegal, but it was fifty shades of immoral and unforgiveable, and I'm so sorry we fell for it and hurt you."

"Well, that's all we have to say," Joe said. "We know you're still reeling from this whole ugly mess. You don't have to respond to anything right now, but if you can ever find your way to forgiving us, please call. We may not deserve it, but we would so love to have our mother back."

"Love you, Mom," Patty said.

"Ditto that," Joe added, and then they were gone.

Bettina felt the disconnect immediately. Whatever happened next was up to her.

The hawk was still in the tree—stunning in avian splendor.

She stood, and when she did, the hawk's head swiveled, fixing its gaze directly toward the window. It was hunting, but wise enough not to let itself become the hunted. If only she'd been this wary.

She took a step forward, and when she did, the hawk took flight. She watched from the window until it was out of sight.

It had chosen that tree, but she was the interloper that changed the plan. Just like David changed hers.

And such is life.

The hawk was gone.

David was gone.

But she was still here, and it was time to move on.

CHAPTER EIGHTEEN

Bettina heard the girls' voices as she came down the stairs. It felt like a lifetime ago when she'd gone up to her room, even though only a couple of hours had passed.

They saw her as she walked in. Saw how swollen her eyes were from crying, and they stopped, waiting for her cue. Then she paused in the doorway, her hands on her hips.

"Well, I just blew up two worlds. I know it's still morning, but does anybody besides me want a drink?"

"I'll take wine," Janie said, and dropped the wreath she was holding.

"I'll have what she's having," Gretchen said.

"What's your pleasure?" Pauline asked.

Bettina's eyes narrowed. "Whiskey. Neat."

"I'm with you," Pauline said.

They all headed for the library, and then the bar at the end of the room. Bettina poured their drinks, and they sat.

Bettina tossed her shot of whiskey back like a gambler right before he laid down the winning hand and started talking.

"The conversation I had with Gary wasn't pretty, but he admitted everything, then tried to excuse his actions. He is so full of bullshit, but I digress. I recorded the conversation without his knowledge and sent it to my kids, along with pictures of the checks and the notebook open to a page mentioning the deal with Gary. They lost their minds, nailed him to the wall, and quit him. I've been so hurt by how my children acted toward me after our divorce, but after this happened, my son said something that really made sense. He alluded to the fact that he and Patty had apparently been as conned by their father as we were conned by David. Gary fed them lie after lie to turn them against me. They were kids, and I was gone. He lied to them, and they believed, just like David lied to us, and we believed."

"Oh wow," Janie whispered. "That's deep, Miss Bee. And very insightful of him."

Bettina nodded.

"What are you going to do?" Gretchen asked.

"With your blessings, invite them to Christmas dinner?" Bettina said.

"Yes!" Pauline said.

"Absolutely," Gretchen said.

"Can't wait to meet them," Janie said.

"Thank you," Bettina said.

Janie glanced at Gretchen. "You are welcome to invite your sister to dinner, too. The more the merrier."

Gretchen's stomach knotted. "She would ruin the whole day."

"Not unless you let her," Bettina said. "And you have us for backup. But that's only if you want."

Gretchen shook her head. "Thank you, but no. The distance between us feels safer. Besides, she doesn't love me. She just loves herself. When the spotlight moves away from her, if even for a moment, she creates drama to pull it back. Besides, I have acquired three sisters this year that I think I'll keep."

"Ah... A true narcissist," Janie said. "Understood. Won't ever mention it again. As for the sisterhood thing... ditto, sugar," Janie said, and then gave Gretchen a quick hug.

Bettina sat in silence for a few moments, and then added. "Want to hear the phone call?"

"Yes!" they echoed.

She pulled up the recording, hit play, and then put it on speaker, and when it was over, they were momentarily silent.

Finally, Janie was the first to comment. "Holy shit."

Gretchen was in shock. "Whoa, Miss Bee. Way to go. You know the old saying, 'revenge is a dish best served cold'. I'll bet he never saw that coming, but he should have. A woman wronged is an enemy forever."

"Hmmm, now *that* last sentence would make a great bumper sticker, too," Pauline said. "You guys are full of them. I'm seriously going to have to explore that bumper sticker stuff as a side business."

Janie leaned forward. "So. After all we've uncovered from opening those boxes, do you feel a measure of justice has been delivered, or does knowing all of this just make things worse?"

Bettina shrugged. "It answers questions. Knowledge is wisdom. Wisdom is growth. It can't all be bad." She leaned back in her chair and closed her eyes, but she was smiling.

"What's funny?" Pauline asked.

Bettina looked up. "Gary's wife. I know how she operates. If she hasn't already done it, she is, at this moment, in getaway mode."

"But why would she want to leave Gary just because he's been found out?" Janie asked.

"Because, knowing her, they were in it together, and now that the bubble has burst, they'll be at each other's throats, playing the blame game, and Gary will never admit he was wrong. Whether she knows it or not, she's toast."

Gretchen nodded. "When there are worms in the apples, no matter how red and shiny they appear, they eventually rot."

After the emotional fall-out from the boxes, they hung a huge Christmas wreath on the front door, and for the time being, called it done.

Gretchen shoved her hands through her hair in disbelief. "Is this still the same day? It feels like forever since we all went upstairs to look for decorations."

"It's the same day, but I know what you mean," Bettina said. "And it's a good thing I'm blonde, because there's got to be a gray streak in my hair somewhere from the shock."

"I know it's cold, but let's get some fresh air. Let's go out for lunch. After digging through all those boxes, it feels like we've been mingling with a ghost," Janie said.

"I need to change," Pauline said.

"So do I," Bettina added, and they all headed to their rooms.

They chose pizza.

The warm air and the mingling scents of baking crusts, spicy sausages, and melting cheese wrapped around them as they entered the restaurant.

"Oh, my gosh, it smells so good in here," Gretchen said.

"And no waiting today. Here comes a hostess," Janie added.

They wound their way through the diners, following the girl with their menus, then took off their coats and put them on the backs of their chairs before they sat.

The room was busy. The tables full of diners, talking, laughing, and even the hints of arguments in low, angry tones. The noise level was just below fraternity food fight, and it was perfect for their moods.

Their waiter arrived and took appetizer and drink orders while they were still trying to decide what they wanted to eat.

As they talked, a family moving past their table suddenly stopped, and then the man spoke.

"Hello, ladies. Excuse me for interrupting your meal."

They looked up, and then Gretchen smiled.

"Sean Royal! Is this your family?"

"Yes. We're just leaving, but we saw you come in. This is my wife, Terrie. My daughter Laura, and of course, Billy, who may look a little the worse for wear, since that slice of pizza he just wrangled. Terrie wanted to meet you and thank you in person for what you did."

Terri Royal moved a step closer to the table. "Mrs. Lowry, it is my blessing to finally meet you. Thank you for saving our son. Thank you from the bottom of my heart. Billy suffered no lasting effects, thanks to you."

"I was just in the right place at the right time," Gretchen said, and noticed Billy smiling shyly at her. "Hi, buddy. Do you remember me?"

"Cookies," Billy said, and grinned.

"Yes. Cookies," she said, and laid her hand on his head, remembering the feel of his hair against her cheek.

"Well, then. We won't disturb you any longer," Sean said. "Hope you all have a Merry Christmas. Thanks to you, we sure will."

"Oh, Gretchen! How special was that?" Janie said, as they watched the family leaving the restaurant.

"Pretty much made my day," Gretchen said, still smiling.

"And a good reminder to get over ourselves," Bettina added.

Pauline nodded. "Right. Everyone has problems. Some get solved. Some we have to learn to live with. And life goes on. I'm having a thin crust sausage and mushroom pizza. Anyone want to share?"

The discussions began, and the meal came and went without any further interruptions. Afterward, they ran errands, picking up groceries, a couple of prescriptions, and clothes from the cleaners. By the time they headed home, their car was as full as they were. Now, all they had to do was get home and unload it.

They put up a tree in the living room and decorated it with ornaments from the generations of Duvalls. Then when they were finished, Janie produced four small boxes and gave one to each of them, keeping the last one for herself.

"What are these for?" Gretchen asked.

"It's an ornament for each of you. Everything on this tree comes from my family, but this is our tree, and we all need to be a part of it. So, next Christmas, when we do this again, you'll have your own ornaments to hang."

"Oh, Janie! How thoughtful of you," Gretchen said.

Janie smiled. "Okay... Open your boxes and hang your ornaments."

And so they did, exclaiming over the small glass angels with clear crystal wings, and tiny gold halos on their hair.

"I'm going to cry," Pauline said.

Bettina frowned. "Nope. Nope. You're not gonna do that, because then I'll cry, and I'm just learning how to put on false eyelashes. I don't want one floating down the side of my face, okay?"

They grinned.

"Oh, is that what's on your eyes? I thought you'd just slept in your makeup again," Janie said.

Bettina grinned. "Shut it. I'm trying new things," she said, and then picked up an ornament hook, and hung her angel on the tree.

The other girls did the same, and then stepped back to eye their work.

The tree was aglitter. The lights sparkled. The holly garland and big red candles on the grand, cherry wood mantle gave the room an old-world appearance. All that was missing was a Yule log on the fire, but they were happy with the gas logs and the flickering flames dancing among them.

"It's perfect! Best ever!" Janie said. "I am so glad we are together. Let's go to the kitchen. I want some of that hot chocolate simmering on the back of the stove, and you can help me with the list of who you want to invite to the Christmas Tea. I've already ordered the invitations. Now all we need are names and addresses of your guests."

They gathered around the table with their mugs of hot chocolate, while Janie had a big notepad and a pen.

"Write down the names and pass it on. You can give me addresses later. All I need right now is a head count, so I'll know how much food to order."

"We could make our own," Pauline said. "I wouldn't mind."

"I know," Janie said. "And your stuff would be so good, but we're not turning ourselves into the chef and wait staff and miss our own party, right?"

"Oh, good point," Pauline said. "I might even go to your stylist at Crowning Glory and get my hair and nails done."

"And something new to wear," Bettina said.

"Something red and sparkly," Gretchen added.

"I don't do red," Janie said. "My hair is all the red I dare wear, otherwise I always look like the cherry on top."

"You *are* the cherry on top," Gretchen said. "Own it."

They kept up the chatter as they wrote names and sipped the sweet, warm chocolate. Then they helped Janie plan the menu of foods to order. It was the biggest event of their lives together, and they didn't want to mess it up.

Later that night, after dinner, Bettina went upstairs, crawled on her bed, and picked up her phone. She was about to take a chance on getting her heart broken again, but she was ready to risk it.

Her first call was to Joe, because he was her first-born. She glanced at the time. A little after nine p.m. Tomorrow was a workday. Hopefully he would be home. She made the call, listening as it began to ring, and then on the third ring he picked up, slightly breathless, but she heard hope in his voice.

"Hello? Mom?"

"Hi, Joe. Yes, it's me. How would you feel about having Christmas dinner with me, here at our house?"

His voice broke. "Oh God—Mom—happy, that's how I'd feel."

"Then consider yourself invited. As huge as this house is, there aren't any extra bedrooms, but I will make reservations at one of the hotels for you and Patty, if that's okay?"

"Yes, it's okay. Anything is okay."

"Okay, send me dates when you and Patty can fly out. I can pick you up at the airport. I hope you can come a couple of days early, so we'll have some time to spend together before the big day."

"Yes, yes. I'll get with Patty about that. Have you spoken to her yet?"

"No, but I will."

"Mom, do not buy us gifts. Being forgiven is the best Christmas present ever. I love you. Can't wait to see you again."

"I love you, too, Joe. I'm going to call your sister now. Text me within the next two days about arrival dates, so I can make that hotel reservation. They'll fill up fast here."

"I will. I promise. Talk to you soon," he said.

"Yes, good. I'll be waiting for your call," Bettina said, and hung up.

Then she turned around and called Patty. It only rang once before Patty picked up.

"Mom!"

"Hello, Patty. I just spoke to Joe and invited him to Christmas dinner here, and I'm issuing the same invitation to you, if you're interested. If you've already made—"

"Oh Mama... Yes, I want to come. Thank you for giving us another chance. I feel so ashamed of how we treated you."

Bettina's heart skipped a beat. This felt positive, and that was a good thing.

"Well, this is going to be us, letting go of the past. I haven't seen either of you in person for over seven years, and I keep wondering how much you've changed, and if I'll still recognize you. You became adults without me," Bettina said.

Patty sighed. "We did get older, and we do look a bit different, I suppose, but I don't think we have done much adulting. I think we got stuck in the spoiled brat stage."

Bettina smiled. She wasn't going to comment on a truth.

"I've already explained the situation to Joe about no empty guest bedrooms, since we're all living in them, but I'm getting you rooms in a nice hotel for the duration of your stay. And I'll pick you up at the airport when you arrive. As I mentioned to Joe, I hope you can come a couple of days early, so we can spend some alone time together before Christmas Day."

"Yes! I would love that. I can make that happen," Patty said.

"So, talk to Joe. Get your travel dates coordinated and get back to me ASAP. The longer I wait, the harder it will be to get good reservations."

"We will, and thank you again! I can't wait to see you. Love you, Mama."

"I love you, too," Bettina said, and disconnected.

Then she laid down with her phone against her heart and closed her eyes.

Please God, let this work. I need my babies in my life, even if they no longer need me.

A couple of days later, Joe sent Bettina a text with their arrival and departure dates. Three days, two nights, and flying home late Christmas day. Bettina quickly reserved rooms for them at the River Center Casino and Hotel. She sent them the info so they could see where they'd be staying. The excitement was building about seeing them again. She had no idea what had happened between Ellie and Gary, and didn't care, but she knew when her kids arrived, if there was anything to know, they'd tell her.

Once the Christmas tree went up in the living room, their Christmas shopping began. Four women, trying to find the perfect gift for each other, within a pre-set limit of twenty-five dollars. Ingenuity led to trips to little boutiques, and craft fairs, and church bazaars, and then the secretive wrappings before putting the presents beneath their tree.

The kitchen was awash in candy making and holiday breads to give as gifts. Gretchen made loaves of pumpkin bread to give to her co-workers and Pauline bought little gift boxes of flavored teas and sent them to the clients she'd worked with. Janie's gift to her clients was the same as it always was—the Christmas Tea, which was now only two days away. Bettina was in the midst of semester finals and had been cramming for days beforehand.

The city was alight in decor, as were neighborhoods.

When Gretchen drove home from work each night, it was like driving through a Christmas wonderland. Everything from Santa and his reindeer on roofs, to blow-up dinosaurs wearing elf hats, were on people's lawns. Homes with blinking lights wrapped around porch posts and dripping from the eaves of houses—to churches everywhere lit up from inside with nativity scenes outside their doors. Glimpses of Christmas trees were visible in picture windows and behind partially opened blinds.

Some people showed off their Christmas spirit.

Others celebrated it from within.

But it was the season to be jolly.

Gretchen had finally taken the test to get a realtor's license, and was anxiously awaiting the results. She came home from work one evening, picked up her stack of mail from the kitchen table, and was sorting through the letters when she saw the return address on a long white envelope. Her heart skipped a beat. She tore into it quickly, scanned the letter, and then let out a whoop.

"I did it! I did it!" she yelled and ran down the hall to show Janie.

"I passed the test. I still have to go through background checks and get fingerprinted, but I passed!!!! I'm going to be a Realtor!"

Janie jumped up and hugged her, laughing with her in her success.

"I am so happy for you, honey!" Janie said. "But I never doubted for a minute that you would pass."

"I've got to tell the others!" she said, and left the office on the run.

Janie sat back down, thinking to herself as she heard Gretchen running up the stairs, shouting out her news.

There you are, David Logan. One more survivor pulling herself up from the pit you tried to bury her in.

The morning of the tea dawned clear and cold. A van from Flowers by Baxter was at their door by nine a.m. with holiday arrangements and pots of red and white poinsettias. Janie let them in, directed where she wanted everything to be placed, and then they were gone.

The caterers came in two shifts. The first ones brought white folding chairs with plush cushions in every seat, and tiny cocktail tables scattered about the living room and foyer for the guests. They set up a punch bowl, and a bowl for eggnog at the cherry wood dining table, with dozens of little cups all waiting to be filled, and then they left.

The second shift would bring the food and drink, and the staff to host it. They'd take over Janie's kitchen, as they did every year, and the show would go on.

Only this year, Janie wasn't hosting this alone, and the delight she felt in sharing this with the girls was bubbling inside her. Not once in all the years she and David were married had he ever been home for one of these. But this year, his wives were. All four of them. It could have been awkward, but instead it felt right.

Janie had already been contacted by the *Dispatch*, asking her if they could send one of their writers and a photographer to get a few photos for the Lifestyles section of the paper. It was the twentieth anniversary of the Duvall Christmas Tea, and they wanted to use it as part of the St. Louis social scene.

She'd agreed without thinking, only later realizing they would face the consequences of winding up in the paper again. Then she shrugged off her worry and thought, why not? At least this time, no police would be involved, and the girls were excited. So, there was that.

Pauline was doing last minute dusting.

Gretchen had done a quick sweep of the front steps.

Bettina was in charge of getting all the lighting just right and making sure the fireplace was on.

And Janie was making sure there were sufficient hand towels in the guest bathroom downstairs, and fresh rolls of tissue on the roller.

The big day was here, and time was running close. It was a bit past noon. The caterers would be here within an hour. The party was from two to five p.m. It was time to put the finishing touches of themselves.

Janie came running up the hall, her curls bouncing, and called a halt.

"Okay ladies, we've done all we can to this old girl. Now it's time for us. Go make yourselves pretty. The party starts at two p.m. sharp, and I want us all together when the first guests begin to arrive. After that, mix, mingle, and enjoy the goodies. There will be someone to get the door after that."

"The whole place is dripping in old school elegance. Thank you for letting us be a part of it," Gretchen said.

"Trust me, I'm the one who's excited you're here," Janie said. "I've always done this by myself... except for Baxter. He always made sure to be here for me."

"But surely David was—" Pauline started, and then snorted. "Bite my tongue. What was I thinking?"

They all knew what she what she meant. David had never been around when they needed him. They turned and bolted up the stairs, while Janie headed down the hall to her bedroom.

Janie stripped down to her undies, and then started applying makeup, pulling out jewelry, and the shoes she wanted to wear, and then looked at her hair and sighed.

"As usual, you are an unruly mess, and I can't do a thing about it. Ah well, if anyone comments, I'll just tell them I'm going for the 'just had mind-blowing sex look', and let them wonder if I already have a new man in the wings."

Then she laughed at her own wit and reached for her dress. Yes, it was awash in silver bangles, and yes, it was the most mini, mini dress she'd ever owned, and yes, her red heels were a couple of shades shy of stilettos, because she didn't want to look like she was walking on stilts. But she was owning the look.

She chose the most outrageous dangle earrings she owned and slipped her mother's ruby cocktail ring on the finger where her wedding band used to be, and then closed the doors to her bedroom, the library, and her office, as she passed them on her way up the hall.

Bettina had the same routine, makeup, hair, jewelry and then her dress. Even though it wasn't an after-five affair, they'd all decided to sparkle, and the black sequined mini-dress she was wearing caught the light, no matter which way she turned.

She left her blonde hair down but clipped back over one ear with a white silk poinsettia, and then added the diamond earrings Gary had given her for their tenth wedding anniversary. There was nothing sentimental about it. Just the need for flash. She had her war paint on and was flaunting the scars on her legs from the dog attack. She wasn't ashamed of them. They were proof she was a survivor.

Gretchen was a vision in red from head to toe, with chandelier earrings and silver heels. She'd pinned up her long blonde hair into loose, messy curls on the top of her head. And right before she left the room, she swiped her lips with an ultra-shiny lip gloss and gave herself one final look.

"Yes, ma'am, I think you will do," she drawled, blew herself a kiss, and left the room.

Pauline's dress was midnight blue and glittered like a night sky full of stars. The front of the dress had a Mandarin collar, quite demure, except for the slit over her right leg that went halfway up her thigh, and the fact that the back of the dress began just below her waist. She looked less like Christmas, and more like a spy about to seduce someone for government secrets.

They came out of their rooms in full stride. Eyed each other quietly, gave themselves a thumbs up, and proceed downstairs,

Janie saw them descending and grinned.

"You have done yourselves proud," she said. "We do not look like broke-ass women anymore."

"We don't feel like them, either," Pauline said.

And then the doorbell rang.

"Ladies, find yourselves a comfortable place to be in the living room. It's going to be a madhouse here for a bit as they get everything inside. And somebody watch for Baxter Williams and let him in. He'll be early, because he feels the need to be the 'man on hand' when the rest of the guests arrive," Janie said, then opened the door to the second wave of caterers.

It was just after one p.m.

CHAPTER NINETEEN

As predicted, Baxter was the first to arrive.

He greeted the girls with a quick kiss on their cheeks, eyeing their appearances as closely as he did the flowers that came from his business.

"Ladies, you are absolutely gorgeous. Where's my little pixie? I need to see if there's anything I can do to help."

"You look very dapper, as well. Not every man can carry off an ascot, but it suits you," Pauline said.

Baxter lightly stroked his gold brocade tie. "A bit of my own holiday glam," he said.

"Janie's in the kitchen with the caterers," Gretchen said.

"We're staying out of the way," Bettina added. "Too many cooks in a kitchen aren't always a good idea. However, they're all safe from me, because I am a terrible cook."

Baxter smiled. "Anyone as beautiful as you should never apologize for lack of anything. God has already blessed you more than enough," he said, and headed for the kitchen.

Bettina blushed, surprised by the compliment.

"He's adorable," Pauline said. "And I think he's not just a client of Janie's, but a true friend as well."

"I think you're right," Gretchen said.

Moments later, Baxter came back with Janie at his side.

"As usual, Janie has everything under control," he said, then pointed out the front windows. "And here come your first guests."

The girls turned to look out the windows.

"They're arriving in shuttles?" Pauline asked.

Janie nodded. "No parking here for a crowd. I get to use a parking lot at a nearby high school. I went to school with the principal. It's only for three hours, and shuttles run back and forth constantly, picking up and returning people to their cars. The shuttles are donated. The owner is one of my clients."

"I am in awe of your organizational abilities all over again," Bettina muttered.

"Okay, ladies. Line up with me at the door to meet the first wave, and then Marty, the handsome young man in the cute red jacket and black slacks, will be the doorman after that," Janie said.

The girls gathered at the door.

"I can't decide if this feels like the receiving line at a wedding, or lords and ladies greeting their guests," Gretchen whispered.

"There you go with your Downton Abbey again," Pauline said. "This is St. Louis, and today we shed the stigma of being David Logan's wives and come into our own."

Gretchen nodded. "Got it."

The doorbell rang.

"Chin up, sisters," Janie said, and opened it wide to John and Shelby Attilla. "Merry Christmas! I'm so happy you could come. You already know Bettina, but do introduce yourselves to the other girls, and find something yummy to eat and drink."

And so the guests filed in, making no attempt to hide their surprise at the elegant women standing beside Janie Logan.

By the time the second of three shuttles had arrived, the party was in full swing. Subdued Christmas music played in the background as wait staff circulated among the guests with drinks and food.

When the doorbell rang, Janie looked up and saw Marty open the door to the duo from the *Dispatch*, so she went to greet them.

"Welcome!" Janie said. "Denise Lawson, isn't it?"

"Yes," Denise said, and this is Patrick, my photographer. Looks like you have quite a party in progress."

"We do. Follow me. I want to introduce you to Pauline, Gretchen, and Bettina."

"Great. I'll want one shot of the four of you together, and then we'll mingle a bit through the crowd and be out of your hair," Denise said.

"No problem, and don't forget to sample some of the goodies before you leave," Janie added, and then escorted them through the crowd to where Bettina stood.

"Bettina, I need to interrupt you for a moment. The people from the *Dispatch* are here. They want to get a photo of us together," Janie said.

"No problem," Bettina said.

"Denise, I think you might remember Bettina from the dog attack. Oh, there's Gretchen. Let me snag her from her conversation," she said, and hurried over.

"Gretchen, my apologies, but the people from the *Dispatch* are here to get some photos," Janie said. "They're over by the fireplace with Bettina. Would you please join them? I'm going to get Pauline."

"Will do," Gretchen said.

Janie glanced across the room, saw Pauline visiting with Florence from next door, and went to get her, too.

"Time out, you two," Janie said. "People from the *Dispatch* are here. I need to borrow Pauline for a sec."

"Go do your thing, dear. I want another glass of punch, anyway," Florence said, and went in search of a waiter.

"How's it going?" Janie asked, as she and Pauline moved through the crowd.

"Wonderful," Pauline said. "I almost feel human again."

"Ditto," Janie whispered, as they reached the fireplace. "Here we are, Denise. This is Pauline Lord, an amazing web designer who recently won a prestigious award for her work. You'll have to ask her for details. This is Gretchen Lowry, who recently passed the test to acquire a realtor's license. And this is Bettina Lee. If she hasn't already mentioned it, I'm going to brag on her as well. She's gone back to college to finish her degree."

Denise's eyes widened.

"Wow! Quite an industrious bunch of women I have before me. So, I want a shot of you ladies in front of the fireplace, for sure."

"There's one more person that needs to be in this photo," Janie said. "Baxter Williams, of Flowers by Baxter. He's always helped me host, and this is the twentieth anniversary of my Christmas Tea."

"Of course," Denise said.

By now, most of the guests realized what was going on and had stopped to watch.

Janie turned and called out across the room. "Baxter! I don't know where you are, but you're wanted up front," she said, and then saw a hand shoot up above the crowd.

"I'm here, darling! On my way!" he shouted.

The crowd parted to let him pass, patting him on the back and telling him to smile for the camera, as he made his way to the end of the room to the grand fireplace.

At that point, Denise stuck Baxter in the middle, and the girls on either side.

"Okay, now think happy thoughts and smile at Patrick," she said.

"That won't be hard. Patrick is cute enough for a multitude of happy thoughts," Bettina muttered.

Baxter snorted, and the girls burst out laughing.

And Patrick got the shots they wanted, grinning all the while.

"Okay! As you were!" Janie said.

After that, Denise and Patrick moved through the crowd, stopping for a photo of John and Shelby Attilla talking to Bettina and catching party goers in the act of eating and drinking. Patrick took photos of Sarah Biggers and her husband visiting with Gretchen, and Florence sitting in a chair by the fire with a young woman in a chair beside her, having a conversation.

It was party perfect, and exactly what they wanted for the Life-styles section. As soon as they left, Janie kept moving through the crowd, chatting with her clients and making a point to talk to the girls' invited guests, as well. She kept an eye on her sister-wives, making sure they were having a good time and being treated with respect.

It was just coming up on four o'clock when she snagged a fresh glass of punch from a waiter's tray, and as she took a quick sip, she felt a hand on her shoulder and turned around.

It was Farrah Welty, the fifty-something wife of Pete Welty, who ran a construction company. Welty Construction was one of her oldest accounts. She appreciated their business and got along great with Pete, but Farrah was a hot mess.

Janie had seen her frowning at the girls more than once during the afternoon and picking up brick-a-brac and figurines about the room, then turning them over to look for markings to see if they were worth money. Janie knew she was sizing her up and had landed on the shady side of envy—just as she did every Christmas Tea.

"Farrah! I'm so glad you and Pete could come," Janie said.

Farrah shifted into pseudo-serious and leaned closer.

"Darling! I just wanted to tell you how dreadful we feel about what happened with your husband and were wondering how—"

Janie frowned. "I'm sorry, but your curiosity and commiseration are six months too late. Today is all about my annual Christmas Tea for my clients. Have you tried one of those prosciutto wraps? They're delicious. Here comes a waiter now. You must try one!"

Farrah flushed, caught out with nothing to say for herself, so she took a canapé from the tray and popped it in her mouth, so she wouldn't have to speak. She meandered to the other side of the room, as Janie moved on through the guests.

Janie noticed Baxter and Pauline head-to-head in deep conversation and smiled to herself, betting Baxter was talking to Pauline about updating his website.

The Christmas Tea was almost over. Another party in the can, so to speak. Guests were beginning to leave, saying their goodbyes. Three shuttle buses sat at the curb, waiting to take party-goers back to their cars.

Janie was at the door, accepting thanks and good wishes, and the girls joined her, thanking everyone for coming and wishing them Happy Holidays all around.

And then they were gone.

"Oh, my God!" Bettina said, looking around at the chaos in the room.

"No worries," Janie said. "Once the caterers remove their things, it will be good as new."

"Thank God," Gretchen said, and kicked off her shoes. "I couldn't take another step in those shoes if my life depended on it."

But Pauline was silent.

"Anything wrong?" Janie asked.

Pauline shook her head. "I haven't talked that much in three hours in my life. I think I'm all out of words. But I have two new clients, so for me, this party became a business meeting, too."

"Is Baxter one of them?" Janie asked.

Pauline nodded.

"I knew it! And none too soon. His website is a bit dated," Janie said.

"So he said, but that I can change," Pauline said.

At that point, another catering van pulled up and began retrieving the tables, chairs, and punch bowls, while the chef and servers were packing up and cleaning in the kitchen.

Within an hour, they were all gone, and the house was so quiet, one could have imagined the house was also sighing with relief.

The girls had all gone to their rooms to change. They emerged later in an assortment of sweats and pajamas, their faces clean of makeup, and their hair in ponytails, all except for Janie, whose hair was still a mess of curls.

They met in the kitchen, grabbed a cold drink apiece, and went into the living room to gather around the fire.

"This was the best day," Pauline said.

"It was redemption day for all of us," Bettina said.

"Truth," Gretchen said.

Janie sighed. "I know. It's always fun, but I have to admit, I have never been so tired smiling in my life."

"People make me tired," Pauline said. "I guess that's why I'm so suited to computer work. It's a solitary job, with no one to answer to but myself."

Gretchen smiled. "We're all so different, and yet we sync, for which I'm grateful."

Their chatter trailed off as they sat cross-legged, staring into the fire.

Sometime later, they heard what sounded like rain against the windows and looked out. It was sleeting.

"Crap. Icy streets," Gretchen said.

"Tomorrow is Sunday. The city will have treated the streets before you have to go to work," Janie said. "In the meantime, I'm going to make scrambled eggs and toast. We haven't had one decent meal today, just party food."

"That sounds good," Pauline said. "You do the eggs, I'll do toast."

"Then Miss Bee and I will clean up afterward," Gretchen said.

"Deal," Bettina said.

They switched off the fire in the fireplace and headed for the kitchen.

"I'm so tired, my butt is dragging out my tracks," Bettina muttered.

"Then park it, sister," Janie said, pointing toward the table and chairs.

"Don't have to tell me twice," Bettina said, and sat, with Gretchen beside her.

Much later, after the food had been eaten and the kitchen cleaned up, they went to their rooms, fell into bed to the sound of sleet against the windows, and slept so hard that they didn't wake up again until morning.

As Janie had predicted, the roads were clear by Monday, and they resumed their routines.

That same week, Bettina got the grades for her semester and gave a little whoop of delight as she announced all A's in her classes.

"Dang girl, how did you do that?" Gretchen asked.

Bettina shrugged. "Learning has always come easy, but I'll be honest, when I began the semester, I was a little concerned that I'd forgotten how to study... Only it appears, I have not. Apparently, it's like sex. A little daunting when you first begin, and then you fall into the rhythm of it and everything you ever knew comes flooding back in a big, swooshing climax."

The three of them stared, their mouths slightly parted, their cheeks just a little bit pink.

Janie was the first to pull herself together. "Well, damn, girl. Was that your real answer or was that wishful porn?"

They laughed, and the moment passed.

But for Bettina, it was yet another step to regaining her sense of self.

Her children were due to arrive tomorrow. She was excited and nervous, and hated that so much time and drama trauma had passed between them. All she could do was head to the airport tomorrow afternoon and hope for the best.

The plane was coming in for a landing.

Patty was gripping Joe's wrist.

"I hate landings," she muttered.

Joe grinned. "I'm kinda fond of them myself, otherwise we'd never get off this plane."

Patty gave him an eyeroll. The plane touched down with a little bounce, and tires squealing as brakes were applied. They were on the ground. One step closer to repairing their relationship.

Joe sent his their mom a text.

We've landed. See you outside the terminal near luggage claim.

Bettina quickly responded.

I'm already parked there. Look for a red Chevrolet Equinox.

Finally, they were off the plane, and on their way to reclaim their luggage.

Bettina's heart was pounding as she sat in her car, watching people come out pulling suitcases and lugging carryalls over their shoulders.

She hadn't seen her children in so long.

Joe had just turned seventeen, and Patty had been fifteen when she and Gary had gotten divorced. She'd rarely seen them during the years she'd worked as a bartender, and then never after she and David had married. It was hard to imagine Joe being twenty-four years old now, and Patty twenty-two.

Joe was a stockbroker.

Patty worked in a bank.

And that's all she knew about their lives. They had a lot of catching up to do, and the rest of their lives to do it right.

And then a group people filed out the door and began dispersing. When she saw a young man with thick brown hair standing a head above the others, her heart stopped.

God in heaven, he has my father's face. When did that happen?

Then she saw Patty standing beside him. Still Patty but grown. She got out of the car and stepped up onto the curb and waved.

They saw her, waved back, and started toward her, and it was all she could do not to weep.

A mother's heart. It can break, but the ethereal bond of children who grow to life within their mothers are alive forever.

Then Joe dropped his bag and swept her up in his arms.

"Mom! You look beautiful. I'm so glad to see you!"

Patty laughed and threw her arms around the both of them.

"Hey, I'm the baby, remember? Don't leave me out of this homecoming!"

Bettina was laughing and crying, and then loading up their luggage, and after another hug apiece, they piled into her car and drove away, talking non-stop.

Bettina could tell they'd been anxious about their reception, and now their constant chatter was the release of nervous energy. Finally, she got a chance to speak.

"I've booked adjoining rooms for you two at the River Center Casino and Hotel. I think you'll like it."

"Casino?" Joe said.

Bettina nodded.

He grinned. "Way to go, Mom. I'm not a gambler by any means, but I have been known to indulge a bit on holidays."

"What fun," Patty said.

"Well, it's just something to do when we're not together, although I plan to spend as much time with the both of you as you can tolerate."

"We can't wait to meet the—uh... The others," Patty said.

"I think of them as sisters. But you can refer to them as my dear friends. And they're anxious to meet the both of you, as well."

"Do they know? About how we treated you, I mean?" Joe asked.

"Oh honey, after all these months, we know pretty much everything about each other. It's how we survived. But you will also be happy to know they're the last three people on earth who will judge you. And just so you know, we don't discuss David with anyone."

"Duly noted," Joe said. "Now, what's on the agenda for the rest of this day?"

Bettina grinned. "First off, I need to tell you how much you look like my father now. I nearly had a heart attack when I saw your face."

"Good," Joe said. "I sure don't want to be a reminder to you of *our* father."

Bettina frowned. "Well, that's silly. Even if you were the spitting image, I'm not that delicate. You two are your own people. Your DNA will never have anything to do with the adults you become, and I'm so proud of the careers you are making for yourselves. And look, that's your hotel up the street. Let's get you registered and into your rooms, and then you have choices. Going to meet the girls and then we go out to dinner somewhere in the city, or if you're both too tired from traveling, we can eat dinner here in the hotel. You two can unwind a bit in the casinos, and we'll start a little sightseeing tomorrow."

"I'd love to meet them today," Patty said.

"So would I," Tom added. "And tomorrow is Christmas Eve. Have you and your friends planned something at home?"

"We're opening presents Christmas Eve and devoting Christmas day to cooking dinner, which we plan to serve around noon."

Patty frowned. "We don't want to take you away from all that. If we wouldn't be intruding, I'd love to be a part of all that with you."

"So would I," Joe said. "From all you've said about them, you rescued each other. They're the family who didn't let you down, and now is no time to quit them just because we had the blinders slapped off our faces."

Bettina smiled. "Wonderful, and they'll be happy to hear this. I'll give them a quick call and let them know we'll be stopping by later after we get to the hotel."

CHAPTER TWENTY

Janie was in her office finishing up the last bit of work she had to do, and then she'd be completely free through Christmas Eve and Christmas Day. She'd just hit save when her phone rang. She reached for it, saw it was Bettina, and smiled.

"Hey, Miss Bee."

"Hi, Janie. I just picked up my kids. I'm getting them settled into their rooms before we go out to dinner, but they can't wait to meet you. Is it okay if we stop by for a bit?"

"Yes! Very okay. I'll tell the girls, and I can't wait to meet them," Janie said.

"Thanks. See you soon."

Janie jumped up and went to look for Pauline and Gretchen, following the sounds of laughter and the scents of something cooking, and found them in the kitchen.

"Oh, my God! It smells heavenly in here. What are you making?" Janie asked.

"Enchilada Casserole, but I kind of went overboard on the size and had to bake it in two dishes," Pauline said. "I guess we'll be freezing one."

"Or not!" Janie said. "Bettina just called. She's bringing Joe and Patty by to meet us before they go out to dinner. If they smell all of this, they might be lured into dinner here."

"Yay!" Gretchen said. "And if they so choose, then I'll just make a bigger salad, and we'll be good to go. I already have chips, guacamole, salsa, and queso ready."

Janie gave them a thumbs up. "But that's only if they want to.

They might prefer to spend some alone time, too. They have a lot of catching up to do."

"They can play catch up in the privacy of the hotel," Pauline said. "Offer them the meal. Then it's their decision, without pressure."

"Will do," Janie said. "I expect they'll be here within the hour. They were already at the hotel when she called."

"No problems on timing here. The casseroles come out of the oven in about thirty minutes, and they'll need at least that long again to cool off before we can eat them."

Joe was in his room and Patty in hers.

The adjoining door between them was open, and Bettina was sitting on the corner of Patty's bed, talking to the both of them as they unpacked, resisting the urge to pinch herself to see if this was really happening.

She'd dreamed of this moment—a reunion—a rekindling of the bond they'd once had. And then Joe said something silly, and Patty burst out laughing, and it was just like before. Her. Them. Together. She didn't know she was crying until Patty saw her.

"Mom! What's wrong? Why are you crying?"

Joe came flying out of his room and into where they were sitting. "What's happening?"

Bettina felt the tears then and looked up in a moment of confusion.

"Sorry. I don't know what came over me. I'm just so very glad to be sitting here, listening to my children's voices again.

They sat down beside her, Joe on one side and Patty on the other, and hugged her to them.

"We've hurt you so deeply. We're so sorry, Mom," Joe said.

Bettina wallowed in the comfort of their arms for only a few moments, and then shook her head.

"Enough of that. I'm fine. Just an overwhelming moment," she said, as she began looking around for tissues.

"Here," Patty said, and pulled a handful from a tissue box near the bed.

"Thanks," Bettina said. "Sorry for the weak moment. This visit isn't about the remnants of my life, it's about rebuilding our relationship. So, if you two are ready, I know the girls are waiting for us."

"You can't rebuild anything until the rubble of what fell down has been removed," Joe said. "And just for the record, that's why we're here. We wrecked it. We came to fix it, and we're behind you all the way."

They left the hotel and headed across the city, with Bettina mentioning points of interest and landmarks they were passing. When she finally drove into the historic district, Patty couldn't quit gawking and pointing.

"Mom! Look at that one. . . Wow. Three stories tall with a widow's walk. And there! These aren't really houses—they're old mansions, but so beautiful, and obviously restored. They are amazing."

"It's one of the historic districts in the city," Bettina said. "Janie's home is in the next block. If you look over the bare tree limbs to your left, you can see the top of the turret on her house."

A couple of minutes later, she pulled into the driveway, and then she parked, smiled to herself at the looks of shock on her children's faces, and opened her door.

"Well? Are you coming, or are you just going to sit there with your mouths open?"

"Holy shit, Mom! You live here?"

"Yes, I do."

"It's a freaking mansion," Joe said.

"And it's time to meet the freaking angel who saved us," Bettina said, and headed up the front steps with her kids at her heels.

She unlocked the door and walked in, then held the door as they entered.

"Hey everybody! We're home!" Bettina shouted, and then they were inundated with hugs and welcomes—greetings beyond anything Joe and Patty had expected.

"Everybody, these are my children, Joe and Patty Vale. Kids, meet the other wives. The little redhead is Janie Logan. She's the angel who took us under her wings. The tall brunette is Pauline Lord, and the other blonde in the family is Gretchen Lowry."

"We're so happy to meet you," Janie said. "Miss Bee, show them where the coat closet is and then join us in the kitchen. We're in the midst of dinner prep."

"Will do," Bettina said, as the trio filed back into the kitchen.

"Holy crap, Mom, they're gorgeous, and they call you Miss Bee. I love that," Patty whispered, as they hung up their coats.

"Mom's gorgeous, too," Joe said.

Patty gave her brother a look. "Well, that went without saying, and something smells heavenly."

Bettina breathed a sigh of relief as she led the way back into the kitchen. This was going far better than she had hoped.

There was a huge bowl of chips on the table, besides bowls of queso, guacamole, and salsa, and a stack of plates and napkins at one end.

"You two must be exhausted from your trip," Janie said. "We have some pre-dinner appetizers going. Have a seat and help your-self, unless you don't want to ruin your appetite for other plans. We're eating Mexican tonight, hence the chips and dips. Shout out your choice of drink. We have bottles of dark ale, a couple of kinds of pop, and always unsweetened iced tea."

"I'll try that dark ale, and nothing ruins my appetite," Joe said, as he reached for a chip and scooped it into the guacamole.

"I'd love anything cola," Patty said.

"I'll get them," Bettina said, and soon, everyone was at the table, talking, laughing, drinking and eating.

"If you've already made dinner reservations somewhere, then that's fine," Janie said. "But if you haven't, and you're in the mood for a low-key meal at home with us, Pauline has two big enchila-da casseroles cooling on the stove, and we would love to have you join us."

"It's Mom's call," Patty said. "If she doesn't already have some-thing planned, I'm really happy here."

"Ditto," Joe said.

Bettina grinned. "I was going to let them pick, and they have, so dinner is solved."

After that, they put the food out on the island, buffet style, left the appetizers on the table to have with the meal, and got up to fill their plates.

For Joe and Patty, who'd been uncertain of the reception they would receive, it was a homey welcome. Soon, they were all back at the table with their food and listening to the chatter between their mother and her friends.

"Janie, you have a beautiful home," Patty said.

Janie smiled. "Thank you. I'm the third generation to live here, and grateful for it."

"I think Janie's life here was calm and quiet before we all ar-rived," Pauline said.

"Lord, isn't that the truth," Bettina said. "We came close to bringing down the house a time or two."

"Other than the fact that we were fodder for gossip for several months, which was not our fault, I think you exaggerate," Janie said. "Besides, I'm the one who opened the door to a total stranger and nearly got myself killed." She glanced at Joe and Patty. "Pau-line and Bettina saved my life."

Patty gasped. "Oh, my God! What happened?"

Janie began the story, and Pauline and Bettina finished it.

"There was blood everywhere, most of which came from Pauline punching the woman in the face and breaking her nose. She had the crazy bitch down in seconds, while I was dragging Janie out of the way," Bettina said.

"And don't forget about that woman who tried to play a con game on Janie, claiming to be David's long-lost daughter," Gretchen said.

Joe blinked. "You're not serious?"

"Oh, yes. It happened," Janie said.

"Was she really his daughter? What did you do?" Joe asked.

Bettina laughed. "Janie called her bluff and never once challenged her claim. Instead, she sent the woman a statement listing what David stole from us and asked how she planned to repay it. The woman immediately withdrew her demands and disappeared."

Joe grinned. "That's amazing."

"I think the most panicked we all were was when the tornado came through St. Louis a few months back, and we thought we'd lost Gretchen," Janie said. We sat here without power for hours and hours, and heard nothing, and were fearing the worst when she finally pulled up in the driveway. They insurance office where she worked had a storm shelter, but they got trapped in it for a bit, and then when she tried to get home, every street was blocked off because of downed power lines or uprooted trees. And she didn't know the city well enough to find backroads."

Gretchen nodded. "It was frustrating, and then I got lost, and I drove and drove until I just stopped my car in the street and cried. A fireman knocked on my window, and then after I told him where I lived, he gave me directions to roads that had been cleared enough for me to get home."

"Oh, my lord," Patty said. "You must have been so scared, because you didn't know what had happened here either, right?"

"Right," Gretchen said. "It was a happy homecoming, for sure."

"Bettina, did you tell your kids about the hoarder?"

"We know nothing about what's been happening to Mom, and it's all our fault," Joe said. "Tell us. What hoarder?"

Bettina sighed. "It's a sad story, but it ended on a positive note." And then she told it all."

"If Bettina hadn't followed her heart, the outcome could have been so much worse," Janie said. "They took the man to hospice, the little dog to foster parents, and the health department went in and cleared out the house."

"You never realize the level of human suffering until you find yourself in the middle of it," Pauline said. "But we have good things to celebrate, too. Janie holds an annual Christmas Tea for all her clients, and I acquired two new clients last week because of it."

"What do you do?" Joe asked.

"I design websites," Pauline said.

"She just won a national award for one of her designs," Janie added. "We're so proud of her."

"Okay, I am in awe," Patty said. "I freak and call tech support every time something happens with mine. I couldn't begin to figure out what's wrong with it, let alone build websites."

"Like mother, like daughter," Bettina drawled.

"Nope. You don't get to belittle yourself again," Gretchen said. "You just pulled straight A's in your classes, missy."

Joe and Patty kept looking from one woman to the other, mouths open in disbelief as each story was told, shocked by all the drama going on in their mother's life that they'd known nothing about. And now this?

"Classes for what?" Joe asked.

Bettina shrugged. "I went back to college to finish my degree. I was doing online classes because of my dog-walking, and then after the attack, I couldn't face the job anymore. I just finished up the semester. I'll enroll with a full schedule next semester, and then I'll finally have my degree—about twenty-five years late, but better late than never, you know."

"I can't believe all this was happening, and we knew nothing," Patty said.

"Which, again, was our fault," Joe said. "I'm proud of you, Mom"

"So am I," Patty said. "And I am so sorry we weren't there for you."

Bettina shrugged. "I have the girls—my sisters. Once we came here, we became our own tribe. We aren't alone anymore."

Joe looked around the table in quiet admiration.

"If one day I ever have daughters, having them born with the grit and guts and determination of women like you would be a gift."

"Both of you, just make sure you raise your sons to be honest, and teach your daughters to be self-sufficient," Bettina muttered.

Patty nodded. "I promise."

"As do I," Joe said.

After that, the evening came to an end.

"This was the best evening," Patty said.

"Yes, it was, and thank you for dinner," Joe added.

"You're very welcome," Janie said.

"We loved meeting you," Gretchen said.

"See you tomorrow evening for opening presents," Pauline added.

"I'll take you back to the hotel," Bettina said. "Just let me get my coat."

"No, Mom. It's late, and it's too cold. I don't like to think of you driving back to the house alone. I'll call an Uber."

"But I don't mind," Bettina said.

"I know you don't, but humor me," Joe said. "We're grown-ass people, and we can get across town on our own."

Bettina grinned. "Fine, then."

Joe made the call, gave them the address, and got a fifteen-minute pickup time.

"The car will be here shortly," he said. "In the meantime, what's on the agenda for tomorrow?"

Bettina wasn't about to set a schedule. "You two just wake up when you want, eat breakfast, and then call me. We can sightsee, shop if you want, and come back here later in the day, hang out a bit, have something to eat and open presents."

"Sounds perfect," they said.

A short while later, their Uber arrived. Bettina stood in the doorway, watching as they drove away, and then went back inside, locking up behind her. She was exhausted, both physically and emotionally.

All she wanted to do was sleep.

Back at the hotel, Joe and Patty were in their rooms, about to crawl into bed and turn out the lights.

"Want me to leave the door open between our rooms?" Joe asked.

Patty wasn't a fan of being alone in hotel rooms and nodded. "At least leave it unlocked."

Joe grinned. "Just like when we were kids?"

"Okay, don't make fun. I don't need you to slay the dragons in my dreams anymore, but I do like to know I have backup... if the need arises," Patty said.

"You got it," Joe said, then shut the door.

Patty turned off the lamp, then slid down beneath the sheets. Today had been a revelation, and when she finally fell asleep, she dreamed her mother was standing on an auction block, being sold off by her father to the highest bidder.

Joe Vale didn't go to bed as quickly.

He was standing before the bathroom mirror, still thinking about what his mother had said, about him wearing his grandfather's face. He remembered his grandparents as being old. He'd never thought of them being young, but it made him feel good about himself. Learning how shameful a man their father was had been a shock Joe was never going to get over. Knowing he was a visible reminder of a good man made it easier to look himself in the eye.

He finally went to bed, happy that their first "meeting" with their mom had been easier than he'd expected, and the next time he opened his eyes, it was morning.

After breakfast, they called their mom, and the day began.

It was a day of sightseeing. Shopping. Hot dogs in a food court at a mall, and then back to their hotel to kick back and relax before getting ready to go back to the big house to open presents later.

They hit the casino with a hundred dollars each, gave themselves two hours to play or go broke, whichever came first, then when time was up, went back to their rooms to see who came out on top.

They all gathered in Joe's room and dumped their earnings out on the bed, one at a time, and started counting. Patty went first.

"Unless somebody went broke, I can guarantee I am the loser," she muttered. "I work at a bank all day, surrounded by vast amounts of money, and go home with none of it. I think I just repeated the process downstairs."

Bettina grinned. Patty was witty, but forever a drama queen.

"Forty-three dollars," Patty muttered. "Two hours of winning and losing, and that's where I'm at."

"Mom, you go next," Joe said, and then they watched as Bettina pulled out a wad.

"Crap!" Patty said. "What were you playing?"

"Just the slots," Bettina said, and counted out five hundred and sixty-four dollars.

Then they both looked at Joe and saw a smile on his face.

"I know that look!" Bettina said. "You were playing poker, weren't you? What did you do? Win a big pot?"

"A few," he said. "I guess today was my lucky day," and pulled out a wad of one-hundred-dollar bills. "Four thousand, six hundred and twenty-five dollars."

"Oh, my God!" Bettina said. "I don't even want to think about you flying home with all that money on you."

Joe laughed. "No worries. There's a branch of my bank here in the city. I saw it while we were sightseeing. If you'll drive by it on our way back to your house, I'm depositing it all."

"Then we better hustle," Bettina said. "The bank may close early for Christmas Eve."

"The drive-through will be open a little later. I think we're good," Joe said, but just in case, I'm ready to leave whenever you are."

Since Bettina was gone for the day, Pauline and Gretchen left to make one last trip to the supermarket for the Christmas Eve festivities, and tomorrow's Christmas dinner, leaving Janie home alone.

It was rare to have the old house to herself, and while she loved not living alone anymore, the quiet of the place settled within her as she took a cup of coffee into the living room and sat down before the fire.

This had been the year from hell for all of them. Sad times. Hard times. But they were all coming out of the dark in their own way. Her knee-jerk decision to invite the girls into her home had been a good one.

She'd thought long and hard about what she would give them for Christmas, and the idea had come to her one night about a month ago when they were sitting around the kitchen table, talking about their plans for the next day before going to bed.

Bettina had been in her pajamas and devoid of makeup. Gretchen wore in her bathrobe with her hair piled on top of her head in a messy ponytail, and Pauline had on the sweats she'd put on that morning and had shoved her computer glasses up on top of her head, having forgotten they were there.

There they were, laughing as if David Logan had never happened, and they'd been friends for life. That's what it felt like to Janie. And that's the moment when she'd known. They would find out soon enough. But not while Bettina's children were here. This was for after, when the four of them were here alone.

She was staring out the window to the street beyond, watching the occasional car drive by when she saw a UPS van turn up into her drive. The driver got out carrying a large, flat box and moments later, he was at the door, ringing the bell. She opened it.

"Delivery for Janie Logan. Apologies from UPS. This box got lost in shipment some months back."

Janie frowned. "Thank you," she said, and closed the door against the cold. She couldn't remember ordering any—

And then it hit her!

"No. No, no, no, no," she muttered, and dropped the box on the floor of the foyer and tore into it.

There it was. A fully lined, hooded sheepskin coat. Size XL. A present for David's birthday that had long since come and gone.

The skin crawled on the back of her neck, then she started screaming.

"Shit. Shit, shit, shit! Not now! Not in this house. Not on this good day. I got rid of you and the secrets in the boxes you hid. Why won't you go away!"

She yanked the coat out of the box, tore off all the tags, and then dropped it back in the box, turned, and ran toward her room.

Moments later she came back wearing her coat and dragging her purse behind her. She would have been shocked by the look on her face as she crammed the coat back into the box and stormed out of the house. But there was a rage inside her that wouldn't go away. She didn't need any fucking reminders of him. She just needed it gone.

She threw the box in her car and drove away, burning rubber as she pulled out into the street and headed for the far side of the city, choking on her own tears as she maneuvered through the traffic of last-minute shoppers. Green lights. Red lights. Yellow caution lights. And cars.

It felt like she'd been driving forever, and then all of a sudden, she was there. Like she'd crossed over into another country. The poverty of the place—the homeless curled up in corners trying to stay out of the wind—the gaunt faces and shoulders of the street people hunched against the cold hurt her heart. This wasn't a holiday for them. It was just another day of trying to survive.

She kept driving, looking at the people, watching for a man who was most in need. And then she saw him standing on a corner, leaning against a building. He was tall and ageless, with whiskers down past his chin, and the only thing he wore passing for a coat was a ragged flannel shirt.

She hit her brakes, then pulled over to the curb and parked. Her hands were shaking as she yanked the coat out of the box, took all the money she had in her purse, stuffed it in one of the pockets, and got out carrying the coat and her keys.

The man saw her coming toward him, then saw the tears on her face. He didn't know what was about to happen, but he was suddenly afraid, and on the verge of running when she spoke.

"Sir. I do not want to offend you, but I find myself with a brand-new man's overcoat that I will never use. I am not a person who believes in wasting anything, and you would be doing me an enormous favor if you'd accept this as a Christmas gift from one stranger to another."

He was in shock. "Uh, lady I—"

"Please," Janie said, as the tears kept rolling. "You need it. I don't. Turn around," she said, and held up the coat.

The man did as she asked, bending slightly to accommodate her tiny stature as he slipped one arm in a sleeve, and then the other.

Then he sighed, feeling the warmth and the weight of it on his body.

"Thank you. Thank you, lady," he said, and turned around, but she was already in her car and driving away.

When he thrust his hands into the pockets for the warmth and felt the money, his heart skipped. He looked down into the pocket at the number of twenty-dollar bills in his hand and shoved it deep, then took off walking. This meant shelter. Enough for a room for a few days. A place to bathe. Food to eat. He didn't know her name, but he would never forget her. A tiny little Christmas elf with a head full of red curls, and tears on her face.

Janie threw the box into a dumpster in an alley, and then headed home. The emotional breakdown had been a long time coming, but she intended it to be her last. By the time she got to the house, both girls were back. She hung up her coat, put her purse in her room, and followed the sound of their voices. They were in the kitchen wrapping presents for Joe and Patty.

"Hey girl. We didn't want Miss Bee's kids to be left out of presents this evening. We got a couple of things for you to give them. Nothing much, but just so they won't feel out of place."

Janie frowned. "Thank you for that. I should have thought of it. I don't know where my head's been."

Pauline paused. "You've been crying. Is there someone I need to hurt?"

Janie shook her head. "No. It was just a momentary thing, and it's over."

"Good. These two things are yours to wrap. The gifts are explanatory, unless you think Joe would rather have the perfume, and Patty, the men's cologne."

Janie grinned, reached for the box of perfume and the scissors, cut off enough red foil wrapping paper, and got busy.

When they had all the gifts wrapped, they carried them to the living room and put them beneath the tree with the others.

"After we open gifts, we're having potato soup and chicken salad sandwiches. Then we'll just have a little plate of Gretchen's fudge and divinity for something sweet."

"Sounds perfect," Janie said, then glanced at the clock. "We have a few hours. I'm going to the office for a bit to check email, just in case there's some emergency pending, and then I'm coming back to claim a seat at the fire."

"Want something to drink?" Pauline asked.

"Not just yet. Maybe later," she said, and left the room.

As soon as she was gone, they began to whisper.

"Something big happened," Gretchen said.

Pauline nodded. "I agree, but knowing Janie, she's not going to talk about it."

"She'll be okay, though," Gretchen said. "She's the smallest, but she's the most steadfast of all of us."

Unaware of being the topic of conversation, Janie went into her office and closed the door. That was the trigger that shifted her into work mode and made the rest of the world disappear.

She stayed there, doing busy work until her emotions had settled, and then went back to join the girls. It was nearing time for opening presents, and they were expecting Bettina and her kids back at any time.

They put the finishing touches on the sandwiches and stashed them in the refrigerator until serving time. The kitchen table was set and soup was warming on the back of the stove when they heard the front door open and the chatter of happy voices.

"We're back!" Bettina shouted.

The girls came to meet them, taking their coats and hanging them up, then shooing them toward the fire.

"Go get warm," Janie said.

"Won't argue about that," Patty said. "My feet are freezing."

"Oh honey, go up to my room and get a pair of warm socks out of the middle dresser drawer. You can open presents in your sock feet, and they'll get warm a lot quicker. It's the first door to the left at the top of the stairs."

"Thanks, Mom," Patty said, and left the room, while Joe and Bettina put more presents beneath the tree.

"Have you had a good day?" Pauline asked.

"We've had a great day," Joe said.

Bettina rolled her eyes. "So says the man who won over four thousand dollars at the poker table this afternoon. And, like the smart man he is, he's already banked it and is planning where to invest."

"That's amazing. Do you play much?" Gretchen asked.

"Hardly ever, and I haven't been in a casino since I turned twenty-one. But I'm good with numbers and odds. Stockbroker and all that," he said.

Patty came back into the room carrying her shoes and wearing a pair of fuzzy purple socks.

"Mom, your room is so pretty, and thanks for the loan of the socks."

"Janie gets credit for the decor. It was like that when I moved in, and you're welcome. Your brother was just bragging about his win."

Patty rolled her eyes. "Did you tell everyone I was the loser?"

"No. And you aren't a loser. It was just a game between the three of us," Bettina said, and then explained the rest of the story. "We each took one hundred dollars and had two hours to spend it. If it was gone before the two hours were up, then you quit playing. If you kept winning and losing, etc., then whoever was ahead at the end of the two hours was the winner with bragging rights. I won a little over five hundred, so I was technically four hundred to the good when I quit."

"What fun!" Janie said.

"It was, but I'm ready to play Santa Claus. What about you?" Bettina asked.

"Yes," they echoed.

Pauline pointed at Janie. "You've had a day. You sit. We'll help pass out presents."

Bettina frowned. "Why was your day hard?"

"Just unexpected shit, and it's over," Janie said. "Time to celebrate!"

Within minutes, all the presents had been passed out, and the opening began. It was like nothing Janie could remember. Bows torn off presents. Wrapping paper tossed aside. Squeals of excitement and delight. A few tears, and the joy of sharing this night together.

Presents were simple but personal. Scented bath salts. Warm house shoes. New fuzzy socks. Books to read. Godiva chocolates. Winter gloves, and the list went on and on.

Bettina gave each of her children a silver-plated key ring with her phone number on it.

"So you won't forget to call," she said.

And they gave her a new red wool coat.

"Every time you put your arms in the sleeves, it's us hugging you," Joe said.

Bettina's eyes welled. "I'll remember that," she said.

Finally, the last present was opened, and nothing was said about missing presents from Janie.

"I'm starved!" Pauline said, as the others were shoving the used wrapping paper and bows into a big garbage bag. "I'm going to get the food out. As soon as you're through in here, come to the kitchen."

Soon, they were all gathered around the table, having soup and sandwiches, and talking about their day. Janie laughed with everyone else but had little to add.

Finally, the evening came to a close. Joe and Patty gathered up their gifts and left in an Uber, with a promise to return for dinner tomorrow the same way.

Bettina waved goodbye at the door, and then closed and locked it behind her before joining the others back in the kitchen. They were still dawdling over wine when Janie finally spoke up.

"I suspect you've been wondering about your gifts from me, but I wanted to wait until we were alone. We came together because David left you homeless. But my gifts to the three of you will make sure you will never be homeless again. Before I knew you, I had come to terms with growing old alone. And then here you were. As of a couple of weeks ago, I had you three added to my will as co-owners of this house."

Gasps of disbelief rolled around the table.

"Janie! Oh, my God!" Bettina cried.

Pauline was pale and in shock, and Gretchen shook, as Janie continued.

"Should I die before you, then it will belong to the three of you. And even if any or all of you get married again and move away, you will still be part owner of this house. But as the voice of caution, I warn you never to tell someone you might marry. If he can't provide a home for you on his own, then he's not the right one. The house cannot be sold unless all of you agree. Whoever is the last woman standing, will be the sole owner. At that time, it will be yours to do with as you choose. My father left a trust fund. If I die first, the money stays in the trust, and my lawyer will continue to administer the yearly allotment as he's done since my father's death. He sees to paying the annual property taxes and homeowner's insurance from it, and leaves a goodly amount each year for unexpected repairs and the upkeep. All you have to do is live here like we are now. Paying utilities, buying food, knowing the house cleaners will still come, and the landscapers will still mow and trim. If another man betrays you, he will never be able to get his hands on this... or the money. He will never inherit, not even if you should die. Your share will simply go to the ones still living. This is your house. You moved into the Broke-Ass Women's Club, but it is officially disbanded. This place is now your home. Merry Christmas, my dear sisters."

They stood, tears rolling, moving in silence as they surrounded her and then wrapped their arms around her. There were no words to explain their jumbled emotions. Only that they'd been given the greatest gift of all.

The gift of love.

Christmas morning began early.

Janie was up at six a.m. to put the ham in the oven, and then she moved to the kitchen windows and looked out. The security lights shed a faint light. Enough to see her garden in hibernation. Leaves were gone from the trees and the bushes. All the flowering bulbs had been cut back to winter. The grass was dormant, and in the dark, the winding paths looked like scattered ribbons upon the ground.

"It's Christmas again, Daddy. I miss you and Mom, but as I'm sure you know, I'm doing well. Thank you for taking care of me— even now. All these years after you've been gone, you are the single reason that I am sheltered and safe."

Daybreak was but a promise on the horizon as she left to get dressed, and when she came back, the others were up and straggling down the stairs for morning coffee and a piece of toast, saving their appetites for the meal to come.

It was a joyous day.

They'd gone to bed with Janie's gift in their hearts and woke up knowing she'd just taken away the last bits of uncertainty from all of them.

They had the formal dining room set with the family china, and a white poinsettia on the sideboard for decor. Bottles of Pinot Noir were in the refrigerator, waiting to be taken to the table. Janie called it elegance without being presumptuous.

"I love it!" Gretchen said. "It's all so Downton Abbey."

"But without the servants and a stiff upper lip," Janie added.

"Bettina has lip enough for all of us," Pauline said, which made them laugh. Even Bettina. She couldn't deny her own sass.

Pauline had baked a Bourbon pecan pie, a pumpkin pie, and an apple pie, while Gretchen and Janie were making side dishes to go with the ham.

Bettina was in charge of salad and had been prepping fresh veggies to assemble later. It was just past ten when Janie took the ham from the oven, set it aside to cool, and put in a sweet potato casserole to bake.

The kitchen was warm and cozy, and the chatter and taste-testing were at an all-time high when Janie happened to look out the window.

"Look! It's beginning to snow. I can't remember the last time we had snow on Christmas. How beautiful!"

They all turned, then rushed to the windows.

"The flakes are huge," Pauline said.

"The air is so still; they look like they're floating!" Gretchen said.

Bettina sighed. "Today is perfect. It's snowing on Christmas

Day. We're not alone, and my children will be our guests. Patty sent me a text about an hour ago that they were getting ready. They should be arriving soon."

And she was right.

The doorbell rang at straight up eleven o'clock, and Bettina ran to answer.

"Merry Christmas, Mom," Joe said, and hugged her.

"Merry Christmas, Mama," Patty said, and kissed her mother on the cheek.

"Merry Christmas, my darlings," Bettina said. "You know where to put your things."

They moved to the hall closet, hung up their coats, and followed their mother into the kitchen.

"Merry Christmas!" the girls said, as they entered the room.

"Welcome," Janie said. "Isn't the snow wonderful? Meander all you want. Dinner will be ready in about thirty minutes or so."

"I choose this room and you ladies," Joe said. "This kitchen is the heart of your home."

"Is there anything I can help do?" Patty asked.

"We're all just waiting on the rolls to bake off, and then we'll carry the dishes to the table. You both can help with that when the time comes."

And so they did.

When they finally sat down in the dining room, the table was full of food, the ham had been sliced, and wine had been poured. Hot rolls were still steaming when Pauline brought them to the table and took her seat.

Janie looked around the table and nodded in quiet satisfaction.

"I'm not going to say a traditional blessing. Rather, I want to acknowledge how blessed we all are to be able to be here together. Thank you for enriching my life, for turning this mausoleum of a place into a home again, and for being the sisters I always wanted. And I guess, if Joe and Patty will allow the familiarity, thanks to Miss Bee, we have also acquired a nephew and niece. Thank you for giving me family again. Now, if everyone will pass their plates to the right, I'll do the honors with the ham."

"Amen to that," they all echoed, and the meal began.

Copious amounts of food were eaten in fine company, as one might say, but when they got down to desserts and coffee, the light-hearted conversation turned a bit serious.

"When I was a girl, my grandparents, who raised me, used to ask everyone at the table to name one thing they have learned through the year that really mattered to them. Could we do that now?" Pauline asked.

"Certainly," Janie said. "And you should go first."

Pauline glanced around the table, her voice trembling with emotion.

"I learned how to stop being afraid."

Gretchen leaned forward. "I learned to trust my instincts."

"I learned not to blame myself for others' mistakes," Janie said.

"I do not need anyone to make me whole," Bettina said.

"I learned to cherish what matters most," Patty said.

Joe was the last, and for a few moments, was silent. Then he looked straight at his mother.

"I learned not to believe everything I am told. And to let old wounds heal.""Those are good lessons for us all," Janie said.

But before anyone else could comment, Joe's phone rang.

"Oh, dang! Sorry." He pulled it out of his pocket to put it on mute, glanced at Caller ID, and then frowned. "It's Dad. Can you believe it?"

"I remember all the times I wanted to hear your voice. Just answer it," Bettina said.

Joe grimaced as he picked up the call.

"Hello."

"Merry Christmas, son. I've been worried about you and Patty. I wanted you to know how much I miss you two, and how much I hate to think of you both spending Christmas alone."

"We're not alone," Joe said.

Silence.

"Are you with your mother?" Gary finally asked.

"You've lost the right to ask that," Joe said.

"I've lost more than that," Gary said. "Ellie left me."

"Surely that's no big deal to you. You can always buy another one," Joe said, then disconnected and put the phone on mute.

Patty frowned. "What was that all about?"

Joe snorted. "Dad just looking for pity. Ellie left him."

Bettina blinked. "Did you just tell him to go buy another wife?"

"Yeah, I did," Joe said.

Bettina's eyes welled. "If you were still a little boy, you'd be getting a gold star for that."

Joe grinned. "Like you put on school papers every time we got an A?"

"Just like that," Bettina said, blinking back tears.

Joe and Patty stayed until mid-afternoon, and then caught an

Uber back to the hotel. They had a late flight out of St. Louis that night and still needed to pack. They left with standing invitations to visit any time they wanted, and a special invitation to come back for Easter.

Bettina cried a little when they left, but it was from relief. She had her children back.

The snow continued to fall, layering the ground in a blanket of white. They put on their coats and walked out onto the back verandah, then stood side by side looking out into the night.

The silence was profound.

They were all lost in thought, remembering their personal trials by fire and the ensuing resurrections.

One by one, they quietly linked arms, united by a crime and a tragedy, to become the sister-wives they were today.

Finally, it was Janie who broke their silence.

"One for all," she whispered.

"And all for one," they echoed.

Then they turned and walked back into the house—into the light.

THE END

9 780795 353468